The Shepherd's Path

The Shepherd's Path

by

David F. Gray

New Leaf Press

First printing: June 1993
Second printing: November 1995

Library of Congress Catalog Number: 92-60940
ISBN: 0-89221-227-7

Author's Acknowledgments

Novels are never the product of just one individual. From first concept to final draft they grow and change, much like a human being. Also, like a human being, they are affected by a great many people. *The Shepherd's Path* is no exception. While the name of David F. Gray may stand alone on the cover, the ideas and suggestions of numerous others have had a hand in shaping it. To that end I would like to thank just a few of those without whose help this little tale would never have seen the light of day.

Thank you Tim Dudley and the New Leaf family for taking a chance on a brand new (and unknown) writer.

Thank you Sandra Sims, producer for the nationally syndicated television program "Action Sixties," for helping me make the right connection at the right time.

Thank you Roy and Barbara Davoll for early guidance, friendship, and the "turtle on the fence post."

Thank you Nancy deLivron for much needed and exceedingly well-done editing.

Most of all, thank you Heidi Powell Gray, for being my beautiful wife, best friend, hardest critic, and wonderful mother of Daniel and Charis. Without your quiet confidence and patience *The Shepherd's Path* would never have been written.

Above all, may God be honored and glorified.

In October of 1990, a federal judge issued a restraining order to certain pastors in the New York area. These pastors were activists in the pro-life movement and had been instigators of several non-violent protests. They, and others, would physically block the doors to an abortion clinic. Hundreds of protesters would effectively shut down the clinic, as well as disrupt major traffic routes. They would also offer sidewalk counseling to women contemplating abortion.

The restraining order not only forbade them to come within 100 yards of a clinic or 15 feet of anyone attempting to enter the clinic, but also ordered them to refrain from saying anything to their congregations that might be construed as encouragement to take part in a protest. This included reading any Bible verses that could be taken even remotely as supporting the pro-life movement. Disobedience would result in a fine of $10,000 per incident. Government officials would be in the congregations, monitoring the services. This action sent shock waves throughout the Christian community.

PROLOGUE
APRIL 30, 1996

Senator Jack Kline sighed wearily and leaned back in his overstuffed leather chair. He was a well-built man in his late thirties, with dark hair and rugged, handsome features. He contemplated the glowing numbers of the small digital clock on the computer screen in front of him, which read precisely 3:00 a.m. The screen, as well as a keyboard and telephone were set into the solid mahogany top of an oval conference table. There were seven other identical setups spaced around the circumference of the huge table. At the moment, four others were in use.

Rubbing eyes bleary with fatigue, Jack studied his companions with a touch of envy. None of them seemed the least tired, even though all had been at it for well over eight solid hours. Jack wished he had their stamina.

Rajijah Indres, for instance, looked as fresh as he did when they first began. Seated at Jack's immediate left, the diminutive Indian "holy man" sat quietly, occasionally sipping his abominable green tea. In his simple native dress no one would guess that he led the largest spiritualist movement in the nation. Next to him sat Christine Smythe, a handsome, dark-haired woman in her late forties. What little Jack knew about her was impressive. Owner and chairman of the board of one of the most powerful multi-national conglomerates in the world, she was involved in everything from military research and development to legalized narcotics. Her pet project was a string of abortion clinics that criss-crossed the nation.

The strange figure seated opposite him Jack knew only by name. The broad-shouldered, gray-haired man had been introduced simply as Dr. Samuel Steiger.

At the head of the table sat Jacob Hill, their leader. To the general public, Hill was unknown. He appeared to be simply one of the thousands of government officials that inhabit the corridors of national government.

Jack did not know many details about Jacob personally, but he did know through painstaking research that Jacob Hill was on his way to becoming the most powerful man in the United States. Congressmen, senators, and even presidents came and went, but Jacob Hill remained. In his years on Capitol Hill, he had slowly built a power base that was as unknown as it was invincible.

Just recently, he had allowed himself to become more visible by assuming control of the Bureau of Religious Affairs. The bureau was an organization set up over a year ago to watchdog large religious organizations. Its purpose was to prevent the scandals that rocked the nation in the late eighties. What most did not know was that Jacob's organization was the single most powerful government agency in existence. It had become, in essence, a private police force for Hill and his cohorts. He was a most formidable man.

Since his first term of office over seven years ago, Jack had come to understand that those who held the real power in the nation were not in politics. It had been sheer accident that he had learned about Jacob — a name dropped at an unimportant cocktail party over five years ago about a petty government official who had far more influence than he should have.

Going more on intuition than anything else, Jack had begun a personal and very secretive investigation that had brought him finally to this room. After following hundreds of false leads and dead-end trails, he had made a startling discovery. Many of the major issues debated on the floor of the Senate or House of Representatives were already decided by this unobtrusive quiet man and his "inner circle." This group literally ran the country. Lawmakers debated endlessly over how to interpret the Constitution while inner circles inside the Federal Reserve controlled the nation's economy. An elite membership buried deep in the Council on Foreign Relations swayed national policy. Jacob Hill controlled them all. He and his innermost circle of confidants worked behind the scenes, content to keep a low profile.

Jack aspired to be much more than a common senator. Since his arrival in Washington, he had had his eyes set on the presidency. Deep within his soul he knew he was destined for immortality. Now the thing he most wanted was within his grasp. This was where the real power was held. This was where he belonged.

As careful as Jack had been with his investigation, Jacob knew. He watched patiently as Jack slowly and tenaciously followed trails Jacob himself had laid. It was Jacob who finally approached Jack. Offering friendship, he drew him into his circle of friends, carefully gaining his confidence. For all intents and purposes, he had treated Jack like his son, and to Jack's way of thinking, his heir. Jack's mind swam with visions of the kind of power he could control. He intended to be a "mover and shaker," a man who bent the world to his will. This group, and more particularly this man, would allow him to accomplish his goal.

"All right, everyone, let's finish this up." Jacob's calm and cultured voice shook Jack out of his dreaming. Glancing around to see if anyone noticed his momentary lapse, he looked toward the head of the table where Jacob sat. Tall, gray-haired, and rapier thin, he looked every inch the leader he was. For a moment, his pale blue eyes met Jack's, and he smiled. "Stay with us, Jack," he said with a small laugh. Jack felt the blood rushing to his face and he began to scratch his nose to hide his embarrassment. The one thing he did not want was for these people to see him as a naive, inexperienced politician. The fact that he was one of the youngest senators to ever hold office only hardened his resolve to fit in.

"Now," Jacob continued, puffing on his pipe as he leafed through the stack of papers in front of him, "are we all understood as to our strategy concerning this bill?"

"We've been over it enough times, Jacob," said Christine. "I think it's time to call it a night."

Jacob nodded and turned to the man at Jack's right. "And you, Raj?"

"Everything is prepared," he replied quietly, his voice a pleasant tenor. The man had no trace of an accent. "We have solid evidence that one of the most popular televangelists in the country has been embezzling funds meant for Third World countries. We will break this story to the media in one week. Also, there are assorted scandals set to explode in several large churches — affairs, misuse of funds, spousal abuse — it should rock the Christian world to its very core." Jacob smiled his thin smile in approval, and turned his attention to Christine.

"I don't anticipate any problem on my end," she said before he could ask. "The conservative movement is dead. Their latest defeat in the Senate has them totally demoralized and ready to disband. We are now in a position to call for a Constitutional Convention. The last barriers have been removed for a complete rewriting of our legal system. We thank our young senator for that."

There was a smattering of applause, and once again Jack had to control his urge to blush. "No problem," he said. "Although I admit toward the end there, it was close."

"Indeed," replied Jacob. "The Pro-life Amendment was defeated by only 12 votes. Nevertheless, you knew which members on which to concentrate your efforts. You have a keen insight into the hearts of others, Jack. It will get you far." Jack's pride spiraled up like a runaway missile. Praise from a man like Jacob was worth more to him than any honor he could receive on Capitol Hill. His head clouded with dreams of the future, and he missed Jacob's next few sentences.

". . . ready to put our final plans into motion." Jacob paused and looked grimly at everyone. "I want us all to understand that this is not a personal vendetta against Christianity or any other organized religion. Frankly, if they would stay out of government affairs, I would just as soon leave them alone, but the the simple fact is, they just won't give up." He frowned, and Jack felt a momentary shudder. He was *very* glad he did not have this man for an enemy.

"The arrogance," Jacob continued, his voice almost a growl. "They presume to condemn those whose moral code does not conform to theirs, and yet the stink of their own corruption raises from their pulpits. Most of them are almost totally without supervision, particularly these so-called televangelists." Again he paused, and this time he smiled. "Granted, we have severely limited their influence in the past decade, but it is not enough. We have to bring them under complete state control. Let me remind you of a saying I heard long ago. 'When government and religion travel in the same vehicle, there is no limit as to how fast or far they can go . . . right over the edge of the cliff.' "

Jack nodded with the others. Jacob had a way about him, a command over the minds and hearts of others. It was almost mesmerizing.

"This bill is the beginning," said Jacob. "It will give the states the right to regulate churches at a local level. In time, even the sermons will have to be cleared through our people." There was a chorus of agreement from the group, Jack joining in with the rest. Jacob held up his hand for silence. "Let me make a prediction," he said confidently. "Within five years, every church of every denomination will be under our control. The 'freedom of worship' will become 'the privilege of worship.' Nothing will be said without our approval, and the beauty of it all is that those idiots in the pulpit will believe it's for their own good!"

Spontaneous applause broke out from the rest of the members of the Inner Circle. Again Jack joined in, but somewhere inside of him, a warning was being shouted. A bell was going off telling him that all was not right — that something was, in fact, terribly, horribly wrong.

SIX MONTHS LATER

"Happy birthday to you, happy birthday to you. . . ."

"Go 'way!"

"Aww, is he grumpy on his thirtieth birthday? You know what they say — 'the sense of humor is the first thing to go!' "

Scott Sampson slowly raised his head out of the hand-knit quilt that covered him. He looked for all the world like a turtle just emerging from his shell. Rumpled brown hair topped an angular face with a set jaw.

Opening one eye first and then risking the other, he saw his wife Beth standing in the doorway of the bedroom. She was a beautiful woman of 27. Scott, now with both baby blues open, took an instant to take in her shoulder length brown hair and petite, five-foot build. Her sparkling brown eyes danced in merriment at his grogginess. The sunlight streaming through the bedroom window behind her gave an angelic glow and radiance to her skin.

"You're enjoying this!" he accused.

"Who? Moi?" she replied in her best "Miss Piggy" imitation.

With a mighty heave, Scott sat up. Glancing over at the clock, he groaned. "Beth, it's seven in the morning, for crying out loud! *Sunday* morning."

"Not just any Sunday morning, lover," she replied with a mischievous grin. "It's the one thousand five hundred and sixtieth Sunday that you have been alive. In other words, light o' my life, you're 30!" Beth shouted these last two words, and before Scott could move, she took a running jump and bowled him over. Landing on top, she proceeded to tickle him, and soon had him helpless with laughter. Scott had no leverage and could not push her away.

"I give!" he cried through the tears. "Uncle! Truce! Stop! Anything!" Finally, Beth let up. She moved over to her side of the bed and sat cross-legged, arranging her pink robe discreetly. She eyed him warily in case he decided to counterattack.

"You don't have to rub it in," he grumped.

"Oh, don't be silly," she replied blithely. "You haven't even reached your prime yet."

"Just remember, in two years, this will be you," he warned. "I *will* get even."

"Two and a half," she corrected. "And you won't get even. You love me too much."

"Hmmmph"

"Now, are you going to get up? I've fixed your favorite breakfast, and if we eat now, we'll make it to church with time to spare."

"What? Don't I get breakfast in bed?"

"No. At your age, you need the exercise!"

Scott lunged toward Beth, but she was too quick for him. With a squeal, she bounded off the bed and back to the door. Shaking her head, she said, "The reflexes are the second thing to go!"

❖ ❖ ❖

Despite Beth's best efforts, they were still late for church. Scott honestly tried to hurry, but there was something about Sunday morning that seemed to demand that he drag his feet.

Be honest, he corrected himself sternly as they left the car in the church parking lot. *You haven't been excited about going to church since you left home.* Two years ago, Dadestrom Electronics, Scott's employer, had realized that Scott had a special talent in designing and programming computers. They had made him an executive and had given him a hefty raise. Unfortunately, they had relocated him and Beth to Cincinnati, close to the home office. For Scott, it had been a traumatic experience. He had grown up in Detroit. The promotion had meant leaving his family, his friends, and the church he had attended all his life.

Admit it, Sampson, he thought, continuing his conversation with himself, *You can't find a church to replace the one you left, so you don't care about going anymore. And if the only reason you went to church in the first place was for your friends and family, then maybe you're not as strong a Christian as you'd like to think!*

Angrily he derailed his train of thought as he and Beth walked through the chilly autumn air toward the Faith Community Church. He envied the way Beth had immediately adjusted to the move. Of course, her father was an Air Force colonel, and relocating had been a way of life. To her, this was just one more place to explore. In fact, it was she who had found their new church home. Scott grudgingly admitted to himself that at least she had found a strong, Bible-centered fellowship. Pastor Herb Niven was a good man who was not afraid to preach the Word. As they entered the foyer, they could hear lively singing, muffled behind the closed auditorium doors.

"Looks like a full crowd," said Beth, standing on her toes to look through the small windows in the swinging doors. "Want to go on in?"

"Okay," replied Scott, "but let's stay near the back."

"I see a good place to sit. Follow me." Taking Scott's hand in hers, Beth pushed through the doors and headed straight down the center aisle. The only empty pew space Scott could see was just four rows from the front. Sure enough, Beth led them there. Ignoring Scott's half-serious glare, she found the appropriate page in the hymn book and pushed it into his hands. Scott made a mental note *not* to wait until her thirtieth birthday to get even.

They sang another verse of "Heaven Came Down" with Scott's rough baritone voice contrasting with Beth's more refined soprano. When the hymn was over, Pastor Niven got up from his seat on the platform to bring the message. Abruptly, Scott was struck at the man's appearance. Normally, Niven was a robust, athletic, barrel-chested man who looked to be more in his mid-forties than the 63 he actually was. This morning he looked to be twice that. Something had brought about a horrible change in him.

He looks a century older, thought Scott to himself. A glance at Beth told him that she had seen it too. Scott watched closely as Pastor Niven began to speak. The message, while biblically sound, lacked his authority and passion. To Scott, he seemed to be going through the motions, as if he were walking in his sleep. Finally, the altar call was given. Even this was done halfheartedly, and no one came forward.

After only two verses of the invitation hymn, the pastor mercifully gave the benediction. As soon as the amen was said, Scott headed for the door. He was surprised when Niven asked everyone to remain in their seats.

"I know this is an imposition," he said, still standing behind the pulpit. "I promise you it will only take a moment of your time." There was a rumble of confusion as the congregation gradually seated itself once more.

Pastor Niven looked at them for a long moment before speaking. Scott reached over and clasped Beth's hand. For some reason, he was dreading what was to come.

"I don't know any easy way to say this, so I'll just read this letter from me to the church." Niven pulled a folded piece of paper from his jacket pocket. He opened it, and swallowed hard. Then he began to read.

"Dear Church Family," he began. "These past 20 years I have labored as your pastor have truly been the best years of my life. Eileen and I have enjoyed your fellowship and been strengthened by your love. Therefore it is with great difficulty that I hereby tender my resignation as pastor of Faith Community Church, effective immediately. I have already spoken with Ned Slade, the chairman of the deacons, and a search committee will be formed within the week. Please know that I love you and wish you all the best. God bless and keep you. Sincerely, Herb Niven."

A stunned hush lay across the auditorium as Pastor Niven replaced the letter in his jacket pocket. He regarded them through tear-blurred eyes for a moment. Just when it seemed that the silence would become unbearable, he turned and left the platform, disappearing into a back room.

The assistant pastor, Galen Manning, hurried to step up to the pulpit. He led the congregation in a second benediction, and ended the service. Beth kept a tight grip on Scott's arm as they made their way toward the exit. Just before they left the building, Scott felt a soft tap on his shoulder. Turning, he saw Ned Slade, the deacon chairman.

"Scott, Beth, I wonder if I might have a word with you, in private."

"What about, Ned?" Scott had rarely spoken to the deacon, and did not feel like talking now.

"I really can't say here," replied Ned. "It'll just take five minutes. Please."

Scott could think of no polite way to refuse him, and so allowed himself and Beth to be guided into one of the church offices. Ned motioned for them to sit in the two chairs provided while he perched himself on one corner of a large mahogany desk.

"What did you think of the pastor's announcement?" he asked.

"What am I supposed to think?" Scott replied, his irritation beginning to show. "The man up and quits, just like that. What's going on?"

Beth, who had remained silent until now, looked at Ned intensely. "There's something very wrong, isn't there?" she asked.

For a moment, Ned didn't say anything. Then he rubbed his eyes, his shoulders sagging as if under a great weight. "Something is very wrong, indeed," he replied. "If Herb had not resigned, he would have been accused of having an affair with Mary Solow."

"The church secretary?!" Scott was incredulous. "Impossible! I haven't been one of the pastor's strongest supporters, but even I know he wouldn't do a thing like that!"

"There's proof," said Ned flatly. "Eyewitnesses, pictures, a concrete case." In addition to being chairman of the deacons, Ned was also a lawyer. He was on permanent retainer to Faith Community. "Everything points to the fact that the pastor is guilty. There's just one problem." Ned paused, then slapped the desk in frustration. "He didn't do it! You're right, Scott. Herb has his faults, but infidelity is not one of them. The simple fact is, someone set out to get him — and succeeded."

Scott bit back the obvious question of "Who?" and asked instead, "Why tell us all of this? We're not that involved here. Shouldn't it be brought before the church body? If you tell them the truth . . ." Ned shook his head.

"There would always be some doubt. As I said, the evidence is quite convincing. Herb didn't want to tear the church apart."

Pausing, Ned contemplated the two in front of him, as if sizing them up. "Scott, Beth, the reason I'm telling you all of this is simple. We are under attack here. Someone is trying to tear this church apart, and I have reason to believe that we are not alone. This scenario is being repeated all across the country, in hundreds of Bible-believing churches. Are you aware of the bill that was passed in Congress a few months ago that requires us to clear all of the sermons through a local government office? Do you know that the state can now dictate to us who can and cannot work here?" Scott stared at Ned as if he were speaking gibberish. Sure, he had heard of Congress passing a new regulatory act, but didn't that just apply to television ministries? What

Ned was saying was far more frightening. Ned nodded, seeing in their faces what they were thinking.

"It hits everyone that way," he said. "That's why we're meeting tonight. The time is coming when it will be illegal for us to meet as a church. We have to get organized, and be ready when that time comes."

"You're talking about an underground church," whispered Beth.

"That's right. Just like in Rome in the first century. Just like behind the Iron Curtain. All that hooplah about the Curtain rusting lasted about 10 years. Now the persecution is worse than ever over there. The Communist party was replaced by a group of dictators who are set on destroying the Church — and the same thing is happening here, right now, right under our noses. That's why we want you to join us. I know that you're new here, but I have a feeling about you. Will you come? It's at 7:30 tonight, at my house."

"Uh, let us think about it, Ned," stuttered Scott. All he wanted to do right now was to get out of that office.

"Sure," agreed Ned. "It's a big decision. Think about it, and pray about it. I hope we'll see you tonight." With that, he got up and opened the door for the Sampsons. Scott almost tripped over Beth's heels in his haste to leave.

They were quiet in the car on the way home. Finally, Beth turned to Scott and asked, "Are we going?"

For a moment, Scott hesitated, then shook his head. "No. I don't think things are as bad as what Ned said, and if they are, then the last thing we need is trouble with the law."

"But if they end up closing the church. . . ."

"Beth, stop it!" Scott snapped. "This is America, for crying out loud! Nobody is going to close the churches. And even if 'they,' whoever 'they' are, did, then what could we do about it?"

Beth didn't reply. Scott could feel her disappointment, but did not know how to make her feel better. The fact was, he honestly didn't believe what he had just told her. Deep inside, he had the feeling that things were going to get bad — very bad. They drove the rest of the way home in silence.

ONE YEAR LATER

"All right, access the 'Gideon' file."

"Accessing. There it is."

"Hmmm. I don't know, Jeff. It's awfully easy to get into. Are you sure dumping it into the community billboard is safe?" Helen Bradley glanced up from the glowing computer display and raised her eye-brows at her younger companion. He was a handsome black man in his mid-thirties.

"Relax, Helen," he answered, his voice a confident bass. "The best way to hide things is in plain sight. The billboard is strictly for public access. It's designed to talk to any computer. In the eighties, computer buffs used them to trade different programs, send messages to each other, and keep current on new developments. Today, everyone uses it. They're a great way to exchange information. Nobody puts anything there they want to keep secret. It's perfect for us."

"Sure. Now everybody and their brother can get into our files. Perfect, he says." FBI Director Jeff Anderson pushed himself away from the desk that held the terminal and arched his back. The resulting cracks and pops inside his well-muscled body reminded him that he had been working on this little project for most of the morning. Not that he minded, of course. He returned Helen's sarcastic look with a smile.

"Since it's so easy, why don't you try it." With a flourish, he stood up and motioned for Helen to take his place. She moved over to the terminal and began to type.

"Let's see. First I access the billboard, right?"

"Right."

"Wait a moment — there it is. Now I call up the general information menu."

"So far, so good."

"Goodness, look at all of those different files. There must be thousands."

"Over ten thousand, actually."

"Show off. Okay, now I type in the file I want . . . in this case, Gideon. Wait a minute. It says bad command or file name. Where is my file?" Jeff grinned, the chocolate skin around his dark brown eyes crinkling.

"It isn't there," he said, obviously delighted with himself. "Go ahead and look — they're in alphabetical order." Helen scrolled down the long list to the G's and saw that he was correct. As far as the billboard was concerned, "Gideon" did not exist.

"So where is it?" she asked patiently.

"Okay," he answered. "Type in data search. Good. Now what does it say?"

"Ummmm, password."

"Now type in Network."

"Okay. There. Now it says enter access number."

"Type 1-2-3-4."

"I'm glad they teach you to count in the FBI. Or does that just apply to regional directors like yourself?"

"Cute. Type the code."

"1-2-3-4. Now it says improper code."

Again Jeff grinned. "Right. Any numerical sequence will be rejected. Now, type the numbers again, only this time spell them out."

"Okay — one, two, three, four . . . now it says enter file name. Gideon, right?"

"You got it." Helen typed the file name, and was rewarded with a list of names and addresses. There were thousands, spanning the nation.

"You see? The file name isn't even on the main menu, and if you don't know the proper way to retrieve the information, you can't get it. As far as the computer is concerned, it doesn't exist."

"Excellent, Jeff. And I suppose that anyone who does have the proper codes can get into the system, from anywhere in the country?"

"Uh huh. This is a national network. It even has a toll-free number. Of course, I'll change the codes and the password to something a little more exotic. These were just for show."

"I should hope so. One-two-three-four indeed!"

"One other thing, Helen. I have the necessary codes to get us into the FBI system using any home computer. It's linked to every major computer in the country — law enforcement, travel, credit bureau — you name it. A small number of us have placed what we call 'back doors' into several of the programs. They give us easy access and don't show that we've been tampering. They're somewhat risky to use, but in an emergency, they might mean the difference between life and death."

"What about your superiors? Will they know that you have been using FBI computers to establish what is essentially an illegal network?"

For the first time, Jeff became totally serious. "I'm good at covering my tracks," he said. "Unless they do what we call a 'class one' search, we're safe. Besides, you would be surprised how many Christians there are in this office alone." He took Helen's hand and squeezed softly. "We're not alone, Helen. A lot of my friends see what's happening, and a lot of them are in so-called 'high places' in the government. We just don't know how to stop it. No matter what we try, things keep getting worse." He shook his head. "I'm afraid all we can do is get as organized as possible and wait for the storm. It's coming, that's for sure."

"I know," Helen replied, looking away. "If things keep going the way they are now, the Church, the true Church, will have to be completely underground within the year. The 'Shepherd's Path' will have to be ready long before that."

"As far as the computer end is concerned," said Jeff, "you will be ready in six weeks. The rest should fall into place soon after that."

"I hope so. I hope we're doing the right thing. The idea of breaking the law scares me."

"Ask the first Christians about that," said Jeff. "They broke the law of the land when they met in secret. The Lord was pretty clear on that subject."

"I know," agreed Helen. She had been a Christian for over 40 of her 63 years. "I just never thought I would see it happen in this country." She stood up and made ready to leave. "I can't tell you how much I appreciate your help, Jeff."

"Anytime, Helen. You know that. We're in this together." Jeff shut off his terminal and began to clean off his desk. "I'd better get going, too. While it might look good for me to be here on a Saturday, I don't want to overdo it. Besides, I've got tickets to the Reds' game. They're back in town."

"I'll see you in a few days, then," said Helen. She slung her purse over her shoulder and without another word, left.

❖ ❖ ❖

Driving back across the Ohio River to her home in Covington proved to be more of a chore than Helen had anticipated. There was a major accident on the main bridge, and traffic was at a standstill. Knowing from experience that it could be a while before things started moving again, she shut down the engine of her small compact and opened the windows. The cool, crisp spring air of April began to blow gently through the car. As she waited patiently for the accident to be cleared, Helen again went over the hundreds of details that were vital for the establishment of what she called 'the Shepherd's Path.' She was still a little skeptical over Jeff's public access system. Perhaps if she copied the entire system into a few other files, just for backup, it might make things a little more secure.

Started by her husband Roy over 10 years ago, the Shepherd's Path now involved thousands of Christians from every walk of life. Across the nation they were linked by a common cause — to establish small, self-sufficient groups of believers that met to pray and worship in secret. Until his death from cancer three years ago, Roy had been a well-known evangelist. Together, he and Helen had traveled the country, preaching the gospel of Christ. He had seen the end of free worship coming in America, and had worked to convince believers of the approaching darkness. Helen shared his vision of a national underground network supporting local cells of Christians, and had carried on Roy's work after his death. The Shepherd's Path was the culmination of that vision. Now, everything was almost in place, and Helen knew deep in her soul that it had happened none too soon. Just six months ago, her dear friend Herb Niven had been forced to resign from his church. Since then, he had disappeared with his family, and Helen could find no trace of him. Scandals had rocked the Christian world left and right, and many loud voices were calling for tighter government control over religious organizations.

"Lord," she prayed softly to herself, "We are about to go through a great trial. I pray we might acquit ourselves well, not denying or forsaking You, as You have never denied or forsaken us. Give us strength to face the days and years ahead. Help us to stand firm in Your Word, no matter what. In Jesus' name, Amen."

Just as she finished praying, the loud blaring of a car horn behind her told her that traffic had started moving again. She started her car, and began to inch her way forward, her mind filled with apprehension at the dark days ahead.

JULY, 2002

A musty twilight was starting to settle over the business district of downtown Covington. The red and green glare of traffic lights contrasted sharply with the orange and blue hue of the rapidly darkening sky. The pungent odor of old exhaust, sewage, and uncollected refuse hung heavily in the dirty air.

On a deserted street not far from the center of town, a battered red LeMans slowly pulled alongside a short row of parking meters. The engine idled for a moment, then shut off. From under the hood came a soft hissing, as if the 10-year-old car was sighing at the indignity of being driven in its latter years. For a moment, all was still. Then, the driver opened his door and got out. Scanning the street for any sign of danger, he walked in front of the car and stepped up onto the curb. Fishing a handful of change out of his pocket, he methodically fed it into the proper meter. Then he moved back to the car.

As Scott opened the door for Beth, his sense of unease at this journey began to grow. Things had been bad enough over the past few years. He had been demoted, and almost fired from Dadestrom. Most of the people he thought to be his friends there had stopped talking to him. To make matters worse, his marriage to Beth was in deep trouble. It seemed that they could not be around each other for long before they began to fight. Most of their arguments were about money, these days. The pay cut from his demotion had played havoc with their budget. They were constantly bickering over everything. Between home and office, Scott was at his wit's end.

The worst part was, he honestly did not know the cause of all his problems. His performance at his job was excellent as usual. He had done nothing to merit the severe reprimand he had received some time ago. All Joe Peterson, his supervisor, would say was that he had somehow violated company policy. When Scott had pressed for a clearer answer, Joe advised him to let matters rest. It was either that or lose his job. Scott knew that if he were to be fired from Dadestrom, no one else would hire him.

He was equally mystified at the decay of his relationship with Beth. There was a time when he could talk to her about anything. His deepest fears, his goals and dreams, everything that mattered he felt he could share with his wife. Now it was different. They still slept in the same bed, but that was the extent of their intimacy. They were two strangers living in the same house. There was no warmth or caring left between them. It felt to Scott like things were broken beyond repair.

As Beth began to climb out of the car, he offered his hand to assist her. Ignoring it, she got out and closed the door behind her. Scott thought about snapping at her, but shoved the urge aside. This was not the time. Instead he scanned the empty street once again. What they were about to do was illegal and highly dangerous. He cursed himself for allowing Beth to talk him into this ridiculous adventure. As far as he was concerned, she had tricked him into coming — she and Ned Slade. He could still hear Ned's strained voice on the other end of the phone. They could not afford a video link, so could not see Ned as he talked to them. Beth had joined the conversation from the bedroom extension, while Scott gritted his teeth and listened in the living room.

"Listen, Scott," he said. "I know this is dangerous. Believe me, I know what could happen if we're caught. The choice is yours. If you want to come, I'll give you instructions on where and when. If not, then you won't hear from me again." Scott could hear Beth's heavy, expectant breathing, waiting for him to answer.

"Tell you what, Ned," he said finally. "Let me know how to get there, and I'll think about it. I can't make a decision like this over the phone."

"Sorry, Scott. Either you're in or out. I need to know now."

Scott had opened his mouth to say most emphatically NO! Absolutely not! It was right at that moment that Beth had appeared at his side. He had not heard her come in from the bedroom. Tears were running down her cheeks, and she silently mouthed a single word — please. Scott had stared at her for a moment, thinking of the past several months of almost constant fighting. He remembered a time — it seemed like centuries ago — when things were much better between them. He had taken a deep breath, knowing he would hate himself for what he was about to do. Still, if it helped bring a little harmony, or even just some peace to their troubled lives, it would be worth it. Without pausing to consider the consequences, he had told Ned that he and Beth would be there. Ned gave them explicit instructions and then had hung up.

Now, just over 24 hours later, Scott was deeply regretting his decision. As far as he was concerned, both Beth and Ned had played on his sense of guilt to get him out here. They had no right to ask this of him. Didn't he have enough problems without flaunting the law like this? Right then and there, he almost told Beth to get back into the car. He would use physical force, if necessary, to get her home. She might hate him for it, but at least they would be safe.

Beth looked up at him, as if reading his mind. Her lips were set in a firm, determined line. She shouldered past him and started down the street. He stood there for a moment, staring after her. He had a wild thought of jumping back into the car and leaving her to her own devices. He instantly rejected the idea, horrified that he had even thought it. There was only one other course of action. Shoulders slumping in defeat, he trotted forward and drew even with her.

Slowly they began to walk down the empty street, trying not to look too noticeable. This section of Covington looked more like the aftermath of a war than a business district.

The city had always suffered from a "little sister" complex, with "big sister" Cincinnati just across the Ohio River. Only small, family-owned businesses had once occupied this particular area. The completion of two ultra-modern malls in the suburbs had been a death blow to them. Now the empty buildings were home to the homeless, the unwanted, and worse, roving gangs. Like vultures, they fed on the remains of the city, terrorizing the weak and the dying. Even the police seemed to have given up. Scott had not seen a single patrol car since they had entered the city — a mixed blessing.

The empty buildings stared at them as they made their way toward their destination. To Scott, it seemed as if the myriad of broken windows each held an invisible threat. They stared at him like the empty sockets of a mammoth skull — unblinking, and seeing everything.

He glanced over at Beth, as if to say "All right, you've made your point, and had your fun. Now let's get out of here." She continued to stare straight ahead, not acknowledging his look. Scott could tell that she was afraid, too.

Suddenly he caught a blurred motion out of the corner of his eye, but when he turned to look, all he could see was a chained and locked door. He was still trying to figure out what had caught his attention when Beth stopped abruptly and gripped his arm. He turned back around and came face to face with hopelessness personified.

Muddy brown eyes that only came up to his waist peered out from behind the dirtiest face he had ever seen. Stringy, oily-black hair fell to pale bare shoulders. Faded cut-off jeans clung to a stick-thin frame. Scott wasn't even sure if this urchin was male or female, only that he/she was the single most pathetic sight he had ever witnessed. Like most people, Scott knew that somewhere in the world children were starving and dying, but he had never come face to face with such need. It galled and sickened him. For a moment, all he could do was stare. Then, on impulse, he reached for his wallet, intending to give the child what little money he had.

"Jo Jo!" The woman's angry voice came from across the street. Instantly the child stiffened. "Get over here, girl! Now! Or else your poppa'll beat you good." The little girl was off like a shot towards the woman. Scott could not see her well in the fading light, but got the distinct impression that she was staring at them.

"Great!" he muttered angrily under his breath. "So much for not being noticed!" He turned around to head back to the car, assuming that Beth would follow. This was no place for them! When he looked back, though, he saw that she was still moving toward their destination. He cursed to himself. Cursing was something he did quite a bit these days, and he had become rather creative at it. For a moment, he debated picking his wife up bodily and carrying her back to the car. He knew it would be the only way to get her back home. He toyed with the idea for a moment, then decided against it. Even in this part of town it would cause too much of a ruckus. Instead, he stood there and watched her retreating back. Finally, sighing the sigh of the much put-upon, he ran forward to once again walk by her side.

"This is not a good idea," he whispered as he drew even with her. Beth did not bother to answer. They had been over this too many times already today. Scott opened his mouth again to complain about the risk that they were taking, but closed it when he saw the deep pain on his wife's face. The sight of that filthy, malnourished child had affected her deeply.

Children were another sore spot in their marriage. Beth wanted to start a family, but Scott flatly refused. He felt it ridiculous to bring a child into this dangerous, war-ridden world. Even at age 36 he did not feel ready for the added burden. With the way their lives were going, they were lucky to barely support themselves, and that was

only after Beth had gone back to work full time. The only "good" thing
that had happened lately was that Scott had been too old for the draft.
The last thing he wanted was to end up in the center of the escalating
Middle East War.

Looking at his watch, he saw that they were running late. It was
almost 7:25, and they had been told to be there no later than 7:30.
Otherwise, they would not be admitted. The sun was just casting its
last rays over the skeleton of the city when their destination at last
came into view. Taking Beth's arm, he quickened their pace. He
wanted off the street, even if it meant going through with this insanity.
He tried to push all other thoughts out of his head. There didn't seem
to be any way out of their troubles, so why worry about it?

"There," he said softly, and Beth nodded.

To all appearances, it was no different than any of the other
dilapidated buildings that surrounded it. Chipped green paint clung to
dirty masonry, and rotted wood trim barely held itself together. Three
stories high, it was a squat, ugly edifice. A litter-covered alley ran
down one side. Only the fact that this business was still open set it apart
from its dying brothers. A cracked and faded sign over the single
revolving door said simply "Mather & Son Used Furniture." Another
sign, this one bright orange and black, hung in one of the two display
windows. It proclaimed to any who cared that the store was open for
business.

Beth began to go through the revolving door, but Scott abruptly
tightened his grip on her arm and forced her to keep walking. She gave
him a half-puzzled, half-angry look as he stopped in front of the
display window just past the door. When he released her, she moved
away from him.

"Just look at the furniture for a moment," he said in a low voice.
They stood there for what seemed like an eternity, looking over a worn
blue sofa and various pieces of imitation wood tables. Inside, harsh
fluorescent lights bathed everything in an ugly greenish tint. In the
back of the store, seated at a high, old fashioned desk that commanded
a view of the entire room, sat a balding, middle-aged man. He did not
seem to notice that he had possible customers. Scott took a deep
breath.

"Beth." Something in the way he said her name caused her to turn
and face him. Her brow was wrinkled in an unasked question. Scott
struggled, searching for the right words that would change Beth's
mind. He was angry and scared. Right now he wanted nothing more
than to go home. "Listen," he said after an endless pause, "I know that

things haven't been too good for us. It's probably mostly my fault." The admission stuck in his throat. A large part of him did not believe it, but he plodded on doggedly.

"If we go in there, we're committed to do something very dangerous." His voice cracked a little, betraying his fear. He swallowed, and brought it back under control. "If we leave now," he continued, "I'll do whatever it takes to make things right between us again." Deep inside his heart a burning shame began to grow. He knew that it was not concern for their marriage that motivated him to speak, but his own fear of being caught. Right at that moment, he would have promised anything to leave. The look Beth gave him told him that she knew it as well as he. She merely continued to look at him, keeping her silence as she had the whole trip. Was that pity in her eyes?

Scott could feel his cheeks reddening with embarrassment. Anger welled up inside, a fitting companion for the shame. Without another word, he turned and pushed through the revolving door. Beth hesitated, then followed a few paces behind. Scott started to head straight for the man at the desk, who was exactly as had been described, but thought the better of it. Instead he turned to the left and began to examine the battered bedroom set that sat nearby. Beth stood waiting in the aisle that led to the back. Scott tried to focus on his instructions, but his head felt as dull as the dirty yellow tile that covered the floor.

Aw, why fight it, he thought in disgust. *I can't win either way. If I don't go through with this, I'm probably gonna loose Beth. If I do, with the way my luck has been, we'll both get caught.* With an air of resignation, he walked back to where his wife waited, his feet dragging. He stopped and just looked at her, searching her face for some sign of affection.

For the first time, he noticed the tiny worry lines at the corners of her eyes and mouth. The strain in her eyes was like a veil, covering the once bright twinkle that he had always loved. The past few years had been rough on her, too.

"Okay, let's do it," he said. Together they walked to the back of the store. The man, who until now had taken no notice of the couple, looked up and nodded.

"Help you, folks?" he asked in a surprisingly high tenor.

"We're not sure," replied Scott with as much nonchalance as he could muster. He moved to stand next to the high desk and looked up.

The top of the old antique was chest high, and the man's head was at least two feet over his own. "A friend of mine told me you might have a roll-top desk. I can't find one anywhere else." The bald man nodded, stroking about a days growth of beard.

"Don't get much call for things like that, these days," he said, a trace of disgust in his voice. "People don't want real furniture anymore." He jerked a thumb behind him, where a doorway was covered with a dirty, dark green curtain. "I got one in the back, but it's buried under a bunch of other stuff. I'll warn you right now, it's in pretty bad shape."

"As long as it's wood, and not some imitation, I don't mind refinishing it." As he spoke, Scott rested his arms on the edge of the desk. Struggling not to look over his shoulder, he carefully reached down with his finger. Still looking up at the man, he drew a small figure in the dust on top of the desk. One straight line, then one curved, connected at the top — the shepherd's staff. The man did not react, but simply reached over to get his glasses which rested on the other side. In doing so, he casually erased the design with his sleeve.

"Come along, then," he said. With more dexterity than Scott would have credited him with, he leaped down off his stool and led them through the back door into a dimly lit, musty smelling stock room. Shelves lined the walls and ran all the way to the ceiling two stories above. Discarded furniture was piled haphazardly all around, giving the feel of a junkyard rather than a place of business. The floor, rotting wooden planks replacing the yellowed tile, creaked as they advanced. About halfway to the rear wall, a rickety, locked door appeared on the right.

The man pulled a jangle of keys out of his pocket and began to fish through them. Finding the right one, he unlocked the door and pushed it open. The resounding "creak" sent shivers through Scott's spine. The opening revealed a staircase descending into the darkness. The man stepped back and motioned them to go through.

"Down those stairs to the left. You know the knock?" Husband and wife nodded. "Get going, then. You're late." Without another word, he turned and went back to his stool. Scott and Beth stood there, looking at one another. Both were nervous and frightened, but neither one wanted to admit it.

"Come on," Scott said in a resigned voice. He led the way down the steps, going carefully in case he lost his footing on the rotten wood. The dim light from above did little to aid him, and he was forced to rely almost solely on touch. He could hear Beth's heavy breathing as she followed behind him.

By the time they reached the bottom, they were in complete

darkness. Scott felt the solid concrete floor under him, and turned left. Almost immediately he found the door. He paused, then rapped softly on the wooden frame. He used the pattern that Ned had given him — three quick knocks, followed by two slow ones. There was a pause, then he could hear a latch being undone. A small sliver of light indicated that the door had opened a fraction.

"The Lamb is returning," said a hushed voice.

"May He come soon," replied Scott. He was grateful that his voice did not crack. The door opened all the way.

"Come in," said the voice that he now recognized as Ned's. The Sampsons stepped into the cellar, the door shutting behind them. After the darkness of the staircase, even the single low wattage bulb hanging naked from the low ceiling dazzled Scott's eyes. It took a moment for him to adjust. When he did, he could make out 12 people in the room. He looked at them for a moment, trying to think of something to say. It hit him suddenly that these people were not what he expected. There was nothing special about the way they looked. He had pictured them to be spiritual giants, so close to God that they would glow or something. Now he saw the truth. These were not heroes, he realized. No one in this room was a "super Christian." They were simply believers who wanted to worship their Saviour.

For a moment, Scott was able to push his fear into the back of his mind. These 12 believers would continue to meet together no matter what the cost. Their faith was far more important to them than their lives. He could feel the strength here in this dirty cellar, but more importantly, he could sense the presence of God. How long had it been since he had been able to do that? It humbled him, but in a strange way, it also gave him strength. He looked at Beth, unable to find the right words. She smiled at him gently, understanding. Then she turned to the small church, and for the first time in hours, spoke.

"The Lord is risen," she said, her voice trembling with emotion. The reply came back in perfect unison, as it had centuries before.

"THE LORD IS RISEN INDEED!"

❖ ❖ ❖

It's nice to know, Helen Bradley thought wryly, *that some things truly never change.* She was sitting in the upper level of the Florence Mall where the fast food restaurants were located. Being dinner time on Friday, the large, open plaza was crowded. A mostly young crowd gathered in small groups around the scattered tables that dotted the area, discussing things that only youth were privy to.

For the past 15 minutes Helen's attention had centered on two of the young people who occupied a table by themselves. The boy, who looked to be maybe 17, had a strained expression on his face. His whole body language bespoke of uncertainty and nervousness. The girl, on the other hand, was aloof and cool, with all of the sophistication 16 had to offer. (Helen knew without a doubt she was 16. Sixteen-year-old girls have a certain look that is unmistakable.) As she watched, the boy shyly took the girl's hand and tried to hold it. Calmly, the girl retrieved her hand, and shook her head.

The boy was about to say something when several of the girl's friends rushed up to their table and pulled her away. They walked off, giggling to themselves as only girls of that age can do. The boy remained there for a moment, obviously hurting, then got up and shuffled off in the opposite direction, the very picture of dejection. Helen smiled wistfully, remembering her dating days. She wanted to go over and put her arm around that young lad and tell him that the object of his affection was probably just as confused and uncertain as he was.

Come to think of it, she thought to herself, *I was probably harder on poor Roy than that. What he must have gone through in order to get my attention.* For just a moment, Helen wished she could return to her past, when the most pressing concern was what to wear to school, or whether or not that cute boy in history class liked her.

"But those days are gone," she told herself firmly. "And I will not live in the past." Strangely, the poignant scene she had just witnessed had lightened her grim mood. It was nice to know that amid today's troubles, the endless ritual of courtship was still being observed, despite what the news people said. According to the media's statistics, usually a teenaged couple slept together, and then had their first date!

She settled back into her seat and checked her watch. It was almost time. She took a last bite of her salad, wishing that it was one of those aromatic hamburgers being served just a few feet away. Actually, what she really wanted was a bite of that chocolate sitting in the display window across the food court. Unfortunately, her metabolism no longer tolerated such things. At age 65, she was in perfect health, and she intended to stay that way, even if it meant a somewhat bland diet. Casually, she fingered the homemade piece of jewelry on her left shoulder. The small replica of the shepherd's staff would identify her to her contact. Helen hoped that whoever it was would be on time. She reached under the table to make sure that her shopping bag was still by her purse. Scanning the milling crowd, she searched for some clue as to his or her identity.

"Helen? Good grief, Helen, is that you?"

In spite of herself, Helen jumped, startled at the masculine voice coming from behind her. She had been concentrating on the eating area, not on the rest of the mall.

Slowly she turned to see a young, handsome, blond-haired man in his mid-twenties. He was carrying a shopping bag identical to Helen's. Despite the man's familiar greeting, Helen had never seen him before.

"Tom! Tom Donahue!" she replied with as much enthusiasm as she could muster. "I haven't seen you in years. You're all grown up now!"

She stood up and hugged her old/new friend, then motioned for him to sit with her. She did not like using her real name in meetings like this, but Jeff had insisted. The best way to hide things, he kept insisting, was in plain sight. On the off chance she was being watched or followed, it would look far more suspicious if she began using an alias.

Technically, she should not even be here. As head of the Shepherd's Path, she was too important to expose herself this way. Less than an hour ago, however, her courier had called, saying he could not make it. He had given no reason, but Helen suspected fear as a strong motive. It had meant some frantic reshuffling to be able to have this meeting at all.

"I can't believe I've run into you in the middle of all this crowd," Tom beamed. He sat down in the seat opposite Helen and put his bag down on the floor beside hers.

He's good, Helen thought to herself.

"We were going to call you tonight and let you know we were in town. This is great!"

"It's wonderful to see you again," said Helen. "How are Sheila, and the boys?"

"They're fine. They're back at the hotel, swimming. We drove straight through from home and they're all a little tired."

"Well, why don't you come over tonight after they're rested?" Helen tried to sound natural, but the truth was she hated meetings like this. She wasn't by any stretch of the imagination an actor. As her "close friend," Tom droned on about family and friends, Helen wondered how much longer she would be able to keep up these rendezvous. Because she was the widow of a former evangelist, she had been forced to register with the local office of the Bureau of

Religious Affairs. She didn't think she was being watched yet, but she didn't intend to start taking chances. Abruptly, Tom stopped talking and Helen struggled to remember his last words.

"I'm sorry you can't come over tonight," she replied at last. "Let's make it tomorrow afternoon, then." Looking at her watch, she continued, "Goodness, it's getting late. I've got to get going." She retrieved her shopping bag and stood. Tom hugged her as she made ready to go.

"Tomorrow, without fail," he said as he helped Helen get her things together. They said their goodbyes and parted, Helen heading toward the east parking lot, Tom going in the opposite direction.

Helen's bag felt heavier, which did not surprise her since Tom had switched bags. The bag he now had contained a much treasured Bible — New American Standard version, both Old and New Testaments. Since the crackdown four years ago, they had become almost non-existent. The Bible drives sponsored by the government had been responsible for their disappearance. On the black market, it was worth over $10,000, and it could mean life imprisonment if either of them were caught with it. If things went as planned, Tom would deliver it to a small body of believers who were meeting tonight. Then he would come over to Helen's house tomorrow to report how things went and receive a new assignment.

Helen did not know where or when the church group was meeting. Although she was theoretically the top person in the Shepherd's Path, she knew the location and membership of only a few scattered churches across the country, as well as a handful of "safe houses" and assorted other contacts. People like Tom knew a few more. No one person personally was aware of more than four. It was safer that way. If anyone were caught and interrogated, only a small part of the network would be compromised. Even if Helen herself were captured, the Shepherd's Path would continue.

Helen reached her car and put her package in the back seat. Curiosity made her look inside. For a moment, she simply stared, then started to chuckle. Someone must have told Tom about Helen's love of chocolate, for the bag contained the largest candy bar she had ever seen. It must have weighed five pounds if it weighed an ounce.

"So much for my bland diet this week," she laughed to herself. "My delicate system will just have to handle a little sugar." She started the car and headed home, giggling. She would have been very pleased to know she sounded just like the teenage girls in the mall.

❖ ❖ ❖

The sub-orbital shuttle sliced through the thin upper atmosphere over the North American continent. Officially, the sleek craft had no existence. Unlike Air Force One, which was constantly in the public eye, this particular shuttle was a phantom, a ghost. There were no exterior markings to identify it, nor call letters to mark its home base. Only the code name "Ayres One" told ground-based controllers that a very private and very classified vehicle was traversing this particular flight path.

The shuttle itself was a marvel of twenty-first century technology. Developed just a few years ago, it was not quite spacecraft, not quite aircraft, but a little bit of both. It inhabited the outer fringe of the atmosphere where it walked the delicate tightrope between gravity and weightlessness. Although still too expensive for commercial use, shuttles like this one were popular with the government. They could cross the distance between New York and Los Angeles in just over an hour.

The interior of this particular shuttle was a study in subdued luxury. An equal space on a passenger vehicle could carry over 300 people in comfort. This was designed for less than a tenth of that. The spacious center cabin was a mixture of burgundies and grays, the plush carpet and concave walls bearing the latter, with the sofas and chairs using the former. A wet bar in the back overlooked four comfortable couches arranged in a conversation pit in the exact center of the cabin. A large viewing screen dominated the front. Across the two aisles on either side of the pit were passenger chairs arranged in single file, a round viewport set into the wall next to each seat. Scattered tables and cabinets made of imported polished teak completed the decor.

In the forecabin was the command and communications center. Here, high technology replaced luxury. The center was capable of tapping into any communications or defense system owned by the United States or her allies. It could also extract information from every major computer network in the country, including those of "unfriendly" powers. Six other places in the world exceeded it in sophistication and effectiveness, and they were all ground-based. The command center was quite literally capable of starting an all-out nuclear war. Exactly seven people knew of its existence.

Although it always carried a full crew complement including seven flight attendants, tonight only two passengers were present.

One sat quietly reading the *Wall Street Journal,* while the other slept, only the slow rising and falling of his chest indicating he was alive.

Senate Majority Leader Jack Kline thumbed through the pages of the *Journal,* his motions restless. Although he could have just as easily called up the same information on either of the two terminals located at opposing corners of the conversation pit, he preferred the feel of the paper in his hand. Try as he might, however, he could not focus on any one article. He lowered the paper just enough to glance at his traveling companion. Jacob Hill looked fastidious even in sleep. Jack envied the man his poise. No matter the circumstance, Hill always seemed to be in complete control of events and surroundings. Although the past six years had been good for Jack and his family, he rarely felt in control. This nocturnal flight to who-knew-where was a good example. Jacob Hill had "requested" that Jack accompany him, and Jack had not dared to disobey. Jacob had literally made him, and he could destroy him as well.

Since his induction into Hill's inner circle, Jack's political career had sky-rocketed. He had risen through the ranks to obtain what was essentially the second most powerful office in the nation. (Many thought it to be the most powerful.) The meteoric rate of his ascent had astonished both friend and foe alike. Now, he was said to be a "shoo-in" for the presidency in '04. He was envied, admired, and just a little feared by his peers on Capitol Hill. The problem was, none of this was thanks to Jack Kline. Each of his victories, every one of his advances, had been carefully orchestrated by the man sitting across from him.

Six years ago, Jack had been naive enough to believe he had been destined for greatness. He truly felt that he had the ability to be Jacob Hill's equal, and perhaps his successor. Why else had the man taken such an interest in him? Now, he knew better. The bitter truth was, he was an average politician who happened to be the special project of a very powerful man. His accomplishments, his victories, all belonged to Jacob Hill, not to Jack Kline. It was a truth he tried hard not to dwell on.

Throwing his paper on the couch, he stood and walked over to one of the passenger seats. Falling rather than sitting into the soft cushion, he reached over and drew aside the small curtain that covered the viewport. An incredible vastness loomed before him. At this altitude, the curvature of the earth was easy to see. Far below, the United States was shimmering in the eerie glow of a full moon. It was a clear night and he could see scattered sparks of light denoting human habitation. Off in the distance he could make out a large city. Since he had no idea where they were going, he also had no idea what city it might be.

How serene it seems up here, he thought to himself, but he knew that peace to be a false peace. The world was in turmoil, on the brink of an all-out war. The Eastern Bloc states were embarking upon the greatest military build up in their history. NATO, plagued with internal strife and ready to disband, was trying desperately to keep up. China was threatening to invade the Middle East, where war was the rule and not the exception. Intelligence sources reported that they could now field an army of over two hundred million. This year alone, over 5,000 American lives would be lost in the never-ending conflict. Unless something was done soon to lance the boil of war, the entire planet was liable to blow.

Domestically, things were little better. The Midwest once again was in the grip of a fierce drought, and it looked as if the latest wheat crop would fail. That meant even longer lines at the stores. Alternate sources of energy were still far in the future. With gas prices at over $5 per gallon, how long could the average American hold out?

To top it all off, since the government had taken control of organized religion, people had started holding private meetings in their homes. They flagrantly violated the laws that were written to protect them. Didn't they see that they were damaging themselves and their country? That would have to stop. Then there was runaway inflation, rampant crime, and the killer plague known as AIDS. All in all, the outlook was bleak.

Jack let the curtain fall back into place and leaned his head back in the seat. Pushing the button recessed into the armrest, he reclined the back to where he was almost laying flat. He turned the small reading light above him off, closed his eyes, and tried to sleep. It should have been easy. The dim lighting, the steady "thrum" of the powerful engines, and the soft hiss of the air conditioning all seemed to whisper "sleep" to his tired mind. Sleep, however, was an elusive ghost that stayed just out of reach.

Six years, he thought wistfully, thinking of his first meeting with Jacob's inner circle. He considered that meeting a major turning point in his life. *Incredible that so much has changed in such a short period of time.* His rise to power, the constitutional convention that had rewritten the face of the nation, the sweeping changes in the law books, all of it seemed a blur. He rubbed his eyes and massaged his temples, but it did little to relieve the tension he felt. He glanced over at the still sleeping figure of Hill, and wondered about his traveling companion. Despite working closely with the man these past few years, he still did not know him. Jacob had taught and guided him, but had not allowed Jack to get too close. The fact was, he was more than a little frightened of Jacob. Many of the changes made in the nation could be traced directly to Jacob's influence.

Take organized religion, for example. Jack had agreed with Jacob that religious groups desperately need to be brought under strict government control. The corruption in many of those organizations was rampant. The average citizen was being bilked out of millions of dollars by some of these con men. He himself had been instrumental in getting the proper legislation passed, but now things seemed to be getting out of control. Instead of simply watchdogging the more suspect groups and regulating their fundraising, Jacob, through the bureau, had literally destroyed them. Jack had watched as he had maneuvered politicians, corporations, a president, and the American public. He was amazed at the man's subtlety and patience. The results were staggering. In the "land of the free," it was now considered an act of treason to even own a Bible.

What's next, Jack thought sarcastically, *the vote?* He realized that Jacob's militant hatred of religion was starting to deeply disturb him. *Forget it,* he told himself sternly. *It's still a free country. People can still go to church, as long as that church is government sanctioned.* Thrusting unpleasant thoughts aside, he again closed his eyes and tried to sleep. Slowly, the engine noise, the dim lights, and his own fatigue overcame him and he drifted into a light doze.

Scott Sampson was in church. There were no "ivory towers," or impressive fixtures. The cellar was cold and the walls were crawling with green fungus. The single dim bulb did little more than reveal the horrid condition of the place. There was absolutely no place to sit, and his legs were already beginning to cramp. Still, Scott Sampson was in church, and, much to his surprise, he was happy. His feelings were a crossbreed of ecstasy and amazement — amazement because he had not felt like this in years, not since attending his home church in Detroit. Ecstasy because he knew, really knew for the first time in what seemed like forever, that God was in this place. Gone, at least for the moment, was the fear that had plagued him all the way here.

Ned had started the meeting quite simply by quoting Matthew 18:20. The 12 worshipers had grown still as Ned's quiet voice said, "For where two or three have gathered together in My name, there I am in the midst of them."

At that moment a quiet peace had come to Scott's heart. There was no doubt in his mind. Almighty God, in the person of the Holy Spirit, filled that little room. Although the dim bulb became no brighter, there was a luminance — that was the only way he could describe it — that permeated the room. His physical eyes could see no better than before, but his spiritual eyes beheld the glory of the living God. At last Scott truly understood the phrase "now we see as through a glass darkly . . . but then shall I know. . . ." As he studied the other members, it was as if he could almost see them as they *would be,* not as they are now. He got a glimpse of what it must be like to be glorified. They seemed covered with the radiance of God. It left him speechless.

He was surprised to recognize several of the group. There was Ned, of course, and his wife Lilly. The Fergusons, Tim and Susie, were there. Scott had remembered them as a husband and wife team who taught the youth group at Faith Community. Off in the corner were two teenage boys Scott remembered from the youth group. *Men,* Scott corrected himself. *If they have the guts to be part of this, they aren't boys.*

Then there was Allan Meyers. Scott knew him as an insurance salesman who attended Faith Community on a semi-regular basis. Allan had called the Sampsons at home soon after they began going to the same church. He wanted to set up an appointment to discuss their insurance needs. Although Scott declined, Allan had nevertheless been gracious and friendly whenever they ran into each other at church. Scott had caught the man's eye when the meeting started and nodded a greeting. Allan did not even acknowledge the gesture. His eyes constantly roamed the room, as if searching for a way out.

He looks like a caged tiger, thought Scott. *I hope he can hold it together while we're here.* He looked back to where Ned was speaking and promptly forgot about Allan in the wondrous time that followed.

After beginning with Matthew 18:20, Ned had then quoted the first chapter of John . . . then the second . . . and then the third! Almost without pause, he had gone on to the first two chapters in First Corinthians, the first four chapters of Ephesians, and topped it all off with the entire book of Second Timothy. Scott stood with his mouth wide open. The man was a walking Bible! What's more, there was no pretense here, no "hot-dogging" or showing off. Ned wasn't trying to impress anyone. The tender and loving way he quoted each verse spoke volumes about his love of Scripture. He caressed each word gently, reluctant to let it go. It set the tone for the service. They were not there to listen to a "message" or a three-point sermon. They had not come to sing three verses of a hymn. They were there to listen to the Word of God. When he finally finished, there was not a dry eye in the group. Ned finished quoting Scripture and paused a moment.

"These are dangerous times," he said finally. "Like the Christians of old, we find ourselves persecuted at every turn. We can no longer meet to worship in the peace and freedom we once enjoyed." He scanned the cellar, looking each person in the eye. At that moment, the entire building could have come collapsing down around them and they would not have noticed. They were completely caught up in the spirit of the meeting. Ned smiled, and his smile quickly widened into a grin.

"That's okay, though," he said, his voice growing with excitement. "Jesus never promised us an easy time of it. In fact, just the opposite! Let us not forget the Apostles who were beaten and thrown into prison. They rejoiced that they were found worthy to suffer for our Lord's sake." There were many nods, and a few smiles from the group, but Ned was not finished. He set his face in a determined look, and once again he had the tiny church's complete attention.

"The Apostles were glad to suffer," he repeated, "but do not forget just what they were glad to suffer *for*. When Peter and John were brought before the high priest and the scribes, they were ordered not to teach in the name of Jesus. Listen to their reply in Acts 4:19. 'Whether it is right in the sight of God to give heed to you rather than to God, you be the judge; for we cannot stop speaking what we have seen and heard.' " Ned's voice grew stern and powerful, although it was not greater in volume than before. While Scott had not known the man well at Faith Community, he had never seen him like this — so confident and assured. He wished he had the man's courage.

"This," continued Ned, waving his arm to encompass the entire room, "this is *not* enough! Let's not get the idea that we are brave, or special because we meet like this. Unless we leave here with the determination not only to live for Christ, but to share His love and salvation with as many as we can, then THIS . . . IS . . . FOR . . . NOTHING!"

The words hit the church like a hammer, each one pounding in the truth. Scott almost physically recoiled from the force of Ned's admonition. The bitter truth hit him like a blow. When was the last time he had witnessed to someone? He thought of the people he worked with, of his neighbors next door. He had been so concerned about his own safety that he had never once mentioned God to any of them. He saw the ugliness of his own selfishness, and it sickened him. What was the use of having a light if he only used it for himself? For a moment, Scott bowed his head in recognition of his own failure. He missed Ned's next few words.

". . . be discouraged. Just remember why we meet like this. We meet to worship, and to gain strength from each other and most importantly, from God. This time together is our refuge, a time to rest in our Lord. When we leave here, our mission begins anew." A look of sadness crossed Ned's face.

"In the years before we lost our freedom, a great number of Christians were involved in politics. Now, I'm not saying this was wrong, but somewhere back then, we lost sight of something important. We became so involved in trying to stop abortion that we forgot to pray and witness to those who performed abortions. We fought so hard to get prayer reinstated in public schools that we stopped loving those who threw it out in the first place. We forgot to care for and love those who stood against us. Now our enemies are multiplied a thousandfold. Will we fight them?"

There was a murmured "no" from the tiny group.

"Paul did not resist when he was taken prisoner and sent to Rome," continued Ned. "He didn't bemoan his imprisonment. Instead, he loved and witnessed to his captors, and many of them were saved. Can we do less?" Again the congregation whispered "no," this time in greater unison.

"Remember," said Ned, "if we were an army, they could defeat us. If we were philosophers, they could debate us, but if we are love, plain and simple love, what will they do with us? They may hurt us, they may kill us, but they will never stop us." There was a strong chorus of "Amens," and Ned looked down at his watch.

"I've talked long enough. You didn't come here to listen to me, but to the Father. I think it's high time we did just that." So saying, he joined hands with the people on either side of him. At his cue, the rest gathered along the four walls, linking hands to form a circle.

To Scott, the prayer time was sweet beyond belief. The presence of the Holy Spirit filled the cellar, stronger even than before. He wished it could go on forever, but knew that it must end soon. Ned led them, and each member stood with him and agreed with him. He prayed for each one of those in the room by name, then he prayed for those who would destroy them. He asked that everyone of them would have a chance to share the love of Christ before they met again. Scott had attended a prayer meeting before, but now knew that he had never really been in a real prayer meeting until tonight.

Oh God, he said silently to himself, but the words caught in his throat. He wanted desperately to ask forgiveness, to turn away from his fear and doubt, to live a strong Christian life, but he simply could not find the right thing to say. His heart breaking, he stood in mute silence. Then finally he asked God for the right things to say. No words came, but suddenly the doubt was gone. He knew, for the first time in his life, that his prayer was being heard. He prayed with his heart, and in the Spirit, with groanings that could not be uttered. It was the first time in his life he had ever prayed this way, and in the privacy of his own thoughts, he poured out his heart to God, asking for another chance to live for Him. He knew inside that his battle with fear was far from over, but now he had a friend to lean on, to fight the battles for him. From this moment on, Scott Sampson would not be alone.

When Ned finished, Scott lifted his head, surprised to find two large tears running down his cheeks. He was not alone. Beth, who held his hand on his right, sniffed a little, and smiled shyly at him. For just a moment, they shared the joy of the Lord. Scott felt his love for his wife blossom anew, and squeezed her hand tightly. She returned the pressure, and leaned up against him. It was the closest they had been in months. Scott looked up at Ned, who was looking at his watch again.

"There was supposed to be someone else here tonight. I was saving it for a surprise, but it looks as if it will have to wait." He held up his hand to forestall further questions.

"I said it was a surprise," he smiled. "Now," he continued, "as wonderful as it's been tonight, we've overstayed our welcome. It's time to break up and go home. Scott, Beth, since you two got here last, you can leave first. Just go back the way you came, and be careful on the streets. This isn't the best section of town."

"I just hope our car is still in one piece," remarked Scott as they edged their way toward the door. There were scattered chuckles at his comment. Scott reached for the door, but paused a moment to look Ned in the eye. "I was scared to death to come here," he said evenly. "The only reason I'm here is because of Beth, and she had to drag me kicking and screaming all the way." For a moment, Scott found he was unable to speak. Ned looked at him, his eyes understanding, waiting for him to continue.

"The thing is," he said in a rush, "this is the best thing that's happened to us in a long time. Will you let us come again?"

Ned laughed heartily. "Welcome to the family, Scott. Count on it. We'll call you when it's time."

For the first time in what seemed like a lifetime, Scott grinned, then laughed out loud. He felt as if he were a child that had just been given the thing he wanted most for Christmas.

He opened the door for Beth, then, just before he walked out, he turned to that small determined group of believers and said, "The Lord is risen."

Once again, the church replied joyfully, "The Lord is risen indeed." With that wonderful greeting ringing in his ears, he closed the cellar door. Again blackness settled over them, leaving them in the stifling mustiness. Scott took a deep breath of the cool, damp air. Even that seemed fresh compared to the cellar. With no ventilation, it had begun to get a little stale toward the end of the meeting. Taking Beth's arm in one hand, he began to grope toward the stairs with the other.

"Can you see at all?" whispered his wife.

"Not a thing," he whispered back.

"Do you think it's safe to leave?"

"Sure. If there was going to be any trouble, it would have come sooner."

"Then would you mind telling me why we're whispering?"

Scott was in the middle of taking a deep breath, and Beth's last remark caught him off guard. He started to laugh, but ended up coughing when he tried to inhale and exhale at the same time. This caused him to forget where he was and he promptly barked his shin against the foot of the stairs.

"Ow!"

"Eeek! That sounded painful."

"It *was* painful," he replied peevishly, rubbing his bruise.

"Funny, I didn't feel a thing!"

"Cute," he said through clenched teeth. "Let's see you navigate any. . . ." Abruptly, he broke off what he was about to say. It suddenly hit him that Beth was joking with him the way she used to — the way she did when things were good between them. For a moment, he remembered how they used to love each other. Tears came unbidden to his cheeks, because he realized that, in her own way, she was telling him that they could be that way again. She was willing to start over, to forgive him for his childish and timid ways. For the first time in ages, he felt a wave of pure, emotional love rush over him. At that moment, he wanted nothing more than to spend an eternity with just her.

"Beth," he managed to croak, and then she was in his arms, holding him tight. It made him feel whole again. Squeezing her with all his might, he realized just how much he had almost lost.

"Beth," he said again, this time lovingly and softly. "Forgive me. Forgive me for being such a. . . ." He would have continued, but her lips found his. The kiss was electric and vital. It was as if they were touching for the very first time, and in a way, they were. His tears mingled with her own and their embrace grew more ardent. Then Beth pulled away, touching his cheek lightly with one hand.

"Whoa, lover." Her voice tinkled. That was the only way Scott could describe it. It sounded like tiny chimes. "Don't you think we should continue this discussion somewhere else?"

"Hmmm? Your place or mine?" he joked, sniffing at the same time.

"Ours," she answered softly, kissing him again. "We've got a lot to talk about. I love you, Scott." Her words thrilled him. Once again, he took her arm and started forward. Beth was right about getting a move on. Soon others would be leaving, and it would not do to have too many going out at the same time. Slowly, they made their way up the rickety staircase. Each step groaned as it accepted their weight. Finally, they reached the landing at the top. Scott felt for and found the door latch. He started to tug it open, and froze. Beth inhaled sharply.

"What is it?" she asked, apprehension suddenly in her voice. She felt it too. Scott tried to answer, but couldn't. His heart was pounding. Try as he might, he could not open the latch. Somehow, he knew beyond certainty that it would be disastrous to go through that door. He felt trapped. There was nowhere else to go. There were no other exits out of the cellar. He took a deep breath and tried to slow his heart rate. Gingerly, as if it were a snake that would bite him, he lifted the latch. Putting both hands on the door, he pulled it gently toward him. When he had opened it about an inch, he leaned forward and put his eye to the crack. It took a moment to adjust to the light spilling in. When he could see, he peered forward.

He could see the doorway they had come through, and the showroom beyond that. The dirty curtain was only closed halfway. There was the bald man — Scott never did get his name — still sitting at his high desk. Everything appeared to be normal. Nothing had changed since they had arrived except that it was now dark outside. He could see the dim glow of street lights through the display windows. He breathed a sigh of relief, but the feeling of impending disaster would not go away. He wanted to get out of there, back to his home and safety, but could not make himself move.

He was just about to force himself through the door when, without warning, the revolving entrance started to spin. In horror, Scott watched as a half dozen men, some in suits, some in uniforms rushed in. Without hesitation, they made straight for the bald man. Scott didn't wait. He knew that they had been discovered. There was no place to go, but he had to try to get away.

"Back! Get back down!" he whispered roughly to Beth. Leaving the door ajar, he grabbed her arm and started down the stairs. It was a miracle they didn't fall. Once, when a step gave way, they almost pitched head first down that dark hole. Only Scott's death grip on the handrail saved them. The dim light coming through the cracked door helped a little, and somehow they made it to the bottom. Scott's first thought was to get back into the cellar, to try to warn those inside. He ran out of time. The door at the top flew open, and the harsh glare of flashlights shone through. Without thinking, he dove into the narrow space between the wall and the staircase. As heavy booted feet thudded down into the cellar, he all but dragged Beth under the stairs. There was a narrow crawl space there, filled with stacks of molding boxes. He found an opening between two of the stacks and slid in, pulling Beth in behind him. Part of him thanked the racket the raiders were making. Otherwise, they would surely have been heard. Heart beating like a runaway locomotive, he crouched down in that filthy space as more and more men filed down the stairs. There was a thud, and some muttered cursing as one official tripped on the step that had given way under Scott and Beth's wild flight. There was a loud clicking sound, as of metal on metal, and Scott realized with a thrill of fear that he was hearing the cocking of firearms. Then came a heavy banging on the cellar door.

"Federal officers! Open this door at once!"

There was a muted shout from inside. Scott thought it was Ned. Then another knock rocked the weak door. One more, and it gave way.

"Everybody, against that wall!" shouted the harsh voice. "Let's go, get up off those knees! Move!"

There was a loud "smack," and then a cry of pain from one of the women. Voices rose in protest, and then a powerful voice took command.

"Everyone, be calm," it said, and this time Scott was sure that it was Ned. "Do what they say. We knew that this might happen. We are in God's hands. Don't fear!"

"Yeah, right," came another gruff voice. "I got yer 'god' right here." Again there came a smack, and this time it was Ned that cried out in pain. Scott closed his eyes and clenched his fists. He had never felt so helpless.

"Please, God, let this be a dream," he prayed desperately, but of course nothing changed. They had been found out, and all they could do was to face the storm headlong."

"Well, isn't this special," mocked the first voice. "What a nice cozy group. Sergeant, cuff these traitors and get 'em into the wagon. Look's like a good night, gentlemen. This is quite a haul, a real feather in our cap. It'll look good to the higher-ups."

"We have to take them all now?" leered the second voice. "This one here, we could have some fun with her." There was a groan of despair. Scott recognized it as Susie's.

"Sorry, Sergeant. Orders are that none of them are to be 'damaged.' They got a little trip ahead of them."

"Too bad. Okay, let's go. Come on, MOVE!"

"What about our rights?" Scott heard Ned ask calmly. "If you're arresting us, we should be read our rights." There was a momentary silence, and when the first voice spoke again, it spoke with a chill that froze Scott's heart.

"You have no rights," it said flatly. "When you decided to have your little meeting, you automatically became a traitor to the state. That means you forfeited any rights to be treated like a citizen. Sergeant!"

"All right, enough talk. Let's go."

The shattered group was led out of the cellar and up the stairs. From the sound of it, the police, or whoever they were, were not too gentle. More than once Scott heard someone fall, only to be struck and ordered to keep moving. Not daring to move, he crouched low. Beth leaned against him, pushing him hard against the cellar wall. They listened as the footsteps thudded their way up the stairs and out the door. The flashlight beams disappeared and darkness returned. For just a moment, all was quiet. Scott was actually beginning to hope that they had escaped. He was just about to move when the cellar door again opened and a single ray of light appeared.

"Nice work," said the first voice, who had evidently remained behind. "Thanks to you, we got the whole bunch."

"Look, you got what you wanted. Is that it? Can I go now?" Scott felt Beth stiffen behind him, knowing her reaction was mirrored by his own. He knew that voice! Allan Meyers!

"Of course. Just as soon as you assure me that we got everyone. Wouldn't want to miss someone, now would we? It wouldn't look good for you — or your family."

Allan's voice had the tone of one totally defeated. "Two others left just before you got here. You must have seen them."

"Nobody came out the front. There's a back entrance, but we had it covered. Are you sure they left?"

"Where else would they go?" snapped Allan. He was obviously under a great deal of strain.

"Don't use that tone with me, Mister. What were their names?" In despair, Scott listened as Allan answered.

"Scott and Beth Sampson. They live on this side of the river, somewhere in Fort Mitchell, I think." There was a muted click, then a burst of static.

"Sergeant!"

"Sir!" The sergeant's voice sounded as if it were on the other end of the phone. The man in charge evidently had a communicator.

"There are two other suspects. They left just before we came in, so start a search of the immediate area. Their names are Scott and Beth Sampson. Call that in to Central and get an address on them, and put out an APB to the local agencies. Let's find them, Sergeant!"

"Yes, sir!"

"Now," said the leader, "is there anything else you need to tell me?"

"No."

"Then go on home, but don't leave town, and be sure to stay in touch. Got that?"

There was a grunt of agreement, and the two went up and out into the store. Below, two frightened people huddled together, their entire world having just crashed about them. Scott had no idea what to do next. There was nowhere they could go. Their house would now be watched, and there was no one at work Scott could trust with his or Beth's life. He closed his eyes and leaned back against the cold wall, trying to make some sense of what had just happened.

Unbidden, the image of Allan Meyers came to his mind, and a sudden wave of anger washed over him. Betrayer! Those officers had called the others traitors, but Allan was the real one. The church had simply stayed true to God. They had sworn their allegiance when they accepted Christ as their personal Saviour. But Allan — Allan had turned his back on his faith and on his friends.

Scott remembered the way he himself had been before coming here tonight. He remembered his fear and anger, but try as he might, he could not bring himself to believe that he would betray the others just to save himself. Why? Why had Allan done this? The more he ran it over in his mind, the more angry and frustrated he got. He also realized that it was getting him nowhere. They were now wanted by the law, and they had to have a plan if they were going to stay free.

"Scott?" Beth's voice, though only a whisper, startled him.

"Yeah?" he said, taking a deep breath.

"Shouldn't we try to get out of here?"

"Too soon," he replied. "You heard what that guy said. They're going to be looking for us. Let's give it a few hours. By then, things may have quieted down enough to leave."

He could tell by the way she was leaning against him that she did not like the thought of remaining under that staircase. For that matter, neither did he. Now that everything was quiet, the other residents of the cellar were beginning to make themselves known. Scott was almost glad that they were in complete darkness. He didn't want to see what was making all those scratching noises. He was suddenly aware that his legs were cramping from squatting between the boxes. Gently, he pushed Beth away and levered himself to a full sitting position on the cold floor. He could feel Beth following suit, settling in once more against him.

"Try to rest a little," he whispered. He felt for his watch and pushed the button that would light up the tiny display. It read 10:30. "We'll try to leave just after midnight."

"All right. Scott, I love you."

"I love you, too. Don't worry, we'll get out of here." Trying to sound confident, he put his arm around his wife and nuzzled her hair. It was going to be a long two hours. Probably the longest he had ever spent in his life.

❖ ❖ ❖

Helen had never been happier. Here she was with Roy, canoeing across the main lake at Versailles State Park. They had spent their honeymoon here, and tried to come back at least once a year since. Just across the Ohio/Indiana border, it was only a two hour drive from their home.

Roy looked wonderful. Tanned and healthy, he was the husband she knew before the cancer made him into an empty, eaten-out shell. He smiled at her as he evenly stroked the canoe across the lake. The sun was bright and warm on the back of her neck. There was not a cloud in the sky. Soon, they would beach the small craft in a spot only they knew about. Helen would prepare the picnic lunch she had brought, and they would spend the rest of the afternoon just being together.

"This is perfect, Hon," she said in a lazy voice. The warm air and slow lapping water had an almost hypnotic effect on her. Roy just smiled and nodded. Off in the distance, thunder began to rumble. Thunder? Helen looked up at the sky, seeing nothing but blue. How could there be thunder with no clouds? Again it sounded across the lake, louder this time, more insistent. It seemed to call to her, demanding her attention. Anxiously she looked at Roy, who continued to smile as if nothing was wrong. He kept paddling the canoe.

CRASH! This time there was lightning, and suddenly the sky was not clear anymore. Huge dark threatening clouds boiled overhead, and the once calm water was now dark and choppy. A large drop of rain smacked onto the deck of the canoe. More followed. Helen felt her cheeks getting wet, and began to get frightened. They should be heading back to shore. She started to say as much to Roy, but to her horror, she couldn't talk above a whisper. CRACK . . . CRASH! The thunder deafened her. The sky was so dark now that it was almost impossible to see. She squinted toward Roy, but could only make out his outline in the murky darkness.

"Roy!" she called desperately. "Roy, don't leave me here. I need you. Don't leave me. . . ." The rain began to pour down with a loud roar, washing everything out. Her world disappeared. "ROY!" she shouted, and sat upright in her bed, completely disoriented. She reached over to touch her husband, but of course there was no one there.

"Oh, Roy," she said softly as memory returned. "Did you have to leave so soon?"

Her cheeks were wet with tears. She just sat there for what seemed like an eternity, wanting nothing more than to go back inside her dream, to spend just a few more precious moments with her mate. Gradually it came to her that the thunder was still banging, its sound muffled through the bedroom walls. Abruptly she realized that someone was beating on her front door. A cold fear gripped her heart. The clock on her night stand read almost two in the morning. In her line of work, a nocturnal visit like this could only mean trouble. She got up and looked out the bedroom window. There were no police cars, at least. Somewhat relieved, she hurried to put on her robe. She made her way into the living room and to the front door. Turning on the porch light, she stood on tiptoe to peer through the peephole. There, his face distorted by the convex lens, was Tom, her friend from the mall. Without hesitation, Helen unlocked and opened the door.

"Helen! Thank God! I rang and rang the doorbell, but there was no answer."

"That's because it doesn't work," replied Helen, standing aside to let her distraught friend in. "Hasn't in a few years. Tom, what's wrong? You weren't supposed to be here until tomorrow, uh, this afternoon?"

"Helen, they got them. They got the whole group." The fear that had hovered unnamed in the back of her mind finally coagulated. This was her worst nightmare come true.

"Okay, calm down," she said as much to herself as to Tom. "Come on in and tell me what happened." She led him into the small but comfortable living room and motioned for him to sit on the sofa. Disappearing into the kitchen, she returned a few moments later with two steaming cups of coffee. Tom sipped his gratefully. The hot black liquid seemed to calm and reassure him. Settling herself on one of the highbacked chairs across from her guest, Helen gave him a few moments to gather his composure.

"All right, Dear," she said in her most comforting voice. "Tell me what happened, one step at a time."

Tom nodded, and then thought for a moment. "When I left you at the mall," he finally began, "I went straight back to the motel. I stayed there until it was time to leave. Sheila wanted to come with me, but I insisted on staying with the original plan. Besides, someone had to stay with the boys." Helen nodded, encouraging him to continue.

"Anyway, I left with plenty of time to spare. I wanted to make sure that the meeting place wasn't being watched. When I got there, I just drove by, checking things out. It was a furniture store, by the way — downtown Covington — bad section of town. Everything looked fine. There were no parked cars along the street, and no one seemed to be hanging around. I even checked out the rest of the neighborhood. Nothing was out of the ordinary, so I parked in the garage that I had been told about. It was a few streets over. I walked the rest of the way. There was a little diner just up the street. From there, I could see the store, so I got some dinner and waited. I wanted to make sure that everything was okay," he repeated, as if trying to reassure himself.

"You did the right thing," said Helen. "Go on."

"Well, I watched the store until just after dark. The only people I saw go in was a younger couple. I'm pretty sure they were part of the church, because they didn't come back out. I finished my dinner and paid my check, then went to the bathroom. When I came back out, there were a few other customers looking out the window. I went over to see what was going on, and. . . ." For a moment, Tom closed his eyes and seemed unable to continue. Helen waited patiently.

"There were police cars in front of the store," he blurted out finally, his voice thick with emotion. "They had their flashers on and a bunch of officers were running inside. I couldn't watch, but I had no choice. There was nowhere to go until they left. A few minutes later, they began to drag everyone out. They were really rough on them. They took them out and put them all into a van. When the van drove off, the officers left began going building to building. One officer came into the diner and asked if any of us had seen a young couple in the last hour or so. When he gave their description, I recognized them as the ones I had seen go into the store before. I guess that somehow they got away. I don't know." Tom stopped abruptly and put his hands into his face.

"I tried, Helen. I honestly tried to get there. If I could have been just a few minutes earlier. . . ."

"You would have been captured along with the rest of them," finished Helen bluntly. "Tom, look at me."

Tom raised his eyes to meet hers. He had a haunted look about him.

"There was nothing you could have done," she told him firmly. "From what you've told me, this wasn't a spur-of-the-moment operation. If you had been with them, you would now be in custody, and we would be a lot worse off."

"I could have warned them . . ." began Tom.

"How?" demanded Helen. "It happened so fast." She thought for a moment. "This was planned. Somehow, the police got wind of this meeting."

"Not the police," corrected Tom. "I saw the uniform of the officer who questioned us at the diner. The emblem said 'Bureau of Religious Affairs.' "

"I know the bureau," said Helen thoughtfully. "I also know they have their own force, but I didn't know they were working on such a local level. I have a feeling that things have just become more complicated."

Tom was silent for a moment, then said, "What about that church? Isn't there something we can do for them?"

Helen shook her head doubtfully. "If they had been arrested by local authorities, I would say yes. We've had some success on that end. From what you say, though, city or state police didn't have anything to do with this. I'll make some phone calls, but I don't know."

"Those poor people," Tom said miserably. Helen stood up and took Tom's cup.

"You can stay here for what's left of the night," she said. "Call Sheila and let her know where you are." She pointed toward the guest bedroom. "Everything you need is in there. Get some rest, and we'll try to figure out what to do in the morning." Without another word, Tom went into the bedroom and closed the door.

Helen put the cups in the sink and retired to her own bedroom. She had tried to sound calm and confident for Tom's sake, but inside her heart was breaking. Another body of believers stamped out! And what about these uniformed officers? Why was the bureau breaking up small groups like this one? They usually left that to the local authorities. She would have to call Jeff first thing in the morning to check this out. Right now, though, she realized that there was only one thing she could do for those poor victims. She knelt beside the bed and began to pray. She stayed there the rest of the night.

❖ ❖ ❖

Jack Kline's world was a blur. Lack of sleep had made the events of the past few days run together. First, there was the phone call from Jacob requesting — no demanding — that he accompany him on "a short trip."

Then there was his furtive departure from Washington in the middle of the night, followed by the sub-orbital flight. Now, here he was, in a black stretch limousine that was navigating its way through an industrial sector several miles outside of Los Angeles. It was close to 4:00 a.m. Pacific time, and still quite dark on the West Coast. Between the hectic events of the past day and the lost sleep, he was in pretty bad shape.

He hoped he had been successful in diverting suspicion from his activities. The senate majority leader simply did not take clandestine trips such as this, at least not if he wanted to remain in office. Already, several of his colleagues were starting to ask some uncomfortable questions — questions about his political ties. Unless his executive assistant, Marcie Cummings, could successfully "throw the hounds off the scent," he could be in for some rough times ahead. He had mentioned this several times to Jacob, but the man had merely smiled and assured him that everything was under control. Jack wanted to believe him, but still he had his doubts.

The limousine made its way down the narrow, sparsely lit street toward who knew where. Although it was still dark, traffic was already starting to build. This part of the city truly never slept. Factories, refineries, and assorted manufacturing plants operated around the clock. Right now, the graveyard shifts were just getting off and the early morning crowd was gearing up for another work day. Jack watched with something akin to envy as the "heart of America," the so-called blue collar workers, went hurrying to wherever they were going.

How long has it been since I've held a regular job? he thought. *One where I go in, put in my hours, and go home. One where I leave my work at the office, and forget about it until the next day.* He thought about it for a moment, and then decided he couldn't remember ever having that sort of job. For as long as he could recall, he had wanted to hold a public office. Even in his high school days, he had worked for his political party. While his friends had been flipping hamburgers and washing cars, he was passing out campaign leaflets and knocking on doors. Politics had been an all-consuming ambition.

"Jack." Jacob's calm, cultured voice cut into his thoughts. Idly, Jack wondered if Jacob ever raised his voice above speaking level.

"Hmmm?" Jack responded.

"There's our destination up ahead on the left."

The car had just rounded a sharp curve. Jack looked where Jacob was pointing past the driver's shoulder and saw a high security fence. Beyond that was a huge steel, glass, and concrete structure that seemed to spread out in all directions. It was a sprawling complex made up of at least four separate sections, all connected to form a rough square. The whole effect was of a complex cube that looked as if it ran on forever. As they approached the menacing security fence, Jack read the single name on the huge triangular-shaped ebony and gold sign, just past the gate.

"Mentasys?" he said aloud.

"Yes," replied Jacob, and Jack could hear a grim satisfaction in his companion's voice. "Have you heard of it?"

Jack tried to wipe the cobwebs out of his tired mind and concentrate. "Isn't that one of Christine Smythe's corporations?" he said at last.

"Correct," answered Jacob. "Mentasys is a multinational corporation owned by our friend Christine. Among other things, it is a supplier of pharmaceuticals to every major hospital in the nation. They deal almost exclusively in drugs which affect the mind — drugs that treat schizophrenia and other mental disorders. They have made quite a few breakthroughs in the past five years."

"So why are we going there?" asked Jack.

"There are a few things I want you to see," said Jacob, glancing sideways at him. "You have proven yourself worthy of our trust, Jack. All of us agree that it's time we brought you into our complete confidence."

Instantly, Jack was wide awake. *By all that's holy, this is what I've been waiting for!* he thought. Excitement suddenly engulfed him like a fire. By "us," Jacob meant his inner circle, the elite. He had worked *for* them for over six years. Finally, it looked as if he would be working *with* them. Now, Jack Kline would take his place within that very circle. He would be someone that mattered. He had wanted this all of his life. His entire political career had been geared solely toward this instant.

He dismissed the doubts and fears that had been plaguing him during the trip. Sure, Jacob had been instrumental in his political climb. He had been with him every step of the way, but not because he was average or could not do it alone. Now Jack understood that Jacob had chosen him because he was *special*. Jack Kline was destined for greatness — for immortality.

Jack's head was reeling with visions of power as the limousine turned off the main street and up to the outer gate. A small guardhouse was located just outside the gate. The limousine stopped and both the driver and Jacob lowered their windows. A no-nonsense guard greeted them coolly.

"Morning, Mr. Hill," he said. "I'll need to see your identification, sir."

Without a word, Jacob handed the guard a small, blank card about the size of a drivers license. The guard took both Jacob's and the driver's ID and inserted them one at a time into a box that stood waist high on a single pole. When Jacob's card went in, a small screen lit just above the slot and glowed with information.

Jack could see a computerized image of Jacob as well as printed information next to it. The procedure was repeated with the driver's card.

Satisfied, the guard handed the cards back. Then he peered past Jacob at Jack.

"You're Senator Kline," he said, nodding. He handed Jacob a small clipboard. "I'll need your signature, Mr. Hill, authorizing him past this point." Jacob took the clipboard and signed in the appropriate place.

"Thank you, sir," said the guard. He retrieved his board and motioned them through. They drove through the well-manicured grounds and toward the complex itself.

"This place is quite unique," remarked Jacob once they were inside the gate. "In addition to manufacturing all sorts of pharmaceuticals, this is also one of the most advanced research facilities in the world."

"What type of research?" asked Jack

"Mental disorders, mainly," replied Jacob. "The staff here has mapped the human brain more extensively than has ever been done before."

Jack's only reply was a noncommittal grunt. They passed a number of small parking lots and finally came to the main entrance.

Here, the limo stopped and the driver got out and opened the door for his two passengers. Jack followed Jacob out of the car and into the main lobby of Mentasys. He saw a reception desk straight ahead and a row of elevators across the lobby to his right. The lobby itself was a pleasant place. Even though it was still dark, the large windows across the front gave a feeling of airiness. Plenty of assorted indoor plants and trees decorated the interior, and the thick royal blue carpet added a touch of luxury.

"Ah, there you are Jacob — and you, Senator Kline. It's good to see you again."

The familiar voice came from Jack's right. He turned to see Dr. Samuel Steiger emerge from a door that was obviously an office. Other than Jacob Hill, Jack did not meet with the other members of the inner circle often. He had not seen the doctor since that fateful meeting six years ago. Even so, the man looked much the same. Tall and broad, looking more like a football linebacker than a doctor, he towered over even Jacob. A shock of jet black hair went well with his ruddy complexion. *What makes you notice him though, are his eyes,* thought Jack as he shook hands. He had built a career on reading people, and the best way to read them was through the eyes. Steiger, though, was an enigma. The man's eyes never seemed to quite focus on anything. It was as if he was always staring at something just out of sight. It gave one the uncomfortable feeling that he was seeing inside you — that all of your darkest secrets were an open book to him.

"Good to see you again, Doctor," said Jack with a smile right off the rack. He did not feel comfortable in the man's presence. "What brings you out to the West Coast?"

Steiger glanced at Jacob, then back to Jack. "I see Jacob hasn't brought you up to date, yet," he replied. "I'll be glad to fill you in on my end as soon as he does." Turning to Jacob he said, "I'll be in Phase One if you need me."

Jacob nodded and Steiger, with a glance toward Jack, left. Jacob motioned for Jack to walk with him. Together they passed the reception desk and turned a corner into a long hallway. Almost instantly, the mood of the place changed. The lobby had been a cheerful place, full of freshness and warmth. Now, the hallway turned stark and cold, with harsh fluorescent lights replacing the cheery atmosphere. Jacob escorted Jack down the hall and turned another corner. Three halls and several turns later, he was hopelessly lost.

"This place is bigger than it looks," Jack said under his breath.

"Over one square mile," replied Jacob, "and that's just the visible part."

"Visible part?"

"Bear with me, Jack. You've been very patient. Soon, all will be revealed." Just as he made this statement, they came to a single elevator. It so blended in with the white wall that Jack almost missed it. Only the bright "AUTHORIZED PERSONNEL" sign to the right of the door drew his attention to it. There were no buttons or other visible controls. Jacob stopped. For a moment, he stood there, as if waiting. Then, with a bit of a flair, not unlike a stage magician at the climax of an illusion, he pressed his hand against the wall just under the sign. Immediately, a square of light surrounded his hand, and Jack heard the unmistakable sound of an elevator motor. He raised an eyebrow at Jacob, who smiled and nodded.

"As you guessed, we are heading to a high security area," he said. "The elevator only operates on verification of an authorized handprint."

"Pretty heavy security for a place that manufactures supposedly legal drugs," remarked Jack. He was starting to get a bad feeling in the pit of his stomach. For an instant, Jacob frowned, and Jack realized he had overstepped his bounds. Then it passed and he smiled again. "I promise you, Jack, there are no illegal substances made here. You have my word on it."

Jack relaxed a little. One of the notable things that Jack admired about Jacob Hill was his sense of honor and honesty. If he gave his word, it would be kept, no matter what the cost. In all the years of his association with this man, he had not known him ever to utter anything that was not the truth. Jacob could destroy a person's career as easily as he could create it, but he would always do it with the truth.

The elevator door opened to reveal a small, paneled cabin. They stepped in and the door closed behind them. Suddenly they were bathed in a soft blue glow that seemed to come from everywhere.

"What the. . . ."

"Weapons scan," replied Jacob to the half-asked question. "Only properly coded weapons will pass — and only the security force here has properly coded weapons." Jack shook his head in wonderment. He knew of such devices, of course. Every airport in the country now had them installed. Such a scanner was much more efficient than the old metal detectors used a decade ago. Not only could they detect metal weapons, but plastic explosives, volatile liquids, and even the newer non-metal pistols that were flooding the black market. The question was, who ever heard of one being installed in an elevator? Whatever Jacob was hiding here, it must be big!

Again, Jacob pressed his hand to the wall. This time, instead of a light, there came a feminine, computerized voice. "Level, please," it said.

"Executive Suite," replied Jacob.

"Voice print confirmed," said the disembodied voice. "Welcome to Mentasys, Mr. Hill." Without another word it began to rise. In less than a minute, they had completed their journey. Jack assumed the door would open, but was again surprised when it began moving again, this time horizontally. He lurched backward as the unexpected movement caught him off guard. Jacob steadied him with a hand to the shoulder.

"Just another little nicety Christine had installed. It will take us directly to my suite."

True to his word, the elevator deposited them in a foyer with only one door. Without waiting for Jack, Jacob took the necessary three steps forward and once again pressed his hand against the wall. This time, the door simply opened inward. Motioning for Jack to follow, he disappeared into the suite.

By this time, Jack did not know what to expect. His lack of sleep and Jacob's little surprises had left him numb. Nevertheless, he still stopped and gaped at the room he had just entered. In stark contrast to the ultra-modern environment he had experienced since entering Mentasys, this place was bathed in antiquity.

He felt as if he had stepped into eighteenth century France. The decor was a study in ivory and gold. The furniture — and Jack had no doubt that it was genuine — looked like it belonged in a palace rather than a manufacturing plant.

Jack slowly walked further into the luxurious suite, trying to take everything in at once. Part of him cursed himself for acting like a gawking tourist. He had visited heads of state, for goodness sake! Expensive surroundings were a part of the game he played.

"Come in, Jack. Make yourself comfortable." Jacob motioned for him to take a seat on one of the highbacked couches as he busied himself at the large desk that sat in front of one wall. He was wearing that small smile he usually wore when something amused him. Abruptly, Jack realized that he was that source of amusement. Angry at himself, and trying not to show it, he sat down.

As he sank into the deceptively comfortable cushions, he again felt sleep tugging at the corners of his eyes. To resist the temptation he examined his surroundings, this time with more detachment. A row of alabaster curtains covered the entire outer wall to his right. Judging from the barely-there dawn light that was starting to peek through, Jack guessed that the whole wall was made of glass. It probably looked out over the entire complex. The wall behind the desk was covered with mahogany shelving. Each shelf contained a small piece of sculpture or one of many sets of leatherbound books. The opposite wall held several expensive paintings. Letting his eyes rove over to where he came in, Jack was startled to discover that there was no obvious door. Only ceiling length mirrors that covered the entire wall. As he tried to figure out just where he had entered, he noticed a stranger sitting on a plush couch. For a moment, he froze, wondering who was in the room with him. Abruptly, he realized that he was staring at his own reflection. As if pulled against his will, he stood up and walked over to stand in front of the stranger. His hair was oily and matted, and a days growth of beard darkened his face. The expensive suit he wore was wrinkled almost beyond recognition.

I hope this place has a bathroom, he said to himself. *I need a major overhaul.* He went back to the sofa. Just as he sat down, Jacob finished whatever he was doing and looked up.

"Jack, what have you heard about the Shepherd's Path?" The unexpected question caught him off guard.

"Uh, nothing, I think," he replied, the confusion apparent in his voice. He hated it when Jacob did this to him. He would keep him in the dark for days or even weeks about his plans. Then, everything would come together at once. Jacob would hit him with a totally unexpected question that left Jack feeling as if he had missed something.

"The Shepherd's Path," replied Jacob, "is something we are trying very hard to find out about."

"As usual, Jacob, you've left me behind." Jack tried to sound flippant to cover up his lack of knowledge, but Jacob only frowned. Jack knew that frown and immediately sobered. "So what is it, then?" he asked.

"Actually, we are not quite sure," said Jacob, satisfied that Jack now displayed the proper attitude. "We have heard rumors that it is anything from a nationwide terrorist organization to a hoax."

"Terrorist?" asked Jack. This did not set well with him. At last count, there were over 1,200 known terrorist groups based in the United States. Most of them were only made up of a handful of people. A few, though, were highly dangerous and volatile, liable to go off at any time. The incident at Macy's department store in New York last Christmas was proof of that. At 7:00 p.m. on Christmas Eve, a bomb had exploded on the main floor, killing 31 shoppers. Six of them had been children. Since then, mandatory security measures had been instituted in all public places, but Jack knew it was only a matter of time before the tragedy repeated itself.

"You said nationwide," he responded. "That implies organization and backing. Any proof?"

"Only rumors," admitted Jacob. Jack was more than a little surprised. Jacob Hill usually had all the answers. "We do know that if they exist, they are based in the Midwest, probably in or around Cincinnati," he continued.

Jack blinked. "That's an unusual place to base such an operation," he said.

"Agreed," nodded Jacob. "It is a bit off the beaten path. Nevertheless, that is where the evidence points."

"What evidence?"

"Small things," said Jacob slowly. "Here, let me show you." He leaned forward in his chair and opened a previously unseen panel in the center of the desk. There was a small whine, as a tiny servo-motor lifted a computer keyboard up level with the desktop. In front of the keyboard, a small monitor appeared. Jacob typed for a moment, and then, without any warning, the shelving in back of him began to split apart. A seam appeared in the center of the wall as either side slowly moved away. As Jack watched, the wall disappeared completely and in its place stood row upon row of every sort of electronic apparatus. There were monitors arranged in neat rows, a communications system, and a large viewing screen in the center. If he had seen the situation room on the shuttle, he would have been struck by the similarities.

Jacob swiveled in his chair and began to press various control board buttons located on a two-foot-wide ledge that had slid out from just under the viewing screen. He ignored Jack for a moment, then turned back.

"You are aware, of course, that since we got organized religion under government control, there has been a tendency for many disgruntled citizens to begin meeting on their own, forming small groups that some have begun to call underground churches?"

"Of course," Jack replied. "I suppose it was inevitable. You will always have a few unsatisfied dissidents. I suppose a policy will have to be adopted in order to deal with it."

"Policy," snorted Jacob with contempt. "What do you think the Bureau of Religious Affairs was formed for? That's our policy."

"I don't understand," said Jack. "The bureau keeps tabs on licensed churches. What does it have to do with uncovering these small groups?"

"First of all, get the idea out of your head that these are small, scattered groups meeting across the country. We have every reason to believe that they number in the tens of thousands, and they are growing."

"What?!" Jack was beyond surprise, now. "Impossible! Certainly we would know about it. An organization that size can't stay hidden."

"They seemed to be well organized," replied Jacob. "It seems they have been preparing for years. As for the bureau's involvement," Jacob shrugged, "in this case, they are acting as an elite law enforcement unit, with orders to track down and arrest as many of these groups as they can discover. One unit uncovered a meeting in a New York penthouse. Through interrogation, we got wind of this network, the Shepherd's Path."

Jack held up his hands. "Slow down, Jacob. Are we talking about terrorists, or just disgruntled churches — and as for the bureau, since when did they become a law enforcement agency? It was my understanding that they were only a watchdog, with orders to report violations to the FBI."

"Perhaps I should say 'potential terrorist threat' instead," replied Jacob. "It seems the Shepherd's Path is an illegal organization, operating outside of the law, supporting the churches that are holding secret meetings. Personally, that strikes me as remarkably terrorist-like. As for the bureau, some things have changed."

"Changed how?" asked Jack carefully.

"Too many suspects were slipping through the cracks," he responded. "The bureau would report suspected meetings, the FBI would act, but it seemed that they often acted too late. True, several people were arrested, but hardly any were prosecuted or convicted. I suspect that there are many sympathizers, perhaps even members of this organization, in the Federal Bureau of Investigation."

"Are you accusing the FBI of supporting a terrorist organization?"

"Of course not!" said Jacob. "But I do suspect that there may be key personnel in that worthy organization that are aiding these people. That's why the Bureau of Religious Affairs was given far more authority. Now, they answer to no one on the outside."

Jack massaged his temples, trying to make sense of his conversation. "Terrorists, or underground churches — which one, Jacob? Are we talking about vicious killers or holy rollers?"

"Perhaps both, perhaps neither." Jacob smiled and flicked a switch. On the center screen, a computerized map of the United States lit up. As Jack watched, several red dots began to appear. Jacob motioned Jack out of the couch. Jack pulled another chair over to the control board and sat down.

"These dots represent groups we have already eliminated," explained Jacob. "Over 200 arrests have been made in the last six months. Out of those 200, we selected 10 suspects for interrogation. These were brought here."

"Here? To Mentasys?"

"Yes," Jacob smiled. "I told you that this was one of the most advanced research facilities in the world. It is now also our main headquarters." He pressed one of the many buttons on the panel and instantly the smaller monitors lit up. One in particular caught Jack's attention. He found himself peering into what looked like a hospital ward. There were 10 beds, 5 on each side. Four were occupied with women, 6 with men. Jack examined them closely and noticed several wires attached to their heads by adhesive tape.

"What are you doing to them?" he asked in confusion.

"This is Phase One of our interrogation process," explained Jacob. "In order for Phase Two to be effective, the subject must be rendered unconscious for at least four weeks. This puts them in a susceptible state. The electrodes you see attached to their heads are connected to a sleep inducer. It directly affects the brain, not only causing a deep sleep, but effectively prohibiting dreaming."

Jack was no psychologist, but he did have a rudimentary understanding of the human mind. "You mean that thing stops dreaming? Jacob, that's not healthy. Dreams are the way we release our fears and tensions. Put a lid on it, and you could cause irreparable psychological damage." Another thought struck him. "Where did you get the authority to use this process? Have these people been arrested? Have they been given the right of due process? You can't just hold them like this."

"I can do just that," replied Jacob grimly. "These people are traitors to our nation, and our cause. They waived any right to be treated like citizens when they declared their allegiance to their God."

"Declared what?" Jack asked in confusion. He had never

heard Jacob speak this way.

"Never mind," replied Jacob abruptly, waving away Jack's questions. "It is enough to know that these 10 suspects could be the key to breaking this so-called Shepherd's Path once and for all."

They sat uncomfortably in silence for a moment. Jack was thinking furiously about Jacob's statement regarding allegiance. He felt sure that he had been on the verge of saying something he did not want Jack to hear. And what was this cause? Jack knew that Jacob had many goals, but this was the first time he had ever heard him speak of a cause as if it were a sacred mission. Jack was uncomfortably aware that there were too many things about Jacob he did not know. Suddenly, sitting there and watching those poor souls, he felt as if he were a tiny cog in a much larger machine — so large that he could never see it in its entirety. It was a disturbing thought. The silence was broken by a soft melody of chimes. Jacob pushed a button and said, "Identify."

The same feminine computer voice he had heard in the elevator now addressed him. "Dr. Samuel Steiger, identity confirmed." Jacob turned a control and Steiger's face appeared on the main screen.

"Yes, Doctor."

"Just thought you would like to know, Jacob, one of our subjects just confirmed the information we obtained earlier. It looks like your gamble should pay off."

"Very good," replied Jacob, looking at his watch. "If everything went as planned, they should be arriving here sometime this morning."

"You haven't heard anything?"

"No. My orders were to make the arrest and get two of the subjects to Mentasys as soon as possible. I want to keep this as low profile as we can. We'll know how it went as soon as they get here." Steiger nodded, and Jacob switched him off.

He glanced at Jack, who was getting ready to ask what this was all about. "I know you have been wondering why I have confided all of this in you," he said with a smile. "The reason is simple. There are those in your circles that are beginning to question the function of the Bureau of Religious Affairs. I need the bureau, Jack. It's my right arm in uncovering these fanatics. I need you to draw off some of the heat. As soon as we nail this network, we will prove its worth. Until then — well — you see the importance of what we are trying to accomplish."

Jack swallowed hard, and tried to formulate an answer, but he could not keep his eyes off the people lying in those beds. He took a deep breath and turned away. There would be no denying Jacob's request, he knew. He had sold out to Jacob Hill years ago. The man owned him completely. Jack wanted power, and Jacob held it out to him. It was a heavy price, but one which Jack now had no choice in paying. Again, Jack felt as if he was in the grip of something much larger than he had ever imagined.

"Of course, Jacob," he finally managed. "You know I'll do whatever it takes to help."

Jacob smiled and clapped him on the back. "I knew I was right about you," he said. "There is literally no limit to the heights you will obtain, Jack. Count on it!"

"What was that bit with the doctor all about?" asked Jack, changing the subject. He suddenly felt dirty and used, and wanted to think about something else.

"Hmmmm? Oh, just a confirmation on a little gambit I started yesterday. We got a tip that an underground group was meeting in the Cincinnati area. While this would ordinarily not demand my personal attention, our informant told us that a member of this network was going to be there. If we can get that person, it would be a major breakthrough."

"Informant?"

"One of many," smiled Jacob smugly. "An insurance salesman in that area. We told him we had enough evidence to convict him of sedition, then offered him amnesty if he cooperated. Needless to say, he did. He let us know where the meeting was being held — in an old furniture store, I believe. Last night the place was raided and the suspects are on their way here."

Looking over at Jack, his smile became a grin. "You look awful," he laughed. "Come, my friend, I'll find you a place to sleep for a few hours and some fresh clothes."

Jack allowed himself to be steered out of that palatial room and back into the elevator, welcoming the chance for rest. He had a feeling of dread that the dangerous game he was playing had just changed, and he didn't know the rules anymore.

3

Scott jerked awake, totally disoriented. So complete was the darkness that surrounded him that for a moment he was not sure whether his eyes were opened or closed. His muscles were cramped and he could not feel his right arm. Panic set in. Legs scrambling against the hard floor, he tried madly to stand up, but something held him down. A heavy weight had trapped his arm against a cold surface. He reached over to push it away, and abruptly realized that it was Beth. Memory poured in, and with it despair. The hopelessness of their situation hit him like an oncoming truck. They were fugitives, with no place to go. He heard a soft groan, and felt Beth stir. Gently he dislodged his numb arm from behind her, and forced himself to move it. Feeling began to return, bringing with it the sensation of a thousand needles biting into his flesh. He gritted his teeth against the pain and continued to move it.

"You awake?" he asked in a whisper.

"Uh huh. I think my foot's asleep."

"So's my arm. Try to stand."

"I can't see anything. Give me your arm."

Scott reached out in the blackness and found Beth's hand. Slowly, he stood, pulling her up with him. Just before he reached full height, he bumped his head on the underside of the staircase.

"Do you think it's safe to leave?" Beth's whisper, coming out of the darkness, had a surreal quality to it. Scott half believed that this whole situation was a bad dream anyway.

"I haven't heard anything upstairs." he replied, listening. He released Beth's hand and felt for his watch. In the total darkness, even the dim illumination of the display caused him to squint.

"It's past three," he said. He forgot to whisper in his surprise. "No wonder I'm so stiff." Again he paused to listen, but heard nothing. "I can't believe anybody would still be waiting around," he said. "Let's get out of here." He felt Beth nod in response.

Slowly, hands outstretched like one born blind, he inched his way out from under the stairs. Beth put both hands on his waist, following. When he reached the opposing wall, he turned to his right and begin to feel his way to the cellar door. In this way, they made it to the foot of the staircase. They started to climb, Scott just in time remembering the broken step. Every creak, every groan seemed to call out for unwanted attention. If someone *was* keeping watch, they would surely hear them. Finally, his outstretched hands found the doorknob. Cringing at the tiniest sounds from the rusty instrument, he slowly turned the knob and cracked open the door. As he had done several hours earlier, he peeked out. This time, he saw nothing.

"Well?" He was so intense on what lay before him that he had almost forgotten Beth. Her one word question made him jump. He tried to will his heart to beat slower.

"It looks deserted," he replied over his shoulder. Indeed, the only light was coming through the display window far in the front, probably from a street light. The rest of the store was in total darkness. He contemplated going out the front door for a moment, but decided against it. He remembered seeing a back exit when they had first arrived.

"Let's go," he whispered. He opened the door all the way and with his hand in Beth's, started toward the rear of the store. Even with the dim glow coming from the front, it was almost impossible to see. More than once, he barked his shins on an unseen piece of old furniture. It got to be a nightmarish routine.

He would take a few steps forward, stub his toe or bang his ankle, change course and try again. By the time they finally reached the rear exit, Scott was gritting his teeth again, this time in pain.

The door was locked and double bolted, and it took him some time fumbling in the darkness to finally open it. Sudden light struck him like a blow! Reflexively he pulled back and shut the door. Spots swam before his eyes from the intense brightness.

"Trouble?" asked Beth, her voice anxious.

"No, I don't think so," he answered, his eyes watering. "There's a light right above this door, that's all. It caught me by surprise. Let me check again." This time he was ready. He peered out into what looked like an alley. From his vantage point, he could see that it ran parallel to the street out front. A rotting wooden fence ran along the back, and he could see the dark sinister shapes of buildings rising on the other side. *Good,* Scott thought. *We don't have to take to the street right away.* Even so, it took all the courage he could muster to leave the relative safety of the store.

Taking a deep breath, he led Beth out into the darkness of the alley. They moved forward a few yards, then Scott stopped. He looked back at that lonely pool of light, and the store behind it. For just a moment he felt a deep pang of remorse for the tiny church that met there. He wondered what was happening to those courageous souls now.

Beth looked over at him, seeing the pain on his face reflected in the dim light. Gently she tugged at his arm. "We have to go," she whispered. "Come on, Scott." He allowed himself to be turned away, leaving the crumbling building behind forever. It was more than likely, he knew, that it had seen its last customer. Local authorities would surely close it down, and it would join its rotting brothers on either side.

Now it was Beth who led the way. Using what little light was available, she navigated past scraps of rotting food and trash piled to shoulder level. There was no breeze in that narrow space and the stench was almost overpowering. Their going was faster than their escape from the cellar, but still painstakingly slow. As the light from the furniture store faded, another dim glow grew up ahead. Scott could now see that it was an access way to the street.

"There," he nudged Beth. Nothing else needed to be said. Scott knew that the open street was dangerous, but both of them were now anxious to be out of the alley. They could hear its inhabitants scurrying through the trash, and more than once Scott felt something run across his feet. They hurried forward and found that another alley did indeed intersect the one they were in. They could see the street about 200 feet ahead. A glaringly bright street light shone at the other end, making the accumulated trash stand out in stark relief. It looked like some fantastic moonscape.

Hand in hand, they started toward the street. Now, instead of being a help, this new light was a hindrance. The other had led them to this adjacent alley, but this one now shone directly into their eyes. They had not gone 10 feet when Scott's foot got caught on an unseen obstacle. He pitched forward, his hands outstretched. He smacked the surface hard. Something crunched under his left hand, and a sharp, piercing pain ran up his arm. Despite their situation, he cried out in pain.

"Scott!" cried Beth, kneeling down beside him. "What is it?"

"My hand," he groaned. "I think I fell on a bottle or something." He could feel warm blood flowing down his wrist. He probed gingerly with his other hand and felt tiny slivers buried in the flesh.

"I don't have anything to bind it," said Beth. "We'll have to get back to the car. Can you walk?"

"Yeah, just a second." He sat there for a moment, fighting the pain and accompanying nausea. Now that his back was turned away from the light, he could see clearly the way they had come. Two large trash cans stood side by side next to the wall on his left. He looked down to see what it was he had tripped over, and froze.

There, protruding from between the cans, was a human leg. He stopped breathing, and found that he could not move. For one terrifying second, his body would not obey him. Then he grabbed Beth's arm with his good hand. His only thought was to get them out of there.

"Scott! What's. . . ." Beth stopped in mid question. She could see the leg now, as well. With surprising strength, she jerked Scott upright. They started to back away, holding on to each other.

"Wha's that?" The blurred voice came from between the cans. "Who's there?" Without another thought as to what might await them, they turned and ran toward the street. Panting for breath, they burst out of the alley and onto the sidewalk. The street was deserted. Only the widely spaced street lights gave any illumination, casting an amber glow over the dark storefronts. A single traffic light a block away blinked forlornly.

"Hold — hold on a second, Hon," said Scott, gasping for breath. He leaned against a brick wall, trying to ignore the throbbing in his hand. Beth moved to stand next to him, all the time scanning the street. Scott fought down the urge to throw up, and slowly caught his breath. He listened intently, but there were no signs of pursuit from behind them. The street remained deserted.

"I'm okay now," he whispered, standing straight. Beth looked at him anxiously, then nodded. Taking his arm, she helped him to retrace their path to the car. It was still several blocks away. The pain in his hand settled down into a steady ache. He held it against his side, trying to stop the flow of blood. Beth held his other arm, half supporting, half leading him. He kept looking back, expecting the owner of that leg to emerge from the alley. No one seemed to be following them, however, and they continued on their way.

"Hey, Rube!"

"Chick, chick, chick. Here, chick!" The voices surrounded them, coming from everywhere.

"Oh, no!" groaned Scott, closing his eyes. He jerked his head around wildly, trying to see in all directions at once. He saw movement out of the corner of his eye, but when he turned, there was nothing there.

"Hey, Mon! She be fine! Want to share her?"

"He's gonna be selfish, Beany. Think we should teach him some manners?"

"Aw, Mon, we don't want to keep her. We just want to borrow her for a while."

"Just keep moving," whispered Scott. He could feel Beth trembling against him. The taunts continued to follow them, never getting louder, never receding. He looked at Beth. Even in this dim, ugly light, he could see the fear on her face. They had had no trouble with gangs on their way in, but now, in the middle of the night, they were attracting attention.

"She got legs, she know how to use them!"

There was a flash of darkness, and, without warning, their way was blocked. Five youths, all much larger than Scott, stood in their path. One was female, the rest male. Two were black, the rest white, and all looked ready to kill. There was nowhere to run. Scott clutched his wounded hand to his side. He was already starting to feel lightheaded from the pain. The biggest gang member — pale, lean, and hungry looking — stepped forward.

"Yo, Home," he said, his voice a rasp, "This be Red Jack turf. No geeks allowed." The rest of the members jostled each other, laughing. They knew that they were in total control. Scott felt the hopelessness of the situation rising around him. He knew what these hoodlums wanted, and there was nothing he could do about it but struggle uselessly. In desperation he pulled out his wallet and threw it at them.

"Take it," he almost shouted. "Take it all, but let us go."

"Whoaaa," said the leader. "Ain't so cheap." He pointed at Beth. "She be nice. Share her and go free." Scott put out his arm to move Beth behind him. He had absolutely no chance against them, but he wasn't about to just hand over his wife to these creeps. As he began to push Beth back, though, she took his arm and moved it down. He looked around in surprise, and was horrified to see her step forward. Her next words stunned him.

"Get-out-of-our-way," she said, each word slow and deliberate. Scott hardly recognized her voice. It was rippling in righteous power.

The leader actually took a step back before he caught himself. Bullying helpless victims was his game. To have this short, fiery woman talk to him in such a commanding tone was beyond his experience. Beth continued to move toward him.

"We are children of the King," she said, "and are under the personal protection of our Lord Jesus Christ. How dare you try to obstruct us. Get out of our way, I said!"

The leader recovered himself. Beth had taken him by surprise, but loud voice notwithstanding, he would have her. His cronies had seen him take a step back. It would be taken as a sign of weakness, and could cost him his leadership. He had to take her now, and kill her man as well. He reached out for her.

As if in slow motion, Scott saw the leader reach for his wife. He started to move toward them, to try to intervene. The leader put his hand on Beth's shoulder, and then stopped. His gaze went from Beth to Scott. Then, slowly, he raised his head to stare somewhere above Scott. A look of pure terror came onto his face. At the same instant, Scott felt a total peace come over him. He felt protected, as if he was encircled with wings. The other gang members followed their leaders gaze. The looks on their faces went from amazement to horror. Then, like a shot, they scattered, flying in all directions.

In a matter of seconds, the Sampsons had the street to themselves once again. Scott stood there, breathing heavily. He did not really believe what had happened. He had been ready to fight a hopeless battle. Then, before he could lift a finger, the battle had been fought and won. By . . . whom? Almost unwillingly, he turned and raised his eyes to where the gang had been looking. Was there something there? It seemed for a moment that he could almost see something. A kind of after-image hung there, but when he tried to concentrate on it, it disappeared completely. He stared a moment longer, then turned back toward Beth. She had not moved, her back still turned towards him. He stepped behind her and put his hand on her shoulder. His touch jolted her out of her trance-like state. Instantly she whirled around, a wild look in her eyes.

"Easy, Hon, easy," he said soothingly. "It's over. They're gone, and I don't think they'll be back."

"What was I doing?!" Her voice was shrill. "I just tried to take on that Neanderthal by myself. Am I that crazy? Scott, what happened?"

"Offhand, I'd say we won." He shook his head vigorously, still dumbfounded by what had just happened. "No, that's not right," he corrected himself. "We had nothing to do with it." Forgetting for a moment his wounded hand, he gripped Beth's shoulders. "They saw something they couldn't handle," he said. "Two somethings. One was a short woman filled to the brim with the Holy Spirit, the other was whatever or whoever was above us." He started to chuckle, then broke into a full-fledged laugh that was part relief, part hilarity. The humor of the situation suddenly came home to him.

Beth stared at him as if he were crazy. "We almost died just now, you idiot," she said, slapping him on the arm. "This is supposed to be funny?"

Her tone was angry, but Scott could see the beginnings of a smile. "If you could have seen yourself," giggled Scott. The more he thought about it, the harder he laughed. "The way you backed him up. Somehow, I don't think he'll be leading his little gang anymore."

On impulse, he hugged Beth hard. "We're not alone, Hon! None of us are alone!" He released her and saw that she was starting to laugh, too. "We may have to go through the fire before this is all over," he grinned, "but we won't be alone." If anyone had been driving by just then, they would have been convinced that there were two crazy people standing on that street. Who else would be shouting and laughing at this time of the night, and in this neighborhood? Why, one of them had even started to dance!

Scott whirled Beth around in circles. Ten minutes ago, he had carried the weight of the world on his shoulders. Now, the burden was gone. A great weight had been lifted. He now knew what was required of him.

"All we have to do," he said, his voice near a shout, "is to stay true! Keep believing, keep praying, keep witnessing. That's all! THAT'S ALL, FOLKS!" His shout echoed off the deserted buildings.

Beth had tears running down her cheeks. She put her hand to Scott's lips. "Okay, Lover, we'll tell the world — tomorrow. Right now, how's about we stop acting like weird people and get our ever-lovin' bodies out of here!"

Scott calmed down a bit, and grasped Beth's hand. "Ouch!" he said in surprise, jerking back. He had forgotten his injury.

"Come on, Scott," said Beth, sobering. "Let's get back to the car. We can fix your hand and figure out what to do there." Scott's exuberance subsided. On cue, the throbbing pain returned. He allowed Beth to take his arm. Together, they made their way back to where they had left the LeMans.

After their experience with the gang, Scott was not surprised by the fact that the car was exactly where they had left it, seemingly intact. He fished his keys out of his pocket with his good hand and opened the door for Beth. Then he got in on the driver's side and sagged into the cool vinyl. After hours of cold concrete, this was paradise! The familiar surroundings were like the return of an old friend thought long lost. Beth rummaged around in the glove compartment and found the first aid kit.

"Here, gimme," she said, taking his hand. "Now turn the dome light on, please." Scott complied, and then gasped when he saw his hand. An angry deep cut ran across the palm. Gingerly, Beth used her eyebrow tweezers to pull out the shards of glass. Scott clenched his jaw, resisting the temptation to jerk his hand away. Patiently Beth removed the slivers, trying to be as gentle as possible. When she was finished, she used the antiseptic spray. The sharp pain almost sent Scott through the roof of the car, but when it passed the throbbing subsided. He sighed in relief. Beth finished her ministrations by adding a plastiskin bandage. Once the wound healed, the organic covering would be absorbed into the skin. Scott examined her work and decided he would live. Now he could turn his attention to the matter of where they could go.

"We have our passports," Beth suggested. "We could try for the tropics, maybe one of the islands."

"Too dangerous," Scott replied. "With all the trouble in Mexico, any North American traveling south of the border is a target."

"Canada?"

"I don't think we can get across the border. By the time we get there, our passports will be revoked." They discussed it for a while longer, all the time keeping watch on the street. Once they had to duck down to avoid being seen by a passing car. It wasn't the police, but they weren't taking chances. Scott's euphoria after the encounter with the gang had worn off, and he was feeling the effects of being up most of the night. He could see that Beth was near exhaustion as well. While helpful, their nap in the store had hardly been restful. His thoughts were becoming muddled and slow.

"Look," he said finally, trying to pull his mind together. "In a matter of hours, we'll be on every major computer network in the country. Our credit cards will be revoked, our funds will be frozen, and we'll be effectively trapped. We need to get away from here now."

"What if it isn't a matter of hours?" Beth replied, the frustration showing in her voice. "What if we're on now? If we try to use our bank cards or credit cards, we could be sending a signal to whoever is after us."

Scott shook his head. "I know how these things work. Computers are fast, but people are still slow. You have to cut through major red tape to get into the system. Even the government has to follow set procedure, and that means getting the right people out of bed. It's going to take some time. We need to act now if we're going to act at all. Otherwise, we might as well go turn ourselves in."

Beth was silent for a moment. "How about my parents in Denver? I know they would take us in."

Scott didn't answer right away. He had already thought of that route, but the truth was, he didn't get along all that well with his in-laws. True, this was a desperate situation, but the idea of showing up on their doorstep begging for help did not sit well. Unfortunately, it seemed to be the only way to go. Her parents might not be too crazy about Scott, but they would never turn their daughter away.

Reluctantly, he nodded. "Let's get to the airport," he said. "We'll get the next flight out and be there by noon."

"Are you sure we should take a plane?" asked Beth. "That's awfully visible. How about a bus, or train?"

Scott thought for moment, then shook his head. "The bus or train will take a few days, and by that time, we'll be plastered over every system in the country. If we take a plane, we'll beat the system. By the time they know to look for us, we'll be safely in Denver with your parents." Beth nodded, showing that she agreed with his logic.

"I don't think we want to try to drive *this* car all the way. If we're lucky, we might get out of the city." She smiled at that, and Scott continued. "We sure don't want to go home and get your car." That brought a pang of sadness and regret to both of them. It hurt not to be able to get to the safety of their own house.

"Okay, you sold me," Beth replied, and settled back into her seat. Scott started the car. Checking carefully in both directions, he made a u-turn and headed away from the furniture store.

The greater Cincinnati airport was located in northern Kentucky, not very far from their present location. They headed out of the city and got on the interstate. Covington sat in the Ohio valley, surrounded by foothills. The airport sat in the high country, away from the city. The interstate wound its way up into the hills, and then headed south all the way to Miami. As he coaxed sufficient speed out of his cranky car, Scott tried to make some sense of the last 10 hours. The raid, Allan's treachery, their flight, all seemed to be a part of some fantastic plot in a 'B' movie. He wasn't sure he wanted to stick around for the ending!

"Scott?"

"Yeah, Hon."

"What about Allan? Why do you think he did what he did?"

Scott fought another bout with the anger that crowded into his mind every time he thought about the man. "I don't know," he replied, forcing his voice to stay even. "It sounded like they may have been threatening his family. You heard the conversation, too."

Beth was silent for a moment, then changed the subject. "What are we going to do when we reach Denver? Shouldn't we call and let my folks know we're coming?"

"No, I don't think so. We'll get a cab or a bus from the airport. It won't take long to get there. Let's don't take a chance calling them. I don't want to waste the time. Besides, what good would it do to worry them?"

"None, I guess." She stretched her arms out, her fingers interlocking. "Right now, all I want to do is sleep for a week." She leaned over and put her head on his shoulder.

"You can sleep on the plane," he said. "Once we get in the air, we should have it made. If they have anything on us, it'll show up at the ticket counter."

"Hmmm. Let me know when we get there."

"Don't go to sleep now. We're almost there. Besides, I need you to keep me from remembering how scared I am."

Beth snuggled against him, squeezing his arm. "You're doing fine, Hon," she said. "I'm really proud of the way you've been handling things."

"Let's just be glad that He's looking out for both of us," Scott said. "I was scared to death to get involved with the church. I'm still scared, if you want to know the truth. The only difference is, I know that we're not alone. God's got His hand in this. Only He knows where He's going to lead us."

"Scott," said Beth, sitting up and looking directly at him, "if you had it to do over again, and this time knew what was going to happen, would you still go through with it?" The question caused him to pause. His ego wanted to say yes, but his new-found closeness with his wife demanded honesty. He had to think about it for a moment.

"I don't know," he finally said. The admission hurt, but he continued on. "I'd like to think so, but I remember how scared I was when we got there." Another pause. "I do know this. I'm not sorry now. What I gained at that meeting. . . ." he shook his head in wonderment, unable to continue for a moment. "I turned back to God, and He gave me back you. I . . . I had forgotten what it was like to be in His will."

He rubbed his eyes, feeling the fatigue. "Now, well, everything may seem wrong, but inside, it feels right." He glanced over at Beth. "Was that what you wanted to hear?"

"No, that was what I wanted to *know.*"

She snuggled back onto his shoulder and they rode the rest of the way in silence. The remainder of the trip took less than 20 minutes. By the time they pulled into the multi-level airport parking garage, the eastern sky was just beginning to lighten.

They got out of the car, and Scott locked it up. He hated to leave it here. Sooner or later, it would be discovered. In effect, he was leaving a trail for their pursuers to follow. On impulse, he opened the trunk and rummaged around in the tool box he kept there.

"What are you doing?" asked Beth.

"Maybe buying us a little time," he replied. He found a screwdriver and proceeded to remove the license tag. Since the screws were rusty, he was a few minutes at this task. Finally, he pulled it off.

"Wait here a second," he said as he got back into the LeMans. Checking to make sure no one was watching, he moved the car over to an empty spot next to the wall. He parked it so the rear end was facing the wall, effectively blocking the view from the back. After emptying the glove compartment, he took the stack of papers he found, including the registration and license plate and tossed them into the nearest trash can.

"They can still trace the car, but it may take them a few extra hours," he explained, walking back to Beth. "By that time, we should be well away."

"Do you have some secret past that I don't know about?" she asked, looking at him with mock seriousness. "Or have you been watching your collection of James Bond movies again? Where did you learn that trick?"

Scott laughed and put his arm around her waist. Together they started toward the main terminal. "Actually, I heard about it on the late news," he explained. "Some drug dealer pulled this trick. It was almost 24 hours before airport security noticed the abandoned car, and another 6 before they identified it."

"Terrific," replied Beth. "What a role model."

"The funny part is, he got caught at the ticket counter. They found over two kilos of marijuana sewn into his pants."

"Marijuana?"

"That was before it was legal," Scott explained. "The idiot tried to use his credit card, and they nailed him."

"Isn't that what we're trying to do?" asked Beth.

"Not exactly," replied Scott, wishing he felt as confident as he sounded. "That guy had been wanted for several days. He should have known better than to try to use any mode of public transportation." He looked at his watch. "Our names shouldn't be on the public network until after nine o'clock."

"Human efficiency, right?"

"Uh huh. Every law enforcement agency in the country should have us by now, but the rest won't. Thank God for bureaucracies." His arm tightened around Beth's waist. "Just be glad it isn't six months from now." He looked at her expectantly.

"Okay, I'll bite. Why am I glad it isn't six months from now?"

Scott grinned. More than anything else, he was thankful for Beth's sense of humor. She could make *any* situation seem brighter. It helped to keep the constant fear in the back of his mind at bay.

"In six months," he explained, "next January, every major computer system in the nation will be absorbed into one gigantic network. Credit agencies, transportation systems, government agencies. . . ." he shook his head at the enormity of it. "There won't be different systems running different organizations. It will be one — count 'em — one system. If that network was on line now, we wouldn't have a chance."

"You mean no red tape?"

"Right, but it's more than that. Your whole life will be available to whoever wants it. Your income, credit rating, relatives, friends, occupation . . . whatever anyone wants to know will be instantly accessible." He chuckled, but there was nothing humorous about his laugh. "You remember all those rumors going around during the late eighties or so? The ones about a super computer called the 'Beast?' "

"I remember one about the 'vanishing hitchhiker,' " replied Beth, unsure of where Scott was going.

"Yeah, I remember that one, too," said Scott. "Somebody would pick up a hitchhiker, and after a few miles the hitchhiker would say something like 'Jesus is coming soon,' and then disappear. It was one of those rumors that was eventually proved false — like the one about the Beast computer."

"Scott," asked Beth, "are you headed somewhere, or are you just talking to prove you're not as terrified as I am?"

Scott started to reply, but saw the half-smile on Beth's face and realized she was joking with him. "Cute," he said with a mock growl. "Anyway, once all of the separate systems merge into one, I've heard that there *is* one super computer waiting to run the whole show. It's either somewhere in Spain, or under the Vatican, depending on which rumor you want to listen to."

"And you think that. . . ."

"I don't *think* anything," said Scott. "I do know a little bit of Bible prophecy, though. It's pretty clear that whoever the Beast is, he's human . . . at least on the outside. A computer can simulate life, but when all is said and done, it's still a glorified adding machine."

"If you say so," replied Beth doubtfully.

"I say so," he replied. "Now, let's see who has the next direct flight to Denver." Together they made their way to the information booths located in the main terminal. There, they were able to find that the next available flight for Denver departed in just over an hour.

"Perfect," said Scott, checking the time. "That puts us there at just before nine, counting the time change." He called up the reservation screen. The screen announced several different airlines and flight numbers. Scott selected the proper one and touched the screen in the proper place. The flight information flashed on the display and he read through it quickly.

"Uh oh," he said under his breath, glad that his body blocked the screen from Beth's view. He had not anticipated this. He called up the main menu again, and looked through it for other flights going to Denver, or any place even close. The next available flight was not until 10:30 that morning. He closed his eyes for a moment, hating the choice that was before him. Then he realized that there was really *no* choice at all. He called back the flight information that he had first looked at, and punched in his ticket request. In answer to the computer's request, he pushed his bank card into the proper slot, and held his breath. He was reasonably sure of what he had told Beth, but not 100 percent. His bank card could have been revoked, if an urgent enough order had been pushed through.

The terminal sat there for a moment, as if deciding whether or not to grant Scott's request, and then began to print out the ticket. He considered fainting with relief, but decided to wait until he was alone. He took the ticket as it finished printing, and retrieved his bank card. Holding both in his hand, he stood there for a moment, thinking about the decision he had just made.

No choice, he reminded himself, and turned back to Beth. "Here," he said, handing her the ticket.

She took it, and then looked at his now empty hands. "Where's yours?" she asked, her voice level.

"Let's go get some coffee," he said, deliberately ignoring her. "I need a jolt of caffeine."

"Scott," said Beth, and this time her voice held a slight tremor to it, "I said, where's your ticket? Tell me. Please."

"Not here," he replied, taking her arm and leading her away from the booths. "Let's go somewhere and sit down. We need to plan." He led her to a small cafe that was just opening. The smell of breakfast food beginning to cook would have ordinarily made him hungry, but right now he didn't have much of an appetite. They found a booth and slid in, ordering two cups of coffee. He opened his mouth to explain, but she beat him to the punch.

"Scott, don't even think about splitting up. There's no way I'm leaving you now."

"Beth. . . ."

"If you think that after all we've been through tonight that I'm letting you out of my sight, you're crazy."

"If you would just. . . ."

"I will not just up and leave you, I don't care what you. . . ."

"BETH!"

Surprised at him raising his voice, Beth quieted down. "Now please just listen to me," said Scott, his voice pleading with her. He knew that if he couldn't convince her to go along with his decision, no force on earth would make her leave him. It warmed him, but frustrated him as well.

"There was only one seat left on the flight," he explained. "The next flight won't leave until mid-morning, and that's just too late. Our only chance is for you to take it and get to Denver. I'll take the car and get there in a few days."

Beth leaned forward and rapped his forehead gently with her knuckles. "Scott, think! That car won't make the trip. You said so yourself. And what if you're spotted? That's a long trip."

"I'll take the backroads. If I nurse it, I think it will get me there. Look," he continued, "they'll be looking for a couple. We'll have a better chance if we separate. You go on and get there, and explain things to your parents."

"No, not in a million years, absolutely not. Forget it, Scott. I'll travel with you."

"Beth, please do this for me. I can travel faster and lighter alone. If I know that you're safe, it will make things much easier for me."

Beth searched his face, as if seeking answers that he did not have. "Scott," she whispered, her voice close to breaking, "please don't do this."

It took every ounce of will power for Scott to remain resolute and firm. They sat there for over half an hour, arguing back and forth. Finally, exhaustion and frustration got the best of him. "Enough, Beth!" he snapped, slapping the flat of his uninjured hand on the table. "You're going, and that's it. I've already bought the ticket, and I can't take it back." He softened when he saw the hurt in her eyes. "It has to be this way, Hon. Please do this for me." Their eyes met, and then Beth looked away. Almost imperceptibly she nodded. Even then, he wasn't sure she wouldn't change her mind at the last instant. She became quiet as the time came for her to leave, almost sullen. Scott tried to talk about other things, to relieve the tension, but she would only answer in one syllable words. Finally he gave up.

Paying for the coffee, they left the cafe and headed toward the departure gate. They held hands but did not speak as they took the shuttle to the airport terminal. Scott had timed it so they would not have long to wait. He didn't think he would have the heart to go through with the separation if he had too long to think about it.

The flight was already boarding when they arrived at the gate. As a last hope, he checked with the attendant at the desk to see if there had been any cancellations. There were none. His last hope defeated, he pulled Beth over to one side as the passengers filed past him. He looked closely at her face, wanting to etch every detail into his mind. Was it just 12 hours ago that they had been barely speaking to each other? Now his stomach was knotted at the thought of letting her out of his sight.

"I'll be along in a few days, Hon, I promise. We can figure out where to go from there. With your dad's military connections, we'll find a place where we'll be safe."

Beth nodded, and then suddenly reached forward and grabbed his shirt by the collar. Pulling her face to within inches of his, she said, "Don't you dare get caught, Scott Sampson. So help me, if you do, I'll get you. What the government does to you will be nothing compared to what I do when I get my hands on you."

Scott opened his mouth to reply, but was silenced when Beth kissed him passionately. Their embrace lasted an eternity, and was over in an instant. Without another word, Beth turned and walked to where the other passengers were boarding. She followed the line as they went through the double doors that opened to the ramp. Scott followed her as far as the doors and watched her as she disappeared down the ramp.

Just before she boarded the aircraft, she turned for one last look. Her eyes met his for a moment, then she turned and was gone. Scott felt as if his very soul had just left him. He stood there staring down the ramp. The last of the passengers boarded, and the hatch to the aircraft closed. She was gone. For the first time since everything had fallen apart, Scott felt alone — totally alone. He knew in his head that God was with him, and would never forsake him, but his heart was telling him that the best part of him had just been ripped out.

"Tough goodbye?" The voice came from behind him. He turned, and saw an older man studying him. The man smiled and said, "I've been watching you and your friend. Seen a lot of hard partings here, but yours took the cake. That your wife?"

"Uh, yeah," replied Scott. He didn't want to be answering questions just now. This man was probably harmless, but he wasn't taking any chances.

"Seems like I'm always saying goodbye to someone or another at this place," the man continued. "This time it was some of my best friends. It gets harder every time. You never know which goodbye could be the last."

Scott nodded, trying to think of something to say, and at the same time looking for a way to leave without seeming in a hurry. He had decided not to watch Beth's plane take off. The sooner he got out of the airport the better, and he wanted to get started on his trip as soon as possible.

"Don't worry, young fella," the man said. He reached out and took Scott's arm with a firm grip. His strength belied his age. "You *will* see her again. Count on it!"

"Thanks," replied Scott uncertainly. He was relieved when the man let go of his arm. "I've got to get going," he said. "I want to watch her take off from the observation deck."

The old man nodded and waved a goodbye.

"Remember what I said now," he called as Scott moved away. "You'll see her again. Count on it!" Scott waved, and made his way out of the terminal. He stopped at the automatic teller and withdrew $1,500, figuring that should be enough to get him to Denver. That accomplished, he headed back to the parking garage.

He had a moment of anxiety when he remembered he had thrown his license plate away. The trash had not been collected, though, and he was able to dig it out of the can. It took only moments to replace it on the back of the LeMans. Soon, he was out of the airport and heading north. Now that he had settled on a course of action, he began to feel better. Beth was safely on her way to Denver, and all he had to do was get there himself. True, it would be a dangerous trip, but he knew he could make it. If he kept to the back roads and state routes, avoiding the interstate, he felt he had a reasonable chance. He would pay cash as he went, so no one would be able to trace him through his credit or bank cards.

The sun was well up into the sky as he pulled into a shabby-looking motel. He needed a few hours sleep and a shower before he tackled the long trip ahead. Judging from its appearance, the motel catered to a clientele that was, to say the least, questionable. This was confirmed when the sleepy, half-drunk desk clerk told him that all of the girls had left for the day and would not return until that evening. Assuring him that he only wanted a room, Scott paid the man in advance. The clerk took the money, not bothering to check Scott's identification. That suited him just fine.

The room was dingy, with cheap wallpaper peeling from concrete block walls. It smelled of stale cigarettes and mold. The shower worked, however, and the bed didn't have anything crawling in it at the time. Scott pulled back the faded red bedspread and turned on the television. Finding the news channel he began to peel off his clothes. He wrinkled his nose at the odor they gave off, wondering if the motel might have a laundry. Stripping down to his undershorts, he stretched himself, luxuriating in the delicious sensation.

With half an eye on the television, he went into the bathroom and started the water running in the shower. He adjusted the faucet for just the right temperature, and stepped in. The hot water tingled on his skin, washing away the fatigue. He leaned forward into the needle spray, letting it wash over his face. Then, taking the wash rag, he soaped himself down. Rinsing, he stepped out of the shower, shut off the water, and dried himself with the one single towel on the rack. Getting back into his undershorts, he went over to sit on the foot of the bed, facing the television. There was a "special bulletin" logo flashing behind the anchor man, and Scott leaned forward to turn up the volume.

". . . is estimated that over 400 passengers lost their lives. Repeating this hour's top story, Pan Am Flight 407, bound for Denver, exploded on takeoff this morning at the Greater Cincinnati Airport." Scott felt his heart freeze. As if in a dream, he listened to the report.

"This is the worst such tragedy in over 30 years. Witnesses say that the aircraft was engulfed in a ball of flame just as it lifted off the runway." The anchor man disappeared, and now the screen filled with the wreckage of a once-proud plane. His voice droned on over the video. "Rescue workers have found no survivors, and it is estimated that all 400 passengers and the flight crew of 12 have been killed." Scott fell forward on his knees, the motel room spinning around him.

Mercilessly, the anchor man continued. "A terrorist group naming itself the 'Christian Liberation Front' is claiming responsibility for the disaster. They are demanding a release of over a hundred political prisoners in the United States as well as an end of government control over all churches. They promise more tragedies such as this. Authorities have named several suspects, including this man."

Scott was beyond feeling now, and could only stare numbly as his own picture appeared on the screen. "If you have any knowledge of the whereabouts of this man, Scott Sampson, please notify your local office of the Bureau of Religious Affairs. He is armed and considered extremely dangerous."

A strangling sound came from the back of Scott's throat. He reached for the television, as if by some gesture he could wipe away the horror that continued to parade before him. A mist rose before his eyes, and he pitched forward. He fell on his face in front of the television and knew no more.

❖ ❖ ❖

Jack paced in the spacious suite that had been provided him, feeling like a caged animal. He had slept for several hours, and it was now late in the afternoon. He had used the Mentasys vid-phone system earlier to try to reach Jacob, but could not get through. The only person he could get to talk to him was Dr. Steiger's secretary. He had assured him that Mr. Hill would be with him as soon as possible. That was two hours ago.

While he had slept, his clothes had been cleaned and pressed. He had found and used a toilet kit in the carpeted bathroom. Physically, at least, he now felt and looked like a new man. The problem was, he could not leave. Although the door to the suite was unlocked, he could not access the elevator. It was another one of those blasted devices that required a palm print. All he could do was pace and wait.

Abruptly, he came to a decision. Jacob might dictate most of his actions, but he still had responsibilities in Washington. He went to the elegant antique desk that sat nearby and picked up the wireless phone that sat there. Clicking it on, he dialed his office in the nation's capital.

There was a series of beeps, then silence. He listened in vain for the telltale computerized tones that would tell him his call was going through.

"Come on, come on," he urged under his breath. Still nothing. He was about to dial again when he heard a voice.

"This is Anne. May I help you, Senator?"

"I'm trying to get through to Washington," he replied indignantly. He had obviously reached the Mentasys switchboard. "Since I can't seem to dial direct, would you mind placing the call for me?"

"I'm sorry, Senator Kline," replied Anne politely. "We are temporarily experiencing difficulties with our communications system. Only local calls can get out of the building at this time. We should be back on line within a few hours. Would you like to try again then?"

"Yeah, sure." He clicked off the phone, and in a fit of frustration slammed it down onto the desk. "I don't believe you for a minute, my dear Anne," he said aloud.

Everything he had been allowed to see so far told him that Mentasys was one of the most advanced facilities in the world. It was inconceivable that its phone system would fail so completely. The simple frightening fact was, Jacob did not want him contacting anyone while he was here. He let out a steady stream of curses under his breath. He was just about to use the vid-phone again when soft chiming announced he had a visitor.

"Come in," he said roughly. The door slid back to reveal a smiling Jacob Hill. Next to him was Dr. Steiger. *About time,* he thought.

"Jack, you look much better," said Jacob, coming toward him. "Are you ready for the grand tour?"

"I'm ready to get out of this room," replied Jack tightly. "Why can't I access the elevator? For that matter, why can't I call Washington . . . and don't give me that story about the system being down."

"Settle down, Jack." The way Jacob said it, he was more amused than offended. "As for the elevator, it was a simple oversight. You were so tired when you got here that I only wanted to let you rest. Now that you're up, we'll get your hand and voice print into the central computer. As for the phones, I don't want you communicating with your colleagues just yet — not until I have a chance to show you what we are doing here and tell you what is required of you."

"Jacob," said Jack evenly, "I have responsibilities — commitments. If my administrative assistant doesn't hear from me soon, questions are going to be asked. I'm sure I've already raised some eyebrows by leaving the way I did."

"Don't worry, Jack, don't worry," soothed Jacob. "Do you really think I would allow anything to happen to you? You are too valuable. I need you where you are. Trust me."

Despite Jacob's assurances, Jack still felt uneasy. He let the matter drop, though. He had seen this man ruin too many powerful figures, Jack's predecessor being one. Jacob had destroyed the man's career piece by piece, making it possible for Jack Kline to become the new senate majority leader.

"You know I trust you, Jacob. I'm just a little nervous, that's all."

"Excellent," replied Jacob, his smile widening. "Now, let us show you what is going on here." He motioned for Steiger, who had been standing by the door quietly, to precede them. The doctor led them to the elevator.

"Main lobby," he said to the computer. They were whisked away and deposited onto the ground floor. Once there, Steiger led them into the office from which Jack had seen him emerge when he had first arrived. It was a sparse room, holding only a simple desk, a couple of filing cabinets, and a few plastic chairs. The walls were a dull white, giving the impression of sterility. Steiger walked behind the desk and pressed his hand over a section of wall. Jack was not surprised this time when a small square of light surrounded his hand. The glow subsided, and a panel opened to reveal what looked like a camera lens.

"Good afternoon, Dr. Steiger," said a feminine disembodied voice. "Please step forward for retina scan." As Jack watched, Steiger leaned forward and placed his eye over the lens. He could see a dull red light escaping from around the edges. When the light went off, the voice spoke again.

"Identity confirmed," it said. "Scanning two other occupants. Please step forward and identify." Jacob now moved into place and repeated the process with the sensor. Once he was identified, he motioned for Jack to join him.

"Look directly into the sensor," he said. "We'll go ahead and get your prints on file." Jack placed his right eye onto the sensor and waited. Once again the red light shone. Jack knew that it was scanning his retina. The tiny patterns of blood vessels there were as distinctive as fingerprints. Unlike fingerprints, however, they could not be altered. The light went out and Jack moved away.

"Retina print not on file," said the voice. "Please identify."

"Kline, Jack," said Jacob. "Code zero zero alpha zero. Command override."

"Command override accepted." replied the computer. Without another word, a six-foot section of wall slid back, revealing a room about the size of a large closet. Jacob stepped in, motioning for his companions to follow. Jack abruptly realized it was another elevator. He followed Steiger inside and turned as the door slid shut. Immediately, the elevator started. Jack, who had braced himself for a fast rise, was surprised when they began moving down. As the seconds passed by and the elevator did not slow, he wondered just how far down they were going. Jacob sensed his question.

"You are too young to remember," he said, "but the Cold War of the sixties bred many interesting facilities. Mentasys is built over one of them."

Jack searched his knowledge of that era, and took a guess. "Missile base?" he asked.

"Very good, Jack," said Jacob approvingly. "But not quite right. This was designed as a command base. The missiles were to be launched from silos in the mountains, but controlled from here. It was discontinued in the seventies. Too expensive. By the way, we are descending over 300 feet, and this elevator is the only way in or out." Jack merely nodded, and said nothing for the rest of the ride down. The ride ended, and they got out. Jacob led them to a small anteroom where several white gowns hung. He indicated that Jack put one on.

"This is a sterile environment," explained Dr. Steiger. Jack suppressed the thousand questions that kept crowding into his mind. He knew that he was close to at least a partial answer. Beyond this small room, he felt, was the hidden purpose of Mentasys, and Jacob's real reason for being here. He donned the white jumpsuit, including the clear hood that fit loosely over his head. Gloves and boots completed the outfit. He took a deep breath, and discovered that there was no ventilation. Already it was beginning to get stuffy. He felt a hand on his shoulder. Looking back, he saw Steiger strapping a small cylinder about the size of a hair spray can onto his arm. He turned a knob, and instantly Jack felt a rush of cool, refreshing air.

"This will last you about 15 minutes," Steiger explained. "For longer visits, we would just hook you up to the central supply. This should do for now, though."

"Gentlemen, if you please." Jacob turned and motioned them through the double doors that stood in front of him. Jack followed, and walked into hell. The room was easily 30 feet by 50 feet, with a high, vaulted ceiling. Everything was white — the walls, the floor, the ceiling — and Jack had to squint at first. The room reeked of lifelessness. There were three other people in the room, all dressed as Jack was, and monitoring several racks of complicated looking equipment. Unlike the canister of oxygen strapped to his arm, the others had hoses running from their suits into receptacles in the ceiling. Jack could see that the receptacles were movable, able to follow the wearer.

His attention was drawn to the center of the room, where 12 huge cylinders, each large enough to hold a human being, were placed in two rows of 6. They were laid horizontally to the floor, and had an unearthly look about them. Each was made of a clear material, and each contained a glowing blue liquid. The blue glow was the only other color in the room, and contrasted sharply with the white.

All this Jack noticed later. Just now, his attention was drawn to the cylinders themselves. Almost involuntarily he drew closer. He inhaled sharply, and then fought the urge to gag. Floating in each cylinder was the naked form of a human being! He bent over to examine the first cylinder in line. It contained the body of a middle-aged man of about 50. His bare face was expressionless as it floated in the blue liquid. Jack let his gaze wander over the still form to the top of the completely shaven head. He noticed that wires were attached to the top of the scalp. On closer inspection, he could see that the wires were actually running into the head. What was going on here? What purpose were these corpses being preserved for?

Just as he was about to straighten up, the body jerked.

"What?" He jumped back, his heart pounding like a jackhammer. Again the body spasmed, as if by electrical shock. "My God, he's alive." Jack's shout was muffled by the hood he was wearing. He backpedaled, putting distance between him and the horror in that cylinder. A pair of strong arms clamped around his chest and held him vice grip tight. He struggled to get loose. He might as well have tried to get away from a gorilla.

"Jack! Jack! Stop that!" He was vaguely aware of Jacob standing in front of him, shouting. "Jack! Get hold of yourself, man!"

Slowly he stopped his struggling. Despite the constant flow of air into his hood, the clear plastic was misted over. He fought to control his breathing. Gradually he succeeded.

"That's better," said Jacob, his voice now as hard as steel. "Of course he's alive. What good is a dead subject? Now, are you finished with these childish hysterics?" Jacob's tone was one of a parent admonishing a naughty child. Cheeks burning with embarrassment, Jack could only nod.

"Very well," said Jacob, nodding to whoever was holding him. He was released, and took a deep breath, trying to get back his equilibrium. Glancing behind him, he saw that the technician who had been holding him had already returned to his former task. Jacob looked hard at him a moment longer, then beckoned him back to the cylinder. Taking a deep cleansing breath, Jack obeyed. Once again he peered into the blue liquid at the body. He noticed that now, instead of wearing a blank expression, the man had a look of unbridled terror on his face.

Jacob studied Jack for a moment, then explained. "The liquid is an oxygenated inert substance that sustains life."

"You mean he's breathing that stuff?" asked Jack in wonderment.

"Yes," confirmed Jacob. "And not only breathing. It also contains nutrients and vitamins that are absorbed directly through the skin and into the bloodstream. The fluid is constantly being replenished, so he can stay in there indefinitely."

"Why?"

"Excuse me?"

"Why is he here?" Jack fought to keep his voice level and calm. The body in that cylinder nauseated him.

"This is Phase Two of our interrogation process," replied Jacob. "Remember my telling you how researchers here at Mentasys had mapped the human brain more extensively than ever before?" Jack nodded.

"Well, this is one of the payoffs. Here, let me show you." Jacob led Jack over to a corner of the room. Here, Jack noticed, a sort of command center was set up. A female technician sat behind a large rounded control panel that contained 12 view screens. There were also assorted readouts that indicated heart rate, blood pressure, and respiration. Jack saw that each cylinder had its own display. At the moment, only 3 screens were active. On one, a young, blond-haired woman of about 30 strolled through a beautiful flower garden. The sunlight shone down on her, making her hair glow and giving her an ethereal quality, as if she belonged in someone's dream. The second screen depicted a family at Christmas. Three children were gathered around the tree, holding hands, and saying the traditional Christmas prayer to St. Nicholas. Off to the side, an older woman with gray hair watched the scene in complete contentment.

The third screen . . . Jack swallowed hard and leaned closer. He recognized the man as the one in the first cylinder. He now understood the look of horror he had on his face. He was being placed in a casket. Friends and family gathered around him, mourning his passing. On the screen, his eyes opened, and he began to move feebly. No one seemed to notice. He was arranged neatly, and the lid was closed. To Jack's utter horror, he saw that it was not a burial, but a cremation ceremony. The casket began to roll forward on a conveyor belt to a blazing furnace. Inside the casket, the man began to struggle frantically. Wisps of smoke began to come up between his legs. In moments, the entire casket was engulfed in flame. Jack looked over at the cylinder and saw that the man was now twitching violently, struggling against the non-existent flames.

"Is that what he thinks he's going through?" asked Jack, pointing at the monitor, his voice rising a fraction. Jacob nodded, then tapped the technician on the shoulder. She fiddled with the control panel a moment, and the screen went blank. Instantly the man stopped jerking.

"Now watch," said Jacob. This time, the technician touched the controls under the monitor showing the blond woman. On the screen, the idealistic scene changed. The sky became dark and cloudy. The woman looked around wildly in fear. The beautiful flowers she had been admiring now withered and died. A mist rose up about her, and dark, undefined shapes moved within it. She began to run. Jack's attention was drawn to another of those infernal tanks. He couldn't make out any features of the person it held, but judging from the thrashing, it was this woman.

Suddenly the shapes in the mist became clearer. Jack had to close his eyes at the obscene caricatures of human beings that leered out at him. The woman screamed, although no sound came from the screen. She tripped and fell, and instantly the hideous beings were on top of her. It became unspeakable. Jack turned away, unable to bear anymore. He felt a hand on his shoulder.

"It's not pretty, Jack," said Jacob, his voice a complete void of emotion. "It is, however, necessary."

"Necessary," repeated Jack, his voice barely above a whisper.

"Yes, necessary," replied Jacob. "What we have accomplished here will change forever the way we perceive the human mind. It will, in effect, bring about a newer and better world. You have yet to see the *real* breakthrough."

Something snapped inside of Jack. He turned on Jacob, flinging his hand away. Somewhere in the back of his mind, he realized it was the first time he had ever intentionally touched this man.

"Newer and better world! Tell me, Jacob," he asked, his voice dripping with sarcasm, "just how is this medieval torture chamber of yours going to bring about a newer and better world?" A warning bell began to go off inside of him. An inner voice was screaming that he was pushing his luck too far, but once started, he couldn't stop.

"Are you planning to re-establish the Inquisition again, is that it? Jacob Hill, grand inquisitor — that has a nice ring to it, doesn't it?" He would have gone on, but without a word, Jacob turned away. At his gesture, the technician at the command center again adjusted the controls, and the screen went blank. The thrashing ceased. Then she left, joining her colleagues at the far end of the room. Dr. Steiger, who had been standing quietly off to the side, went with her. Jack stood there, breathing heavily into his hood. He wondered just how much oxygen he had left.

When Jacob turned back to face him, he recoiled at the rage now manifested in his face. "How dare you presume to judge me," he said, his voice low and dangerous. "You have no understanding of what is being done here, and yet you have the audacity to place your outdated morals on my activities." Jack had never seen Jacob like this before, and he was beginning to get frightened. He understood that he had just made the most dangerous man in the world angry at him. He knew with utter certainty that Jacob could and would have him killed if it suited his purposes.

"Jacob, I. . . ."

"Quiet," hissed Jacob. "Look around you, *Senator.*" The way he said it made a mockery of Jack's title. "Every subject in here is a convicted felon. Over there is a mass murderer, and there," he pointed to the far cylinder, "is the leader of an insurrection. The rest are known traitors to the state. With this process, I can extract every bit of information that is stored in their pathetic minds." He held up his hand and clenched his fist. "I can squeeze everything out. Nothing gets held back. Do you understand, Senator? For the first time, we have an absolutely foolproof interrogation process. Phase One inhibits their dreaming and puts them in a susceptible state. In Phase Two we take the deepest fears from the depths of their minds, and make them come alive. We didn't put those scenes there, they were already in place. We just brought them to the conscious mind. We can pull whatever we want out, and there is absolutely no room for error."

His anger now spent, Jacob once again was the picture of self-control. "It's time for you to see the rest of it," he said calmly. "Come with me."

Without waiting to see if Jack followed, he turned and left. Jack's fear and nervousness were growing. He knew that somehow, he had just crossed a line. Like a dog brought to heel, he followed Jacob out of that nightmare of a room. *This can't be happening,* he thought as they stripped off the protective suits and returned to the elevator. Earlier this morning, Jack Kline had imagined himself destined for greatness. He would allow the Inner Circle to make him the next president of the United States. More importantly, he would become a member of that same Inner Circle. Now, he was wondering if he would live to see the dawn of the next day. Jacob Hill demanded total obedience and complete loyalty. Anything less was unacceptable.

The two men ascended to ground level. Jack thought he would be taken back to his suite. Instead, Jacob led him down a series of halls to a large double door. A small panel next to the doors informed him that this was a conference room. Jacob opened both doors and ushered Jack inside. Much to his surprise, Jack saw that the entire Inner Circle was assembled. There was Christine Smythe, who owned Mentasys, and Rajijah Indres. The only one missing was Steiger. It looked for all the world like a hearing, and Jack was the defendant.

"Come in, Senator," said Christine, her voice dangerously flat. "We have much to talk about." Without a word, Jack walked into the room and took an empty seat at one end of the oval table. How often he had dreamed of being a part of this group! Now, he felt like a man convicted of murder about to be brought to trial.

"We understand," said Indres, "that you do not approve of our, shall we say, research here at Mentasys." Jack wondered how they could have found out so fast, then realized that there must have been cameras in Phase Two. They would have watched the whole scenario play itself out. There would be no denying his actions.

"There must be a better way to get the information you need . . ." he began. Indres held up a hand, and he fell silent.

"You must understand, Senator, that gathering information is really secondary here," he said.

This threw Jack off. "I don't understand," he said in confusion.

"While the information we will obtain will be invaluable," continued Indres, "particularly in dealing with this so called Shepherd's Path, it is not the primary purpose of Mentasys."

"I thought you wanted me to take the 'heat' off your people while you tracked down this terrorist network," said Jack, "to give you a chance to justify the added powers of the Bureau of Religious Affairs."

"That's only a part of it, Jack," said Jacob, who had taken a seat at the other end of the table. "Granted, this network is something that must be eliminated. It encourages thinking which is non-conforming to our vision of the future."

"And what is that vision?" asked Jack. He wanted to keep the subject away from his actions of a few minutes ago. "You've never really made that clear." Jack had followed Jacob because of the power the man wielded, but it had been some time before he realized that Jacob considered power as merely a means to an end. Over the years, Jacob had hinted at some sort of master plan that unified the Inner Circle. Jack had hoped to be an integral part of it, but had never gotten Jacob to confide in him.

"Look at the world we live in, Jack," said Jacob by way of answer. "The most conservative estimates say that we will be in the middle of World War III within one year. That war will almost certainly be waged with nuclear weapons. Our goal," and he waved at the rest of the circle, "is to avert that catastrophe. A noble cause, wouldn't you say?"

"Of course," agreed Jack. "But what does that monstrosity," the word slipped out before he realized it, "have to do with bringing about world peace?" He was speaking of Phase Two, of course.

"It has brought about the development of a major tool for our use," replied Jacob. "I'll tell you about it in a moment. Now, we here, and countless more scattered across the globe, are moving toward our ultimate goal of a one world government."

"What!?" The exclamation burst out of Jack before he could contain it.

"We now have the ability to begin the formation of a single government that will hold complete authority over this planet," Jacob explained.

"Impossible," said Jack. "Fifteen years ago, I might have believed you, but now . . . like you said, we'll be in the middle of a world war by 2003. I don't care how many people you have in 'high places,' it's not going to happen."

"Jack," said Jacob, shaking his head, "I had such high hopes for you. Yours would have been an important voice in the new order. Now, though, judging from your reaction to Phase Two, you're just not willing to pay the price necessary to obtain greatness." He nodded at Christine Smythe, who in turn picked up a small black box sitting on the table in front of her. Jack had wondered what it was. She passed it over to him, and he opened it. Inside, on what looked like crushed velvet, was a tiny computer chip about the size and shape of a pea. He touched it lightly, then looked at Jacob, his face a question.

"*That* is the result of Phase Two," said Jacob. "It was brought about by intensive study of the human brain, and is the tool I mentioned a moment ago."

"So what does it do?" asked Jack.

"It's an implant." This time, it was Christine that answered. "It is placed in the cerebral cortex, right at the juncture of the spinal column and the brain. It has the ability to enhance desired behavior."

"Mind control," said Jack, aghast. This went against everything he believed in. Jack wanted power. He wanted to have a place in history, but this — this was obscene! It went against every fiber of his being. He had worked for decades to bring organized religion under strict government control because of the way he perceived they controlled the minds of the masses. He had sold out to this group, this Inner Circle, in return for their help to bring this about. Jack now saw that their power and influence went deeper and further than he had thought. He had imagined them running a nation, and they were out to control a world. He had thought them to be a small group, and now he saw them as a worldwide organization.

"This world system has to be brought under one government," said Jacob, picking up where Christine left off. "And the government has to be brought under one leader. It is the only way to keep this planet from exploding. This pod will be implanted in hundreds of world leaders. It doesn't even take an operation, just an injection with a hypodermic. Once implanted, the pod itself does most of the work. It's what we call a bio-chip. Part of it is actually organic. It will grow into the cortex and become a natural part of the brain. By the way, you're wrong, Jack. It doesn't control the mind, it frees it."

"It taps into the hidden resources of the mind," added Indres, "and allows the individual to see more clearly. It releases the full potential of the human brain! Some of the subjects we have already implanted have displayed marked tendencies for telekinesis, and two have actually demonstrated an ability for telepathy. Think of it, Senator! Mind-to-mind contact! This is truly the beginning of the New Age!"

"So what we have," added Christine, "is simply a device that enables people to 'see more clearly,' as Raj puts it. They are not controlled. They are now simply 'awake.' They see the importance of our vision and will be in a position to bring it about."

Jack felt like a drowning man who had just been thrown an anvil instead of a life preserver. Things were rapidly getting out of control. He became even more frightened when the double doors opened and Dr. Steiger walked in. Behind him were two impressive looking security guards. They moved to stand behind Jack.

"What's going on?" he asked, the panic rising in his voice.

"I had hoped not to have to resort to this," said Jacob, shaking his head. "I had hoped you would join us of your own free will."

"Jacob, give me a little time," said Jack desperately. He was grasping for anything that would keep him alive. "You hit me with this all at once. You can't expect me to just jump in with both feet on something this big."

"Unfortunately, that is *exactly* what I expect from you. Why else have I brought you this far, Mr. Speaker?"

Jack started to speak, but Jacob continued. "You have been monitored since you came to Mentasys," he said. "The results are not good. You are not wholly with us, Jack, and I can't have someone in on this that isn't wholly with us."

"You can't just get rid of me," said Jack through clenched teeth. It was a last effort to save himself. "You can't just get rid of a United States senator!" Inside, Jack knew he was very wrong. Jacob Hill and his Inner Circle could do just about whatever they wanted.

"Jack! I'm not going to get rid of you," protested Jacob mildly. "I've put too much time and effort into you, and I don't want to see that wasted. No, you are still very important to me. You see, you WILL support me unconditionally. All it will take will be a simple operation." Jacob nodded to the two security guards, who moved to stand on either side of Jack.

"No!" He jumped up in a desperate move to escape, but there was nowhere to run. The guards pinned his arms, and Dr. Steiger came forward. In his hand was a syringe.

"We haven't perfected the injection process yet, so I'll have to put you out for a while," said Steiger.

"Please, Jacob! Don't do this to me!"

"I'm truly sorry, Jack," said Jacob, "But you leave me no other choice. Don't worry. The operation is completely safe, and relatively quick. You will be back in Washington within 24 hours."

As Jack watched in horror, Steiger forced his sleeve back and plunged the syringe into his exposed arm. Almost instantly, a growing numbness began to come over him. The room began to swim and grow blurry. The last thing he saw was Jacob looking at him with his empty, expressionless eyes.

4

"Helen, calm down." Jeff watched as his friend paced from one end of the dingy warehouse office to the other. This particular warehouse was owned by a member of the Shepherd's Path and was not far from the furniture store that had been raided two nights before. Hidden in strategic places throughout the cavernous building were small caches of Bibles and other materials that were routinely distributed to churches across the nation.

It was also used as a safe house. Behind the office was a small concealed room that served effectively as a hiding place. More than one fugitive, whose only crime was to attend a non-sanctioned church service, had stayed there until he or she could be moved to a safer location. Places like these were scattered across the country. Just now, though, it only had two occupants. Jeff Anderson sat behind a battered desk and watched as his companion worked herself into a lather.

"Calm down?" Helen stopped her pacing and turned to confront her friend. "Calm down?" she repeated. "Jeff, have you been paying attention to me at all?"

"Of course I have," replied Jeff soothingly. "But there's only so much I can do right now. Everyone I can trust is either looking for this Sampson guy or trying to uncover some lead to this 'Christian Liberation Front.' Until we get something else to go on, all we can do is wait."

"Wait!" Helen turned and resumed her pacing. "We just lost one of our churches. It looks like they were betrayed from the inside — one of their own members, for goodness sake. Was it this Scott Sampson? Tom identified him as one of the last people to enter the building."

"With a woman," added Jeff. "Presumably his wife. Helen, we

have no proof that it was Sampson who blew the whistle on the church."

"We have no proof that it wasn't him," she snapped back. "He's wanted in connection with that terrorist bombing at the airport. A man like that could have easily turned in his own church." She threw her hands up in the air in frustration. "Why don't you *do* something instead of telling me to wait?"

Instantly she regretted her harsh words. "I'm sorry Jeff," she said quickly, reaching out to touch his arm. "We've lost churches before, but never this close to home. I know you're doing your best."

Jeff waved away her apology. "If you want my professional opinion," he said, "I don't think Sampson is a terrorist, or an informer, for that matter. He doesn't fit the profile."

"How do you mean?" asked Helen. She stopped her pacing for a moment and sat on the edge of the desk.

Jeff thought for a moment, gathering his thoughts. "I ran a check on him," he said finally. "Standard procedure in these cases, even if the Bureau of Religious Affairs is handling it. It seems that he was having a rough time on his job. Got a demotion a year or so back for no apparent reason. I have a hunch it might be because both he and his wife belonged to a local church in this area."

"That's no indication of where his loyalties lie," commented Helen. "In fact, it could mean just the opposite. If he was bitter enough about his job, he could be driven to betray a church — possibly for money."

"Agreed," said Jeff. "But there's more. He doesn't have any priors, not even a parking ticket. Never been in trouble, and no known affiliations with questionable groups. He moved here from Detroit. He's clean there too, by the way. Been married for over seven years, wife's name is Beth."

"Was that his wife he went to the meeting with?" asked Helen.

"We're pretty sure," replied Jeff. "We're getting Tom to ID her now, and should have an answer momentarily."

"This still doesn't clear him," said Helen.

"I know," agreed Jeff, "but there's one final fact. The airline just released the passenger list off of that flight that blew up. His wife was on it."

Helen was quiet for a moment. "Are you sure?" she asked finally.

"We have her name, and a person matching her description was seen boarding. Hopefully, we'll be certain when we see the computer tapes from the airport." It was standard procedure for all airport gates to be constantly monitored by surveillance cameras. All activity was recorded onto computer disks.

"So if Sampson isn't our informer, who is?" asked Helen.

"We're checking the arrest records from the raid," replied Jeff. "It's slow going because the Bureau of Religious Affairs is keeping a tight lid on their actions. If we can get a list of who was taken in, and compare it with who was actually arrested, we might be able to finger the culprit." He shrugged. "It's a long shot, but it's the only one we've got."

"We have to know," said Helen, getting up from the desk and resuming her pacing. "If someone like that were to go undetected, there's no end to the damage they could do."

"I know," said Jeff. "Helen, I've already got as many people working on it as I can without arousing suspicion. For the last time, all we can do is wait!"

"I know, I know, Jeff, but knowing that doesn't make it any easier."

"Tell me about it," he grunted. "Half my job is spent waiting on one thing or another. Trust me, it never gets any easier."

"One thing I can always count on you for is encouragement," said Helen. Her voice dripped with sarcasm, but she smiled to remove the sting from her words. Jeff grinned in return.

"Do you really need me here?" she asked, changing the subject. "I should get some other things done today. I've got a courier coming for a run to St. Louis and. . . ."

"And nothing," said Jeff. "Until we get this mess straightened out, we don't make another move."

"Jeff," said Helen. "We can't shut the entire network down because of one raid. There are too many people depending on us."

"Until we know more, that's exactly what we have to do," said Jeff. "Look at the facts," he continued, holding up his fingers and ticking off points. "One, we've got an informer on the loose. He's probably not part of the network, but only probably. Two, we've got a terrorist bombing that has killed a few hundred people and drawn national attention. The terrorists are calling themselves the 'Christian Liberation Front,' and have demanded the release of known underground church members. Now, it's a fairly well-established fact in government circles that a lot of people are holding secret church meetings. Granted, the Shepherd's Path seems to have escaped detection so far, but we can't be sure that will continue to be the case. Now, if you add everything up, what does the answer come out to?"

Helen did not have to answer. The expression on her face told him she had figured it out.

He nodded grimly. "It's going to be open season on believers," he said, confirming her worst fears. "What we have gone through up till now," he said quietly, emphasizing each word, "will be nothing compared to what's coming."

"Like lambs to a slaughter," said Helen, her voice almost a whisper. They sat in silence for a moment, each contemplating the approaching darkness.

Abruptly, Jeff brightened up. "However," he said, rubbing his hands briskly, "we are, as they say, not finished yet. We still may identify our traitor. If we can do that, we can resume operations, albeit at a lower level. Also, if we can prove that this terrorist thing has nothing to do with Christians, things may ease off a little."

Helen shook her head. "What you call 'operations' are people, Jeff. Some of these groups meeting haven't seen a Bible in months, even years — and what about those in hiding? We can't just. . . ." She was interrupted by the beeping of Jeff's private line. He held up a hand to silence her as he took his phone out of his pocket and flipped it open.

"Anderson," he said into the receiver. Helen could hear muffled speaking coming from the tiny speaker, but could not make out any words. Jeff listened for a moment, then spoke. "Have you got a positive I.D., then?" Another pause. "Okay, get on it. And David, keep a low profile. The last thing we need is to draw attention to ourselves. Good luck." He closed the phone and put it back in his pocket.

"Well?" asked Helen.

Jeff didn't answer for a moment. He sat thoughtfully, staring at nothing.

"Jeff, what is it?'

"Hmmmm? Oh, sorry Helen. I just — never mind. We identified the informant. He was at the meeting, taken to bureau headquarters, but not arrested. David, the agent I was just talking to, did some checking. It looks like the bureau was putting pressure on him — threatening his family, that sort of thing."

"Was it Sampson?"

"No. Sampson and his wife were there as legitimate worshipers. This guy's name is Allan Meyers."

"I don't know that name," admitted Helen.

"Doesn't matter," replied Jeff. "We know who he is now. He won't be anymore trouble. . . ." Jeff trailed off, and again turned thoughtful.

"Jeff, what is it?" asked Helen again. "There's something else, isn't there?"

"I don't know," said Jeff, frustration creeping into his voice. His hands clenched and unclenched themselves. Biting his lower lip, he tried to put his feelings and fears into words. "I just get the feeling that there's something going on, something very very big. The clues are all there, but they won't fit together."

"What clues?" asked Helen.

"Well, take our Mr. Sampson," he said. "We know now that he was simply attending the meeting at the furniture store — he had no ulterior motive. Then he's supposed to bomb a passenger flight? The one his wife just boarded? I don't think so! It looks like someone is using him for a scapegoat.

"Next, there's the Christian Liberation Front. Who are they? Evidence points to the Church, but we know that's not possible. Therefore, someone is deliberately making it look like the Church is responsible. Why? Just to begin a new offensive against us? Are we looking a major persecution in the face?

"Finally, there's the Bureau of Religious Affairs. In the last few years, it seems like they have become a law unto themselves. Who do they answer to? I thought it was supposed to be the FBI. Now, they're acting more like a privately owned force than a government institution. Somehow . . ." he groped for the right words. All he had were vague suspicions and hunches. "Somehow," he repeated, "it seems as if all this should be related. It's almost as if a single guiding hand is directing everything, but I can't make the pieces fit."

Helen listened patiently to Jeff. It wasn't the first time she had heard someone voice suspicions about a mammoth conspiracy. It had been a popular theme on the Christian talk show circuit over a decade ago — when there had *been* Christian television. Many had voiced opinions about secret societies. From what she remembered, they were supposed to be responsible for everything from both world wars to their current dilemma. They were supposed to be all-seeing, all-knowing, just short of God — and, as far as Helen was concerned, they didn't matter at all.

"Jeff, if a single hand really is running things, how does that effect us?"

"Well," he began, "we probably should. . . ."

"I'll tell you what we probably should do," interrupted Helen. "We should 'probably' keep doing exactly what we are doing. One of the responsibilities God has given us is to help nurture infant churches.

Most Christians were caught flat-footed when the crash came, and now they need what we have to give. Our other job is to win souls, and we need to keep doing it. Let's not forget that, okay? All of this cloak and dagger stuff has its place, but we're here to be a 'light to the world,' and no secret society is going to stop us from doing just that."

Jeff looked at Helen for a moment, then grinned. "That's why you're in charge of this whole shebang," he said. "Me, I get caught up in the mechanics of the operation, and tend to forget just why we put ourselves through all of this. Okay, Helen, you made your point. We've learned what we came to learn. Let's get out of here. I've got to get a watch put on Allan Meyers' home."

"Why?" asked Helen as Jeff walked her to the door. "I thought you said that now that we know who he is, he can't hurt us any more."

"Think it through," answered Jeff. "Meyers set up the church Scott and Beth Sampson attended. Somehow, they managed to escape. Scott puts his wife on a flight to Denver, presumably to someplace safe, and it blows up, killing all aboard. Somewhere out there is a man on the run. He's just lost his wife, he has no place to go, and nothing left to lose. What happens if he finds out it was Allan who betrayed them? Allan is directly responsible for Beth Sampson's death."

"You don't think, . . ."

"Like you said, people have cracked under less pressure. I'm not taking any chances. The Bureau of Religious Affairs is combing the country. There's nothing I can do there, but if he shows up at the Meyers' home, we'll get him — hopefully before he does something drastic."

"I hope you're wrong," said Helen as they left the office and headed out through the warehouse.

"I do, too," replied Jeff, "but I have a sinking feeling that Mr. Sampson may just try to kill Allan Meyers."

❖ ❖ ❖

The sun was just setting on the community of Crestview Hills when the man moved out from under the cover of the trees. The sound of children at play could still be heard as they tried to squeeze in a few more rounds of hide-and-seek before the call to supper. Lights were beginning to appear in various windows of the upper middle class homes, and people began to settle in for the night. The summer air was turning pleasantly muggy.

The man had hidden by one of the many lakes that dotted the area during the day, peering out of a small glen of pine trees. Now he moved onto the deserted road to observe one particular house. He certainly did not belong here. If he had been seen in daylight, he would surely have been reported. Two days growth of beard covered a pale, drawn face. He wore faded jeans, and a short sleeve blue cotton shirt that looked as wrinkled as he did. Eyes that were dead to any emotion, save maybe hatred, scanned the surrounding area. The fading light made it difficult to see, but he was patient. Finally, when satisfied that no one was watching, he began to stalk toward the house he had chosen.

Scott Sampson had only one thought in his mind now. He wanted to make Allan Meyers pay for shattering his life. Everything else was secondary. He fully expected to be arrested tonight, perhaps even killed. He didn't care. His whole being was geared toward ending the life of a betrayer. As he slipped across the street and into the front yard, he felt the lump of metal in his jean pocket press against his thigh. He had paid cash for the small caliber hand gun. The serial number had been filed off, and the street hustler he had bought it from had only cared about the color of Scott's money.

The past two days were a blur to him. He had left his car in the motel parking lot, not wanting to take any chances of being spotted — and frankly not caring about keeping it anymore. A bottle of cheap dye and a tube of instant sun tan foam, bought at a local drugstore, built a simple disguise. For hours, he had hitched his way haphazardly back toward town. He was in a daze, and had no clear idea what to do or where to go. When he had regained consciousness on that motel room floor, his emotions were gone. Through the haze in his mind, he knew vaguely that he should be mourning Beth, but try as he might, he could feel nothing. He could not even remember what his wife looked like. Something inside of him had broken off. Something special, something precious, had been lost. If he carried through with his plans tonight, it would never be regained.

His last ride had spoken about the tragedy at the airport. Scott had remained silent, but the mention of the bombing brought his ordeal back to the forefront of his thoughts. Like a tidal wave, the hopelessness of his situation threatened to engulf him. He had cast about for an anchor, and a face had presented itself — Allan Meyers. Now at last the emotions came, but they were of anger and hatred. This man had cost Scott everything he held dear. It was unfair that he sat safely at his dinner table tonight while Scott was hunted like an animal. He had to pay! Scott had bought the gun, and now, two days after his life fell apart, he was ready to use it. The sun was completely down now and night was beginning to cover the peaceful neighborhood.

"Enjoy your home, Allan," whispered Scott to himself. "Enjoy your home and family, for this is the last night you will ever spend with them." He knew that his prey was home. He had seen him arrive from work several hours ago. He had not come out since.

While he was waiting under the trees, Scott had studied the house carefully. It was a split level model, attractively built with tan bricks and white wooden trim. A large two car garage sat on the first level, while above it were obviously the bedrooms. The rest of the house comprised the second, middle level. On the far side, the neighboring house stood. Two large windows faced the Meyers' house, and Scott doubted he could go in that way without being seen. The opposite side was better. A tall hedge ran between Allan's house and his neighbors. A single window in the center of the wall would allow Scott to slip in quietly.

He made his way into the front yard, noting the child's bicycle lying next to the door. He didn't want to hurt Allan's family, so he would somehow have to isolate him. Without hesitation, he walked swiftly into the side yard. Now he felt more secure. The hedge blocked the view from the side, and the house that sat across from the back yard was not visible from this angle. He crouched down low, leaning against the rough brick. The window that would be his entrance was dark. Slowly, he edged under it. Once again, he made sure no one was watching from the street. It was now completely dark. He could hear an orchestra of crickets playing their nightly sonata, and could see the flaring of a thousand tiny lightning bugs in the night. Once, a millennia ago, he would have enjoyed the sensations they brought. Now, they meant nothing.

Carefully, Scott peered into the window. The curtain that covered it was separated about two inches in the middle. Although it was dark, he could get a rough idea of the layout of the room. There was a little light coming through the door that stood opposite him. It was a fairly large room, almost 13 feet square, and looked to be a study. On his right were shelves of books that stood from floor to ceiling. To the left, across the room, was a desk that faced the books. Behind the desk was an open door that revealed a shallow closet. The door that opened out into the rest of the house was half open.

It was time. Scott reached up and pushed gently at the window. It was the type that slid up rather than out. Locked! He considered his options for a moment, then produced a small screwdriver from his pocket. It took only a moment to force the blade between the window and the lock. Moving carefully, trying not to make any excess noise, he slid the screwdriver forward. He could see the latch begin to move, then his tool lost its purchase and he jerked forward, thudding against the glass. Quickly he ducked out of sight, his heart pounding. Expecting the curtain to be drawn back at any moment, he quelled his urge to run. Forcing himself to sit quietly, he waited. Nothing happened. Once again, he raised himself and used the screwdriver. This time he was successful, and the latch slid back.

Just like in the movies, thought Scott with grim humor. *Call me "the cat."* He giggled under his breath. "Looks like you forgot to put the cat out tonight, Meyers, and it's going to cost you." His giggle threatened to become a full-fledged laugh, and he shut it off. It would not be the laugh of a sane man.

He put the screwdriver away, and again tried the window. It slid easily upward, opening wide enough for Scott to slide through. It took him only seconds, and he was inside the house. He brushed the curtain aside and crouched in the darkness, listening with every fiber of his being. He could hear the sounds of a family at dinner coming through the door. Quietly he lowered the window and secured the latch. Then he rearranged the curtain. On tiptoe, he crossed the study and stood by the door. He leaned forward just enough to see out. The study opened out into a hall that ended in a bathroom on his left. To the right, the hall ran into the rest of the house. Soft, yellow light shone around the corner at the far end, indicating a kitchen. Judging from the level of noise, the dining room was on the other side of the kitchen. Straight across the hall, another door opened into a large master bedroom. There was a small table light burning brightly on a night stand that stood next to a king size bed.

Scott remembered from his time at Faith Community Church that Allan had two children. His daughter was about 10 years old, and his son in his late teens. He could hear four distinct voices coming from the dining room, although he could not make out any particulars of the conversation. The whole family was home, then. That was too bad, but it could not be helped. Scott was not about to be detoured from his purpose.

He backed off from the door and closed it slightly, leaving just enough of an opening for ample light. Taking one more quick survey of the study, he padded over to the closet behind the desk and opened the louvered doors. It was filled with cardboard file boxes stacked almost to the ceiling. Taking a deep breath, he began to move the boxes, one at a time. At any moment, he expected the light to click on and Allan to be standing there. He began to sweat as he rearranged the boxes. The dim glow from the hall made his task almost impossible, but he kept at it. Finally, he cleared an empty space just big enough to squeeze into. He paused for a moment, then went back to the study door. The clatter of dishes in the sink told him that dinner was over. Carefully he peeped out of the tiny opening, trying to see down the hall. There was a sudden movement, and before he could draw back, Allan himself appeared. Scott yanked his head back behind the door, sucking in his breath. If Allan had seen. . . .

He could hear the muffled footsteps as Allan came toward him. With a sinking realization he saw that he had not closed the closet door. The boxes were now crammed every which way, obviously disturbed. Allan would see immediately that something was wrong. Scott waited, listening as Allan drew closer. He heard the footsteps as he came even with the study door. There was a pause, and Scott tensed. His fingers went of their own volition to the gun in his pocket.

Click! A bright light shone through the crack for an instant, then disappeared. Scott nearly fainted with relief. Allan had gone into the bathroom! He slumped against the door, and immediately it shut with a dull "thunk."

That tears it! he said to himself, disgusted with his carelessness. Surely Allan had heard that. Gently he opened the door again. There was no change. He could still hear the rest of the family somewhere at the other end of the house, talking happily among themselves. He felt a brief pang of regret for what he was about to do to them, but shoved it aside. *Think about what Meyers has done to you,* he lectured himself grimly. This was the man who had destroyed his life. There would be no mercy.

Leaving the door, he went back to the closet and slipped in. He had just closed the door behind him when he heard the toilet flush. A moment later there was the sound of running water. When it shut off, the bathroom door opened. Scott heard a brief shuffle, then the study door opened. By putting his eyes right up against the slats in the louvered doors, he could see out. Allan stood there, outlined by the bathroom light. He paused for a moment, as if checking out the room. Then he walked over to the desk. A floor lamp was sitting off to one side, and Allan disappeared for a moment as he turned it on. A soft glow flooded the study, and Scott leaned back from the closet door. He didn't think Allan could see him, but no sense in taking chances. Now Allan reappeared. He moved over to the window, moving the curtains aside and checked the latch. Satisfied, he shut the study door and sat behind his desk. Rummaging through the drawers, he pulled out a stack of papers, and began to leaf through them. Scott could not believe his luck. His intended victim had just gift wrapped himself!

Slowly, carefully, not even daring to breathe, Scott put his hand gently on the closet door and began to push. It would not do, he knew, for Allan to hear him just yet. He had visualized this moment over and over again. He knew exactly what he would do, and what he would say. The door resisted for a moment, then began to move. Allan's chair was less than 24 inches away. The slightest sound would alert him. Patiently, Scott continued to push. The door moved, opening a millimeter at a time. Once, Allan put his papers down and arched his back. Scott could hear it pop as he froze, hand still on the door. Allan twisted back and forth, relieving the pressure around his sagging middle. Then, with a deep sigh, he went back to work.

Scott resisted the urge to draw in a deep breath. He waited, unmoving, while Allan pored over his work. Finally, he started to push again. The minutes dragged on, each one an eternity. Every second the door opened wider. It took over five minutes to make an opening wide enough to squeeze through. It seemed like a year, but at last it was done. There was now nothing between Scott and Allan. With the same patience he had used with the door, Scott reached into his pocket and pulled out the pistol. His hand grasped it tightly, as if it were a lifeline to his sanity. He was starting to sweat, although it was cool in the study.

Slowly, deliberately, he brought the gun up to where it was level with the back of Allan's head. His mind was giddy with the thought of revenge, but somewhere in his soul, a voice was calling, demanding attention. Part of him, the part he had turned off since Beth's death, wanted him to listen, wanted him to respond. He ignored it. Clenching his jaw so tightly that it hurt, he brought his thumb up to the hammer and pulled it back. It answered with a resounding "click." At the same time, Scott took a step forward out of the closet. Allan jumped at the noise, and swiveled around in his chair. He was met by the barrel of Scott's pistol not three inches from the bridge of his nose. Scott had dreamed of this moment. He had pictured Allan's face when he understood that he was about to die. Nothing, however, could prepare him for the delicious satisfaction that flowed through him when he saw Allan's look of shock that turned rapidly into terrified realization. Revenge was sweet, indeed!

"Hello, Allan," said Scott, pleased that his voice sounded as casual as if they had just met for coffee. Allan's mouth opened, closed, then opened again. He tried to talk, but could only respond with a squeaky whine. Scott feigned surprise.

"Nothing to say?" he asked in a mocking tone. "You always had plenty to say before." Carefully, Scott edged away from the closet and toward the study door. From this vantage point, he could see the entire room. There would be no surprises. Carefully he locked the door.

"You had plenty to say when you tried to sell Beth and me life insurance. 'What a great deal I can get you,' you said. You were never at a loss for words when you prayed out loud in church. Those were great prayers, you know. I'm sure everyone was impressed." Scott motioned threateningly with his gun. "You especially had a lot to say," he continued, his voice beginning to rise, "when you betrayed us the other night. When you gave the police our names and address. When you took away our lives." His arm stiffened, the gun now pointed right at Allan's forehead.

"Wait!" Allan squeaked, his voice cracking. "You don't understand."

"I was *there*, Allan! We were under those stairs in that filthy cellar when you sold out." Scott was yelling now, not caring who heard. It would all be over in a moment.

"I heard you tell them everything." Allan's face drained of blood as he listened to Scott. His eyes kept flicking from the barrel of the pistol to Scott's eyes. He licked his dry lips, and tried desperately to think of something, anything to say. He opened his mouth, but Scott wasn't through.

"Did you hear about that plane blowing up, Allan?" Scott asked, now lowering his voice to normal. When Allan didn't answer, Scott took another step forward, bringing the gun within inches of his face. "Answer me!"

Allan nodded rapidly, as if speed could save him.

"Well, my wife was on that plane. I put her there to get her away, and it blew up. Now, who do you think is to blame for that?" A groan escaped Allan's lips. He knew there was no answer to that, just as he knew he was staring death in the face.

"Who . . . is . . . to . . . blame, Allan?" Scott's words came one at a time, each one spat out like a bullet. Allan realized that he was waiting for an answer.

"The terrorist who. . . ." Slap! Allan jerked back into his chair, the force of Scott's openhanded blow staggering him. When his vision cleared, he saw Scott towering over him. The hand that held the gun was trembling, and Scott had a wild look in his eyes.

"Wrong answer, Allan." The gun steadied, once again centered on his forehead. "Last chance. WHO IS TO BLAME FOR MY WIFE'S DEATH?" Allan felt gingerly at his jaw. It still stung, and he could feel a small trickle of blood. He licked his dry lips, and struggled to speak.

"I am," he finally managed to say. He knew he was signing his own death warrant, but also knew that Scott would accept no other answer.

"Very good." Scott nodded his approval. "Now you can die with a clean conscience. Doesn't it make you feel better now that this is out in the open?" Allan sagged in his chair in utter defeat. He put his head down on the desk. What little self-control he had left deserted him, and he began to cry, quietly at first, then in great wracking sobs. Scott watched impassively. He felt a twinge of guilt, but suppressed it immediately as he pictured the explosion that had killed his wife.

"They — said — they — would — take — muh — my family." Allan struggled to get the words out between sobs. His whole body seemed to be convulsing. Scott began to feel uncomfortable. This was exactly the reaction he had wanted, but now the sweetness was wearing off. In its place was a growing emptiness.

"Mu — my kids, they threatened my kids."

"Stuff it, Allan!" said Scott sharply. "Tell it to Beth. For that matter, tell it to the rest of that little group. Who knows what they're going through right now, just because you didn't have the guts to stay true." For a moment, Scott moved the gun away. He leaned forward on the desk, and smiled. Instinctively, Allan leaned away. Scott's smile was that of a shark's when it was closing in for the kill.

"Give me one reason," he said in a low voice. "Give me one reason to let you live, and I will." He brought the gun back around. "But make it a good one, Allan."

Allan chewed his lower lip. He tried desperately to think of a way out, a way to escape, but could not force his mind to function. His heart was pounding like a trip hammer. He knew that Scott, in his half-crazed state, would not accept any reason he might give. The only hope was his wife or kids. Surely they had heard the commotion!

"Sorry, Allan," said Scott, sliding off the desk. "Time's up, and you lose. Better say your. . . ."

"ALLAN!" The shout came through the locked study door, followed by a heavy thud. "Allan, what's going on?! Who's in there with you? Allan, open this door, now!" It was Allan's wife. Scott knew his time had run out. He sighted down the barrel of the pistol, to the bridge of Allan's nose. Allan's eyes widened in panic.

"Allan! Jerry's calling the police! Open the door, now!" Scott set his lips in a thin line. This was it! He looked at the quivering human sitting in front of him. This would be a mercy killing! Allan was a waste. Worse, he was a traitor to his God and his church. It was only right that he be put out of his misery.

"THUD" The study door shuddered, its thin construction threatening to give way. It was now or never. Scott clenched his teeth, took a deep breath, and pulled the trigger. Reflexively, he closed his eyes, waiting for the bang. He had never shot a gun before, and did not know what to expect. What he did *not* expect was — nothing — no sound, no jolt to his arm — nothing. He opened his eyes, and saw the situation unchanged. He still held the gun to Allan's forehead, and Allan still sat there, waiting for the end. His hand was trembling. It seemed to be no longer attached to his body, and would not obey his commands. He focused every ounce of his being on his trigger finger, willing it to contract, to pull the trigger. Nothing! It would not move, no matter how hard he tried. It was as if some irresistible force had taken control of his arm and would not let him fire. He closed his eyes, and in an eternity that lasted no time at all, fought a battle.

Suddenly the tiny voice in his soul that had been crying for his attention came to the forefront of his mind. "So you would kill this man?" it asked.

"He deserves to die," Scott answered.

"Undoubtedly," agreed the voice. "He deserves to die, and many who die deserve to live. Can you give them back their lives?"

"That's ridiculous," replied Scott in annoyance. Why wouldn't this blasted voice go away and let him do what he had come to do?

"You cannot give back life," continued the voice relentlessly. "But you are ready to take a life. Have you been appointed this man's judge and executioner?" Scott had no answer to that. He knew he wasn't here for justice, but for vengeance. He tried to shut out the voice, to drive it away, and was surprised when he was successful.

That takes care of that, he thought in satisfaction. Now he could get on with business. Only now there was another voice. It was at once compassionate and commanding. It spoke softly, yet would not be ignored.

"Father," it said, echoing down through the ages. "Forgive them, for they know not what they do!" It was the voice of utmost love, and gentleness, and yet it tore through Scott like a hot iron. It burned him, and in its burning, healed him. It was the voice of his Saviour.

Scott blinked, and realized he was back in the real world. Allan was still there, waiting. Someone was banging on the door, and off in the distance he could hear police sirens. He swallowed hard, and knew what he had to do. The anger was still there, as was the desire to punish this man for the horrible grief he had caused. Now, though, there was something else. The part of Scott that was lost two days ago had been restored. He remembered his own fear on the way to that ill-fated meeting, and he found he could now understand Allan. Slowly, he put aside the anger and hatred. Just as slowly, he lowered his arm. Allan saw the gun go down, and blinked in confusion. He looked at Scott.

Scott looked back, searching for words. The sirens were now closer, and whoever was banging at the door had almost battered it in. His time was gone. He moved toward the window, hoping no one was waiting for him on the other side. As he opened it, he realized he had to say something to Allan. His next words were the hardest he had ever spoken in his life. He turned to face his former enemy.

"Allan," he said, each word a struggle, "I had no right to do this. I know it's a lot to ask, but will you forgive me?" Instantly, Scott felt a tremendous burden lift from his shoulders. He had not even realized it was there, but now that it was gone, he felt as if he could soar!

Allan just stared at him, not understanding. Finally, he managed to croak, "I — I forgive you?"

Scott nodded. "Just like I forgive you," he said softly. "After all, if Jesus could forgive those who crucified Him, can we do less? Will you forgive me?"

For a moment, Allan didn't move. Then, as if in slow motion, he nodded. Scott nodded in return, a ghost of a smile playing across his face. He took the pistol, and made sure the safety was on. Then he tossed it underhanded to Allan. Allan barely managed to catch it. He held it gently, as if it were a poisonous reptile. Then he opened his desk drawer and laid it inside.

"Go," Allan said. "I'll tell them it was a thief, or something. I promise." Scott nodded, and began to climb out the window.

"Scott!" Allan called, and Scott turned back. "Thank you," said Allan, the words coming straight from his heart. There was nothing else to say. Scott nodded, and dropped through the window. His feet had just hit the ground when he heard the police sirens reach the front of the house and stop. He could see the reflection of their lights on the hedge, and could hear the car doors slam as they got out.

There was only one avenue of escape. He headed away from the street, into the back yard. The lights from the house lit his way. He skirted the edge of the yard, following the hedge. He had just reached the border between Allan's house and his rear neighbors when his eye caught a sudden movement inside the hedge. He turned to look, and was knocked flat on his back by a flying tackle. His assailant ended up on top of him. Scott struggled to get away, but was hopelessly pinned. His opponent had greater strength and size. The darkness masked his face, and Scott could only wait to see what would happen next.

Suddenly, the weight on his chest disappeared. Scott took a deep breath, and then was hauled ruthlessly to his feet. A voice whispered harshly in his ear. "You want to live?" it asked. "Then don't say a word. Follow me." Like a shot, the dark shape took off weaving back and forth.

Scott stood there in indecision for a moment, then began to run after the mysterious figure. Whoever he was, he was fast, and Scott had to struggle to keep up. They left Allan's house behind, going from yard to yard in a mad dash. Their route took so many turns and twists that Scott lost his bearings completely. He caught glimpses of swimming pools, picnic tables, and badminton nets on that wild dash. He listened for signs of pursuit, but heard nothing. Perhaps Allan had told the truth. Perhaps he did indeed mislead the police. Only time would tell.

Finally the mysterious shape stopped. Scott pulled up behind, gasping for breath. He wasn't in bad shape, but the past few days had taken their toll, and the adrenaline rush that had gotten him this far was wearing off. He was feeling dizzy and slightly nauseous. "Where . . .?" he gasped. "Where . . .?" he tried again, but had to pause to breathe.

"Shut up!" the man whispered fiercely. He pulled out a small dark object about the size of his hand. "This is Snoopy," he said into it. "The red baron is in the neighborhood. Request immediate pickup."

There was a pause, then a feminine voice came from the object. "This is Lucy, Snoopy. Pick up in 10 minutes. Repeat, 10 minutes. Be there, or be square!"

Scott's guide replaced the communicator back into his pocket, then grabbed Scott's shoulder. "Come on," he said, and once again took off at a dead run. Scott groaned, knowing that he could not match his pace. Then he heard a sound that chilled him. Dogs. They were somewhere in the distance, but seemed to be getting closer. The police were tracking him. Instantly, the adrenaline surged again. He would pay for this later, but for right now, all he wanted to do was get away.

His guide had gotten about 10 paces ahead of him, and was widening the distance. Once again it was helter-skelter through private yards. Several times they crossed empty suburban streets and splashed through the edges of glimmering moonlit lakes. It seemed to go on forever. The sound of dogs receded, then grew louder, then receded again. Finally, when it seemed he couldn't go on any longer, they emerged from yet another yard and ran smack up against a tall, chain link fence.

The man halted, then began to climb. "Move!" he yelled over his shoulder, and Scott followed suit. He grasped the fence, his barely healed hand twinging. He could hardly get a grip, the cold metal biting into his flesh. His guide reached the top and flipped himself over with the ease of a gymnast. He dropped the 10 feet to the ground to land expertly on the other side, and waited impatiently. Scott continued to climb. A lancing pain shot through his arm as he reached the top. Barbed wire! He resisted the pain and pulled himself up. Long red gashes appeared on his arms and chest. With a mighty heave, he pulled himself over and dropped. His mysterious friend was there to catch him.

He looked around in the darkness and realized he was standing underneath rows of bleachers. He was led out from under them and into a wide expanse of grass that he recognized as a football field. Across the field was the dark shape of a high school. Together with his guide he trotted out into the middle of the field. It was wide open, and there was a full moon.

Feeling exposed and vulnerable, he turned to his rescuer and heard him muttering under his breath. "Come on, Lucy! Where are you?" Off in the distance Scott again heard the baying of the dogs, but at the same time, another sound announced itself. This was a dull whup! whup! whup! and it was coming from overhead. Scott strained his eyes upward and found a large dark shape descending towards him. There were no lights, but he recognized the shape of a helicopter. Just what was going on?

He felt a tug on his shoulder and followed as his guide led him off toward the side. Scott watched in amazement as a helicopter set down dead center in the football field. Automatically he ran toward it as if he had known the plan all along. The side opened, and a pair of hands reached out and helped him aboard. The door slid shut, and with a lurch, the helicopter lifted off.

Scott lay panting on the floor, feeling like he was going to throw up. The cuts on his arms and chest burned, and his lungs felt like they were on fire. He rolled over on his back and sat up. The noise from the rotor was almost deafening, but he tried to talk anyway. He felt as if he had just stepped into some kind of spy thriller, and he wanted some answers. There were three people, including himself, in the cramped cabin. His guide sat cross-legged in the rear, and another, smaller person squatted next to him. They appeared to be having a conversation. In the dim light of the cabin, he could see that they were both dressed in black body stockings and caps. They looked like some sort of commandos in an action movie.

"Who are you?" shouted Scott. It wasn't an eloquent question, he knew, but it got the point across. His fellow passengers ignored him.

"Hey!" He shouted at the top of his lungs, and this time they turned toward him. "I said, who are you? Where are you taking me?"

The smaller person got up and came over to sit next to him. From the way she moved, he could tell she was a woman. She leaned forward to yell in his ear. "We're friends," she shouted. "We're taking you to a safe place, and we'll answer your questions there. Okay?" Scott nodded, and she patted him on the shoulder.

"Just relax and enjoy the ride. You've had a rough time." A tiny glow appeared in her hand as she produced a small flashlight. He did not resist when she examined his arms and chest. The angry cuts were starting to look worse.

"We'll get those taken care of soon. Can you hang on?" Scott shook his head yes, and she walked back to the other man. He wrapped his arms around himself, and leaned back against the cold metal wall. The cabin was not pressurized, and the wind whistling through the seams in the door was beginning to chill him. Worse than that was the rough ride. He felt as if he were in a truck with bad shocks instead of an aircraft.

He tried to settle in for what he assumed would be a long ride. It came as a surprise, then, when his stomach lurched as the chopper started a rapid descent. No more than 10 minutes had passed since he had scrambled aboard. The man who had led him this far now came over and knelt down to face him. In the dim light, he could tell that he was a young man, probably younger than Scott. Wisps of blond hair stuck out from the cap, matching a thick mustache. The younger man regarded Scott for a moment, as if judging whether he was worthy of all the trouble he had been put to.

Finally he spoke. "We'll be landing in a few seconds," he shouted. "Once we're on the ground, you'll get out. You'll see a blue van about 50 yards away. Head straight for it. Walk, don't run. Get in.

Inside, there will be a black man. He'll take care of you from there. Understand?"

Scott nodded, and the younger man clasped him on the shoulder, giving him an affectionate shake.

"You showed a lot of guts back there in that house," he said. "Don't worry, we'll get you to where it's safe." With that, the man stood up and disappeared into the pilot's cabin. The woman came over and made ready to open the door. Seconds later, the chopper touched down with a gentle bump. Instantly, the door slid back. Scott was on his feet quickly, and the woman helped him down. They had landed in some sort of empty field, probably back in the hills. Straight ahead, just like he had been told, was the van, barely visible in the moonlight. He started to turn back to the woman, but she pushed him forward.

"Get going," she called. The chopper revved its engine and made ready to take off again. Scott started to jog toward the van.

Just as the helicopter took to the sky, he heard a shout. "God be with you!" There was a loud roar, and the chopper took off.

Scott turned to watch it for a moment, wondering just who had saved him. Then he lit out across the field, stumbling more than running. Each step was agony. The pain in his arms and chest was almost unbearable, and his energy level was non-existent.

The windows of the van were darkened. In the pale light of the full moon they stared back at him, empty and foreboding. A wild impulse came over Scott. Suddenly, all he wanted to do was run, to get away from the madness that had been his life over the past few days. Only the fact that his body would stand no more abuse prevented him. He knew that even if every cop in the city was breathing down his neck, he could run no further. He came even with the van, and leaned against the cool surface, panting for breath.

All was quiet for a moment, then the door on the rider's side opened. "Scott Sampson?" a deep male voice questioned. Scott nodded, then realized that he probably could not be seen.

"I'm Sampson," he gasped, sucking in air. In the back of his mind, he knew that admitting to his name was dangerous. If the man in that van was with the police or any other authority. . . . Scott shrugged his shoulders. The truth was, right now he was just too tired to care.

"Get in, Scott," said the voice kindly. "You're almost home."

"Not likely," he muttered under his breath. It was highly improbable that he would ever see his home again. Like a bolt of lightning, emptiness and longing welled up inside of him.

No time for that, he told himself ruthlessly, and climbed into the van. He settled in the captain's chair, sinking into the crushed velvet material. It was the first time he had sat down since reaching the Meyers' house. Exhaustion threatened to overwhelm him. To counteract it, he sat up in the seat and looked over at the driver, who was staring back at him.

"All set?" he asked. He was indeed a black man, well-built, judging by his silhouette.

"Where are we going?" Scott asked, not really expecting an answer. As if in reply, the driver started the van and pulled smoothly out into the deserted back road. When no other answer was forthcoming, Scott began to scan the countryside. If he hoped to pick out some sort of landmark, he was disappointed. They were deep in the back country. He could see the lights of the city off in the distance. If their current direction was any indication, they were heading toward it. The sweat he had worked up during that torturous run was beginning to dry. It was cool in the van, and he began to chill. He shivered involuntarily. The driver saw this, and jerked his head over his shoulder. "There's a jacket in the back seat," he said.

Scott found the brown windbreaker and slipped it on. Although slightly too large, it was well lined. He wrapped it around himself, feeling warmth creep over him. Turning to the driver, he asked, "Are you going to tell me anything at all?" He tried to keep his voice steady, but there was an edge of frustration to it. He wondered if he should be afraid.

The driver simply shrugged. "I know you've had it rough, Scott, but hang in there. Believe me when I tell you, you're among friends. All of your questions will be answered tonight. I promise."

Something in the man's voice made Scott want to trust him. He leaned back in the chair and watched the trees whisk by. His eyes wandered to the glow of the dashboard. There, under the windshield, was a clipboard with a yellow, legal pad. A pen hung from a string next to it. On impulse, he picked up the pad. The driver saw him, but made no move to intervene. Squinting in the dim light, he drew a straight vertical line. Without a word, he handed it over to the driver. The driver took it, and stared at if for a moment. Then, chuckling, he added the curved line at the top, forming the shepherd's staff. He passed the pad back.

"Like I said, Scott, you're among friends. Now, we've got about a half-hour ride in front of us. Why don't you recline that chair and get some rest? You look like you could use it."

Scott didn't need any more persuasion. He found the control, and leaned back. The pain in his chest and arms was still there, subsiding into a dull throb. He closed his eyes, but as exhausted as he was, sleep would not come. His wounds would not allow him to get comfortable. Worse, he had too many questions. Things were happening too fast. He was riding an emotional roller coaster, hanging on for dear life. It had been a wild ride so far, and a tragic one. What was next?

The van sped through the night, drawing ever closer to the city. The areas they were passing through were showing more and more signs of habitation. Soon they were back in Covington, heading toward the river. At first, Scott thought they were going over into Cincinnati, but just before they reached the bridge, the driver turned. Then they were passing a series of warehouses. Scott's stomach tightened. He didn't know Covington all that well, but he did recognize his general location. Only a few miles away was a certain furniture store. He closed his eyes, as if blotting out the city could blot out his memories.

The van came to a stop at last, in front of a huge metal building. The driver reached past Scott and opened the glove compartment. Rummaging inside for a moment, he brought out a small remote control. He pushed the single button, and a huge reinforced door began to roll up. Scott strained to see inside, but it was pitch black. Without waiting for the door to finish moving, the driver edged the van forward into the darkness. The headlights picked out stacks upon stacks of crates arranged in small islands. There was just enough room for the van to enter. It crept inside and came to a full stop. The driver shut the engine off and closed the door behind them.

"Let's go," he said, and climbed out. Scott followed suit, wincing at the pain the movement brought. The headlights were left on, and Scott followed his guide past the first stack of crates. The light diminished rapidly, forcing the driver to produce a small flashlight. He waited as Scott drew even with him, then continued on. Scott was led deeper into the warehouse, until finally they came to a small wood frame office standing against the rear wall. A curtained window allowed light to peek through, indicating the presence of others inside. Without hesitation, the driver opened the door and ushered Scott inside.

The small office was sparsely furnished with a single desk and chair. Other than the curtain across the single window, there were no other trappings. It smelled of unfinished wood, slightly musty. A single light hung from the bare ceiling, bathing everything in its hard glare. Scott came in slowly, feeling as if he were an exhibit at some sort of museum.

As the driver shut the door behind him, he became aware of another person standing in the far corner behind the desk. An elderly woman with silver hair watched him with a mixture of relief and suspicion. He returned her scrutiny, getting the impression of an immovable, unshakable object. It was immediately evident that this person was in charge. There was a single chair in front of the desk, and she motioned for him to take it. When he had done so, she moved to sit behind the desk. For a moment, they simply regarded each other warily, like a pair of boxers at the beginning of a match.

Scott was not one to rely on first impressions, but of one thing he was certain — this was not a person to be trifled with. She had the easy assurance of one used to being in charge. Her eyes bored into his, demanding total honesty. Yet, underneath her stern exterior, he could sense both compassion and love. He found himself liking her, and had to remind himself to keep up his guard. This lady, he knew, could be a tremendous friend, or a dangerous enemy. The driver leaned against the door, watching the two. He displayed a vague air of amusement at the scene playing out in front of him.

"Mr. Sampson," she said finally. Scott nodded, unsure of what to say. She continued to regard him quietly. Then, as if reaching a decision, she leaned back in her chair and sighed. "If you knew the trouble we went through to get you here," she began, but Scott interrupted. He had been kept in the dark long enough.

"Excuse me," he said, lifting his hand as if he were in school, "but just *why* have you brought me here. Who are you people?"

He looked back at the driver, who smiled and motioned toward the woman. "She answers the questions," he said. Scott turned back to face her, his eyes questioning. Again he was met with that penetrating stare.

"As to who we are," she said, "my name is Helen, and that," she motioned toward the driver, "is Jeff. The reason we are here at this late hour is because you decided to shoot Allan Meyers. That wasn't very nice, you know."

Scott stared at her, unable to formulate a reply.

Helen continued. "We thought, or rather Jeff thought, you might try something foolish like that." Helen's face softened for a moment, and she smiled gently. The compassion Scott had sensed now manifested itself. "We're very sorry about Beth," she continued. "I said you were foolish, but given the same set of circumstances, any one of us might have acted the same. Thank God you didn't go through with it."

Scott did not say a word. Inside he was in turmoil. Who *were* these people? How did they know about Beth? He sat very still.

Jeff walked past him to stand next to Helen. "Actually Scott, you should know who we are," he said. "Your use of the staff says that much."

Scott debated briefly whether or not to say anything else. Inwardly he shrugged. As much as they knew already, it made little difference. "I thought it was just a signal of recognition between believers," he said.

"It is," agreed Helen, "and much more. It's the symbol for the Shepherd's Path. One of the symbols, anyway."

"The what?" asked Scott in confusion.

"The Shepherd's Path," said Jeff, "is a loose network of believers. We're trying to help people like you — people whose only crime is to profess a belief in Jesus Christ, and who claim Him as Lord."

"Help? How?" asked Scott.

Helen shrugged slightly. "By doing whatever we can," she replied. "Sending Bibles to underground churches who have none, hiding believers who are being hunted, playing courier, messenger, and a hundred other things."

"How did you find me?" Scott wanted to know.

This time, it was Jeff who answered. "We knew you were at the furniture store, and weren't arrested. We also knew it was Allan Meyers who betrayed the group." His voice dropped. "I got the passenger list off Flight 407, so when the Bureau of Religious Affairs issued an arrest warrant for you, it was obvious they were looking for a scapegoat. I played a hunch that you knew it was Meyers who set you up, and thought you might show up at his house sometime."

"You should be a detective," snorted Scott.

Helen chuckled softly. "He is, actually," she said.

Jeff shook his head. "Even so, we almost blew it. I've had two agents watching the Meyers home for the past 12 hours, and somehow you managed to slip past both of them. David, the man who got you out of there, saw you at the last minute. He tried to stop you, but you were too fast. He watched that whole scene with you and Meyers from outside."

Scott rubbed his eyes. He was fading fast, and could not think straight. "Why?" he asked in frustration. "Why all that trouble for me? You had a helicopter, for cryin' out loud!" He ran his fingers through matted, oily hair, wincing at the pain in his arms. His movement caused the jacket to fall away from his chest, revealing his blood soaked shirt.

Helen saw his wounds for the first time, and blanched. "Jeff," she cried, springing forward, "why didn't you tell me he was hurt? Get the first aid kit out of the van. Quick!"

Jeff threw his hands in the air. "Idiot," he said, referring to himself. "They called me from the chopper and told me about that. Scott, I'm sorry. I forgot. I'll be back in a minute."

As he left, Helen reached under the desk and fiddled with something out of his sight. There was a soft "click" behind him. He turned to see a four foot high opening appear in the back wall. Helen motioned for him to go through. Past the door, Scott found a tiny room, more of a closet than anything else. Against the opposite wall was a cot. Next to it stood a plastic night stand with a small shaded light. Across from that was a sink.

At Helen's command, he shrugged out of the jacket and began to unbutton his shirt. The blood had dried, causing it to stick to his cuts. He peeled it off, gritting his teeth at the pain.

"How did that happen?" asked Helen, as she helped him.

"We went over a barbed wire fence," he replied. He sat down heavily on the cot, causing it to creak under his weight. Jeff returned with the first aid kit and gave it to Helen, then left to keep watch outside. She went over to the sink and dampened a cloth that was hanging there, then came to sit beside Scott. Quickly she washed the angry looking welts. Then she pulled a vial of antiseptic spray from the kit.

"This is probably going to hurt a little," she said, breaking the safety seal. She began to apply it. The stinging wasn't too bad compared to the pain he had already endured, but the sterile odor assaulted his senses.

Instantly, he was transported back in time to two nights ago. He was sitting in his LeMans with his wife. He could feel Beth's gentle touch as she wrapped his injured hand. He tensed, sucking in a quick breath to prevent himself from losing control.

"Almost done," said Helen, mistaking his tensing for pain. She finished with the spray and applied the plastiskin strips. The numbing agent in the strips went to work immediately, and within seconds, the pain was gone. Scott let out a deep sigh. He was actually beginning to feel human again! The absence of pain was an indescribable pleasure. It almost made him forget his situation.

Helen surveyed her handiwork with satisfaction.

"You should be able to get some rest now," she said. "As far as I could tell, there was no infection. You should heal nicely."

"Thank you," replied Scott, really meaning it. He leaned against the wall and closed his eyes.

Helen studied him for a moment, then patted his shoulder. "We've talked enough for one night. I've got to leave, but someone will be keeping watch outside all night. Get some sleep, and we'll decide what to do in the morning."

She got up and opened the low door, but before she left, she turned back toward him. "What happened tonight, Scott? At the Meyers' house, I mean." Scott thought for a moment, trying to put into words what he was feeling.

"I was reminded about some things," he said slowly. "Like the price that was paid for my salvation." He struggled, trying to communicate his thoughts. Finally, he gave up. He was just too tired. "I was reminded about who I was," he said simply.

Helen nodded, understanding. "We'll talk more tomorrow," she said. "I'll come back with some food, then. Good night, Scott."

"Good night," he replied, and watched her disappear through the door. He sat there for a moment, then carefully pulled back the blanket on top of the cot and crawled in. He lay there, looking up at the ceiling, thinking about what he had just said. He *had* remembered who he was. He had been healed of his hatred and lust for revenge, but there was still one thing he had to do.

He crawled out of the cot and lowered himself to his knees. "Oh Lord," he prayed, "forgive me for the hatred I kept in my heart. If You forgave those who crucified You, can I do less for those who killed Beth?" He swallowed hard, fighting back the tears. "I don't know why You have allowed all of this to happen," he continued, "but I thank You for delivering me from my enemies. And Lord," he hesitated, wondering if he could do what he knew he should do. He thought of all he had been through — the pain, the loss, the grief. If he went through with this, there would undoubtedly be more. *Was it worth it?* he asked himself. The answer came back from his heart immediately. Yes! Absolutely!

"Lord," he began again, "if You can still use me, then I'm willing. Whatever the cost, Lord, use me." It was the first time in his life he had ever prayed that way. A great peace flooded through him as he made his commitment. This was right, this was good. Somewhere in the back of his mind, a very human part of him was afraid.

It tried to call attention to itself, to worry about all of the terrible things that could happen, but it could not stand against that powerful peace.

Scott finished praying, and climbed back into the cot. He lay there for a moment, then reached over to the night stand and switched off the lamp. Total darkness descended, but this time it was a peaceful darkness. His thoughts turned to Beth. For the first time since they had parted, he could remember her face. He could see it in his mind, perfect in every detail. She was so beautiful.

"Beth," he whispered. At last, the tears began to flow. The grief that had locked itself away deep inside was finally able to express itself. He sobbed quietly, his heart aching over his loss, but the peace remained. He could feel the presence of the Holy Spirit, comforting him. For some reason, he remembered the old man at the airport. "You *will* see her again," he had said, and he knew with a calm certainty that he was right. He *would* see his beloved wife again. She was as alive now as she was two days ago, and before too long he would join her in the presence of his Lord. That blessed hope gave him the strength to go on. The tears rolled down his cheeks and on to the pillow, soaking it. Now his body began to take over, demanding rest. With his physical and emotional wounds at last healing, ready for whatever might come his way, Scott Sampson quietly cried himself to sleep.

5

"And in conclusion, it is imperative that our government agencies, particularly the Federal Bureau of Investigation and the Central Intelligence Agency, cooperate completely with the Bureau of Religious Affairs in the handling of this present crisis. In the 10 days since the bombing of Flight 407, over 100 new threats have been made by the Christian Liberation Front. It is imperative.... Good grief, Marcie, why do you keep staring at me like that?" Jack looked up from his hastily scrawled notes to see his executive assistant blink in surprise at his comment. He had given her no indication that he was even looking at her.

"Sorry, Boss," she said, not sounding at all sorry. "You just seem different, that's all." An attractive, middle-aged woman with fiery red hair and a petite figure, she had been with Jack since before his election to the Senate. Her personality matched her hair. Jack had hired her not only because she was competent, but honest and outspoken as well.

"Different?" he asked, leaning back in his swivel chair. They were in his office, just a few hundred yards from the Capitol Building. "In what way?"

Marcie shrugged. "Can't put my finger on it," she said. "You just seem to be more, I don't know, dynamic, I guess. Where did you pick up this 'go get 'em' attitude?"

"You don't get this job without that kind of attitude," replied Jack, smiling.

"I know that," said Marcie, aggravated at being told the obvious. "You just seem to be," again she hesitated, then said, "more of what you are. I really can't put it into words."

Inwardly, Jack was pleased. He indeed knew that he had changed, for the better. "Let's finish this speech after lunch," he said, gathering up his notes. "I won't deliver it until tomorrow, anyway."

Marcie nodded and got up to leave. "Do you think Congress will go along with you on this?" she asked, adjusting her horn-rimmed glasses. "You're asking for a lot."

"They have no choice," said Jack shortly. He waved her away, but just as she got to the door, she turned, a mischievous smile playing at the corners of her mouth.

"Something I've always been curious about." she said. "Who came up with the name 'Bureau of Religious Affairs,' anyway?" Jack was surprised at the unexpected question. He squinted a bit, studying her aura. It flickered a pale green, which indicated she was amused.

"I don't know," he answered. "I guess it's the logical thing to call it."

"It just seems strange that we have the FBI, the CIA, but it's always the Bureau of Religious Affairs. Isn't that weird?" Now Jack saw where she was heading. It was an old joke.

"Very funny," he said. "I can just see the logo now. Capital letters over the bureau's seal. BRA. Has a kind of ring to it, don't you think?" He grinned at her, going along with the gag, but now Marcie was looking back at him in bemusement.

She shook her head slightly. "Are you sure you're all right, Senator? We can put this off till tomorrow morning, if you like. Why not take the rest of the day off?"

Again Jack checked her aura. A pale twinge of pink, indicating worry, was replacing the green. He shook his head, wanting to reassure her. "I'm fine, Marcie," he said, meaning it. "In fact, I've never felt better. Go have some lunch, and we'll get back to work in about an hour." Still radiating concern, Marcie left.

Jack allowed himself to grin again, knowing it was out of character. He had something of a reputation for over-seriousness. The fact was, though, he truly never *had* felt better. Since his return from Mentasys over a week ago, he had been a new man. The implant opened up a whole new world for him to explore — the world of the mind. His newly found ability to see and read a human aura, or in layman's terms, the emotional "halo" that surrounded every person, was just one of the benefits of the bio-chip. Others were manifesting themselves daily. While he could not actually pick up on another person's thoughts, he could get a distinct impression of what they were thinking just by concentrating. No one could lie to him now, and in his line of work, that was a priceless skill to have. He felt as if he had been asleep all of his life, and had just recently awakened. His mind was clearer, and sharper than it had ever been — and all of this was thanks to Jacob.

Jack's heart welled with love and devotion at the thought of his friend. He felt ashamed of the way he had acted at Mentasys. True, the methods being employed were harsh, but necessary. Information must be obtained, and what had been learned at that facility would forever change the world. He could see it very clearly now. Mentasys was but one small step in Jacob's overall plan. Jack felt his eyes misting with tears of joy at the thought of that plan. A united planet! One world, at peace, sharing its resources equally. No war, no famine, no disease — Utopia! A grand scheme indeed, and he was an important part of it! It was all he could do to keep from dancing around the office in his happiness.

Abruptly, Jack's alarm watch sounded, reminding him he had a lunch date with his wife. She would be meeting him at their favorite place, just a few blocks away. He felt to make sure he had his wallet. Then, whistling a tune he had picked up on the radio that morning, he left his office.

❖ ❖ ❖

Marcie Cummings watched Senator Kline leave as she ate lunch in her office. It was situated across from the senator's, and she had purposely left the door open. She waited a good 10 minutes after he had walked past, to make sure he was out of the building. He would be gone now for at least an hour. Leaving her half-eaten tuna sandwich on her desk, she slipped quietly into the senator's office. Locking the door behind her, she moved over to the desk and began to leaf through the drawers.

Marcie knew her boss. She had worked closely with him for the better part of eight years. During that time, she had come to care deeply for him and his family. She had seen him at his best, and at his worst. Like everyone else, she had been astonished at his meteoric rise through the echelons of government. She knew Jack Kline was good, but not that good.

Although they had never shared a bed (some on Capitol Hill thought otherwise), in many ways, she knew him better than his wife. One thing was certain, he was not himself. The Jack Kline she had served faithfully for so long had changed. It wasn't something she could easily identify, but the change was there nevertheless, and she was worried. He had been acting — well — creepy. The way he looked at her, it was as if he could read her thoughts. Something was wrong, and she was determined to find out what it was. If he was in some sort of trouble, she would do everything in her power to help. Quickly she looked through the desk drawers, searching for anything out of the ordinary. Forcing down the feeling that she was betraying him, she sat behind the desk and thought.

"What's going on, Jack?" she whispered quietly. Abruptly she reached a decision. He had taken some sort of emergency trip a week ago. No one knew where he went, and it had raised several eyebrows in Congress. He had assured her it was necessary, and classified. In other words, mind your own business. For two days, he had literally disappeared off the face of the earth. Very well, she would begin her search there. She picked up the phone and punched in a certain number. It rang on the other end twice, then there was an answer.

"DuPont Investigations," the bland female voice said.

"Terry DuPont, please," said Marcie. "Senator Kline's office calling."

"One moment." There was a click as she was put on hold, followed by sleepy elevator music. A moment later, there was another click, and a deep male voice answered.

"Terry DuPont."

"Terry, it's Marcie."

"Hi, Marcie. What skullduggery does the great Senator Kline want me to perform for him this time?" Terry DuPont was a private investigator on permanent retainer to Jack's office. He had come in very handy in obtaining information that was not readily available, or ethical.

"It's not for the senator, Terry," replied Marcie. "It's for me this time."

"Wow, Marcie, I really don't have time for a new client. In fact, I'm backlogged as it is. Why don't you let me refer you to the Remington Agency. They're very good, and I'm sure they can help you."

"Terry," said Marcie urgently, "it's got to be you. You're the only one I can trust. There's something wrong with the senator, and I need you to find out what it is." There was silence on the other end.

Finally, Terry spoke. "That sounds pretty serious, Marcie. What kind of 'wrong' are we talking about?"

"If I knew that, I wouldn't be talking to you," she snapped, and immediately regretted it. "I'm sorry, Terry, but this whole thing has me upset."

"I can see that," answered Terry slowly. "Why don't you st. the beginning. Tell me anything that might have a bearing on this, n matter how trivial."

Taking a deep breath, Marcie began. She filled Terry in on everything, ending with his mysterious trip. "I think that's the key to it all," she finished. "When he got back from wherever he went, he had changed." Her voice cracked a little. "Terry, I think he might be in some sort of trouble — big trouble."

"Okay, settle down," said Terry. "Let's think about this. Do you think he might be cheating on his wife? Keeping a mistress on the side somewhere?"

"No," replied Marcie emphatically. "I would be able to tell if it were that. Besides," she went on, her voice dropping, "if he were going to do that, it would be with me, and we settled *that* issue years ago."

That brought a small chuckle from the detective. "Okay, let me look into it," he said. "I'll do some nosing around and see what I can come up with."

"Thanks, Terry," said Marcie in relief. DuPont was the best in the business, and his discretion could be trusted. "Just send the bill to me personally."

"Not this time, Marcie," said Terry. "The senator is my friend, too. This one's on the house."

"That means a lot, Terry," said Marcie. "I don't know how to thank you."

"The tone in your voice just did. I gotta go, now, but don't worry. I'll keep in touch."

"Bye, Terry, and thanks again." Marcie hung up and sighed a sigh of relief. She had gone past the worry stage and done something. It felt good. Carefully, she made sure everything was back in place in the senator's office, then slipped back into her own. All she had to do now was wait.

❖ ❖ ❖

Terry Dupont replaced the receiver and sat thoughtfully at his desk. He had known something like this was bound to happen, but had not expected it to come from Marcie Cummings. She had always impressed him as the ideal organizer, but lacking in the initiative department.

"She's better than I thought," he said to himself as he picked up the phone again. He dialed a certain long distance number known only to a handful of people. He waited impatiently as it rang several times. Finally there was a click as a connection was made at the other end. There was no answer, as Terry had expected. Instead, there was one long, shrill tone. This lasted for exactly three seconds, then silence. Carefully, he punched in a five digit code on his keypad. Again the tone sounded, followed by a series of musical notes. Finally, there was another ring. This time, when the connection was made, there was a human voice.

"Sierra Foxtrot Nevada," it said without any preliminaries. It was a male voice, totally devoid of emotion.

"Delta Five Five Delta," replied Terry in the same tone. Again there was a pause, then another voice answered. This time there was human feeling in it.

"Mr. DuPont, what can I do for you?" This voice was somewhat higher in pitch than the previous one.

"Problem, sir," replied Terry respectfully. "It seems that some- one close to Kline is getting suspicious. They want me to investigate the trip he took a few days ago."

"Hmmmm. Who is it?"

"His executive assistant, Marcie Cummings," said Terry. "She knows something is different, so she called me. She knows she can trust me," he added wryly.

"Indeed," responded the voice in the same tone. There was a brief pause. Then it continued. "We need one of our own people in her position anyway. I think it's about time to arrange an 'accident' for Miss Cummings."

"Would you like me to take care of it, sir?" asked Terry.

"No, I don't think that would be proper," said the voice. "This presents an opportunity for some excellent publicity. We will handle it from this end. I understand certain — materials — are already in place for just such an occasion. You have done well, DuPont. It will be reflected in your next bonus."

"Thank you, sir," said Terry. "I just want to do my part."

"You have done that, and more. I knew we chose well when we put you in Kline's circle of associates. Now, is there anything else?"

"No, sir. I'll continue keeping an eye on our senator. If anything else pops up, I'll call you."

"Very well, DuPont. Until next time."

The phone went dead, and Terry replaced it on its receptacle. Leaning back in his chair, he puffed out his cheeks and blew a sigh of relief. In his line of work, he had been forced to kill before, but he didn't like it. He was very glad that he wouldn't be involved in Marcie's fate.

"I'm sorry, Sweetheart," he said softly. "It's nothing personal. You just got yourself in the way of some very powerful people. I'm truly sorry." Shaking his head in regret, he went back to work.

❖ ❖ ❖

"I am Wolf, of the Christian Liberation Front. Listen carefully. In exactly 15 minutes, a bomb will explode in the offices of Senator Jack Kline." Marcie listened in growing horror to the voice on the speaker phone. She was back in Jack's office, helping him finish his speech. It was late in the day, almost five o'clock. The call had just come through the switchboard.

Jack, sitting behind his desk, motioned to get her attention. "Get security," he mouthed silently.

Quickly, Marcie picked up the second phone on the desk and keyed in a three digit number. "Phone tap, Senator Kline's main line," she whispered hurriedly to the security chief. "Trace, if possible." She put the phone down, and listened to the man who had identified himself as "Wolf."

"We demand that Senator Kline back off of his position of religious persecution. We demand the return of total freedom of worship in this country. At the present time, we estimate that over 3,000 citizens are being held against their will because of their religious beliefs. We demand their release. To demonstrate our commitment, we will explode a bomb in the senator's office building in one hour. To demonstrate our compassion, we give this warning. Comply with our demands, or the next time there will *be* no warning." The phone went dead, and Jack and Marcie sat there staring at each other for just a moment.

Then Jack grabbed the other phone and called security. "Did you get it?" he asked urgently.

"Sorry, sir. Whoever it was, was using a scrambler. That makes it impossible to do a trace. They know their stuff."

"Yeah," agreed Jack sourly. "What are the chances it's a hoax?"

"I wouldn't want to bet my life on it, sir. Would you?"

"Of course not," snapped Jack. "Okay, evacuate the building, and call the Bureau of Religious Affairs. It's their bailiwick."

Marcie watched as Jack hung up.

"Get the backup files out," he ordered. "Then shut down everything. Make sure the whole system is safeguarded."

"That won't help much if a bomb really does go off," she observed.

"Of course not," agreed Jack. "But it will stop someone from entering the system while we're not here. Now get moving."

Exactly one hour later, Marcie stood beside Jack and watched with the rest of the office staff as a bomb deactivation team left the building, rolling a pot-shaped, armored canister. A tall, blond-haired agent for the bureau came over to speak with them. He had introduced himself as agent Lynch.

"Our friends from the CLF were thorough," he said, nodding to them. "We found three separate explosives in key parts of the building. They were set to go off in sequence. If they had, the whole building would be dust by now." He shook his head, as if in confusion.

"Exactly what time did you say this threat happened?" he asked Jack.

"Almost an hour ago," he answered. "Why?"

"What we found in there was a precision set up. It would take at least two people who knew what they were doing to pull it off. More importantly, it takes time to accomplish. Judging from the dust we found on the bomb casings, they had been set for at least a week."

"You mean we've been working around those — things — for days?" demanded Marcie. She paled at the thought.

"Exactly," said the Lynch. "The question is, why now? Any ideas, Senator?"

"It's no secret that I'm planning to ask for emergency powers for the bureau in order to deal with the CLF," answered Jack. "I'm scheduled to address a combined session of Congress tomorrow, in fact."

"That's probably it, then," said Lynch. "If you don't mind my suggesting so, sir, why don't you let us put you and your staff in protective custody?"

"No!" said Jack adamantly, just as Marcie was opening her mouth to say "Yes! Definitely!" "I will not be bullied by terrorists. It's time to close up shop anyway. I'm sending everyone home."

"I wish you would reconsider, Senator," said Lynch.

"Sorry, Mr. Lynch. If I let this Christian Liberation Front know that they have succeeded in intimidating me, they will continue to do so. I *won't* allow that."

"Yes, sir. In that case, I am assigning agents to keep an eye on you." He raised a hand to forestall Jack's objections. "You won't even see them. They'll follow you home and keep watch outside your house tonight. Think of your family, Senator. It's a reasonable precaution."

"All right,"Jack agreed. "I suppose I can go along with that. Just be sure they stay out of the way."

"You won't even know they are there," assured Lynch. "I'm also assigning agents to the rest of your staff. Without anything else to go on, I'm assuming everyone is a target."

"Good idea," said Jack. "That okay with you, Marcie?"

"As far as I'm concerned, you can lock me up until this whole thing blows over, but," she added, as Jack started to speak, "I'll settle for someone keeping watch at my place."

"You live alone, don't you?" Lynch asked. Marcie nodded.

"Fine," he continued. "If you just wait here for a moment, I'll go make some arrangements." Lynch walked off, leaving Jack and Marcie watching as the bomb squad gently placed the canister into a special trailer.

"You sounded a little scared there," said Jack finally. "You want to come home with me? Jenny is making enough dinner for one more."

"Thanks, but I'll pass," replied Marcie. "Right now, all I want to do is go home and lock the world out. It has not been a good day. You need to get home, too." She pointed at the dozen or so news teams gathered a discreet distance away. "I'm sure Jenny has seen this mess already. You need to get home to her and fill her in."

Jack shrugged. "You learn to take these things in stride in this business. It's part of the game. I'm sure Jenny has figured out I'm fine."

Again Marcie was disturbed by Jack's words. It seemed the change in him was growing by the hour. The Jack Kline she had known would have been outraged by the attempted bombing. He would have taken it as a personal insult. Not only that, but the first thing he would have done, once the situation had stabilized, would have been to call his wife. He would have been frantic to assure her that all was well. She dearly hoped Terry would be able to find something that would help shed light on this change.

"*You* take it in stride," she said with dry humor, masking her concern. "I'm taking my car and going home. Good night, Senator."

"Don't go yet," said Jack. "Here comes Lynch. Let's see what he has for us. Besides, you have to help me run the gauntlet."

Marcie sighed the sigh of the long-suffering. "I was hoping you would forget to ask," she said in a resigned tone.

Lynch returned to inform them that they had each been assigned an agent. They would be waiting to follow them home. That settled,

Jack and Marcie, with Lynch in tow, headed toward the police barrier. Like hounds on a fresh scent, the reporters who had been restricted behind the line, converged on the three. Their questions overlapped each other, making it almost impossible to understand them.

"Senator, does this attempt have anything to do with your stand on organized religion?"

"Senator, would you be willing to speak with leaders of the CLF to try to negotiate some sort of settlement?"

"Senator, what about the rumor that. . . ."

"Senator, will you comment on. . . ."

"Senator. . . ."

"Senator. . . ."

Somehow they threaded their way through the mass of reporters. As they got to the street, a black limousine pulled up. A no-nonsense looking man in a gray suit and dark glasses got out and opened the door for Jack. As he reached the car, Jack turned and motioned for quiet.

"I will give a full statement tomorrow at a press conference," he said over the din. "For now, let me say that this incident in no way changes my stand on organized religion or terrorism, nor will I negotiate with terrorists. Thank you." He turned to get inside the limousine, motioning for Marcie to follow.

"I'll get you over to your car," he said into her ear as she got in.

"Thanks," she replied. "I owe you one."

She was driven to her car, which was parked in a lot just half a block away. Waiting next to the compact Saab was a nondescript black van. Leaning against it was another of those stern-looking agents in the obligatory gray suit and dark glasses. He opened the door for Marcie and introduced himself as Agent Peter Crawford. Waving good-bye to Jack, Marcie got into her Saab. It started smoothly, and within seconds she was heading home, followed by the van. It was well past six, and the rush hour had long since died down. She made it home in less than 30 minutes. She pulled into the driveway of her two bedroom home on the outskirts of Washington proper. Many of her friends had tried to talk her into buying a condominium. She was single, had a good job, and didn't need the aggravation of home repairs and upkeep. Marcie was just old-fashioned enough, however, to want to come home to a real house. While she was not married, and her family lived 1,500 miles away, she still wanted the hominess that only a house could bring.

She got out, and Agent Crawford followed her up to the front door. He was carrying a rather large briefcase. Marcie found herself uncomfortable with this stranger in such close quarters. They reached the front door, and she brought out her keys. Crawford moved to stop her.

"Please," he said, holding out his hand. His voice was flat and unemotional.

"Excuse me, I — oh!" Realizing what he wanted, Marcie reluctantly handed him her keys. Carefully, Crawford inserted the proper one into the lock. Then he took a device that resembled a fountain pin out of his pocket and held it up next to the lock. It immediately beeped and a tiny light at the tip glowed green.

"Electronics detector," he explained in answer to her unasked question. "Ninety percent of all explosives are rigged electronically. This would detect any such device."

"What about the other 10 percent?" asked Marcie. As if in answer, Crawford carefully ran his hands around the door frame. Marcie shook her head, not quite believing that there was someone at her house checking for bombs. It did not seem real. Crawford finished his inspection, and carefully turned the key. It opened normally, and they were inside.

"Wait here," he said, and was off checking out the rest of the house. It was a simple design. The front hall led directly into a small living room. From there, it branched out into opposite directions. Left were the kitchen and bathroom, and right were the two bedrooms. Marcie watched as Crawford went through the living room and headed into the kitchen. She knew the search was for her own good, but resented it nevertheless. Having a total stranger examining her personal belongings made her feel violated. She waited impatiently in the hall, listening to Crawford check the cabinets. In a few minutes, he reappeared and headed into the master bedroom. Assuming the rest of the house was okay, she stepped forward into the living room and plopped on the couch. It was over 10 minutes before she saw Crawford again, this time heading into the guest bedroom. Strangely enough, he was only in there for a few minutes before heading back out.

He came back into the living room and smiled reassuringly. "Everything's fine," he said. "I'll be going now, but if you need me, I'll be in the van outside. Here," and he handed her a number written on a small business card. "That's the number to the van. By the way, I'll be monitoring your calls tonight."

"Swell," said Marcie dryly.

Crawford caught the disapproval in her tone, and shrugged. "Just doing my job, Miss Cummings. We can't take chances with these people. You understand, don't you?"

"Yes, of course," replied Marcie in resignation. "I just don't have to like it. Thank you, Agent Crawford." She smiled in apology for her attitude. "I'm really glad you're here. I feel a lot safer. It's just been a long, frightening day."

Crawford nodded in understanding. "I'll say good night, then," he said, moving to the door. "Remember, if you need me, just call."

With that, he left. Marcie stared after him for a moment, then sighed deeply. At least she was home. Right now, all she wanted was a quiet dinner, a shower, and about an hour inside her favorite novel.

Going to the kitchen, she picked a dinner out of the freezer and tossed it into the microwave. On a night like this, she was *not* going to cook! While it was in the thaw cycle, she took her shower and put on her nightgown. It was still early, but she wanted to get comfortable. By then, her dinner was ready. She ate in front of the television, replaying the evening news on her video disk recorder. It always gave her a secret thrill when she saw herself on TV. Because of her close association with Jack Kline, it happened quite often.

Using her remote control, she fast forwarded to the section she was looking for. Sure enough, there was the senator's office building, big as life. A crowd was gathered outside, watching the action. She saw the bomb squad come out, carrying their canister. Then, smiling, she watched herself as she walked next to the senator, helping him elbow his way through the crowd of reporters. Through it all, the news commentator kept up a running dialogue. He paused only when Jack turned to face the cameras and give his brief statement. When the story was finished, the newscast ran a special report on the Christian Liberation Front — who they were and what they hoped to accomplish. Marcie had already heard this before, and turned off the television. She ate the rest of her meal in silence.

Throwing away the disposable utensils and plate, she brushed her teeth, got her book, and settled into bed. The soft mattress conformed to her body, and she stretched in contentment. She had just found her place in the novel when the phone beeped. She looked over at the night stand and realized she had forgotten to bring the wireless receiver to bed with her. Throwing aside the covers in irritation, she padded into the kitchen and picked up the receiver.

"Hello," she said, trying to keep the annoyance out of her voice.

"Sorry to bother you, Miss Cummings," said Agent Crawford, "but I left my briefcase in the second bedroom. Do you think you could get it and bring it to the door?"

"All right," said Marcie. "Give me a minute. Where did you leave it?"

"Just inside the closet," he replied. "Sorry for the trouble."

"No problem. I'll meet you at the door." Marcie hung up and went back into the bedroom.

Strange place to leave it, she thought, as she opened the door to the large walk-in closet. Feeling along the wall, she found the light switch and flipped it on. It took a moment for her to realize what she was seeing. The briefcase was there, sitting on the floor in the middle of the closet. It was open, and Marcie moved closer to examine it. What she saw stopped her heart. The inside was filled with electronics. Wires, chips, four long cylinders, and a timer. She didn't have to be a bomb expert to know that she was staring death in the face. The timer read four seconds and was counting down to zero.

In the final moments of her life, time slowed to a crawl. She realized three things. One, Crawford had to have set the bomb. Some twisted sense of humor must have made him wait till the last second to tell her, so she would know what was going to happen to her. Two, the Bureau of Religious Affairs was not what it seemed, and three, Jack was in mortal danger. Even as these thoughts raced through her head, she ran for the front door. She almost made it. Just before her outstretched hand touched the doorknob, the bomb went off. The entire house disintegrated, severely damaging the two on either side. Marcie never felt a thing. From several houses down, Peter Crawford, special operative for the Bureau of Religious Affairs, watched in satisfaction. Smiling at a job well-done, he started the van. He would have to lay low for a while, then pick up a new identity. It didn't matter. Peter Crawford was only one in a long list of aliases. He would take a month or so off and then be ready for reassignment. He was dreaming of skiing in Switzerland and warm Irish coffees as he drove off.

❖   ❖   ❖

It was past 11:00 when Jack got the call. His wife Jenny came into the family room where he was sprawled out watching the replay of the bomb threat that afternoon. Her face was sheet white as she handed him the phone.

"What is it, Jenny?" he asked, not liking the look on her face.

"Something terrible has happened," she whispered. Jack felt a cold fear grip his insides. It took a great deal to jar his wife, and when she reacted like this. . . . Mentally he scanned the whereabouts of his family. Jack Junior was upstairs studying, and his daughter Sandy was over at her best friend's house. His parents then? He sat up and took the phone gingerly, as though it would bite him.

"Hello," he said, his voice betraying his fear.

"Senator, it's Agent Lynch."

"Yes, Mr. Lynch." Inwardly he breathed a sigh of relief. This had nothing to do with his family, but work instead. No matter how terrible, the news couldn't be as bad as he had first thought. He smiled at Jenny reassuringly.

"Senator, I hate to be the one to tell you this," said Lynch, his voice low and solemn, "but there's been an incident. The CLF has set off another bomb."

"Oh God, no," he muttered. "Another flight?"

"No, sir." There was a pause. "I'm afraid they hit Miss Cummings house. They used enough explosives to level it."

"Marcie?" Jack asked weakly.

"I'm sorry, sir. She had no chance."

Jack could only sit and stare at the phone. Marcie? It couldn't be true. He had just watched her on television, at his side as she had been for years.

"Sir? Senator? Are you still there?"

"Ye — Yes," Jack answered thinly. "Are you sure she was in the house when it. . . ." He couldn't continue.

"I'm sorry, sir. We're investigating now, but we are almost certain that she was inside. The agent we assigned has also vanished. We think he's been kidnaped and fear the worst."

"I don't — understand," said Jack in confusion. "I thought you people were supposed to protect her."

"Senator, what can I say?" said Lynch, sounding tired and frustrated. "We tried. I lost a good agent, too."

"I'm sorry," replied Jack, not caring at all about Lynch's friend. "Where are you now?"

"I'm at her house, or what's left of it."

"I'm coming over," decided Jack, rolling out of the couch. "It should take me about 30 minutes."

"Senator, with all due respect, there's no need for you to be here," said Lynch. "You don't need to see this."

"I DO need to see it," Jack replied, almost shouting. "My friend has just been killed by animals — animals, do you hear? If I don't see it, I won't believe it, I won't *feel* it. I've got to feel it, Lynch. I've got to know that she's dead." He lowered his voice to a dangerous whisper. "We're going to get them, Lynch. Do you understand? We're going to get the monsters that did this!"

"I'm with you, Senator," said Lynch vehemently. "I'll be waiting for you here." With that, Lynch hung up.

It took Jack almost 40 minutes to drive to Marcie's house. So intent was he on his thoughts that he missed the exit off the Crosstown. When he turned onto her street, he could see the fire trucks and police cars, their red and blue lights flashing in a complex rhythm. He had to show his identification to an officer who was blocking the street several houses down. When he got through, his heart sank. During the trip over, he had had the wild hope that Lynch had been mistaken. Perhaps he had the wrong house, or maybe Marcie might have survived the explosion. After all, she could have been in another part of the house. When he saw the wreckage, he knew better. It was Marcie's house, all right — or had been. Not even a shell was left. The houses on either side were heavily damaged as well. One had a huge gaping hole in its side, and the other was missing a large chunk of roof. Jack spotted Lynch standing in the front yard talking to a young woman. He headed toward him.

"Get forensics on this right away," Lynch was saying. "I want a positive I.D. by morning."

"Yes, sir," replied the woman, and hurried off to comply. Lynch saw Jack as he approached and nodded.

"You found M — ," he found he could not say her name. He tried again. "You found a body?"

"Out here in the front," said Lynch, pointing to a spot about halfway to the road. "From what we can tell, it was blown through the front door and out onto the lawn."

"Was it her?" Jack asked in a whisper.

Lynch shrugged. "It was pretty disfigured, but definitely female. We'll have a positive I.D. in a few hours, but I'm betting it was her. I'm sorry, Senator."

Jack just stood there, feeling numb and useless. A strange lethargy was settling over him. Somewhere deep in his mind, he knew he should be feeling something, but all emotions had fled when he spoke to Lynch. His mind was sluggish and unresponsive, and he struggled to speak. "Are you sure that it was the CLF?" he asked with an effort.

Again Lynch shrugged. "We got a call from this 'Wolf,' claiming responsibility. Until there's any evidence to suggest otherwise, we go on that assumption."

Jack opened and closed his mouth several times before he was able to speak again. "So what do you do now?" he asked, his voice devoid of any emotion.

"What we've been doing ever since the CLF announced itself — track them down. Our primary targets are these underground churches that keep popping up." Lynch studied Jack carefully. "I'm told that you know of the 'Shepherd's Path,' Senator. The feeling at headquarters is, the two groups are working together. They may even be one and the same. If we can lay our hands on one of them, we'll have a starting point. Until then. . . ."

Jack nodded slowly, trying to pierce the haze that surrounded his mind. The longer he talked to Lynch, the more dense it became. "I understand," he said thickly.

Lynch looked closely at him. "Are you okay, Senator? Why don't you let one of my agents drive you home? I know that this has really hit you hard."

Jack shook his head no. "I'm fine, really. I guess there's really nothing for me to do here. I just had to come and see for myself." He drew a shaky breath, as if struggling with some unseen foe. "Good night, Lynch. Call me as soon as you have something, please?"

Lynch nodded once sharply. "Count on it, Senator. I promise, we'll get the monsters who did this."

"I know you will," replied Jack blandly. He tried to smile, but gave up the effort and shuffled toward his car. He was almost halfway there when he heard Lynch shout for him to wait. He turned to see the agent trotting after him.

"Miss Cummings' family should be notified," he said as he drew even with Jack. "Normally, we would handle it, since she has no relatives in the area, but I figured that you. . . ." He trailed off, leaving the rest of the unspoken sentence hanging in the air between them.

Jack thought about it for a moment. He really should call Marcie's parents. After all, it would be better if they heard the news from a friend rather than a total stranger, wouldn't it? He tried to concentrate, to focus his mind and will on formulating an answer. His thoughts were disjointed. It seemed that something was scrambling them around in his brain. Strange. Today he had felt so in control, so sharp. What was happening to him? He squinted, trying to read Lynch's aura, but nothing would come. He realized that Lynch was waiting for him to answer.

"Why don't you handle it?" he finally said, as if talking through cotton. "I really didn't know her parents all that well, and you have all of the facts."

Lynch simply looked at him a moment longer before nodding an affirmation. Without waiting for him to reply, Jack turned and covered the rest of the distance to his car. He did not notice or care that Lynch continued to stare after him as he drove off.

The ride home was a blur. Jack existed in a limbo, as if his mind, emotions, and will were being put on hold. His body ran on automatic, finding its way home.

When Jack turned onto his street, he saw that there were several news vans parked outside his house, obviously waiting for him. The glare of their television lights hurt his eyes. Word traveled fast in this city. Slowly he pulled up to his driveway, ignoring the shouting reporters. He used the remote control to open his garage door, and parked the car inside. The reporters still shouted questions, but he ignored them. Let them shout all they wanted! He didn't have to answer. They could wait until tomorrow.

He shut the garage door and went inside. Jenny heard him and met him in the kitchen. She had obviously been crying. She had always been very fond of Marcie. He looked at her for a moment, then moved to embrace her — not because of any feeling or thought. It simply seemed to be expected of him. He always did what was expected of him, didn't he? Jenny held him for a moment, then pushed away. She brushed away a strand of prematurely graying hair and looked a question at him.

"They're pretty sure she was in the house when the bomb went off," he said. "They found a woman's body, and they think it's her." Jenny closed her eyes, trying to control her emotions.

"My God, Jack! I can't believe it! Marcie was like family." Her voice trembled. She tried to control it, but a sob escaped. "What if we're next? What if our house goes up in flames, Jack?" She started to cry again. Jack put his arm around her shoulders and guided her to their bedroom.

"We'll be all right," he said mechanically. "They've beefed up the guard on our house, and you and the kids will have round-the-clock protection."

Jenny started to say something, but Jack interrupted. "Jenny, it's late, and this whole thing has been awful. We're both exhausted, and need some rest. Let's go to bed, and talk about it in the morning."

Again Jenny started to protest, but Jack shook his head. "Please, Jen. Do this for me. Just wait until morning, okay?"

Jenny hesitated for a moment, then said okay. She got into bed and pulled the covers up. Jack changed into his night clothes and joined her. He gave her a perfunctory kiss good night, and turned out the light. What was happening to him, he wondered? He should be feeling something — anything — but his whole being was a void. He lay there in the darkness, his thoughts going nowhere. Finally, he drifted off to sleep.

He did not dream. The implant prevented it, just as it had prevented his mind from functioning normally on certain, specific occasions. Tonight was one of those occasions. There were things that his masters did not want him to get too close to, and Marcie's death was one of them. Tomorrow, he would be back to normal. He would remember little of this evening. His newly found abilities would return, and he would meet his new executive assistant. The fact that he would have no say-so in hiring him would never cross his mind. He would grieve for Marcie, but leave the investigation of the bombing to the bureau.

That would be tomorrow. Tonight, Jack Kline slept. Deep inside his mind a very important part of him screamed in agony, like a caged animal. It tried to get out, to free itself, but could not. It tried to throw off the grip of the implant. The implant, in turn, sensed his resistance and moved to counter it. There was a brief battle, and his mind lost. Ruthlessly, the implant bound his will, imprisoning it. It writhed in agony, but could not escape. Finally, exhausted by its effort, it gave up the struggle and slumped in defeat. Through it all, Jack slept, never knowing that he was a prisoner in his own body.

❖   ❖   ❖

Early the following day, Jacob Hill sat alone in his suite at Mentasys and studied the image of Agent Crawford, which was displayed on the central monitor. He was speaking with him via direct satellite link to New York, where Crawford was preparing to fly to Switzerland. Such calls were expensive, but Hill gladly paid the price.

"Judging from the reports, you have done very well, Crawford." Jacob Hill smiled thinly at the image of the agent. As always, he was meticulously dressed in gray suit and tie.

"Thank you, sir," responded Crawford. "It *did* go well. Did they identify the body?"

"Just a few hours ago," replied Hill. "It was definitely Cummings. As I said, well done."

"What about Lynch? He's heading up the investigation. Could he be trouble?"

Now Hill frowned slightly, and Crawford realized he had overstepped his bounds. He operated on a need-to-know basis only. "Sorry, sir," he said. "I was just wondering why he isn't working for you. He's pretty high up in the bureau, after all."

Hill relaxed a bit, his smile returning. Inwardly, Crawford breathed a sigh of relief.

"Let me tell you a secret, Crawford," said Hill, leaning back in his chair. "There are relatively few of *my* people actually working inside the bureau itself. The organization heads, of course, and a few scattered agents. The rest are there solely on their own volition."

"I don't understand, sir."

"The best way to get people to do what you want is to let them think that they are acting on their own free will. The agents of the bureau are a dedicated group. They are convinced of the danger of uncontrolled religious organizations, and are committed to keeping them under tight reign. Our agent Lynch is just such a man. He would never be part of a conspiracy such as ours. He will, however, work hard to do his job because he honestly sees religion as a threat to personal freedom. In that context, he serves me far more effectively than if he were to be 'in the know,' so to speak."

Crawford's brow wrinkled in thought. "Couldn't he be dangerous?" he asked after a moment.

"Indeed he could," agreed Hill. "That's why his immediate supervisor and the agents under him all belong to me. They control him, and properly controlled, he is of great value."

"Whatever you say, sir," said Crawford, not really understanding. He looked at his watch, then backed up. "I've got to get on board," he said. "My flight leaves in a few minutes."

"Very well," said Hill. "Again my compliments on a job well done. Your Swiss account should be more than adequate to cover your expenses over the next few months. Enjoy your vacation."

"Thank you, sir," replied Crawford. "You know where I'm at. I'll be ready when you need me again. Goodbye."

"Goodbye," said Hill, and broke the connection. For a moment he sat facing the wall of screens, contemplating the progress of his work so far. Things were proceeding rapidly, and would continue to do so. Hill was not a man given to emotion. The work he carried on was begun many generations ago. Now, though, it was coming to its final phase, and even he felt the thrill of the coming culmination. His immediate predecessor had told him that this would happen in his lifetime. He was but one in a long chain of servants, dating back for centuries, but he would be the last.

"Mr. Hill?" His watch intercom interrupted his thoughts, carrying the voice of the Mentasys receptionist. It was an expensive toy, and, he realized, a bit self-indulgent, but he considered it a reasonable vice. He thumbed the mike button.

"Yes, Doris."

"You wanted me to tell you when your conference call was ready," said the dark-haired receptionist. "All of the participants are standing by and waiting for you to join in."

"Thank you. Please see that I am not disturbed for the next hour."

"Yes, sir." Doris broke the connection, and the most powerful man in the United States took a moment to compose himself. In his position as the head of his Inner Circle, he assumed the role of absolute dictator. Now, however, he must change that mindset. For this conference, *he* was the servant, not the master.

Taking a deep breath, he touched the proper controls and the screens lit up. Instantly, five of them displayed images of his fellow servants. Each was of a different race and nationality, and each was his equal. Between the six of them, they controlled the economy, and thus the course, of the entire world. They were called the Sextuaget by their master.

He nodded to his cohorts, and then fixed his eyes on the center screen. Power incarnate stared back at him. Hollow eyes that could decide his future in an instant regarded him keenly, as if passing judgment. The face and scalp was completely devoid of hair. The skin had an Oriental flavor, though the rest of the features were heavily Nordic. The overall effect was one of sharp contrast. He was known to this elite group simply as Brennon.

"Greetings my friends," he said, surprising Jacob once again with his high tenor voice. He had always felt that a man who wielded such power should be a bass. "Things are proceeding well," he continued, inviting comment with an upraised eyebrow.

The man on the screen furthest to the left spoke. His features marked him as Arabic, and his name was Rhys. "The Middle East is ready," he said in a sharp, clipped accent. By Brennon's command, their common language was English. "Thanks to pressure from the European Common Market, the economy of the entire region is about to collapse. Add to this the resentment of the United Arabic States to the presence of American troops in both Iran and Israel and you have an explosive situation. It will require only the proper touch to ignite it."

"Very good," said Brennon. "Brosolov?"

The short, stocky Russian nodded, then spoke. "We need more time to deal with the Siberian situation, but other than that, everything is as planned."

"How much time is required?" asked Brennon, his voice taking on a dangerous lilt.

Brosolov blanched, then consulted something or someone just off screen. "Not more than 12 months," he replied, looking back at Brennon.

"Twelve months," he mused. "It must be accomplished in no more than 8."

Brosolov swallowed hard and nodded. "We can succeed in eight months," he agreed.

Brennon then asked for and got reports from each of the other members of the Sextuaget. All amounted to the same thing — a world teetering on the brink of world war. Jacob waited patiently for his turn, knowing he would be the last. This did not rankle him. Members of this circle had long ago submerged their egos for the greater good.

"Jacob," said Brennon finally, "tell me how things are in the Western world."

Reluctantly Jacob tore his eyes away from Brennon's. They were hypnotic. Although the face gave the impression of a man in late middle age, the eyes were ancient. They could grab and hold a person, much like a cobra held its prey in a trance.

"The pattern is set," he said. "By this time next year the United States will be in the middle of the worst depression of its history. When it is forced to escalate the Middle East conflict, it will be totally unable to bear the expense. Thus, the government will have no choice but to seize private assets for the 'duration of the emergency.' This will move them one step closer toward a totalitarian state. We now own key people in every area of the government. The implants are a success and will greatly ease our task." Others of the Sextuaget nodded in agreement.

"And what of the suppression of Christianity?" asked Brennon.

Jacob found this difficult to answer honestly, but one lied to Brennon at his peril. "We will have it stamped out by the end of the year," he said carefully. "We have managed to change the jargon of the American people. The term 'religion' is now substituted for 'Christianity.' Thanks to the Christian Liberation Front and the

Bureau of Religious Affairs, we have it in a stranglehold."

"You have not told me everything," warned Brennon. "The United States was the last bastion of freedom for practicing Christians. Have they been controlled?"

"Mostly," said Jacob, beginning to feel the heat of Brennon's gaze. "There are still pockets of resistance, but we hope to have them cleaned out soon."

"You speak of it as if waging a war," said Brennon, "and well you should. Mark this well, Jacob Hill. You have done well in guiding the United States toward a dictatorship, but this is only secondary. The rest of you," and his eyes swept the rest of the Sextuaget, "remember this. Our greatest enemies are not governments, or tyrants, or economics. These can be manipulated and controlled. The greatest threat to our plan is Christianity. It must be stamped out, obliterated. Is that understood?" There were nods from everyone, and Brennon went on, now addressing just Jacob.

"I understand that you are having problems with this so-called 'Shepherd's Path.' "

Jacob's heart froze for an instant. If Brennon took this as failure, his usefulness, and his life, were over. "We are dealing with it," he answered carefully. "They are a minor annoyance, nothing more."

"They are *not* a 'minor annoyance,' " interrupted Brennon. "They are a dangerous threat, Jacob. They are organized, and they are nationwide — perhaps even worldwide." Those ageless eyes narrowed. "You must remember this, Jacob. There are two major traits distinctive to Christians. One: they reproduce themselves. It only takes one Christian to produce another. Two: they are never more dangerous than when pushed into a corner — persecuted is their word for it. Do not underestimate them, Jacob."

"Yes, sir," replied Jacob meekly. "I will not rest until they are eliminated."

"Make it your first priority," agreed Brennon. "Gentlemen," he said, addressing the rest of the group, "you still have much work to do. Remember, the entire planet must be brought to the brink of a war that will cause complete annihilation. Nothing less will serve our purposes. Are we in complete agreement?" The Sextuaget nodded as one.

"Then I will no longer keep you from your duties." Without another word, the connection was broken. Jacob sat and stared at the now blank monitors. He realized that he was breathing heavily, and a thin sheen of sweat covered his forehead. Angrily he wiped it away, forcing himself to control his breathing. It would not do for any of his underlings to see him like this.

Jacob Hill was the type of personality whose anger and fear displayed itself in the extreme of cold aloofness rather than heated outburst. His normal icy demeanor reasserted itself in seconds. Once composed, he punched a code into his wrist-com. There was a short buzz, then Steiger answered.

"Doctor, what is your status on our new guests?"

"Proceeding at a normal pace," responded Steiger. "They should be going into Phase Two within four weeks."

"We need to pick up the pace, Doctor," said Jacob firmly. "I need answers immediately." He could almost hear Steiger's brow wrinkling in anxious confusion.

"To do so would be to risk permanent damage to the subjects," Steiger said finally. "Even then, I can't guarantee the outcome. There have been some . . . abnormalities."

This time it was Jacob's turn to wrinkle his brow. "Explain," he said shortly.

"I can't just yet," said Steiger. "All I can tell you is, some of the subjects are not reacting normally to Phase Two."

"How so?"

"Well, somehow they are resisting the suggestions we are sending them. They're okay if the setting in their mind is peaceful, but when we induce fear and horror, they are not reacting normally."

"They are fighting it?" asked Jacob.

"No, they're *enduring* it. I don't know how to describe it. To most people, the greatest horror is being utterly alone and defenseless. That's the scenario we try to induce. It makes the mind more pliable and readable, driving it into a state of catatonia. Once we achieve that, we can extract any information you want." There was a pause. "The problem is, they aren't getting as scared as they were before. The monitors show them in their dream state. Everything is functioning properly, and the scenarios are just as frightening as always. They just seem to be taking it in stride. Some of them are speaking to something or someone — we can't be sure who. It's almost as if someone is in there with them, keeping them company. Very strange."

"So increase the power of the mind probe," said Jacob.

"We're doing that," replied Steiger, "but you must remember that this is not an exact science. If we push too far too fast, we'll lose them totally. Their usefulness will be at an end."

"Doctor," said Jacob, running out of patience, "I do not need a run-down of your problems. I need answers to my questions. Get them!" Without waiting for Steiger to reply, he broke the connection.

He punched in a new number. This time, after the buzz, there was no answer. He had expected none.

"Come to my office immediately," he said to the silence. Again he broke the connection, then turned away from the monitor wall and rested his elbows on the desk, steepling his fingers. Things were about to heat up. He detested rushing his schedule, but now he had no choice. Brennon would expect him to have things well in hand the next time he called. If he did not, he would likely be replaced.

He opened the panel in the top of the desk and activated the keyboard and monitor that were recessed there. Signing in to the mainframe, he called up the information he was looking for. The screen displayed what he privately called his flow chart. Even members of his own inner circle had not seen it. It contained a graph that charted the overall flow of his part in Brennon's plan. On the left side, in a vertical column, were several categories, including government, economics, business, public opinion, and a host of others. Along the top, certain target dates were indicated, reaching back as far as 1976, when he had assumed his current role from his predecessor. Different colored lines flowed horizontally across the graph, steadily rising, though some occasionally dropped. He studied it for a moment, then began to change some of the target dates, moving several up by a factor of several months. When he had finished, he touched a control and the chart realigned itself, conforming to the new information.

"Indeed," he said softly to himself. The new schedule was risky, but could be accomplished. He started to fine tune it, but was interrupted by the door chime.

Saving the new information, he shut down his terminal and closed up the desk. Swiveling in his chair, he activated the security camera hidden just outside. There, waiting patiently, was a rugged looking man with a thick black beard. He was well over six feet tall, and dressed casually in jeans and plaid work shirt. Recognizing him, Jacob thumbed the hidden control next to the monitor controls and opened the outer door.

"Come in," he said calmly. The bearded man entered, and without hesitation crossed the suite and took a seat in front of the desk. He remained silent. Jacob regarded him for a moment, then nodded.

"I've been reading about your exploits. You have become quite famous." The big man shrugged and said nothing.

"The threat against Jack Kline, and the subsequent death of his assistant were well executed. I congratulated Crawford a short time ago. Let me extend the same to you." Again silence.

"Just idle curiosity," said Jacob, "but I must ask. How long ago were those bombs placed in the senator's office building?"

Now for the first time, the mysterious man spoke. "Six weeks," he said shortly.

Jacob nodded in approval. "I suppose that other key areas are, shall we say, equipped as well?" he asked.

"Of course," said the man, a trace of scorn now coloring his voice.

"Very good," said Jacob, taking note of the tone of the man's voice. He was undoubtedly formidable, and Jacob decided it was time to make it clear who was in charge. "I'll remind you of who you are working for, sir. I will also remind you that I know who you are. You may head a very impressive and organized band of terrorists, but you can be replaced. Do you understand, Wolf, or should I say Mister Harry Belmont, of Sacramento, California?" Jacob put as much authority and menace into his voice as he could, which was considerable.

It had the desired effect. The man known as Wolf locked eyes with Jacob for a moment, then looked away.

"That's better," said Jacob, smiling his thin smile. "From now on, you will *not* use that tone of voice with me. Is that clear?"

"Yes."

Jacob raised an eyebrow.

"Yes, sir," Wolf amended, not meeting his eyes.

"Better," said Jacob. "Remember your roots, my dear Wolf. But for me you would be just another white supremacist, waving your pathetic swastikas in parades and killing the occasional black man or Jew. I have elevated you above that. With the bureau supporting your people, you can go anywhere and accomplish anything. Thanks to your demolition training in Special Services, you are a valuable asset to me. We are playing out quite a scenario, don't you think?"

"Very subtle," agreed Wolf. "You have my people, the Christian Liberation Front, running amuck, performing the worst terrorist acts this country has seen since the Muslim attacks of the nineties. The Bureau of Religious Affairs is heroically pursuing them, always a step behind. Caught in the middle are the ones taking the blame for the whole mess. Very pretty."

"Very pretty indeed," agreed Jacob. "And quite effective. As it stands now, Christianity will be totally obliterated within six months. Even churches already state sanctioned will have to shut down.

Things are proceeding as planned, which brings me to the reason of your visit."

Wolf leaned forward unconsciously, his blue eyes bright pinpoints of light.

"I want you to step up your timetable," said Jacob. "You have seven congressmen to hit within the next three months. I want them *all* eliminated by the end of *this* month."

Wolf frowned. "That's a bit risky, sir," he said slowly. "Even with the bureau keeping the heat off our backs, we still have to watch out. A few FBI guys have been snooping around on their own, as well as a lot of local authorities. I think they might be suspicious why the bureau hasn't put away the CLF yet."

"Nevertheless, I want you to do it," said Jacob. "If anyone gets in your way, eliminate them. Besides, the bureau will have some arrests soon."

"You have some information on the Shepherd's Path?" asked Wolf eagerly.

"Not enough, yet," admitted Jacob, "but it's now only a matter of time. We are getting close. The arrest I spoke of, however, will be that of one of our scapegoats."

"Scott Sampson," said Wolf. "You know where he is?"

"We traced him and his wife to Cincinnati International Airport, where he put her on Flight 407. He popped up a few days later at the home of one of our informants, Allan Meyers. We almost had him then, but he eluded our agents. We believe he had help, and it appears that help came from the Shepherd's Path. Since we believe they are based in that area, it is reasonable to assume he has made contact with some of the ringleaders. When he next shows his face, we'll have him."

"If he *has* made contact . . ." began Wolf.

"Then he will be of even more value to us," finished Jacob. "And he will tell us everything he knows."

"All right," said Wolf, sensing that he was dismissed. "I'll get things in motion from my end. You should see results within five days."

"Make it three. I want to see the first of those congressmen taken out by then."

"Very well, sir," said Wolf. He started toward the door, but turned back. "You know," he said, "it's a shame Sampson's woman had to get on that flight. You could have used her to get Sampson."

"Really, Mr. Wolf," said Jacob, frowning disapprovingly. "Do you really think me as inefficient as to miss an opportunity like that?" He turned and activated a monitor. The 12-bed ward of Phase One came onto the main screen. There was Doctor Steiger, hovering over his charges. He looked not unlike a vulture waiting for his dinner to die.

"We knew that Mrs. Sampson was on that flight before it ever took off. While we missed her husband, we were able to secure her." He turned the control of the observation camera. It centered on one particular bed and zoomed in.

"She will be quite useful," he said with satisfaction. The camera finished zooming, and there on the screen was Beth Sampson, deep in an artificially induced dreamless sleep, and very much alive.

Scott stood in front of a dirty mirror studying his reflection. He was still in the hidden room at the warehouse, where he had lived for the past 14 days. Before him was the face of a stranger, slowly shaking his head. His once fair skin was now darker by several shades, and his hair had been dyed a deep, jet black. A thick mustache was beginning to fill out on his upper lip, and contact lenses turned his once bright blue eyes into murky brown. The whole effect was quite disorienting.

"Mrs. Sampson wouldn't know her only son, now," he said to himself. Absently he rubbed his finger tips together, barely feeling the molecule-thin plastiskin that covered them. This had been the final touch in his disguise. The covering effectively changed his finger prints. Within a few days, he was told, it would chemically bond to his own skin, making the change permanent.

"Unbelievable," he said to no one in particular. With the exception of a lone security guard, who was also a member of the Shepherd's Path, he was alone in the warehouse. Jeff had left him strict instructions not to go outside. Instead of cooling off over the past two weeks, the hunt for him had heated up. There had been that bombing in Washington (Jeff had brought in a small television for him to watch, as well as a Bible) and just a few days ago one of the congressmen from Kentucky had been ruthlessly gunned down in his home in Frankfort. Each time, the mysterious entity known only as "Wolf" had claimed credit for the atrocities in the name of the Christian Liberation Front. The president had declared a state of emergency, and Congress had granted unprecedented powers to the Bureau of Religious Affairs for the duration of the crisis. All in all, things looked bleak.

In spite of everything, though, Scott felt better than he had in days. His wounds had healed, and he had rested and eaten well. Jeff had put him on a strict exercise program that had slowly brought his strength back. More importantly, he had found peace with God. Beth's loss still hurt like a kick in the stomach, and more than once he had cried himself to sleep, but he was healing. The process would be slow and painful, and he would carry regrets with him for the rest of his life. He *would* heal, though, and his newly found closeness with the Saviour sustained him and comforted him.

His new friends helped, too. His fondness for Helen was growing daily. He had never met anyone like her. Her dedication and courage astounded him. Once, jokingly, he had told her that if they had been the same age, he would have married her. Without missing a beat, she had responded that she was out of his league. Mouth hanging open, he had simply stared at her. Taking pity on him, she had patted him on the arm and said, "Don't worry. I was out of Roy's league, too." That was the first time he had run up against her deadly and offbeat sense of humor. When he had mentioned it to Jeff later, the agent simply shrugged and said something about "plowboys pulling on number one guns." Scott gathered that Jeff considered him out of her league, too.

Jeff was turning into another friend, although in a different way. It was he who had formulated Scott's new look. Scott had never met an FBI agent before, but had always thought of them as grim and serious. Jeff certainly was that, but also a great deal more. He was unstoppably dedicated to the Shepherd's Path, and to Helen. Scott had no doubt that he was willing to die for his beliefs and loyalties. There was a quiet strength inside of him that could only come from God. It awed Scott, and made him just a touch envious. If he had that kind of strength, he could take on the world, and win!

Scott was equally in awe of the Shepherd's Path. Just days ago, he had felt completely and utterly alone, with no help in sight. He had known that other Christians existed, but had no idea where to find them. Now, through the Shepherd's Path, he had thousands of friends! All were brothers and sisters in Christ, and spanned the length and breadth of the nation. It was staggering! Scott had no idea what was going to happen to him, but he was sure of one thing. He wanted to join these people. They were *doing* something — something important, and he wanted to be a part of it. They were in the thick of the battle. The question was, would they have him?

His thoughts were interrupted when the red warning light over the door began to flash. He looked quickly at his watch, which read 10:30 a.m. That meant it was probably Jeff, who had promised to be here by then, but he could not be sure. Quickly he doused the light on the night stand. Darkness descended, interrupted rhythmically by the amber glow of the warning light. He debated unscrewing it, but decided not to waste the time. He went to the wall that separated the secret room from the office and pushed a certain panel. It clicked open, revealing a space just wide enough to squeeze into. Even if this room was discovered, no one should notice that the separating wall was somewhat wider than normal — he hoped.

Through the thinness of the plywood, he could hear someone moving around in the office. Then there was the sound of the small door opening. Scott tensed, waiting.

"It's okay, Scott. It's me, Jeff. Come on out." Sighing in relief, Scott pushed open the panel. Jeff stood there by the bed, having just turned the light back on. When he saw Scott, he shook his head disapprovingly.

"Wrong, Scott," he said, his tone matching his face. "You didn't wait for me to give the recognition signal." Inwardly Scott groaned. That had been the most important thing Jeff had insisted on. He was under strict instructions not to reveal himself to anyone who did not give the proper recognition codes. Trying to hide his embarrassment, he searched for an excuse.

"I recognized your voice, Jeff," he said lamely, "and I could hear you were alone." Scott could see he wasn't buying it. Jeff reached into his pocket and pulled out a small electronic device about the size and shape of a pocket calculator. He pushed a button.

"It's okay Scott," came Jeff's voice from the device. "It's me, Jeff. Come on out." Scott could hear no difference between it and Jeff's real voice.

"Digital voice recorder," Jeff explained. "Standard FBI issue." He tossed it to Scott. "Neat little toy. It can sample any voice you want. Just have the subject say a few words into it, and it does the rest. Once it has your voice on file, it can be made to say anything." His face hardened. "NEVER," he said sternly, "never respond to *anyone* without the correct signal." Scott held up his hands in surrender.

"You've made your point," he said. "A man who is laden with the guilt of human blood. . . ."

" 'Will be a fugitive until death; let no one support him.' Better, Scott. A little late, but at least you got it right. How's the rest of your memorization coming?"

"Rough," admitted Scott. "I feel like I'm back in Sunday school again. It's been a long time since I had memory verses."

"The stakes are a lot higher, too," replied Jeff, "but it could save your life someday. This month, the recognition signals are being taken from the last five chapters of Proverbs. You need to have them memorized by the time you leave here."

"Wouldn't it be easier to just have two or three verses to choose from? Seems like there's a lot of potential for mistakes."

"True," agreed Jeff, "but it would be too easy for someone to crack that system. That's the same reason we're phasing out the shepherd's staff. Too easy to recognize. This way, there's no set signal. Your contact will simply choose a verse at random, and all you have to do is respond with the following verse."

"The bad guys could memorize Scripture the same way we are," commented Scott.

"Again true," Jeff grinned. "That's the beauty of the system. Personally, I don't think the bad guys will figure this out too soon — but even if they do — well, memorizing God's Word has a tendency to change bad guys into good guys." Scott had to chuckle at the way Jeff put it.

They shared a smile for a moment, then Jeff sobered. "Never forget, Scott," he said, "that there are no bad guys, only lost guys. Those people hounding us and trying to destroy us need Jesus Christ in their lives. It's our responsibility to share Him with them. Otherwise, we're no better than they are. All of this," he spread his arms, encompassing the tiny room, and by symbolism, the entire network, "would be just so much cloak and dagger, if we don't proclaim the gospel of Christ. Understand?"

"I do," nodded Scott. "For the first time in a long time, I really do."

"Good! Enough said. Now," he continued, rubbing his hands briskly together, "let's see about getting you out of here."

"I'm more than ready," said Scott, with deep feeling. Though functional, the warehouse was hardly a place for an extended stay. Scott was grateful for the protection it offered, but felt that if he had to remain much longer, he would be climbing the proverbial walls. Jeff grinned at his reply.

"Feeling a little crazy, eh? Well, I've done some checking, and Helen's made a few calls," he said. "There's a place in Tarpon Springs, Florida, that would suit you, I think. We have several families down there that could take you in for a while. How would you like to be a dock worker?"

"Never been one," said Scott doubtfully. Frankly, the idea didn't appeal to him. He was a creature of air conditioned offices and computer terminals.

Jeff noted his hesitation. "It's your choice," he said, shrugging. "The thing is, it's a very closed community — mostly Greek. That's why we darkened your skin, by the way. Our families down there are full-blooded Greeks, and will absorb you into their culture. You could disappear there for years if necessary. How about it? At least give it a try."

Abruptly, Scott realized how self-centered he was being. These people were risking a great deal for him. What right did he have to spurn their offer? Somewhat embarrassed, he nodded in agreement. "That sounds good," he replied. "My geography is a little off, though. Just where is Tarpon Springs?"

"Around the Tampa Bay area, on the Gulf," said Jeff. "The big problem is, how do we get you there? It's a good thousand mile trip."

"My disguise. . . ."

"Would be worthless if you are picked up," finished Jeff. "Even if your I.D. checks out, and it will, they'll still take retinal prints. We can't change those. They'll have you identified in minutes." They were silent for a moment, then Jeff sighed.

"Helen and I talked about this last night," he said. "It's too risky to take a flight, but I think we can put you on a bus. They are on the same computer network as the airlines, but security isn't as tight. Also, if anything goes wrong, you can get off a bus. Try doing the same thing in a plane."

"Right," replied Scott wryly. "How long a trip is it?"

"If you were to go straight through, it would take just over 24 hours," said Jeff. "However, in your case, we think it would be better to make the trip in short hops. I've got your route mapped out, and we'll go over it in just a minute. How's that sound?"

"Fine," said Scott. Actually, it was beginning to sound better and better. Now that he had an idea of what he was going to do — a plan — he was anxious to get going.

"It's settled then," said Jeff. He reached into his jacket pocket and pulled out a small wallet. "Here," he said, handing it to Scott. Inside were several forms of identification, including a drivers license and several credit cards. The name on the license was Gregory Andropolos, and the picture looked enough like Scott to be his twin brother.

"Is this a real guy?" he asked.

"He was *very* real," answered Jeff. "In this case, he died about three months ago."

"I'm going to be walking around with a dead man's identity?" asked Scott incredulously. "Pardon me, but isn't that a bit risky? All anyone has to do is run a check, and poof," he threw his hands up in the air, "I'm history."

"Relax Scott," replied Jeff. "As far as any government agency is concerned, Gregory Andropolos is alive and well. Let me explain." He motioned for Scott to sit down on the cot. "My office investigates hundreds of homicides a year. A lot of times, one will surface that suits the needs of the network. Normally the victim will be a loner, with no family or friends. When that happens, well, I won't give you the details, but to satisfy your curiosity, it only takes a small bit of tampering to erase a death certificate. When we need to smuggle one of our people to a safer location , we just pull out one of these I.D.s we have on file. Usually, with a minimum of disguise we can make a fairly close match.

"Wait a minute," interrupted Scott. "I don't know anything about the capabilities of the FBI, but I do know a lot about the computer systems the government uses. It takes more than just saying a particular person is still alive to convince them. What about taxes, social security, census — there must be a hundred details that could give you away."

"Like I said, Scott, I won't tell you all of our secrets." Jeff frowned. "The fact is, you know too much already. The only reason you met Helen and me is because we needed to find out about you. Why was the Bureau of Religious Affairs using you as a scapegoat? What makes you so special?"

"Well," asked Scott. "Did you find out?"

"Actually," Jeff replied, "there was nothing special about you."

"I could have told you that," said Scott, a hint of sarcasm in his tone.

"Don't take it personally," said Jeff. "You just happened to be in the wrong place at the wrong time. Since you managed to elude them during the bust — that was a neat trick, by the way — they used you to their advantage.

"I could be a spy for the bureau, you know. What do you guys call it? A 'plant'? "

"You've been watching too much television," grinned Jeff. "Of course, the idea has occurred to me. That's why I ran a thorough check on you before we picked you up. That's why we kept you here so long. We had to know if we could trust you." Jeff shook his head, and shrugged. "Even if you aren't a spy," he continued, " you could still hurt us badly. You know too much. That's why we want you to disappear."

"Yeah, I can see that," said Scott. "I guess I owe you guys a lot. One question, though." He looked at Jeff expectantly.

"Well?" asked Jeff.

"Do you trust me now?" he said, looking Jeff straight in the eye. "I mean, do you still think I might be a part of this terrorist group?"

Jeff smiled grimly and shook his head. "As a matter of fact, I never did," he replied. "You don't fit the profile. When David told me about that little scene in Allan Meyers' house, I was sure you were being set up to take the fall."

"So you trust me, then?"

"I believe that you are who you say you are," said Jeff. "You're on the run, your only crime is to have attended an illegal gathering, and you need help." Jeff looked closely at Scott. "Why do you want to know, anyway? It should be enough that we've hidden you, and are getting you to someplace safe."

Scott hesitated. He knew that he didn't have to say anything. All he had to do was to keep his mouth shut, and he could walk away from here. Chances were that he could probably make it all the way to Florida, and disappear into another world. Part of him was screaming inside of him to do just that. *Get away!* it said. *Haven't you suffered enough? Haven't you lost enough? What more could God want from you? Take their help, and leave!*

He couldn't do it. Maybe the Scott Sampson of two weeks ago could have, but too much had happened since then. True, he had suffered a tremendous loss, but he had also experienced a deep personal growth. Above all, he had made a commitment to God.

"I want to join you," he blurted out. The words came quickly. He knew that if he stopped, he would not be able to start again. "I want to be a part of what you are doing." He smiled a deprecatory smile. "I'm not much, Jeff. Like you said, there's nothing special about me. I just know that I want to be a part of this."

Jeff looked hard at Scott for a long moment, then shook his head. "You don't know what you're getting into," he said finally. "This isn't a one shot deal — do a couple of missions and you're through. It's a lifetime commitment. Look around you, Scott. Things aren't going to get any better."

"I know," said Scott, getting up off the cot and moving to stand face to face with Jeff. The agent stood a good four inches taller. "I was never much of a Bible student, but I think we both know we are living in the last days. I want in — all the way in. I want to count for something. I want to put what I've been taught all these years into action. I want — ," he groped for the right words, "I want to make a difference," he finished.

Jeff just looked at him, as if trying to gauge the depth of his commitment. Scott returned his gaze, not flinching.

Suddenly, Jeff grinned, showing a wide expanse of teeth. "Helen was right," he said, clapping Scott on the shoulder. "She said by the time you left here, you would want to join up. Okay, Scott, you want in, you're in."

"That's it?" asked Scott in surprise.

"Yep," replied Jeff, his smile growing larger. "What? Did you think that maybe we have a boot camp set up somewhere for new recruits?"

"I don't know," said Scott. "I guess I thought it would be much harder."

Jeff shook his head. "Every believer is a part of us, Scott. After all, we serve the same Lord, don't we?"

Scott nodded silently.

"We don't require our people to be experts at this," continued Jeff. "We just need them to be committed — committed enough to put their lives on the line. I think you have that kind of commitment. At least, you're starting to get it. Like I said, if you want in, you're in!"

Scott felt a shiver run up his spine, part fear, part exhilaration. There would be no going back now! Like Jeff said, he was committed! "So what do you want me to do?" he asked, trying to sound casual.

Jeff was not fooled. "Exactly what we talked about earlier. You're headed for sunny Florida."

"But. . . ."

"AND," continued Jeff, holding up a hand to silence him, "you'll be making a few stops along the way." Turning his back, he opened up the small door and stepped out. In a moment, he was back, holding a small suitcase. He threw it on the cot and opened it, revealing assorted clothes and toiletries. Ignoring Scott, Jeff ran his hands along the bottom of the suitcase. There was an imperceptible click, and he removed what proved to be a false bottom. Inside, neatly packed, were 10 small Bibles, each no bigger than a dime novel. Involuntarily, Scott raised his eyebrows and whistled.

Jeff nodded. "You're looking at about $100,000 worth of contraband. If you're caught with it, it could mean life imprisonment."

"If I'm caught, I get the chair for committing an act of terrorism," said Scott drily.

"True enough," grinned Jeff. "We want you to deliver these to selected towns along your route. I'll give you the locations to meet each of your contacts. You'll be expected, and you know how to be recognized."

Scott could only stare at the precious cargo. "There was a time when you didn't have to hide them," he said softly.

Jeff nodded. "There was also a time when too many of us took this beloved Book for granted," he said. "But times have changed. Will you do this? Many of the people you will meet haven't seen a Bible in a long time."

"I'll do it," answered Scott. "Gladly."

He watched as Jeff replaced the false bottom and closed the suitcase.

"Keep it with you," he said, handing it to Scott. "It's small enough that you can carry it on the bus, so don't put it with the other luggage." He looked at his watch. "Let's get to the bus station," he said, ushering Scott to the door. "I've got a map in the van. We can go over your route on the way."

Together, they made their way out of the warehouse. Scott waved to the security guard. He felt a pang of regret that he had never met the brother who had kept watch over him the past two weeks. They stepped outside, and he had to squint at the unaccustomed brightness. He took a deep breath of semi-fresh air. He was just about to get into the van when a sudden thought struck him.

"Hey, wait a minute!" he called to Jeff, who turned to face him. "How come you already had those Bibles packed in my suitcase? You didn't know that I would ask to join."

Jeff actually looked embarrassed. "*I* didn't," he admitted, "but Helen did. Don't ask me how, but she did." With that, he turned away and got into the van.

Scott stood there for a moment, just staring. *How about that?* he said to himself, and got into the van.

❖ ❖ ❖

Exactly 35 minutes later, Scott found himself alone at the Covington bus station. It was like most bus stations, dirty and run-down, and had that air of decay that seemed to hang over most of Covington. Cement floors and dull gray walls made up the decor, with five stained wooden pews lined up in the center of the large waiting area like yard lines on a football field.

Jeff had made sure that he understood his itinerary, and then left with a warning. "Remember," he said, "you don't trust *anyone* until you have exchanged proper signals. In fact, it won't hurt to go through it twice. Let them give one, and answer it, then you give one, and let them answer." He gripped Scott's arm with a reassuring strength. "It's not just you alone anymore, Scott. Others are depending on you. Remember that."

With that, he was gone. Scott had wanted to see Helen one more time, to thank her for all she had done, but Jeff had flatly refused. It was too dangerous, he said, for her to be directly involved with him. It had saddened him to think that he would likely never see her again.

He sat quietly on the back pew, casually looking over the map that Jeff had given him. With half an eye, he scanned the station. Only a handful of people were scattered across the mostly empty space. This suited him fine. He had already resolved not to speak unless spoken to. The last thing he wanted to do was to draw attention to himself. Instead, he reviewed his travel route.

His ticket only went as far as Cynthiana, Kentucky, less than 75 miles away. This had been part of Jeff's plan. He told Scott to take his journey in short hops, taking his time and distributing the Bibles along the way. He would make a pre-arranged contact in Cynthiana this afternoon, and spend the night. From there, he would head for Somerset, another 150 miles south. The procedure would be repeated, and the next day he would be on his way to Kingston, Tennessee. Then would come Woodrow, Hogansville, Bainbridge, Chiefland, and finally Tarpon Springs. All told, the entire trip should hopefully take nine days. During that time, Scott would make contact with nine small underground churches, bringing them Bibles and encouragement. It would be quite a dangerous challenge.

"Ladies and gentlemen, bus number 176 for Knoxville, with stops in Cynthiana, Somerset, and Whitney City is now boarding." The tired voice of the attendant came across the intercom. Scott hurriedly gathered his things and stood up. He was relieved to see that no one else was moving to join him. He made his way toward the huge double doors in the back of the station and out onto the landing. The stench of diesel fuel assaulted him, and he had to force himself not to hold his breath. Several buses were lined up there, and he had to search for the right one. He found it at the end of the row, a tired, old bi-level job that badly needed a coat of paint. He climbed aboard, ignoring the musty odor that replaced the smell of diesel, and moved toward the back. It was less than half full, for which he was grateful. He found an empty row and slid in to the window seat. Lifting his suitcase into the rack above his head, he reclined the chair back to a comfortable position.

Within a few minutes, the engine revved and the bus pulled out. Scott watched as first the station, then the rest of the dying city went by. Strangely enough, he felt no regret at leaving northern Kentucky, even though the area had been his home for the past several years. Too much had happened — too many memories. It was almost as if a heavy burden was lifted when the city fell behind.

The bus turned south on State Route 27, and the country began to open up. Beautiful rolling hills replaced the drabness of pavement, and bright green trees began to multiply. Summer was in full bloom. Scott slid back the huge window and drank in the fresh air. It smelled bright and alive, and seemed to cleanse his lungs with every breath. For just a while, he cast aside grief, and simply enjoyed the sensations that traveling in the country brought.

The first leg of his trip was accomplished without incident. Cynthiana was a bustling town, comparable in size to Covington. Unlike Covington, however, it had managed to stay alive and prosperous. There was a feeling of cleanliness there that Scott found refreshing. He left the bus station, carrying his precious suitcase. Jeff had given him explicit instructions on where to be and when to be there. Since he had arrived about 10 minutes early, he took his time walking toward the appointed rendezvous. It was near the center of town, in a small public park. His watch told him that it was just past one o'clock, and there were still several folks enjoying their lunch hour. Gripping his suitcase tightly, Scott made his way toward the center of the park, where he found a large statue of some long ago hero. There was a wooden bench next to it, and he sat down, scanning the area. No one seemed to take any notice of him. All he could do now was wait.

"Excuse me, but do you have the time?" Scott jumped at the high feminine voice that came from over his left shoulder. He had heard no one approach. Looking back, he saw a cute, blond-haired girl no older than 12. She wore denim jeans and a bright blue cotton shirt. A red knapsack hung from one shoulder. She was smiling, her blue eyes studying him appraisingly. It took him a moment to realize that she was expecting an answer.

"I beg your pardon?" he responded brilliantly.

"I said, do you have the time?" she asked, moving around to stand in front of him.

"Oh, yes, of course," said Scott, regaining his composure. "It's five after one."

"Thank you," replied the girl politely. She made no move to leave, but instead sat down on the bench with Scott, placing her knapsack in between them. "I'm supposed to meet my boyfriend here," she explained. "Is anybody sitting here?" she asked after the fact.

"Hmmmm? You are." His reply caused her to wince.

"I mean, are you with someone? Is this seat saved?"

"No, I'm alone. Just got into town, actually." Her question made him slightly uncomfortable. He really did not want this girl hanging around. It might make his contact nervous about showing him or her self. At the same time, he could not leave this place. He might miss them altogether. He thought about it for a moment, then shrugged inwardly. Best to remain here, he thought. Perhaps her boyfriend would come soon.

"Are you a Mexican?" asked the little girl, peering at him closely. She was sitting crosslegged, looking at him carefully.

"No," said Scott in surprise. Then he remembered his altered appearance. "I'm — er — Greek." He wished she would go away.

"Wow!" exclaimed the girl. "Can you tell me about Greece? I've seen pictures in school."

"Uh, no. I was born here," he stuttered. Jeff had given him a false biography to go with his new identity, and he struggled to recall it. "I mean I was born in Detroit," he amended. "I've never been to Greece."

"Oh," said the girl, obviously disappointed. She sat in silence for a moment. "Do you have friends here?" she asked finally.

"No, I'm just passing through," replied Scott. "I'm on my way — south." Again the girl was quiet. He thought she was done, but she piped up again after a moment.

"Are you thirsty?" she asked. Scott was surprised and gratified that she was evidently finished with the personal questions. He also realized that he was indeed quite thirsty.

"As a matter of fact, I am," he replied. She smiled at him and rummaged around in her knapsack.

"Here," she said, handing him the water bottle that appeared in her hand. Scott took it gratefully and put the spigot to his mouth. Cold fruit juice splashed into his throat, quenching his thirst. He took a couple of gulps and handed it back.

"Thank you," he said, wiping his mouth.

"That's okay," she replied. "You're a nice man. Sheriff Caine says to always be nice, even to my enemies. He says, 'If your enemy is hungry, give him food to eat; if he is thirsty, give him water to drink.' I hope fruit juice is okay instead of water." She looked at him expectantly.

"Sure," said Scott. "It was fine. Sheriff Caine is a smart. . . ." Suddenly the girl's words came home to him and he turned to stare at her full face.

"What did you say?" he asked, his voice rising. The girl was all wide-eyed innocence.

"I said," she replied, "That you're a nice man." She turned away and returned her water bottle to the knapsack. Scott's mind was in a whirl. Had he just heard right? Mentally he ran through the chapters in Proverbs he had had to memorize. Sure enough, this little 12 year old had just quoted, word for word, Proverbs 25:21. *She* was his contact? One side of his brain said surely not! No one would send a little girl out on something as dangerous as this! The other side wasn't so sure. What if she *was* here to meet him? What should he do?

Conflicting thoughts warred inside of him, washing back and forth. He finally decided to take a chance. He watched as the child finished arranging her knapsack, then spoke.

"Sheriff Caine sounds a lot like my dad," he began as she turned back to him. He prayed desperately that he was doing this right. "He used to say that if you're nice to someone who doesn't like you, 'you will heap burning coals on his head.' " He smiled wanly, half hoping the girl would not know what he was talking about. She merely sat there, looking at him, as if waiting for something else. Scott could not imagine what.

"Well?" she asked finally.

"Well what?" he asked, confused.

"Aren't you going to tell me the rest of it?"

"Huh?"

"The rest of it." Her voice lowered, practically hissing. "Are you going to say the rest of the verse, or what?"

"I don't know what you're . . . Oh!" Abruptly, Scott remembered that he had left out almost half of his reply. " 'And the Lord will reward you,' " he said quickly. He was so rattled that he forgot Jeff's advice and did not use a counter sign.

Satisfied, the girl nodded. "That's better. This is your first time, isn't it?"

"Sort of," he admitted reluctantly. He hoped she would not see him blushing.

"Thought so," replied the girl. "Don't worry, you'll get better. Now, are you ready to go?" Scott nodded, and she gathered up her knapsack. Taking his hand, she led him out of the park and through the center of town. It was a busy day there, with numerous people coming and going. Scott felt both visible and vulnerable as his pint-sized guide led him to wherever they were going.

"My name's Marion," she told him as they passed a hardware store. She was leading him toward a large, columned, three-story building that squatted at the end of the street. It looked like a courthouse. A police car was moving slowly toward them. Although the officer inside appeared not to take any notice of them, Scott found himself getting decidedly nervous.

"What?" he asked, not hearing her. Aggravated, the girl tugged at his arm.

"I said, my name is Marion. What's yours?"

"Sco — er — Gregory," he answered, catching himself barely in time. The girl shook her head knowingly.

"That's not your real name. Too bad you can't tell me what it is."

This was getting out of hand, he thought as they drew ever nearer to the courthouse. First he was accosted by this — this child. Then she leads him down the middle of a crowded town, casually chatting about his fake identity. He began to scan the area in earnest, looking for a way to disappear. The courthouse stood at the end of the street they were now on. On either side were rows of two-story buildings housing places of business. Parking meters lined both sides of the street, and several cars were parked along the curb. Not too promising, he thought, if he had to make a break for it. They reached the cross street opposite the court house.

"Come on!" said Marion, yanking at his hand. "The light's green." Before he could protest, she half dragged him across the intersection and up to the concrete stairs that led to the entrance. With a dawning realization, he realized that she was actually expecting him to go inside.

He pulled up short, causing her to stop. "I can't go in there!" he whispered urgently, pulling her toward him. "I'm a wanted man!"

Marion looked at him as if he had just remarked that the sky was blue. "I know that," she replied. "Didn't they tell you *anything* before you came here?"

"Very little," he admitted.

Marion shook her head at this. "The sheriff always says, 'If you want to hide something, put it in plain sight.' " She gestured toward the courthouse. "That's in plain sight, right?"

"Well. . . ."

"So that's where we're hiding. Now come on!" Marion released his hand and started up the stairs, leaving Scott with two choices. He could follow, or he could walk away. There would be a bus going to his next destination later that afternoon.

Marion turned, and saw him still standing there. "Come ON!" she demanded, actually stamping her foot with impatience. What finally helped Scott decide was a perverse curiosity. He simply *had* to know what was going on. If a church was truly based here, right under the noses of the local law enforcement, then these were people he wanted to meet. Besides, it sounded as if the sheriff himself was involved. He took a firm grip on his suitcase and an even firmer grip on his courage and followed Marion up the steps.

Marion obviously knew her way around. Boldly, as if she owned the place, she led through the foyer, up one flight of stairs, and down a long hall. She stopped before a door that was clearly marked SHERIFF. Underneath was the name Marshall Caine. Without missing a beat, Marion opened the door and went in. Scott followed, constantly trying to look in every direction at once.

Inside was a fairly large outer office outfitted in royal blue. A secretary sat behind a desk that held a computer terminal and various other objects. She looked up and smiled at Scott's self-appointed friend.

"Hi, Marion," she said sweetly. "Sheriff Caine is inside. He said that if you came to go right in." So saying, she resumed her work, ignoring Scott completely. Marion nodded, and motioned for him to follow. Scott was beginning to understand why this little girl had been sent to meet him. He also understood why she was so confident. Was the entire city government in on this?

He followed her into the inner office. This one was decorated in much the same way the outer office was. Royal blue carpet contrasted with ivory painted walls. Two large portraits graced the wall opposite him. One was of the president, and the other was of the governor of Kentucky. To his left were shelves containing trophies, plaques, and countless other awards. Under the portraits sat a very large desk, and behind the desk sat a very large man. Marion ran over to the man, who pulled away from the desk, and promptly hugged him.

"Hi, Sheriff," she said.

The man returned the hug, then ruffled Marion's blonde hair. "Hi, Marion," he said in a deep voice that matched his physique. "Did everything go okay?" His gaze turned to Scott questioningly. Scott was caught by the intensity of that look. *Here is a man to be reckoned with,* he thought to himself. He was middle-aged, seemingly in his late forties. His light brown hair and chiseled features gave an aura of perpetual youth. Slowly Marshall Caine set his little friend back down on the floor and stood, revealing a six foot six frame. He nodded toward Scott.

"Sheriff, this is Gregory," said Marion eagerly, "Except that his name really isn't Gregory."

Marshall smiled down at Marion. "Good, Honey. Why don't you head for home, now. Your mom and dad will be worried about you. Tell them that everything went fine."

"Okay," said Marion, and bounced out of the office.

The two men studied each other for a long minute. Then the sheriff spoke. " 'A man who hardens his neck after much reproof will suddenly be broken beyond remedy,' " he said, wasting no time.

Inwardly, Scott breathed a sigh of relief. He didn't really believe that Marion would betray him, but there had been a tiny bit of doubt. Mentally he repeated the verse that Sheriff Caine had given and then gave the counter signal. " 'When the righteous increase, the people rejoice, but when a wicked man rules, people groan.' "

The sheriff nodded and smiled, motioning for him to sit in one of the two cushioned leather chairs that were placed side by side in front of the desk.

Scott hesitated, remembering Jeff's advice, then said, " 'Do not boast about tomorrow, for you do not know what a day may bring forth.' " Now it was his turn to look at Chief Caine expectantly.

Caine blinked in surprise, but recovered immediately. " 'Let another praise you, and not your own mouth; a stranger, and not your own lips.' " He smiled as he finished the quotation. "Can't say as I blame you," he said, again motioning for Scott to take a seat. "This isn't exactly the place one would expect to make contact with a fellow Christian — at least not in this day and age."

"No, it isn't," agreed Scott.

"Jeff Anderson teach you that?" asked Caine. Scott nodded. "Thought so," he said. "He was always cautious. I worked with him on a few cases, years back. He's the one who brought me into the Shepherd's Path, in fact."

"Oh," said Scott. He was not really sure how to respond to this man.

Caine sensed this, and leaned forward, getting down to business.

"I know who you are," he said bluntly. "Jeff got word to me over the computer network. I've made arrangements for you to stay overnight, and we'll have you on your way tomorrow at the crack of dawn." He frowned, then asked, "Have you been following the news?"

"Not since yesterday," replied Scott.

"It's not good. What we've been going through before was a summer storm — now we're bracing for a hurricane. Thing's haven't been too bad here in Cynthiana. We're too small to attract much notice."

"Your being the sheriff can't hurt too much either," commented Scott drily.

"True," smiled Caine, "but as I said, that's about to change. The Bureau of Religious Affairs is setting up shop here, and I've been informed by the mayor that they'll have complete authority in matters of underground activity." He raised an eyebrow at Scott. "They have stepped up their search for you, too," he added. "If you're curious, it's worth $100,000 to the individual who turns you in."

Scott's heart sank. He had hoped that things would quiet down when he didn't surface anywhere. It was all a bad dream, he thought.

Caine caught the look on his face and made a decision. "Come on," he said, slapping the desk with the palms of his hands and standing. "They haven't caught us yet. Let's get you over to the safe house. I understand that you have a tremendous gift for us."

He led Scott out of his office to an elevator. Taking it to the ground floor, they walked to the other side of the building where several unmarked cars were parked. Sheriff Caine picked one out and got in, unlocking the door for Scott. Within minutes, they were driving back down the street he had originally followed in.

Scott took the opportunity to get to know his new friend a little better. "Marion said that the best way to hide things was in plain sight," he remarked.

Marshall chuckled. "She has a bad habit of listening too much to the sheriff," he said. "Like I said before, small towns like us have escaped the worst of the Persecution — up until now, that is."

"The Persecution?"

"That's what it's being called. I don't know who started calling it that, but it's caught on. A little too dramatic for my taste. Anyway, we really haven't had too many problems here. I know who can and can't be trusted on the force. Those who can't, I make sure are working on something else when our churches meet."

"You have more than one?" asked Scott in surprise. Somehow,

he had imagined that each town or city would only have one church.

"Of course. More than you would think, in a town this size. Anyway, we don't have to worry too much about the local law." He shook his head sadly. "That's about to change now, I guess. With the bureau moving in, things are going to get a lot more dangerous."

"I guess so," said Scott. Marshall seemed about to say something else, but changed his mind. They rode in silence for a while. At length, he turned into a large subdivision just outside of town. He motioned toward the glove compartment.

"Open it," he said. Scott did so, and among other things, found a long strip of cloth. "Cover your eyes with that," he said.

"Huh?"

"I said, cover your eyes with that. You don't need to see where we are going. This is a safe house we're headed for, and it needs to remain a secret. Once we're inside, you can take it off."

"What about you?" asked Scott as he tied the cloth over his eyes. "I can identify you and Marion."

Although he could not see him, he could feel Marshall smile. "In the first place, you can only identify me. I'm a widower, and I don't have any children. In the second place, I have contacts all over. If you were to be caught, I would know. I've long since planned my escape route."

"And what about Marion and her family?" asked Scott.

Marshall laughed a full fledged laugh. "Marion is not even a girl," he replied, the amusement evident in his voice. "Nor is he a child. And I don't think you could pick him out of a line up."

Scott was amazed. "Wo-o-o-ow," he said quietly, drawing out the vowel. "She — er -he sure had me fooled."

"That's the idea," said Marshall. Scott felt the car round a curve. It bumped slightly as it obviously pulled into a driveway. There was a pause, then he heard the sound of a garage door being opened. It stopped, and Marshall eased the car forward, bringing it to an easy halt.

"You can get rid of that blindfold now," said Marshall, getting out of the car. Scott did so and took a look around. They were in a typical two car garage. The walls were lined with old furniture, lawn tools, and other items that always accumulated in such a place. Scott got out and followed Marshall through the only door and into a laundry room. From there he was led into a small bedroom. Light peeked around a single, shuttered window.

"You can stay here for a while," said Marshall. "I'll be back to get you in a few hours. We're having a meeting later this evening, and I think it would be good if you join us. I'd like you to give your gift to the whole church, not just me. Are you up for that?"

"Okay," replied Scott reluctantly. He could not help but remember the last time he had attended such a meeting.

"Good," said Marshall. "I'm afraid I'll have to ask you to stay in this room. There's no one here, but you don't need to see what the rest of the house looks like. Are you hungry?"

"I haven't eaten since this morning," said Scott, aware of the empty feeling in his stomach.

"Just a second, then." Marshall disappeared for a moment. When he returned, he was carrying several sandwiches and a pitcher of lemonade. "Help yourself," he said, setting the food down on a small table. "I've got to get going. I'll see you in a little while."

With that, Marshall left. Scott finished off two of the sandwiches, then opened his suitcase. After making sure the Bibles were safe and secure, he stretched out on the small bed against the wall and settled himself in for a long wait.

❖ ❖ ❖

It was almost dark when Marshall finally returned for him. Scott had followed instructions and stayed in the bedroom. The first few hours had not been so bad. After he had eaten he had taken a short nap. After that, he had worked on his memorization. Jeff had suggested he start with the Book of John next, and by the time Marshall walked in he had committed the first two chapters to memory. The afternoon and evening dragged on, however, and when Marshall arrived, he was more than ready to leave. Between the time he had spent at the warehouse, and now this, he fervently hoped he would never see a small room again!

Once again Scott was blindfolded and led to the garage. After they had driven for several minutes, he was allowed to take it off. He saw that they were somewhere in the open country, heading along State Route 27. He did not ask their destination, and Marshall did not volunteer any information. Instead they talked about their lives before the Persecution. Scott was surprised to learn that Marshall had been a captain in the Middle East during the late nineties.

"A tough time," he said, reminiscing. "The heat was the worse part. During the day it got up to 110 degrees. We were in more danger of heat prostration than we were of the enemy."

Scott listened attentively. He had registered with the selective service, but had never been called up. A small part of him was envious of Marshall's experiences. "Did you see any fighting?" he asked when his companion paused.

"Some," he admitted. "I was in Israel at the time of the big push to Turkey — that was the Third Gulf War, you know, although I tend to think of them all as one big mess. Still, I saw some fighting along the West Bank . . . mostly terrorist stuff, nothing real big." Another pause, then, "I lost some good friends there. Our headquarters were bombed by one of the splinter groups of the PLO. They were almost impossible to stop." He sighed at the memory. "We fought an enemy we couldn't see."

Scott was silent for a moment, suddenly feeling uncomfortable. He changed the subject. "How were you saved?" he asked.

His question caused Marshall to smile. "The same way you were," he replied innocently. "By accepting Jesus Christ as my personal Saviour."

"No," said Scott, "I mean, where were you. . . ." He caught Marshall's smile and groaned. "I hate being a straight man," he said, shaking his head.

Marshall chuckled, then sobered. "I'm sorry, Scott," he said. "I shouldn't joke with you about that. It actually happened when I was in the Middle East. I visited Jerusalem on leave. I really didn't believe in anything at the time. I was seeing the sights like any other tourist. Then I visited the Tomb." He paused, his mind re-living that time.

"No matter what you believe," he continued, "you can't go there and not be moved. I bought a Bible and started to read it. Before too long, I knew that what I had been looking for all my life was Jesus. It was that simple."

Scott nodded, and was about to relate his own salvation experience when he suddenly realized something. "Hey! You just called me by my real name!" he said in surprise.

Marshall nodded.

"And you said earlier that you knew who I was. Just how did you know that?" demanded Scott.

"Easy," replied Marshall. "I've been on the Computer Net. Your friends in Cincinnati let us know you were coming just yesterday. They gave your name and description, so we would be looking out for you. After I left you at the safe house, I activated the Net and sent a picture of you back there. They confirmed it was indeed you, Scott Sampson, terrorist on the run."

"I'm not a terrorist," objected Scott vehemently.

Marshall raised a calming hand. "I'm sorry, Scott," he said earnestly. "I didn't mean it. Sometimes my sense of humor doesn't know when to stop. I know you're not responsible for the things they're blaming you for. Forgive me?"

"Yeah, sure," Scott said after a moment. "It's just that, too many bad things have been happening. I lost my wife, you know. The government is blaming me for the explosion in which she was killed. It's still too soon to talk about it easily."

"I understand," said Marshall. An uncomfortable silence settled into the car, each man alone with his thoughts. Fortunately, the ride ended soon after. Once again Marshall insisted that Scott be blindfolded before they reached their destination. He could feel the car making several turns before it finally stopped.

"We're here," announced Marshall, shutting off the engine. "You can take that off now," he said, referring to the blindfold. Scott did so, and saw that they were in the middle of a densely wooded area.

"Let's go," Marshall said, getting out of the car. Scott retrieved the suitcase from the back seat and followed suit. Soon he was tramping through the thick undergrowth. Marshall had a small, dim flashlight, but it did little to light the way. Scott was continuously tripping over dead branches and protruding roots. The tennis shoes he was wearing did little to stop his ankles from being scratched and bruised. Time seemed to drag on. Scott lost track of how long they walked. Once, they were challenged. A loud male voice sounded from the darkness, causing Scott's heart to miss a beat. Marshall answered the challenge with a verse, which was in turn answered with the proper following verse. They were allowed to continue.

"Not much further," said Marshall over his shoulder, a few minutes later. Scott did not reply, as he was concentrating on finding his way. The only other illumination came from the full moon over head. It shone through the branches of the tall, dark trees, casting pale pools of light that glimmered mysteriously.

Without warning, the trees and undergrowth suddenly disappeared and Scott found himself in the middle of a small clearing, no bigger than a large house. In the exact center sat a small cabin that looked as if it would be more at home in an earlier century. There was no light coming through the two windows that adorned the front, and no smoke was rising from the chimney. The porch that ran the length of the front seemed like some ominous mouth that could swallow up the innocent passerby. Nevertheless, this seemed to be their destination. Marshall extinguished his light and continued forward, the moon illuminating his way. Scott fell in close behind.

"This is a hunter's shack," he explained in a low voice as they neared the cabin. "There's hundreds of them around here. During the season, they're constantly in use. Right now, though, they're deserted, and perfect for us." They reached the wooden door, and Marshall gave a complicated knock. There was a moment of silence, then there was an answering rap. The door opened slightly.

" 'A fool always loses his temper, but a wise man holds it back,' " came a spectral voice.

Marshall was ready. " 'If a ruler pays attention to falsehood, all his ministers become wicked.' " Again there was a pause.

Scott could not help it. Suddenly he was back in the basement of that dilapidated furniture store, Beth by his side. He could feel her pressing up against him, her body alive and warm. He remembered the passionate kiss they had shared in that cellar, and the promise of more to come. Something wrenched his gut 180 degrees around inside of him. He hurt so bad he felt as if he were going to die. At that moment, part of him wished he would, so the pain would stop. Marshall, unaware of his agony, stepped forward and disappeared into the darkness. Scott was left standing there on the porch, re-living the pain and hurt.

"Scott? Are you coming?" Marshall's voice came out of the darkness. Still Scott stood there, as if rooted to that spot. He wanted to go home. He wanted to go back to his house, and find Beth there, waiting. He wanted to feel her in his arms again, or just hear her voice. He ached to have just a few minutes alone with her, to tell her the things he should have said years ago.

"Let's take it all back, God," he pleaded silently. "Just give me the last two weeks back. Just say that they didn't count." It was irrational, and somewhere deep inside he knew it, but the wave of emotion that washed over him left him helpless in its wake. He wanted his wife back. He knew that she was gone from him, just as he knew that someday she would be restored. She was more alive now than she had ever been, and she was with God. He *would* see her again. He told himself all of this, and more, but it did not stop the hurt.

"Scott?" A gentle hand touched his arm. "Scott, are you all right?" The physical touch of another human being jolted him out of his memory. He blinked his eyes, and saw the concerned visage of Marshall Caine in the moonlight.

"What?"

"Are you all right? Aren't you coming in? The rest are waiting."

Scott took a deep breath, returning to the present. He couldn't change the past, he realized. Regrets were useless, and in his new line of work, dangerous. As much as it hurt, the past was unchangeable, etched in stone. The only thing that mattered was the present — the here and now. He would deal with the pain later, when he had the time. Right now, there were people waiting on him. He had made a commitment, both to God and to his friends, and he was going to do everything he could to honor it. He reached down to where Marshall's hand rested lightly on his arm and gripped it tightly. "Sorry," he said softly. "My mind was somewhere else for a minute. Let's go."

He allowed Marshall to lead him into the darkness. He could sense, rather than see others there with him. Marshall closed the door behind them. There was a scuffling, then the sound of a match striking. In the near total darkness, the blaze of the single match was dazzling. In its half-light he could see several dark shapes standing around the perimeter of the cabin. The person holding the match was a young woman. Her dark eyes sparkled in the match light as she lifted the glass chimney off an oil lamp that sat on a round wooden table in the center of the room and lit the wick. The level of light in the room increased significantly. Scott could now see the faces of at least 15 worshipers of all ages scattered about the room, sitting on the floor. There were no chairs. Each of the group was staring at him, waiting expectantly. Scott worried for a moment that the light might be visible from outside, but then saw that the windows were covered with heavy black cloth.

From behind him came Marshall's voice. "The Lord is risen," he said softly.

"The Lord is risen indeed," replied the people in unison.

A small smile wormed its way to Scott's lips. But for the different faces and different location, he felt as if he was indeed back in the furniture store. The memories this time, though, were good ones. He remembered the wonderful time that he had experienced, and the special way that God had touched him. He would never be the same again.

The small group was still watching him, as if waiting. He felt he should say something, but before he could speak, Marshall strode past him and moved to stand beside the light. All eyes shifted from Scott to him. Scott expected to be introduced, but Marshall surprised him. Without a word, the big man dropped to his knees. The rest of the group followed his lead, as did Scott.

For the second time in his life, he experienced the pure power of prayer. Marshall led, but others joined in at times. It was like a choral concert. There were many parts, and what could have been total confusion became perfect harmony. God was the Conductor, leading them, cuing each part with precision and perfection. One voice was raised, interceding for a lost son, while another prayed for a Christian brother whose fear prevented him from being a part of the group. Through it all Scott remained silent, allowing himself to experience the movement of the Holy Spirit. After all he had been through it was like a balm on his troubled soul.

In time, as needs were met and petitions were given, the praying ceased. The worshipers did not stop gradually, dying away one by one. Rather they stopped all at once, as if on cue. The Conductor simply ended it, as if laying down His baton. The sweet fragrance of the afterglow permeated the room, filling each participant with contentment. The tiny church was happy. God was there. All could feel His presence. They had accomplished much in that time. Prayers were spoken that would be answered.

Scott was surprised to find he was sweating. With the windows closed and so many people crammed into the small space, it was getting rather stuffy. Marshall evidently felt the same. While he covered the lamp with a bushel basket, he motioned for one of the men to open the door. A wave of cool, summer night air swept inside, causing the group to breath a collective sigh of relief. Scott took a deep breath, feeling the sweat cool his forehead. Everyone simply sat there for a while, enjoying the fresh scent of nature and the closeness of each other.

When the cabin had aired out, Marshall signaled for the door to be closed. He lifted the bushel basket off the lamp, restoring the light completely. He stood by the table, looking at each member before he spoke.

"We have all been thankful for the relative freedom we have had here in the country," he began. "Compared to our brothers and sisters in the larger metropolitan areas, we've had it easy."

"I hear the chief of police is being bribed by the underground church," quipped someone from the back of the room. There was a soft chuckle as the group enjoyed the joke.

Marshall laughed along with the rest. "Of course he is," he said jauntily. "Haven't you seen his new Mercedes?" Again everyone laughed. Marshall held up a hand for silence. "Seriously, we *have* been pretty blessed. I have a bad feeling that is about to change, though. Now that the cities are more or less under control, officials are spreading their operations into smaller towns like ours. For those of you who don't know it yet, the Bureau of Religious Affairs is opening an office in city hall. We are going to have to be very, very careful."

Somber silence greeted this announcement. Looks on peoples faces ran the gauntlet from outright fear to grim determination.

Marshall motioned for Scott to come and stand next to him. "This is Scott," he said, putting an arm around Scott's shoulders. "He's here from Cincinnati." Scott was startled. He thought his identity would remain a secret. He looked at Marshall in surprise.

"I know, Scott," he said, squeezing his shoulders reassuringly, "but it's important that these people understand what might be in store for them. The Persecution hasn't really reached us here, but it's coming."

Scott nodded, giving Marshall his permission to go on.

"You won't recognize our friend here," he continued, "but you all know him. His picture has been in the news quite a bit. This is Scott Sampson, the man accused of bombing that plane that exploded." Muted gasps of astonishment met this announcement. Scott shifted uncomfortably, aware of the new scrutiny he was now under.

"I want Scott to tell you exactly what happened to him," said Marshall. He nodded to Scott, and sat down crosslegged on the floor. Haltingly at first, then with growing assurance, he related his experiences. He started with going to the meeting at the furniture store, and ended with his rescue by members of the Shepherd's Path. Although he did not name names, he left nothing else out. He spoke of his fear, of losing Beth, and of his unreasoning rage. When he finished, there were many who were openly weeping.

Marshall stood again. "Thanks, Scott," he said gently. "That's not easy to hear, and I know it's not easy to tell." Scott was about to sit back down, but Marshall restrained him. "What you heard was the bad news for tonight," he told the church. "However," he continued, a mischievous smile playing at the corner of his mouth, "there is some good news. Some of you know about it. Most of you don't." He turned to Scott. "I think it's time, now. Don't you?"

In telling his story, Scott had actually forgotten his primary purpose for being there. A thrill of excitement ran through him. If these people truly hadn't seen a Bible in a while, this was going to be a pleasure. He picked the suitcase up off the floor where he had set it, and laid it on the table. As the church watched curiously, he opened it and released the catch on the false bottom. With a flourish, he lifted the small Bible out, holding it up for all to see.

There was a stunned silence.

"Here," said Marshall, taking the Bible reverently out of Scott's hands. He held it carefully for a moment, as if he was holding a dream that could be taken from him at any moment. Then, gently, he opened it, thumbing through the pages. He found a place, and quietly began to read.

"In the beginning was the Word, and the Word was with God, and the Word was God. All things were made by him, and apart from him nothing came into being that has come into being." He would have continued, but his eyes became blurred. Two large tears rolled down his cheeks, falling onto the open pages. With the tenderness of a loving father holding his infant child, he brushed them off.

Still not speaking, he handed the Bible to the person nearest him. The young lady, the one who had lit the lamp, took it and continued to read. "In him was life, and the life was the light of men. And the light shines in the darkness and the darkness did not comprehend it."

She turned, and passed the Word of God on to the next believer, an older man with graying hair. He had to move close to the light in order to see, and even then had to squint. "There was a man, sent from God, whose name was John," he read in a high unsteady voice. "He came for a witness, that he might bear witness of the light."

One by one, the members of that small underground church held their new treasure. Each one read a verse from the first chapter of John. Scott watched in silence. He had felt gratification before in giving a gift, but nothing compared to the incredible, soul satisfying feeling that was engulfing him. To see these brave people so overwhelmed by this — it was indescribable. He wanted it to last forever.

At last, each member had held the Bible and read a few verses. The last one to read handed it back to Marshall, who put it in his jacket pocket. He turned to Scott, and smiled. "No other words are necessary, right?" Scott could only nod.

Marshall looked back at the group. "It's time to go." A soft groan of disappointment met this announcement, causing Scott to smile. He didn't want to end it either! "We'll arrange another meeting soon," continued the Sheriff. "Stay in touch with your contacts for when and where. Until then, be careful!" He opened the door and looked out. "Coast is clear, everyone. We'll go in twos, just like always."

Gradually the members left. Each one stopped on his or her way out to thank Scott for his sacrifice. It warmed him, but also made him slightly uncomfortable. These precious folks were treating him like some sort of hero, and he was anything but! He exchanged hugs and handshakes with them, all the time wishing they would stop looking at him as if he were something special. Finally, the last one was gone, and he was left alone with Marshall.

"It's been a great night for us," said the sheriff, standing at the door with Scott and looking out at the moon drenched forest.

"Hmmmm," Scott mumbled, not having anything to say.

"These people will always remember what you have done for them," said Marshall. "You saw how much having this Bible meant to them." He patted his jacket pocket.

"And you?" replied Scott softly.

"Yes," agreed Marshall. "After the big Bible drive a few years ago, it became next to impossible to find one. I'm glad that someone had the foresight to hide a few."

"It still amazes me that they became so scarce," remarked Scott, staring out into the night.

"The bureau was thorough," said Marshall. "Peoples' houses were broken into, supplies were confiscated — it was quite a major operation. We should have seen it coming."

"Some did," reminded Scott.

"Yeah, they did. Thank God!" They lapsed into silence for a moment. As they watched the night, a tiny pinpoint of light flared for a moment, then was gone.

"That's our signal," said Marshall. "Let's go."

Once again, Scott found himself fighting through dense undergrowth. This time though, he didn't mind the scratches on his ankles or the mosquito bites on his neck. His purpose here was accomplished, and his heart was light. Tomorrow would bring another leg of his journey to safety, complete with new hazards and dangers. Tonight, though, he would enjoy his feeling of accomplishment. He would give thanks to God for the privilege of being allowed to be a part of this.

As they made their way back to the car, Scott realized something. Tonight had made him feel better than he had ever felt before. He would look forward to doing this again — and again. He wouldn't mind at all if God allowed him to work at this for a while longer. In fact, he wouldn't mind a bit if he did this for the rest of his life.

INTERLUDE

Beth Sampson existed in an acid fog. She wandered alone and helpless in a black and white limbo that allowed no color or life. It surrounded and burned her, causing pain that was not pain. Trapped inside her mind, she struggled in vain to find a way out. No sound penetrated her tiny world. No thought or dream was permitted to exist. She was utterly isolated and alone. Surely hell could be no worse than this.

The dreams and thoughts were there, she knew. She could sense them, just beyond the skewed horizon, always out of her reach. In her mind she would wander back and forth, seeking a way out. She had no sense of direction, no idea of which way to turn. When she tried to call out, to attract attention, her voice died in her throat.

Somewhere deep in her subconscious, a warning light was flashing frantically. Part of her knew that she must escape from her mental prison soon, or go insane. If only she could dream! If only this horrible void could be filled with something — anything! Even a tormentor would be welcome company. She had to have something to latch on to. She needed an anchor — a rock. If she could not find it, she would never regain control of her mind.

"Beth." The gentle voice pierced the glowing fog as if it were not there. It seemed to come from every direction.

"Where are you?" shouted Beth, surprised that she could now hear her own voice as well.

"Where I have been since you were eight years old," replied the voice. "Here with you. I made you a promise, remember? I will *never* leave you nor forsake you. Don't you believe me?" The voice held a gentle hint of reproof.

It didn't matter to Beth. She recognized the voice now. Suddenly, the prison of her mind was no longer terrifying. The fog disappeared, replaced with a soothing light that seemed to enfold and hug her. She was no longer alone.

"My Lord and my God!" she cried out, falling to her knees.

"I am with you, dear heart. Do not despair. You must go through a test now, but you will not go through it alone. Here, take My hand."

"I can't see it, Lord," Beth said to the light.

"When have you had to see Me to know that I am there?" asked her Saviour. "Reach out with your faith."

Beth did so, and felt a strong, firm hand take hers. Gently it lifted her to her feet. As she stood, the brightness disappeared, to be replaced with a beautiful garden. After the harsh nothingness of limbo, the vivid colors were breathtaking. Greens and blues, accented with every other color of the rainbow met her eyes. She felt her tortured mind heal as she beheld the beauty. She turned to see the smiling face of her Lord, Jesus Christ, looking down at her. Tears welled up in her eyes at the love that was shining out of His eyes.

"My Lord and my God," she repeated, whispering it this time.

"No trial or temptation will come upon you that I will not give you the strength to bear," said the Lord. "Be strong and of good courage, and you will prevail. Others are also being put through the fire. Some will wither and burn, and some will be refined like pure gold. In but a little while, you will be with Me forever. Until then, rest here."

So saying, He led her into the garden. Beth walked beside her best friend, feeling very much like a little girl with her father. In perfect peace, she chatted with her Saviour as they strolled through the beautiful garden.

7

"Anderson, just what the heck do you think you're doing?" Jeff ground his teeth involuntarily at the tone of voice his boss was using. Janet Wilder, a fair-skinned woman in her late thirties stared at him from the screen of his office vid-phone, waiting for an answer. Her dark eyes snapped angrily at him, and her thin mouth was set in a grim frown.

"I'm trying to do my job," he replied as evenly as he could. Inside he was seething at being called directly from main headquarters in Washington. It amounted to nothing more than a reprimand.

"Your job," said Wilder sternly, "is to follow procedure. Were you not instructed that the bombing of Flight 407, in fact *any* activities of the Christian Liberation Front, were to be handled solely by the Bureau of Religious Affairs?"

"I was merely assisting them in their investigation," he answered formally. He was still amazed at the speed that his boss had heard about his actions, even though he had tried to keep things quiet.

"They do not need your assistance," snapped Wilder. "If they did, they would ask."

"May I remind you," said Jeff, his anger beginning to show, "that it has been over two weeks since the bombing? What have they accomplished since then?"

"That is not your concern, Anderson." The two glared at each other for a moment longer.

"Look," Jeff said, attempting to put some friendliness into his voice, "all I did was to try to requisition some logs from the airport. I wasn't even able to get them, so what's the big deal?"

"The big deal," answered Wilder, "is that the head of the bureau's local office has registered a formal complaint against you. Do you realize just what that means? Do you realize how much influence the Bureau of Religious Affairs has now? They want your head, and to tell the truth, I'm inclined to give it to them."

Jeff held his silence and his temper. He had never gotten along with his supervisor, and she did not care for him. It had been dislike at first sight, although he had made several sincere efforts at first to smooth things over. She had rejected each of his attempts, and had become more and more belligerent as the months had passed. He had heard rumors from friends in Washington that she wanted him out. He did not want to believe that it was because of the color of his skin, but things pointed in that direction.

"What do you want, then?" he asked, keeping himself under tight control. "A formal apology? No problem. I'll call the guy right now."

"Forget it," she snapped back. "It's already been done, for all the good it will do. I made it myself, both to the local chief, and to one of their people here. I don't like having to do that, Anderson."

"Then what. . . ."

"They weren't satisfied with just an apology," continued Wilder, ignoring his half-asked question. "They are sending a special agent to interview you."

"What? Why?" A hollow feeling began to form in the pit of his stomach. If he was going to be the subject of an investigation, things could get bad.

"Why?" repeated Wilder. "I'll tell you why. You've been running an unauthorized investigation into the Christian Liberation Front. Even worse, you've kept it a secret, like you're trying to hide something. The Bureau of Religious Affairs takes a very dim view of that. To tell you the truth, I think they may suspect you of conspiracy."

"That's ridiculous," Jeff said heatedly. "All I did was try to get a few computer records. Since when does that make me a conspirator? And since when can the Bureau of Religious Affairs dictate policy to the FBI?" He could tell by the way Wilder glared at him that he had struck a nerve.

"Look, Anderson," she snapped, "I've got better things to do than argue with you. Ask the agent they're sending. His name is Lynch, and he should be there within 24 hours. Wilder out." With that, she broke the connection.

Jeff sat and stared at the blank screen. *Things are getting tight,* he thought. Much tighter than he had realized. It might be time to grab one of the network's ready-made identifications and run. He could be out of the country within hours.

"No," he said aloud, rejecting the idea. The time to run might come, but it wasn't here yet. The Shepherd's Path still functioned, and he was still a part of it. He would continue to do his job. He knew where his loyalties were. Even though Wilder had expressly forbidden it, he would continue to build a file on the Christian Liberation Front. The Bureau of Religious Affairs was using them as an excuse to gain more and more control. If his office could destroy their threat, he could force the bureau to back off. It might cost him his job, and possibly much more, but he would worry about the consequences later.

He activated the computer terminal that sat on his desk next to the vid-phone and went to work. Airport security had flatly refused to hand over copies of the boarding logs, but he still had other leads to try. When electronics failed, people often supplied answers. He had to work quickly. If his efforts were detected, the plug would be pulled. He had to accomplish as much as he could before this Agent Lynch arrived to complicate matters. The first thing to do would be to track down each and every attendant that had been on duty the night Flight 407 had exploded.

Gaining access to the airport personnel files wasn't hard. The FBI system had a direct line to all public transportation facilities. He called up the work schedules of the proper night and area, noting the names of each employee listed. There were four of them, three men and one woman. He wrote down each name on a small pad, then started to call up the personal files of each individual. He tried one of the men first. The name listed was Steve Delmont, age 27. Jeff found his file with no problem but was surprised to see that Mr. Delmont no longer worked for the Greater Cincinnati Airport. He had been terminated due to unsatisfactory work habits, the file said. There was no hint of where he might have gone.

Frowning quietly to himself, Jeff keyed up the next name on his list, a young woman named Sheryl Lynn. Again he found the same thing — employment terminated, with no other explanation. The last two on his list simply had left, giving no indication of where they were going. Sitting back in his desk chair, Jeff mulled over this new information. Each of the attendants working that particular gate on that night were gone.

Going back to the first name on the list, he jotted down Mr. Delmont's home address and phone number. He saw that it was a non-video line, and so used his conventional phone to make the call. He was not too surprised to hear a recording at the other end, stating that this particular number was no longer in service. Going to Ms. Lynn's file, he saw that she lived alone in a small apartment complex. He got the number to the office and called.

"Royal Oaks," answered the feminine voice. "This is Angela speaking."

"Yes," said Jeff. "I'm trying to reach one of your boarders, a Ms. Sheryl Lynn, but the number has been disconnected. Can you tell me if she's still there?"

There was a moment's silence, then Angela said, "I'm sorry, but Miss Lynn is no longer with us."

"Can you tell me how to get in touch with her?" he asked. "It's a matter of some importance."

"I'm afraid that Sheryl didn't leave a forwarding address," replied Angela. "In fact, she didn't even let us know she was leaving. Her brother stopped by and said there was some sort of family emergency and she had to return home to Toledo. He paid her rent and took care of moving her things."

"I see," said Jeff slowly. He did not like what he was hearing. He knew from her personnel file that Sheryl Lynn was an only child. "Thank you anyway," he said, and broke the connection. This was getting him nowhere, he realized. He knew without checking that each former employee would have a similar story. Things were taking on sinister proportions. Why would it be necessary for these people to disappear? There was only one answer, he knew. They had seen something that night that could not be made public. Someone wanted them out of the picture. It was vital that Jeff somehow uncover just what they had seen. He debated bringing in help, but rejected the idea. The small core of Christians that worked in his office took enough risks. He would handle this alone.

His only recourse was to somehow lay his hands on the elusive computer logs. A formal request to the bureau had only gotten him in trouble with his Washington superiors. Perhaps he could try an end run around them. If he talked directly to airport security, he might have more success. His decision made, he headed out of his office. This would have to be a personal visit, he knew. No phone call would work.

❖　❖　❖

Exactly two hours later, Jeff sat in a small security office, waiting for a meeting with the assistant security chief. It was getting on in the afternoon, and he was becoming impatient. For the past hour and a half, he had been busy hacking his way through red tape. This was his third stop in the long line of people he had had to deal with. Things were not going the way he had planned. He had hoped for a friendly little chat with the security chief, and instead was being given the run-a-round. His hopes of maintaining a low profile were dwindling.

As it turned out, the head of airport security had resigned just a few days ago, and the department was in the middle of a massive reorganization effort. The office in which he was waiting was a mess. File folders were stacked in two huge piles on top of the small desk. The wicker trash can next to it was overflowing with litter, and most of the drawers of the three squat filing cabinets that sat behind the desk were left open. Jeff wondered how they got any work done. He had almost decided to give up when the door opened and a short, aging man with gray hair and a slight stoop entered the office. He was wearing a rather rumpled blue security uniform that looked as if it had been slept in.

"Mr. Anderson?" His voice was a nondescript tenor.

"Yes," answered Jeff, rising. He stood a good six inches taller than the old man.

"I'm Hiram Brinn, senior guard on staff here."

"Excuse me," said Jeff, irritation beginning to creep into his voice, "but I'm waiting to see Mr. Carey. I was told he was in charge here."

"Oh, he is, he is," agreed Brinn. "He sent me to tell you that he would be unable to meet with you today. Seems he had a last minute call he had to see to."

"Great, just great!" The frustration that had been building inside all day finally exploded. First Wilder was on his case, now this. He turned away from Brinn, his arms folded in anger. He always did this when he was about to lose his temper. If he didn't, he was liable to hit something. He turned back around to see Brinn studying him carefully.

"I've just wasted two hours here, getting nowhere," he explained tightly. "All I wanted was a few minutes of your boss's time. Was that too much to ask?" The old man scratched his cheek thoughtfully.

"Probably was, the way things are now," he replied. "Ever since Mr. Rooney left, things have been pretty confused."

"Mr. Rooney?"

"He was security chief here until a week ago. Just up and quit, with no notice. It's kind of thrown things into a tizzy."

"I noticed," said Jeff. He was thinking furiously. Could Rooney's quitting have anything to do with the other four airport employees?

"If you don't mind my asking," said Brinn, "just what do you

182 • DAVID F. GRAY

want here? Is what I heard true? You with the FBI?" Mentally Jeff groaned. He had wanted to keep this quiet, but it looked as if everyone here knew who he was. If word got back to the Washington office. . . .

"I just wanted to pay a courtesy call to your boss," he replied, thinking fast. "Since the bombing, we've been updating our procedures. We thought it would be a good idea to be on a first name basis with your department."

"I see," said Brinn slowly. "So you're working on the bombing, too?"

"Not directly," answered Jeff evasively. "I'm just trying to open up channels of communication for the future. Make things easier all around."

"Oh." Brinn was silent for a moment. "I thought the Bureau of Religious Affairs was handling those type of things," he said at last.

"Only if they pertain to the Christian Liberation Front," said Jeff, "Or other fanatic religious groups." He wasn't able to quite keep the disdain out of his voice, and Brinn picked up on it.

"Don't like those folks, eh? Well, you're not alone. They sure turned this place upside down," remarked Brinn. "Questioned everyone, including me."

"They find anything?" asked Jeff.

"Not that I know of," said Brinn, shrugging. "Of course, you would know more about that than me."

"The Bureau of Religious Affairs doesn't include my office in on its findings," said Jeff sarcastically. Brinn only nodded, a curious look on his face.

Jeff found himself liking the old-timer. "Well, I'd better go," he said, edging past Brinn toward the door. "I appreciate your time. Would you tell Mr. Carey that I'll try to touch base with him next week sometime?"

Brinn made no effort to move aside. Instead, he gripped Jeff's elbow with such a surprising strength that Jeff was forced to turn and face him. Brinn's eyes were boring into him, as if trying to read his mind. After a moment, he released his grip on his elbow. "You say you're with the FBI?" asked Brinn softly.

"Yes," answered Jeff in the same tone. *What did he want?*

"And you're not connected with those people, the Bureau of Religious Affairs?"

"Not at all," replied Jeff. His heart began to beat faster. He could sense that Brinn wanted to tell him something — something that could be important. Brinn simply looked up at him for a moment, as if struggling to make a decision.

"Walk with me for a minute," he said finally. He opened the door and motioned for Jeff to follow. Jeff found himself being led through the middle of the airport. The crowd was sparse at that time of day, and no one seemed to take notice of them. He followed Brinn out of the terminal and through an access passage. This led to a large room full of conveyer belts that were humming away, carrying all sorts of baggage. The din from the machinery was almost deafening. They crossed through to the other side. Now Brinn led him through a series of double doors, the last one ending in a stairwell. Jeff stopped abruptly.

"Where are we going?" he asked as Brinn started down the stairs.

"Just a little further," replied Brinn. He turned to face Jeff. "The bureau took things apart after the bombing," he said, his voice echoing in the stairwell. "They confiscated *everything*. Not only that, but I think they're behind Mr. Rooney leaving. He was my friend as well as my boss. A few days before he quit, he gave me something. He said to give it to someone I could trust — someone in a position to do something." He turned and headed down the staircase. "From talking to you, Agent Anderson, I can tell that you've got no love for the bureau. I think maybe you need to see what it is that I got."

"What is it?" asked Jeff cautiously. Brinn might trust him, but he wasn't sure that he trusted Brinn.

"I can't tell you," was the answer. "I have to show you. This way — just down these stairs." Brinn continued down, and Jeff had no choice but to follow. The stairs emptied out into a long underground hall lit by rows of fluorescent lights. Jeff was led about halfway down the hall to a single door. Brinn produced a key and opened it, disappearing inside. Jeff followed, and found himself inside an air handling room. The gigantic machinery was running, making a sound that was similar to television "white" noise. Brinn had to shout in order to be heard.

"When Flight 407 blew up, Mr. Rooney immediately pulled all the logs for that night. He figured he would have to hand them over sooner or later, but he wanted to get a look at them himself, just in case he saw something that others might miss."

Brinn paused, then went on grimly. "Well, he saw something, all right. And whatever it was, it caused him to disappear. He didn't just quit. He wasn't that kind of a man. He just didn't show up for work one day. They found a resignation letter on the airport manager's desk, typewritten, with his signature."

Brinn shook his head. "He was forced to quit," he said, his tone allowing no argument. "Just before he left, he gave me this." Brinn opened a small panel on the side of the air handler and pulled out a small package the size of a credit card and about one quarter of an inch thick. It was wrapped in brown paper and tied tightly with string. He handed it to Jeff.

"Go on, open it," encouraged the security guard. Jeff did so, and found himself holding a tiny video cassette. He looked at Brinn questioningly.

"Mr. Rooney made copies of the boarding logs for Flight 407," said Brinn. "I've seen them myself." He looked hard at Jeff. "I'm taking a big chance giving them to you. For all I know, you could be with the bureau. I don't think so, but you could be. What's on there is dangerous to whoever holds it."

"Why?" asked Jeff, weighing the cassette in his hand. "What *is* on it?"

Brinn shook his head negatively. "You'll see for yourself. Now you've got to leave. Think you can find your way back out?"

"Sure," said Jeff. "Aren't you coming with me?"

"Nope," replied Brinn. "I'll wait here for awhile, then head back to 'C' terminal. That's where I'm on duty. You just get out of here and take a look at that tape."

"All right," said Jeff. He turned to go, but stopped. He reached into his jacket pocket and pulled out his card. "If you need me, call me at that number," he said, handing it to Brinn. "But do me a favor. Memorize the number and lose the card. Okay?"

"Thanks," said Brinn. "With all that's been going on here, I may just need it."

Again Jeff turned to go, but had to stop one more time. The aging security guard had taken a huge chance in trusting him. Jeff found himself liking him, and he could not leave without sharing the love of his Lord. "You seem like a good man," he began. "Have you ever made peace with God? If you were to die tonight, do you know where you would spend eternity?"

Brinn looked at Jeff as if he had just turned into a cobra and was ready to strike. "Sheeesh!" he exclaimed. "You must be crazy! I've already done enough to get myself in deep trouble. Now you want me to get religion? Are you crazy? In this day and age?" He shook his head violently. "Go on, get out of here. I don't need any of that."

Jeff opened his mouth to reply, but Brinn pushed him toward the door.

"I said get! I don't want no more trouble. I've done enough. Go on. Go!" With that, Jeff found himself back in the hall. He felt a deep sense of regret at Brinn's attitude. Brinn was a good man, but being a good man just wasn't enough. Sadly Jeff shook his head and headed back the way he had came in. He had no trouble finding his way out of the airport, and soon he was on his way back toward the office.

❖ ❖ ❖

Most of the day staff had left by the time Jeff returned to his office. Only a skeleton crew remained on duty during the night, taking calls and responding to emergencies. He rode the elevator up to the fifth floor where his office was located, glad for the emptiness of the building. Even his secretary had left for the day.

He shut and locked his door, and even though he was high above the streets below, he pulled the blinds over the single window. Turning on his small desk light, he pulled out the cassette. He turned it over in his fingers for a moment, then set it on top of his desk. Reaching into the bottom drawer, he pulled out a portable hand held VCR. Slipping the cassette into the opening he pushed the play button.

"Okay, Mr. Rooney," he said softly. "Let's see what was so important that it caused you to make an illegal dub of those logs." He turned on the play button and sat back. The tiny screen on the VCR came to life. It took him a moment to orient himself to the view. He was looking down on the boarding area. The camera was placed directly above the gate, allowing it to record the faces of each passenger as they went past. The lens on the camera was wide angled, giving a fisheyed effect. He could see the entire section. At the bottom right hand side of the screen, the time was superimposed. It read 7:00 a.m., a good hour before the flight departed. He fast forwarded until the clock read 7:45 and pushed play again.

Now the passengers were beginning to board. Jeff watched as they filed in orderly fashion through the gate. Suddenly his attention centered on a familiar face. There in the lower part of the screen was Scott Sampson. He was walking toward the gate, arm in arm with someone who was obviously his wife. Both were standing so that they were facing the camera.

"Beth Sampson, I presume," he said softly. He watched as the couple stood there looking at the gate. They clung to each other tightly, not wanting to let go but knowing they must. It gave Jeff a profound sense of regret as he watched the tragedy play itself out on the screen — especially since he knew the end of the story. The two lovers tore themselves apart. Beth walked quickly through the gate and disappeared. Scott stood there watching, a total picture of dejection. Beth must have turned and waved just before she stepped on board, for Scott raised his hand in farewell. He held it there for just a moment, then lowered it.

"My friend, I am truly sorry," whispered Jeff quietly. A single tear found its way down his dark cheek. He had never married, but he did know what it was like to say goodbye to someone he loved. Even on that tiny screen he could feel Scott's pain.

The tape continued to play. Scott turned away from the camera and seemed to be speaking to someone. Jeff frowned and rewound the tape, watching the sequence again. Sure enough, Scott was talking as if someone was standing directly behind him. The only problem was, *there was no one there!* In fact, no one was standing within several feet of him. Strange. Jeff rewound the tape and viewed it one more time, but could see nothing new. Filing it away in his mind with "things to be checked out later," he let the tape roll.

Another five minutes went by. Scott was gone, heading into the worst time of his life, and the rest of the passengers had boarded. An attendant whom Jeff recognized from his file as Delmont was standing at the check-in desk, finishing up his work. Everything appeared normal. Jeff was just about to fast forward again when suddenly things began to happen. As he watched, four men in dark suits rushed into the boarding area. One of them stopped only long enough to flash some sort of identification to the attendant, then quickly caught up with the others. They headed straight for the camera, and then disappeared through the gate. *Just what was going on?* wondered Jeff as the tape continued to play. The boarding area was empty now except for the attendants. Delmont's co-workers had now stepped into the frame, their curiosity evident. They didn't have to wait long. Within just a few minutes the four men reappeared. This time, they had someone else with them.

"Oh, God," whispered Jeff. The way he said it, it was a prayer. Although her back was now toward the camera, Jeff had no trouble recognizing Beth Sampson. She was practically carried off the plane. Two men on either side held her arms, while the other two walked in front. Beth was a picture of utter defeat. She sagged against her captors, only to be yanked upright. Quickly and efficiently, she was escorted out of camera range. Jeff could only stare at the screen.

Scott's wife had not been on that plane when it had exploded! She had been taken off by these — these men.

Quickly Jeff rewound the tape to just before they barged into the boarding area. He watched carefully as they reappeared. When the one flashed his I.D., he stopped the tape, freezing the image. Unfortunately, the resolution was not good enough to be able to recognize the type of identification. *Well,* he thought, *there were ways around that.* He inched the tape forward frame by frame, taking in every detail of the four men. He did not recognize them.

"Okay," he said quietly, "let's see what we can find out about you." So saying, he fished out a special cord from the bottom desk drawer and plugged it in to the VCR. The other end went into the computer. He activated the screen and called up the video enhancement program. When the computer came on line, he fed the images of the four men into it, instructing it to record them for later. Then he stopped the tape where the one man displayed his identification. Freezing the video, he placed the cursor on the I.D. itself. He then gave the command to enlarge it 100 times. The computer recorded the image, then signaled that it was working. Jeff sat back and waited. The enhancement program had helped him on a number of occasions. Although not admissible in court due to the wide margin of error, it nevertheless had identified more than one suspect well enough to at least give him a start.

Within five minutes, the program ran its course. He punched in the necessary codes in order to call up the enhanced video, and then watched as it appeared on the screen. It didn't come up all at once, but rather line by line on the computer screen, from top to bottom. Long before it was finished, though, Jeff's suspicions and fears were confirmed. Although the computer was not able to bring out the man's name, the name of the organization at the top of the card was clear and legible.

"So the bureau caught up with you, Beth," he said softly. "You almost made it, too. I'm sorry. Now the question is, what do I tell Scott?"

Best leave that problem for tomorrow, he decided. He needed to let Helen in on this. It was too risky to contact her directly, he knew. If the Bureau of Religious Affairs was sending someone to talk to him, he needed to be extra careful. The safest way to tell her would be through the network. He unplugged the VCR from the computer and started to remove the cassette. On impulse, however, he decided to watch the tape one more time. Seeing Beth removed from the plane was certainly a shock, but it wasn't enough to cause four airport attendants and a security chief to up and disappear. There must be something else.

Jeff did not like the thoughts that were hanging in the back of his mind. They were so outrageous, so frightening that he did not even want to recognize them as suspicions. Once more he sat through that five minute segment of tape. He watched every detail as the agents boarded and then returned with their captive. Suddenly, what he was looking for jumped up and bit him in the face. Unbelievingly he watched the sequence yet again.

"I must be blind," he said in amazement. He had found what he was looking for. Four agents boarded ill-fated Flight 407. One of them was carrying a small briefcase. Four agents then returned, with one very frightened young woman in the middle of them, only now, there was no briefcase. The pieces finally all came together in Jeff's mind and formed a very ugly picture. It all added up. Now at last he understood why airport personnel had disappeared. He also knew why he had been unable to obtain the boarding logs. This was not a terrorist action. The Christian Liberation Front was running wild in the United States, having just assassinated another congressman along with a federal judge. They were *not,* however, responsible for the bombing of Flight 407.

Jeff rubbed his eyes, feeling tired beyond his years. He understood now what was going on. The Bureau of Religious Affairs had used Flight 407 to extend their authority and influence, but Jeff now knew that the bureau was *responsible* for that very same flight going up in flames.

During his career with the FBI, Jeff had seen all sorts of heinous crimes. Murders, kidnappings, even corruption inside his own department. Whatever evil could be imagined in the mind of man he thought he had seen. This was different. The Bureau of Religious Affairs was the single most powerful agency in the United States, and they were blowing up airplanes. This didn't just indicate some power-hungry individual trying to gain influence. This pointed to a conspiracy of massive proportions.

Up until now, in his work with the Shepherd's Path, he had seen those who were persecuting Christians as not necessarily evil, just misguided. The United States government was still a democracy — albeit just barely. There was always the slender hope that things could reverse themselves. Even the Bureau of Religious Affairs could be brought back under control. Or so he had hoped. This tape changed everything. An arm of the government that was supposed to be enforcing laws was in fact making them. The checks and balances of democracy were no longer in place.

Suddenly the vague suspicions that had been nagging Jeff for years coalesced and solidified. He had told Helen years ago that it seemed as if some single force was guiding America on its present course. Even with good men and women in important seats of government, things continued to get worse.

Jeff had always been good at deductive reasoning, and he had an uncanny ability to make strong, intuitive leaps based on limited information. He made one of those leaps now. Logic told him that the bureau was not only enforcing policy, it was *making* policy. Intuition made him ask just who it was that was controlling the bureau. Someone, or a group of someones, was pulling the strings.

"Okay, first things first," he said to his empty office. He once again activated his computer and, using the procedure he had designed years ago, accessed the Network. This was the nerve center of the Shepherd's Path. A nationwide computer network linking thousands of individuals and groups, it existed right under the collective noses of those who would snuff it out. Over the years it had been an invaluable tool. Jeff found the file that was reserved for Helen's use alone. When he opened it, he saw that she had not yet logged on for that day. Good. That meant that she would be accessing it before the night was over. She would find his message waiting for her.

Slowly he began to type a carefully worded message. The code that they had worked out was limited, and he could only give her the bare bones of what he had discovered. They would have to talk soon.

❖ ❖ ❖

Deep inside the electronic bowels of the FBI headquarters, a tiny relay received a short burst of information. It sat thinking about it for awhile — almost one-third of a second — and then acted according to its programming. It was instructed to observe all computer activity, and to trigger a warning should certain conditions arise. They did.

The relay triggered a single phone line, entering a pre-set number. It was answered almost immediately on the other end. There was a micro seconds' exchange of recognition codes.

Then this second computer, almost one thousand miles away, in Washington, DC, began to access the FBI mainframe. Burrowing deep into its heart, it bypassed with ease the security systems. Like a technological vampire, it began to drain information. Soon, it started to flash its "I have something interesting" signal.

Now, for the first time, human beings were brought into the picture. One agent, Stephen Lynch, was informed that the "tattletale" he had had planted in the FBI computer was activated. Lynch was en route to Cincinnati by plane to meet with FBI agent Jeff Anderson. Suspicions had been aroused when Anderson had started asking the wrong questions. Now those suspicions were confirmed.

Lynch watched as the readout of his handheld computer informed him of Anderson's illicit computer activities. Lynch was a professional, and as such admired professional work. He was impressed that Anderson had somehow managed to acquire classified information relating to bureau investigations. He was also interested to see that Anderson was using some sort of public billboard. Quickly he entered a set of commands on his keyboard. He instructed the tattletale to break into the billboard and access whatever information was there. The plucky little program got to work.

Well, Mr. Anderson, we will have much to talk about when we meet, he thought. He made sure that the tattletale was still in place, then signed off.

❖ ❖ ❖

Jeff finished typing his message to Helen and was about to sign off when a small red dot in the upper left hand corner of the screen began flashing.

"What th. . . .?" The question went unanswered when he realized what was happening. His throat went dry. It was the "bug alert" he had installed a while back. It was designed to warn him of someone tapping into his guarded files, and right now, it was doing just that.

"No!" Quickly he began to use the keyboard. His first impulse was to shut down, but he knew that that would not work. Just shutting down his terminal would solve nothing. The source of the leak had to be traced and expunged immediately. If he let it go, sooner or later the bug would access every piece of information he had hidden. That meant a large part of the Shepherd's Path would be compromised. Jeff was not a man given to panic, but for the first time in a long time, he felt a hint of fear as he tried to trace the source of the intrusion. In a way he welcomed it. The extra surge of adrenaline caused him to think faster and clearer.

"Come on, come on," he whispered savagely as his fingers flew over the keyboard. He put the "bug alert" through its paces over and over. Nothing. There was nothing in the system that should not be there. The little dot disagreed. It continued to flash, warning of a breech in the system.

"Think! THINK!" he whispered savagely to himself, trying to find an answer. Then — "Of Course!" Like a shot he was out of the office and heading down the hall. The elevator was still there, but he took the stairs instead. As he bounded down them two at a time, he tried to remember where the main junction was that tied the mainframe to the outside phone lines.

Within less than a minute, he had reached the basement. Urgently he traced the ducts that ran in all directions, looking for his goal. He found it almost immediately. The main junction was set into the wall, almost three feet off the floor, looking like a fuse box. Quickly he tore it open. He was not a technician, but he had a broad working knowledge of electronics. The computer told him that there was no intrusive program working from the inside. That meant that the bug was physical in nature, probably some sort of relay. It would be activating a line to another computer that in turn would access this one. A simple and elegant plan. The most disturbing part of it was, someone inside this building had to have planted it.

He scanned down the long rows of wiring. He had a good idea of what he was looking for. It was part of his training. If it existed, it had to be here. There! Once he saw it, it was obvious. Smaller than a thumbnail, it rested between two sets of wires, joining them. Without hesitation, he reached down and tore it off. He took just a moment to study it. A tattletale! He had used them himself. They were simple, easy to install, and frighteningly effective.

There wasn't a moment to lose. He checked once more to make sure there were no other relays, then sprinted back toward the stairs.

Jeff was in excellent shape, but even he could get winded taking five flights of stairs at a gallop. By the time he got back to his office, he was gasping for breath. Falling into his chair, he swung over to face the monitor. Sure enough, the red dot had stopped flashing. Utter relief flooded through him, followed immediately by sharp concern. Just how much had the intruder gotten hold of? There was no way to tell without tapping into the network, and he would not take the risk. The presence of one tattletale said that there could be another. He was not about to jeopardize his brothers and sisters in Christ until he had a system by system check run on the whole mainframe.

Slowly his breathing quieted. He began to pay for the adrenaline rush that had energized him just a few moments before. He put his head in his hands, feeling his whole body tremble.

"Man," he said to himself, "there's got to be an easier way to make a living!" The bit of forced humor did little to alleviate the blanket of concern that had settled over him. Even now, the worst of the situation came home to him. Somebody knew! Somebody knew about the computer network that linked the Shepherd's Path! That meant that they probably knew about the Shepherd's Path as well. Even if no information had been stolen just now, whoever was on the receiving end of that relay knew there was something there.

A soft groan escaped Jeff's lips. No matter how good security was, any computer system could be broken into in time. Not only that, but he himself was now a suspect. When this Lynch arrived, he would do more than question him. He would probably have him arrested on the spot. There could already be a warrant out for him now. Maybe it was time to run after all. He could access one of the ready-made identities from any public terminal. Then he could have new I.D.s forged within. . . .

"Oh no!" Jeff felt utter despair. Like a lightning bolt, it hit him. He had been on line with Helen's personal file when he had discovered the tattletale. If they could trace that. . . .

"Helen!" There was no time to worry about the cost now. He had to get in touch with her fast! He activated his vid-phone and punched in the number. Years ago he had insisted that she get a video line herself. Part telephone, part fax, part computer, it was quite useful in their work. Now, he hoped desperately, it would save her life. "Oh God," he prayed more fervently than he ever had in his life, "let me get to her in time. Please!"

❖ ❖ ❖

Once again, Agent Lynch was interrupted during his flight to Cincinnati by the persistent beeping of his port-a-comp. He flipped open the plastic cover and punched in his name and access code with the tiny keyboard.

The two pieces of information displayed caused his eyebrows to go up a notch. One was the name of the person to whom Anderson had been trying to communicate. The other. . . .

"So, Mr. Anderson, you discovered the tattletale. I'm impressed." Indeed, he knew he was dealing with a formidable opponent. Checking the time, he saw that it would be another 30 minutes until he landed. That made it at least an hour before he would arrive at FBI headquarters in the city. Far too long. A man of Anderson's talents would be long gone by then. He pulled out a small handset and plugged it into the port-a-comp. Activating a direct line to the Bureau of Religious Affairs office in Cincinnati, he was soon talking to the local chief.

"Get a warrant out for Agent Jeff Anderson," he told him. "I want him picked up immediately. Tell your people to use caution. He's a suspected member of the Christian Liberation Front. He will be armed and most certainly dangerous. As of five minutes ago, he was in his office. You should have the address." There was a short pause as the bureau chief verified this information.

"Done," came the harsh voice. "What next?" Although Lynch had never met the man, he pictured a stern, severe-looking man in his late forties.

"An even bigger fish," he replied. "Her name is Helen Bradley." He touched a control on the keypad. "You should be receiving the information now." Again there was a pause.

"I've got it," said the chief. "Hmmmm. Just a moment, Mr. Lynch." Lynch leaned back into the comfortable padded flight chair, waiting. Two minutes passed, then. . . .

"The warrants have been issued, Mr. Lynch," said the chief. "It turns out that Helen Bradley is already on file here. She was married to an evangelist some years ago, and so had to register with us."

"Interesting," commented Lynch.

"Yes, sir. I've already assigned personnel to both cases. They're on their way now."

"Good," said Lynch. "I'll be there in less than an hour. Until then, keep me informed." He broke the connection and snapped shut the port-a-comp. Things were going faster than expected. With any luck, he would be able to nail a major part of the Christian Liberation Front by tonight. That should please his superiors. It certainly pleased him. A cold anger was burning deep his heart. It had been there ever since he had lost a fellow agent in that bombing that had killed Senator Kline's secretary. It was about time to even the score.

❖ ❖ ❖

Helen returned from the store later in the day than she had planned. Lines at the supermarket were getting worse. Even with food coupons, she was never assured of getting the supplies she needed. Government officials and media people weren't calling it a famine yet, but it was only a matter of time. With the breadbasket of the country still drought-stricken, things would continue to get steadily worse. Wistfully she thought of the succulent Sunday roasts she used to fix for her family. She could almost smell the odors of cooked meat and potatoes mixed with the sounds of family gathering for a time of togetherness. These days, one was fortunate to get a bit of horseflesh every now and then. Even as she thought these thoughts, she chided herself. With all that was happening, she had not gone hungry yet. The Lord had supplied, and would continue to supply. She had no cause for complaint.

She was actually smiling as she gathered her two bags from the back seat of the car and headed for the front door. Things might be materially tough, but spiritually the harvest was being reaped at an astonishing rate. True, this past month six small churches had been stamped out, its members ruthlessly carted off to who knew where. Reports of brutality against believers were common, and there had been a steady stream of refugees using the Shepherd's Path. Still, the Spirit was moving in a great way. Souls were being added to the kingdom of God at an astonishing rate. The more the government pushed, the more the family of God grew. As it always had since its birth, the Church thrived on adversity.

Helen felt a moment's pride as she opened the door to her house. In the last year, thousands of Bibles had been distributed through the network, and hundreds of believers moved to places of relative safety. For some reason, she thought of Scott Sampson. That young man personified everything the Shepherd's Path stood for. Just an average human being, reared in a soft, middle-class society, he nevertheless had a deep, hidden courage that only needed a dash of adversity to bring out. He had already demonstrated that courage more than once. She wondered where he was now, and what he was doing. Her thoughts were interrupted by the shrill electronic noise of her vid-phone. Dropping her groceries on the kitchen counter, she went over to where the vid-phone sat on the table and activated the screen.

She was more than a little surprised to see Jeff's face staring anxiously at her. A chill of fear made her shiver. He never called her. He would consider it a dangerous breach of security. Something must be terribly wrong.

"Helen!" Jeff didn't wait for her to speak. "Thank God! Listen. Someone, I think it's the Bureau of Religious Affairs, has tapped into the network. I don't know how much they know, but I'm almost positive they're on to both of us. You've got to get out of there and in to one of the safe houses." Helen sat down in one of the kitchen chairs heavily. It took a moment for the full impact of what Jeff had just told her to set in. Discovered? Somehow it didn't seem possible.

"Helen? Did you hear me? You've got to get out of there. Now!"

"Jeff," her voice was almost a whisper, "are you sure?" She couldn't bring herself to believe it.

"Positive," answered Jeff. "I've already taken a big risk in contacting you. Get out. Get to a safe house, and wait. I'll find you. I promise. We'll disappear into the network and keep our heads low for a while, but we've got to move now. Do you understand?"

"I understand, Jeff," replied Helen heavily. She was quite resilient when she had to be. The initial shock of Jeff's news was already wearing off and she was mentally making plans for her escape.

"Good," nodded Jeff. "I'll get out of here and get things rolling. Don't worry. I promise that we'll. . . ." and the line went dead. Helen stared at the blank screen for a moment, then jumped up from the table. She knew that she could have minutes, maybe less to get out of her house. Already it might be too late. If the call had been disconnected from this end, they were probably already here. She grabbed her car keys and headed for the front door. No time to pack, no time for anything. Just get to the car and go. She would drive to a public parking lot and leave it. From there she could take a bus to one of the many safe houses she knew about.

Her keys jingling in her hand, she opened the front door — and ran headlong into two dark suited men. They were simply waiting for her. There was no talking — no "you are under arrest" speech. She wasn't even read her rights. As far as the government was concerned, she had no rights. Instead, they each took an arm and escorted her to their car, which was blocking hers in the driveway. Once there, she was handcuffed and made to sit in the back seat.

Through it all, Helen said nothing. There was no need. She thought of her Saviour as He was being crucified. He hadn't said anything either. There was no better example to follow. They had her. There was no hope of escape, no chance of letting anyone know that she was in custody. She could only hope that Jeff had gotten away.

The two agents got into the front seat, and she was driven away from the only home she had known for 40 years. It was over.

❖   ❖   ❖

Jeff was closer to cursing now than he had ever been during his Christian life. Ten seconds ago he had been talking to one of his best friends, warning her of impending disaster. Then the line went dead. If it had been cut at her home, then she was already in custody. If the connection was broken from this end, he estimated that he had minutes of freedom left. He had to get out of there, and fast.

He wanted nothing more than to rush over to Helen's home. If she was there, he would get her to a safe house. If she wasn't, he would find out where she had been taken — somehow. The problem was, he knew that was *not* what he should be doing. Helen would be the first to agree — the Shepherd's Path came first.

If he tried to rescue her now, while the computer network was being breached, a lot of good people would suffer. He had to prevent that now, before irreparable damage was done. The network had to be destroyed, the system crashed, and he was the only one with the time and tools to accomplish it. It was a bitter pill to swallow.

"Then get on with it, idiot," he said aloud. His voice was harsh in his own ears. He had designed this system to aid fellow believers. Now he would wreck it. For the last time, he activated his terminal. It took only moments to access the community billboard. He went through the recognition sequence quickly, trying to ward off the feeling that he was murdering an old friend. A lot of people had been helped by its information.

He finished the sequence and accessed the system. There it was — all the information he needed to travel to wherever he wanted to go in relative safety. False I.D.s, safe houses, hundreds of churches across the nation, this month's recognition verses — everything. He sat looking at it for a moment, then, fingers trembling, he typed in a single command — ARMAGEDDON. He hesitated before pushing the enter button. When he did, there would be no second chance. The computer would not ask "Are you sure?" Once entered, the password would activate a virus that had lain dormant these many years. It would quickly infest the local system here in Cincinnati. Then, via the phone lines, it would transmit itself to every public access billboard in the nation. It would only affect the Shepherd's Path network. Within hours, the entire system would cease to exist.

He pushed the button. Years to build, and seconds to destroy. The screen went blank. For some absurd reason, he felt there should have been something else. Warning sirens going off, lights flashing, some indication that an important tool had been lost. Instead he just sat and looked at a blank screen. He was jarred out of his thoughts by the beeping of his watch. It was six o'clock. Time to go. He had fulfilled his duty to the Shepherd's Path. By performing the amputation, he had saved its life, at least for the moment. Now it was time to try to reach Helen, and see to their safety.

Quickly he rifled through his desk, making sure that there was nothing there that could incriminate anyone involved with the Shepherd's Path. Carefully he wrapped the airport tape back up and stuffed it in his pocket. He wasn't quite sure what to do with it. It wasn't legal evidence, but, in the right hands, it could be very convincing. The problem would be to find those right hands. Then he got up from his desk and headed for the door. Just before he left, he paused to take a last look around. There was a time when all he wanted was to be an agent for the FBI. He had considered it the ultimate accomplishment in his life when he had been named head of this local office. Now, he knew better. There were higher callings, and better things to devote one's life to. He would never regret his decision to follow Jesus Christ, no matter what the cost. He turned off the light, and, without looking back, walked away.

❖   ❖   ❖

Once inside his car, Jeff made straight for Helen's house. He knew that he was probably heading into a trap, but he didn't care. He had to know, one way or the other, what had happened to her. He thought about using official FBI channels, but decided against it. If the Bureau of Religious Affairs was after him, his own people would soon be right behind. True, there were several Christians on his staff, but now all of them would be closely watched. The rest would be hurt and angered by what they would consider a betrayal. He would have to stay a step ahead of them if possible.

On the way, he turned on his car communicator, but found only static. *So it's starting already,* he thought to himself. Just to be sure, he tried his hand-held communicator and found the same result. His com-channel had been shut down. He was cut off. That meant that pursuit would be close behind. He would have to make this quick.

He reached Helen's without incident. Her car was still in the driveway, and for a moment he had a wild hope that she still might be inside. Quickly he got out of the car and practically ran to the front door. It was open, and without hesitation he stepped inside.

"Helen! Helen, are you here?" His shouted call only met with silence. He rapidly searched the house and found nothing. His worst fears were confirmed when he saw two bags of groceries sitting on the kitchen table. She was gone. There was nothing to do now but try to make good his escape. If she had gotten out, he would know sooner or later. If she was captured, he would try to find her. He still had many resources he could utilize. It wasn't over yet.

He spotted Helen's keys on the table where she had left them, and scooped them up. He would take her car, leaving his here. It might buy him a few hours. Within minutes he had switched his car for Helen's and was off again. He had only driven a short distance when he saw that he was being followed. Jeff had been an excellent field agent before he became deskbound. Those tailing him were very clever and very subtle. They were using at least three different vehicles, but he nonetheless spotted them. Of course they were following him, he realized. They had been waiting for him at Helen's. He had incriminated himself just by going there. That meant they had Helen. It also meant that they were expecting him to run. They would follow him, hoping that he would compromise more of the Shepherd's Path.

"All right," he whispered through gritted teeth. "All right, you want me? Then see if you can keep up." He made it out of the neighborhood and set a course back toward Covington. He felt fairly confident that he could lose his pursuers in the maze of back streets and alleys. Keeping an eye on his rearview mirror, he eased the car up to the speed limit. Sure enough, they stayed with him. He had them pegged.

The first vehicle was an old beat up pickup, at least 10 years old. Although it looked decrepit, Jeff had no doubt it could leave Helen's station wagon in the dust. He could tell just by looking that it was modified for pursuit. The second was a silver compact car — a Sussex — one of the newer models, and the third was a sporty red Corvette.

Jeff watched as they took turns following him. Having been a follower on several occasions, he knew exactly what they were doing and how they were doing it. The pickup would tail him for a while, always staying a few cars back. Then the Sussex would appear from an intersecting street and join the pursuit. The pickup would then veer off and stay with them on a parallel street. That would last a few minutes, then the whole process would start again, this time with the red Corvette. It was a standard three car routine, and usually highly effective. Jeff was on to them though, and so had the advantage. He was relatively sure that he could lose them given enough time. He had only one major worry. It was possible, although unlikely, that the bureau might have called in satellite assistance. If that happened, he might as well park the car in front of the bureau's local office and give himself up.

Every city in the nation now had several surveillance satellites in high orbit above it. Each was capable of reading the title of a paperback book lying on the ground. He could not hide from that kind of technology.

Jeff didn't think this was the case, since he was being tailed. Why waste the time playing such an intricate cat and mouse game if they didn't have to? Satellite surveillance took time and planning. They probably couldn't swing it on short notice. He knew, though, that it could begin at any moment. The worst thing that could happen would be if those following him would suddenly disappear for no apparent reason. That would mean he was tagged with the satellite. He had to wrap this up fast.

He made it into the seedy section of Covington with his followers intact. He had tried a few small tricks on the way, although nothing flamboyant that would get their suspicions aroused. He just wanted to see if the boys were paying attention. They were. They stayed with him, all the time weaving their intricate pattern. Jeff felt like a mother duck leading three very unruly ducklings.

Things changed once he was inside the decrepit city. He was heading casually along a four lane street, staying with the flow of the light afternoon traffic. Suddenly, without warning, he hit the gas. Helen's car was no speedster, but the wagon did have a good sized engine. It surged forward, leaving his tailgaters in his wake.

"Okay, boys," he said aloud. "Playtime's over. Let's see how good you really are!" He gunned the car down the street, weaving haphazardly in and out of traffic. The angry blaring of auto horns followed him. In his rearview mirror he saw the Corvette gaining on him. On its best day, the wagon was no match for it, but Jeff had a few moves left.

He hit the brakes and yanked the wheel hard to the right. The car skidded, throwing him against the door. Smoke rose from the tires as the car fishtailed around. Again he floored the gas pedal, and the wagon was off again, this time in the opposite direction. He watched as the Corvette swung furiously around and started after him again. Jeff smiled as he imagined the conversation going on between the three cars. They must have expected him to run. Cut off from his headquarters, alone and vulnerable, he would head straight for other members of the network, expecting them to help him escape. He would unintentionally betray another part of the network. Now that plan was scrapped. They knew he had pegged them. They also knew that they were tailing a professional. Their only option was to bring him in now and let the interrogators get what they could out of him.

"Sorry, guys," he said to the gaining Corvette, "but I'm not going to play your game." With that, he swerved suddenly down an alley. He was taking a big gamble. Losing a tail like this was a little like playing chess. Not only did he have to know where his opponent was at all times, but he also had to anticipate his next several moves. He was fairly sure that the pickup and the Sussex were one street over, in the opposite direction. Nothing was for certain.

The wagon caromed down the narrow alley, its fenders scraping the concrete sides. Sparks flew as metal struck stone. Jeff winced at the thought that this wasn't his car, then put it out of his mind. Wherever she was, he doubted that Helen would care too much. The Vette stayed with him, matching him move for move. It was less than 20 yards away now. If he guessed wrong, either the Sussex or the pickup would be blocking the end of the alley just about now. He could see the entrance to the next street. It remained clear and open.

"Time to lose you," he said through his clenched teeth. He shot out of the alley and onto a potholed two lane street. Immediately he wrenched the car left, narrowly missing a Volvo on one side and the building on the other. There was no sign of the other two vehicles, but the Vette was still with him. He watched as it skidded out of the alley. It was more maneuverable than the wagon, and so had gained on him. *Time to get desperate,* he thought. He let the Vette get close. He could see the two agents in the front seat. Their faces were determined, and one of them was on the radio. Soon the Sussex and the pickup would be there as well. He felt under his jacket for his .45 pistol. Regulations demanded that he always carry it. Then he braced himself against the floorboard.

"Come on, come on, just a little bit closer." He urged the Corvette on, as if he were a spectator at a football game. The Vette drew nearer, coming to within a few feet of his bumper. Jeff waited for a beat longer. Then, he jerked his foot off the gas and hit the brake. The force jolted him against the shoulder strap. The men in the Corvette weren't so lucky. Their car was faster and could make the turns more easily, but it was also paper thin. Fiberglass met solid steel. The front end of the Vette crumpled like paper. Jeff was flung back against the headrest by the impact. He shook his head to clear it, then released the shoulder strap and opened the door. He knew he might have only seconds before the agents in the Corvette recovered. He jumped out of the wagon and pulled out his .45. In all his years with the FBI he had never been forced to take a life, and he didn't intend to start now. Aiming quickly and surely, he fired. Three lead slugs slammed into the vulnerable engine of the Vette. The fragile frame shuddered with the impact, and he could hear a hissing coming from somewhere inside of it. It would not be following *anyone* for a while.

The two agents looked stunned for a moment.

Then, faces set in grim determination, they pulled out their own weapons and began to climb out of their car. Jeff hopped back into the station wagon and gunned the engine. He could feel his heart pumping with the surge of speed. He took a deep breath to clear his head.

"One down, two to go," he said. He had to chuckle a little at the faces of the two agents. They had actually thought he was going to fire at them. Didn't they know *anything* about the people they were trying to stamp out? Obviously not! He turned right at the next intersection, then left at the next, all the while keeping watch for the other two vehicles. The gloves were off now, he knew. By simultaneously wrecking the Corvette and firing his weapon, he had changed the rules. Instead of wanting to arrest him, the other agents would now come out shooting. That meant stray bullets flying all over. An innocent bystander could very well get hurt. The only way to avoid that was to avoid his pursuers. He wished he was driving his own car. The communications gear inside it was sophisticated enough to tap into the bureau bands.

"Make do, Anderson," he lectured himself. "Make do." A sudden idea hit him, and he acted on it immediately. He knew Covington pretty well. Just two streets over should be what he was looking for. He cut across 14th Street, all the time looking for the Sussex or the pickup. Still no sign of them. It took him just two minutes to find what he was looking for. A five-story parking garage stood at the next intersection. At this time of day, and in this part of town, it was almost empty. He stopped just before the entrance ramp, and checked the area. He still had not seen the other two vehicles, and was beginning to get worried.

Either these guys were not all that good, or they had given up. Neither explanation sounded right. Could they have called in satellite surveillance after all?

"This is ridiculous," he said to no one in particular. "I'm going to have to go find the guys who are supposed to be following me!" He was about to do just that when the pickup rounded the corner just a few blocks ahead. Traffic here was almost non-existent, so they should see him immediately. He waited another second to make sure, then hit the gas. The tires squealed as he muscled the car into the garage. The wooden barrier was down, and he didn't have time to stop for a ticket. The barrier snapped as he hit it, the jagged edge that was left scraping along the length of the car. *Sorry Helen,* he thought. Chalk up one more scratch! He hit the up ramp going twice the recommended

The wagon protested as he wound upward. It wasn't built to take tight turns such as this, and more than once hit the concrete walls. Helen's car was beginning to acquire a bit of a weathered look! Jeff rolled down his window and listened. Sure enough, he could hear the squealing of tires over the racket he was making. The pickup was following. He had one shot at this before the Sussex arrived.

The wagon screeched to a stop on the fourth level. Getting his bearings quickly, he pulled the car up to the exit. Just then, the pickup burst up the ramp. The agents inside saw him. Jeff could see that one of them was on the communicator, undoubtedly telling those in the Sussex where he was. Soon they would be blocking the entrance to the garage. This had to work.

Jeff jumped out of the wagon and sprinted toward the stairs. He could hear the doors of the pickup opening. Just as he reached the exit, a section of the wall next to him exploded, sending shards of concrete everywhere. Somehow they missed his eyes, cutting into his cheeks instead. He could feel them burning as he threw open the door and slammed against the inside wall. He was just barely inside when another bullet followed, smashing into the opposite wall.

The door closed with agonizing slowness. Jeff could hear the footsteps of the two agents as they ran toward him. His only hope was if they assumed he was going to try to escape on foot. They had to hit the door on a dead run. He waited, heart pounding. The footsteps reached just outside the door. Then it was flung open and two youngish men spilled through. The force of their entry took them past Jeff, and they didn't see him for a moment. A moment was all he needed. The first agent went down with a blow to the back of the neck, unconscious but still breathing. The second turned, bringing his weapon around. Jeff saw that it was not a pistol, but a small machine gun. Not terribly accurate at a distance, but more than adequate in close quarters like this.

In Jeff's mind, seconds slowed to a crawl. He could see everything in perfect detail. The machine gun swung around to center on his chest, the face of the agent showing both triumph and terror. Jeff had never taken karate or judo, or any other exotic form of hand-to-hand combat, but he knew how to disarm someone. As the gun swung up at him, he moved forward toward the agent. Reaching across his body with his right hand, he grabbed the wrist that held the gun. In the same motion, he swiveled around, his back now facing his opponent. His elbow came up and thrust back, meeting solidly with the nose and mouth of the agent. He crumpled, letting go of the machine gun and falling to the floor. Jeff caught the weapon, and turned to face the fallen agent. There was no need. The poor man was bleeding fiercely from both nose and mouth, and he was down for the count.

Carefully Jeff felt for a pulse, and found a steady beat. No permanent damage. Satisfied, he examined the machine gun. Small and deadly, it glimmered in the dim light of the staircase. Carefully he removed the firing pin and then the ammo clip. He placed the now useless weapon on the lap of the agent, then searched the other. This one carried the conventional .45 pistol, a twin of Jeff's own. Again he removed the clip, searching the unconscious agents for spares. Each man had two extra, which he confiscated. He was about to leave when a sudden thought struck him. He remembered the Bible stories from his Sunday school days, particularly one about King Saul and soon-to-be King David.

Taking a deep breath, he pulled out his own pistol. Once more he removed the ammo clip and the firing pin. Then, carefully, he laid it on the agent's lap next to the machine gun. Digging into his pocket, he pulled out a withered copy of his own personal New Testament. He held it for a moment, almost caressing it. He had kept it in his desk, buried under a pile of other papers. It was dangerous to keep it there, certainly, but he could never bring himself to part with it. It was one of his most prized possessions. Opening it to the Book of John, he set it down on top of the machine gun. It looked totally out of place there, with so much lethal hardware, but somehow, he knew it was the right thing to do. It was time to go. He left the two agents there, sleeping peacefully. Let them digest his actions when they woke up!

The pickup was still running where the agents left it. Flipping a silent salute to the wagon for a job well done, he slipped inside the pickup and settled himself in. The whole incident in the staircase had taken less than five minutes. If he had guessed right, the Sussex would now be in place, blocking the exit to the garage. They had also probably called in backup. He knew the Bureau of Religious Affairs, though. They hated to use the local police. They would call on their own for help, and that would take a little time. He still had a chance to pull this off.

Carefully he maneuvered the pickup down the exit ramp. When he got to the first floor, he slowed to a crawl. By now, the agents out front would be getting anxious. They would be out of communication with their comrades, and not know what was going on. He planned to capitalize on their confusion. As he rounded the last turn, he opened the window and leaned out. Yes, the Sussex was there, right where he wanted it to be! It was now or never. He slammed the pickup into gear and hit the gas. It sprung forward with surprising power. He had guessed correctly in assuming it had been beefed up. It barrelled off the ramp and through the exit barrier. The last two agents were standing outside of their car, their weapons drawn and pointed right at him. Without hesitation, he caromed forward, catching the agents off guard. They had been expecting a station wagon, not one of their own vehicles running them down.

Just before it seemed he was going to hit the Sussex broadside, Jeff wrenched the wheel left. He had aimed precisely. The pickup smashed into the front fender of the Sussex, effectively taking out the wheel underneath. The pickup suffered damage, but it could still move. Jeff was tempted to wave at the agents as he drove off, but was too busy watching where he was going and dodging bullets at the same time. He was very glad that there was no one else on the street at the time!

Reaching the first intersection, he cut hard right. Now out of sight of the Sussex, he slowed down and contemplated what to do next. He knew that he had only won a brief respite. Soon the bureau would be hunting him again. Now that he had taken out six of their own, it would get a lot worse. He had to disappear, and now!

He ran through the location of the safe houses he knew about. There were seven relatively close by. If he could make it to one of those, he could plan his next move.

Suddenly, the enormity of all that had happened that day caught up with him. His trip to the airport, the discovery of the bureau's involvement in terrorist acts, seeing Scott's wife get off that plane — everything had happened at once! He had to get somewhere where he could have time to sort everything out. He made his decision. Just about 8 miles from here, in one of the few residential sections left in Covington, was the closest safe house. He would go there. He sped up a little, thinking about how to get there safely. One thing was certain — he could not leave a bureau vehicle parked in front of where he would be hiding! Just up ahead, a public bus was moving slowly in the same direction.

"Good enough," he told himself. He moved past the bus and found the next stop. Turning into a vacant dead end street, he parked the pickup out of sight. Throwing the keys as far from it as he could, he hurried to the stop. He arrived just as the bus pulled up. The door opened and he got on, breathing a sigh of relief that he had the correct change. The bus was not heading in the direction he wanted, but that was okay. He planned to go in several random directions before he set a course for the safe house. He settled back in the hard cushioned seat and watched the city go by.

❖ ❖ ❖

It was dark when he finally reached his destination. It was a simple, single story wood frame home, small and comfortable looking. The only way it differed from its companions was that it was somewhat better kept. Jeff checked the address with the number he had remembered, then opened the chain link fence that surrounded it and walked up to the front door.

Twenty years ago, this had been a nice neighborhood. Time and wear had taken its toll. Most of the houses he could see were fading fast, just like the rest of the city. He stood for a moment on the small porch, then knocked. Immediately a dog started barking from inside. Jeff could tell from the bark that it was a small dog and represented no threat. He could hear a shuffling sound, then silence. He knew he was being regarded through the peephole. He was suddenly conscious about the way he looked. His clothes were rumpled and unkempt, and the scratches in his cheeks from the bullet ricochet were burning slightly. At this time of night, in this neighborhood, he couldn't blame the residents for being wary. He waited for a moment, then knocked again. The dog, which had stopped barking, started again. This time he heard a "shush" that undoubtedly came from a human throat.

"Hello?" he called, trying to make his voice sound as unthreatening as possible.

"What do you want?" came an answer from inside. Male, he thought, probably mid-sixties.

He didn't waste time with explanations or pleasantries. Either he had the right house, or he didn't. There was only one way to find out.

"That which is born of the flesh is flesh, and that which is born of the Spirit is Spirit." He was quoting from the third chapter of John. Word had gone out over the now defunct computer network that recognition signals were to be taken from the first three chapters of John. He hoped that these people had got the message. There was a brief pause, then an answer.

"Do not marvel that I said to you, You must be born again." Instantly the door opened to reveal a short stoop-shouldered man who looked indeed to be in his mid-sixties. His skin was a shade or two darker than Jeff's, and his wrinkled face showed concern and bemusement.

"Don't just stand there, son," he said, "come on in." He moved away from the door and let Jeff pass. Jeff found himself ushered in to a tiny living room filled with the clutter that only years of living in the same place can bring.

"Have a seat," said the old man, pointing to a worn couch. Jeff sat down, easing back into the stiff cushions. The old man moved to sit across from him in a high backed chair. He studied the fugitive FBI agent for a moment.

"Looks like you've been through the ringer, son," he said, observing the cuts on Jeff's cheeks. Jeff only nodded.

"Well, I'll get you some stuff for that. You're on the run, I guess." Again Jeff agreed with a nod. "You can rest here," said the old man. "Been a lot of believers come through this old house. Haven't lost one yet. You sit there and relax, and I'll get you some spray. You hungry?"

"Very," replied Jeff, speaking for the first time. He hadn't eaten since lunch.

"I'll get us some food, then. I'm feeling a little empty myself." With that, the old man left the room. When he returned, he was carrying a first aid kit in one hand, and a bowl of delicious-smelling hot stew in the other.

For the next hour, he enjoyed the company of this very interesting man. He did not ask his name — that would not be safe — but that did not stop them from sharing experiences. Jeff felt as much at home here as he had at Helen's. He would be able to stay here for a few days at least. Somehow he would find a way to get a message to his fellow believers in his office. Then he would get a message to Scott about Beth, and above all, find out where Helen had been taken. Given time, he could. . . .

The front door of the tiny house was shattered. It flew open, breaking into several pieces. Six men rushed through the now broken door. Before he could react, Jeff found himself looking down the barrel of an entirely too big gun. The old man was trussed up quickly and half-carried out of his own house. Jeff had never seen the man holding the gun before. There was a look of triumph, and respect in his face.

"You're good, Anderson. I'll give you that," said the man. "You almost pulled it off. If you could have been quicker at the garage, you would have made it."

"How?" was all Jeff was able to ask.

The agent smiled and answered. "Big brother was on the case," he said, pointing to the sky. "We were able to get it on line just before you left the garage. Even then, you almost gave us the slip. Like I said, you're good."

The agent motioned to one of his cohorts, who promptly hauled Jeff to his feet and handcuffed him. Jeff didn't try to resist. There were too many of them, and he was too tired. They had used the satellite! Everything he had gone through was for nothing! His shoulders slumped in defeat. He was led to a car that sat alongside the road in front of the house. Just before he was pushed in, another agent came running up and spoke to the one in charge — the one that had complimented Jeff.

"Mr. Lynch, what should we do with the other one?" Before Lynch could answer, Jeff spoke up.

"He only wanted to help me," he said quietly to Lynch. "He can do you no harm."

Lynch regarded Jeff for a moment, then nodded to the agent.

"Let him go for now" he said. "We know where to find him again." The agent nodded, and left. Even with the shock of sudden capture, Jeff was surprised. He turned to face Lynch.

"Thanks," he said, meaning it. "You didn't have to do that."

Shrugging, Lynch replied, "He's small potatoes. You're the one we wanted. Besides, he's not going anywhere. Now get in."

Jeff was pushed into the back seat, the door slamming out his hope of escape. He leaned back and closed his eyes as the car drove off. He tried to pray, but could not form the words. His heart beat the question he could not bring himself to ask. Why had God allowed him to be caught now? If he had to be captured, why not before, in the garage, or at Helen's? Why was he allowed to endanger the old man? Why did he have to go through all of that? With these questions swirling around inside of his mind, he was taken off into the night.

Scott reclined the window seat in the rear of the bus back as far as it would go. With a tired sigh, he tried to arrange the lumps in the cushions to accommodate his body. His muscles ached in a dozen places, and his brain felt mushy and slow. The last three days had been a blur of open country roads, clandestine meetings, and quick, on-the-go meals. The meetings were an entire story in themselves. He had found himself in locations ranging from an abandoned cabin in the middle of nowhere to a classroom in a local high school. Each stop was unique, and would remain in his memory for the rest of his life.

His eyes closed with fatigue as the bus pulled out of Woodrow, a barely-there spot on the map that was worse in person. It seemed that the town had died, and just did not know it yet. It was a filthy, decaying place that made Scott want to find a bath and scrub his top three layers of skin off, just to be rid of the stench. It was well past midnight. Although he wasn't scheduled to leave until later that morning, his contacts here wanted him out of town as soon as possible. It seemed things were getting dangerous in the area, and no one wanted him around to draw attention. This had been the one low point of his journey so far. Apart from the ever present danger of being caught, Scott's trip had been one of the most satisfying experiences of his life — until now. His stay in Woodrow had not gone well. After the success of Cynthiana, and after that Somerset, it was a bitter disappointment.

He felt sleep tugging at the corners of his eyes and let his thoughts wander. The family that had sheltered him in Somerset popped into his mind. He had never learned their names, but they had treated him like one of their own. A husband, wife, and two teenage daughters, they lived in one of the few suburban communities that made up the area. He had been surprised when they had taken him to a meeting in broad daylight. He had ended up on a high school campus, just after noon. Seeing the students hurrying to and from classes brought back memories of his own carefree high school days. At least they seemed carefree to him now. Upon further reflection, however, he remembered dreading final exams, being left out of cliques, and a general feeling of loneliness. Once his memory was brought into sharper focus, he was very glad his high school days were over. He did *not* want to go through that volatile age again!

The steady hum of the bus motor lulled Scott, and his mind drifted back to the high school in Somerset. The school had been around for a long time. The plaque in front informed him that it was built in the early sixties. Once inside the three story main building, he had been led to a small classroom on the second floor. He remembered the distinctive odor that all schools acquire over the years. Part musty, part old, part body odor, it had struck a cord deep inside of him. In a way it had comforted him. It had felt good to know that some things had not changed beyond recognition — yet.

Inside the classroom there had been 23 people. Although Scott had been warned about the size of the group, he had still been surprised. After his disastrous experience in Covington, and the clandestine meeting in Cynthiana, he was astonished that these people could gather so openly, especially since he had been told that the principal was a devout atheist. He later discovered that several Christian teachers and the principal's secretary had spent months secretly manipulating the class schedule.

Officially, the meeting he attended was Human Development 101, a public sex education class. In addition to the regular students, many adults who were seeking their high school diplomas also attended. As far as the school was concerned, they were there to further their education. As far as those attending were concerned, they were there to worship their Lord. Scott had found it funny that the subject that had caused so much uproar among Christians in the previous decades was now being used to disguise a Bible-believing, fundamental church.

As he entered the classroom, one of the daughters had leaned over and whispered in his ear, telling him that he would be asked to speak. That should have put him on his guard, but he had only nodded and taken a seat close to the front. He was again surprised when he was called up right at the beginning. He expected everyone to open in prayer like Marshall Caine's group had done.

Instead he was asked to step forward and introduce himself.

Even though he had done it before, he was still trembling when he opened his suitcase and pulled out the small Bible. He held it up for all to see, but this time, there had been no gasps of astonishment like before, nor had they passed the Bible around from person to person. Scott had stood there, holding the Bible, not sure what to do next. He suddenly realized that these folks were expecting him to bring them a message. They did not know that this Bible was theirs! Somewhere along the line, communications had failed. They had known he was coming, but did not know why.

At a loss for words, he had simply handed the Bible to the group leader, a dark-haired slender man no older than 25. The leader had looked at him in confusion for a moment, then started to smile a very special smile. It was that smile that Scott was coming to look forward to at each stop. He had nodded a confirmation to the entire group, and suddenly was swamped by hugs and slaps on the back. Everyone, it seemed, wanted to touch him, to thank him. The rest of the time was spent reading Scripture and in prayer. The group feasted on passages from all over the Bible, reveling in their new treasure. Scott had accomplished his mission here and had made several life-long friends.

Then came Woodrow.

Bright and early the next day he was back on the bus headed south. He was full of confidence, thanks to the success he had enjoyed so far. He rolled into the small town early that afternoon. It was not quite what he had expected. Where Cynthiana was bright and cheerful, Woodrow was dull and lifeless. The same sun shone on both places, but there was an aura of heaviness that lay on the town, a feeling of doom and despair.

Following his instructions from Jeff, he had dialed the number he had memorized. It took a while for him to convince the person on the other end that he was genuine. Even answering several quotes from all over the Book of John didn't satisfy the old woman who had answered. Finally he was instructed to go to a certain abandoned farm house several miles outside of town and wait. Not wanting to take a cab or bus, he had walked the distance. It was after six when he finally got there. The farmhouse was indeed abandoned, the windows boarded and the front door padlocked. Tired from the walk, and not knowing what else to do, he found a place on the front porch where he could rest. From his vantage point, he had a wide-angle view of the country road but could not readily be seen.

He waited there for almost three hours. It was dark, and well past nine, when someone finally came for him. He had not eaten since before noon and was getting hungry. Unfortunately the old woman who showed up did not offer him anything to eat. Scott thought it was the same woman he had spoken to before, but could not be sure. She had driven up in a rickety old pickup truck with one headlight out. Cautiously she approached Scott, holding a flashlight in one hand and a small caliber pistol in the other. The pistol made Scott nervous. Still he tried. He squinted at the light shining directly into his eyes and smiled reassuringly, holding both hands in front of him. He was easily a good head taller than her, even taking into account her slight stoop.

She looked him up and down, as if pronouncing sentence. Finally she spoke. "You on the run, Boy?" she had asked in a low, rasping voice.

"I'm headed south," he replied, nodding. "Friends gave me your number before I left."

The woman continued to examine him, then shook her head. "You've come at the wrong time," she said flatly. "Things have been bad here. Two of my best friends disappeared last week. I'm probably next. Our group stopped meeting a few days ago. We decided to break up. I'm afraid we can't help you here."

Scott's heart had broken at the hopeless tone in the woman's voice. "Maybe I can help you, then," he replied, reaching very slowly into his hip pocket. He had removed a Bible from his suitcase before she had arrived, and now he pulled it out. Stepping forward, he held it out to her.

For a moment, she wavered. Then she took it from his outstretched hands. With the utmost gentleness, she flipped through the pages. In doing so, she moved the flashlight, pointing it upward. Scott got a glimpse of her wrinkled face and saw a struggle between conflicting emotions — part of her longing to hold the Bible, the other terrified of keeping it.

Finally, she pushed it back into his hands. "Sorry," she said roughly, "but I can't take this."

"I don't understand," began Scott. "I thought. . . ."

"You thought wrong," interrupted the woman, a dangerous edge in her voice. The pistol was not quite pointed at Scott, but not exactly pointed away either. The flashlight came back down and her face was once again in darkness.

"Do you know what's been going on here?" she asked. "We can't go out of our houses without looking over our shoulders. We don't dare speak to each other in public. We should have stopped meeting weeks ago. Maybe then my friends wouldn't have disappeared! You can't know what we've sacrificed!"

Scott sensed her disgust as she finished her speech. For a moment, he felt sympathy for her and for her plight. Then he remembered the unstoppable courage of Jeff Anderson, and the unflinching dedication of Helen Bradley. Those two were in positions to lose far more than this poor frightened woman, but they did not waver. He thought of his own sacrifice — the loss of his wife. His sympathy disappeared, to be replaced by pity. He remembered trying to encourage her, to convince her to take the Bible in spite of her fears, but she would have none of it. She had insisted that he be gone before the next day. Within an hour, he had found himself alone at the bus station, dropped off by the old woman without so much as a goodbye or God speed. She had simply driven off into the darkness. After a long two hour wait, he had boarded his bus and was off again. The visit to Woodrow had left a bad taste in his mouth.

He shifted his position in the passenger seat, trying to ignore his growling stomach. He had bought a soda and a bag of potato chips at the station, but the snack did not satisfy him for long. He tore his thoughts off Woodrow. The darkness was complete outside, broken only by the occasional homestead.

A melancholy loneliness settled over him as the trip progressed. The pain of losing Beth was always there, waiting for a quiet moment to come forward. He wished he had someone to talk to, to share that pain with. He wondered how Helen was, and Jeff. What were they doing at this moment? Probably, he knew, getting someone to safety, or sending out a load of Bibles to churches across the nation. Right then, he wanted nothing more than to be with them.

With an effort of will, he concentrated on the immediate future. His early departure from Woodrow had forced a change in plans. He would now arrive at his next stop, Hogansville, Georgia, at about three a.m. instead of the planned one p.m. the following afternoon. He didn't want to call anyone that early, so he would have to wait at the bus station for several hours. There was one good thing in this, he reflected. He had been somewhat apprehensive about traveling through Atlanta in the middle of the day.

Even after years of redesigning and rerouting, the big southern city still had mammoth traffic problems. Had he stayed with his original schedule, he would be getting there during the noon rush. Now he would get through in the middle of the night. The last thing he wanted was to be stuck in traffic in a major metropolitan area. He hadn't seen a newscast since leaving Covington, but according to Marshall Caine, they were still searching hard for him.

Slowly, the thrum of the bus and the darkness gently rocked Scott to sleep. His last thoughts were of the old woman in Woodrow. No doubt she, as well as her friends, had suffered. Still, it was heartbreaking that she had given up. Scott could understand. He remembered his own fear the night he and Beth had attended their meeting. It was something he had to wrestle with on a daily basis, but he had not given up. He only hoped that somehow that little old woman would find the courage to keep going. Being stamped out by the forces of the enemy was one thing — letting your light die because of fear was something else entirely.

❖ ❖ ❖

Scott awoke as the bus jerked to a stop. Slowly he came to, shaking the cobwebs out of his head. He looked out the window, and saw that it was still dark, and that he was at some sort of terminal. The harsh glare of the station lights caused him to squint. *Time flies when you're sleeping,* he thought as he gathered up his suitcase and made ready to leave. A quick check of his watch stopped him short. He had been asleep for less than two hours. This trip should have taken at least twice that long. Where was he? The voice of the driver suddenly came on over the speaker.

"Ladies and gentlemen, we're sorry for the delay, but due to circumstances beyond our control, we have been forced to make an unscheduled stop here in Atlanta. Hopefully we will be on our way in a matter of hours. For you that have connections to make, we apologize. The rest of the line has been notified, and arrangements are being made. We do ask that you remain seated until we have been cleared to leave. Thank you."

Scott sat back down heavily. Atlanta? He looked outside at the terminal, wondering what was happening. His question was answered all too soon. Two men in gray suits came out of the terminal and crossed the parking area to Scott's bus. As he watched, they came on board. Scott shifted his attention to the front, where they were now talking to the driver. He was beginning to get nervous.

The two men finished their conversation and began to move slowly down the aisle. They stopped at the second row of seats, where the first passengers sat. Leaning out into the aisle, he distinctly heard one of them say, "Identification, please."

Quickly Scott ducked back into his row. His mind was racing, trying to figure out what to do. He took a deep breath to calm himself. They might not be looking for him, he knew, but he wasn't about to take a chance on that. He pulled up his suitcase and held it close, watching as the two men came closer. There was nowhere to run. If they decided to take him in, and search his suitcase. . . .

Thinking fast, Scott opened the suitcase. The bus was only about half full, and no one was in his row. That, coupled with the darkness, might hide him long enough to hide the Bibles. He raised the false bottom just a few inches and stuck his hand into the hidden recess. Two at a time, he pulled out the remaining Bibles and stuffed them into the cracks between the seats. Then, setting his teeth, he pulled hard at the plastic false bottom. It wasn't hard to rip out, and Scott slid this underneath the seat next to him. Looking up, he saw that the two men were almost halfway to him. Quickly he closed the suitcase and placed it back down at his feet. He breathed a sigh of relief that he had kept it there and not in the compartments overhead. Heart pounding, he pulled out his phony identification and waited for the men to get to him. It didn't take long.

"Identification, please." The man spoke to Scott the same way he had spoken to the other passengers. He looked tired, and somewhat bored. Scott took this as a good sign. They must be checking all of the bus routes, not just this particular bus. The man was holding up a badge in a black leather wallet, signifying that he was with the Bureau of Religious Affairs. Hoping that the man would not notice the slight tremble to his hand, he dropped the plastic card into the outstretched palm. The man took it and inserted it into a piece of equipment about the size of a small radio. There was a moment's pause, then he handed it back.

"Thank you," he said, and returned to the front of the bus. Again there was a brief conversation with the driver and the two agents left, returning to the terminal. Scott considered fainting with relief, but decided against it. The bus was still not moving. This wasn't over yet.

Ten more minutes passed. Then, one of the agents returned. Scott could see that it was the one who had asked to see his identification. He boarded the bus, and spoke in a loud voice from the front.

"Ladies and gentlemen," he said, "We need to verify some of your identifications. Please do not be alarmed. This is strictly routine. As you have probably heard, there is a nationwide manhunt for a known terrorist. We have had reports that he could be headed in this direction, and so are checking all of the public transportation routes. Your cooperation is appreciated, and expected. Now, would the following persons please go inside the terminal. You will be instructed as to where to go from there." With this, the agent looked down at a clipboard he was carrying.

"Will Smith." A young man of about 20 got up from the front, looking rather scared. He squeezed past the agent and left the bus. "James Dover." Another young man, perhaps the companion of the first, followed. The agent resumed his task, calling out seven more names. Each one he called showed signs of surprise and fear. Scott held his breath as each name was called. He was beginning to hope that he would be passed over.

"Gregory Andropolos." The name hit him like a punch in the stomach. He let out a sharp sigh. Then, since he could do nothing else, he stood and walked forward. He left his suitcase by his seat. Perhaps he would pass the inspection and be able to return, but he doubted it.

Once inside the terminal, he saw the others who had been called off standing in a loose group next to the ticket counters. All of them looked frightened. As soon as he joined them, the second agent appeared and led them down a narrow hall. He stopped at the end where two doors faced each other on either side. Motioning for the group to go into one, he disappeared into the other. Scott followed, looking back the way he had come. The second agent was there, trailing after them.

The room was plain, the only furniture being hard metal and plastic chairs. The white walls blended almost perfectly with the white ceiling and white tile floor. There weren't enough chairs to seat everyone, so Scott motioned to one of the others to sit. He leaned against the wall opposite the door. The rest of the group spread themselves out, looking more confused than scared. Just a few minutes had passed when the first agent opened the door and stuck his head inside.

"Will Smith?" The young man stood and nodded. "This way, please," said the agent, and opened the door for him. Will left the room and the door was shut again. Scott wondered what was going on across the hall. Certainly some form of identification process. He looked around and saw that the chair that Mr. Smith had just vacated was in a direct line with the room next door. Maybe he could get a glimpse at what the agents were up to from there. He had no sooner sat down when the door opened again. The same agent leaned inside.

"James Dover," he said, and the second young man got up. The agent opened the door wider for Mr. Dover to pass through. For just a few seconds, Scott got an unobstructed view. Will Smith was standing there, framing the doorway, waiting for his friend. He wore a look of happy relief. Evidently he had passed the test. Scott strained to see past him, and his heart sank. There in the room was a table, and on the table was an electronic apparatus. Scott recognized it from Jeff's description — a retinal scanner! There was no mistaking the eyepiece or the rest of the configuration. Jeff had described it too well.

The door shut, and he was left with the dwindling group. There was nothing he could do, he knew. They had him. Once he peered into that eyepiece, he would be positively identified as Scott Sampson. It would be all over. His fingers drummed on the arm of the chair. *Think!* he practically screamed at himself. There must be an alternative. Surely he could do something other than just wait meekly to be arrested!

Once again the agent opened the door and called one of his fellow passengers forward. As Scott watched, she was taken into the next room like the others. As the door shut, he noticed something that made him sit up straight. *Both* agents were inside the other room *with the door shut.* He remembered the bored look the one who had taken his identification had worn. They had obviously been doing this for several hours — even days, and were starting to get careless. On impulse, he activated the stopwatch function of his watch. A wild idea had sprung into his head, full-blown and ready to act upon. He knew that if he sat and thought about it, he would lose his nerve. His only chance was to act now. Besides, what more could they do to him if he tried to run? He had nothing to lose.

The agent stuck his head inside again and called out another name. As soon as the door shut, Scott started the timer. The next few minutes were the longest of his life. His plan would crumble like a stale cracker if he was called in next. His only hope was if the agents were calling in the passengers in the order they were taken off the bus.

Two minutes!

Scott tried to picture the layout of the terminal in his head. He had only seen a small part of it. If he turned right out of the hall, he should end up in the front of the building. From there he would have to find a way out of the immediate area. The problem would be, of course, that his phony identity was now useless. Once the agents discovered him missing, they would start a thorough search of the immediate area. His name and description would be on every major system within minutes. His only asset was that he had enough cash to get him out of the city, so he didn't have to rely on credit or bank cards.

Three minutes!

The adrenaline was beginning to race through Scott's system, causing him to think fast and clearly. Everything else seemed to run in slow motion. His mind worked furiously, trying to think of any transportation that would get him to his destination. A tapping jarred him back to reality, but it was only one of his fellow passengers tapping his foot nervously on the floor.

Four minutes!

He grasped his left wrist, holding his watch tightly. Surely the agent would be coming in soon! He started to tap his toe on the floor, in rhythm with his neighbor, but forced himself to stop. He could not take much more of this! How long did a retinal scan. . . .

The door opened. "Alicia Roberts," said the agent, still looking bored and half asleep. A middle-aged woman rose and left the room. The door shut. It was now or never. Scott restarted his watch. Then he rose and walked quickly to the door. Looking back, he saw his fellow passengers staring at him.

"Tell those guys that I had to go to the john or else there would have been an accident!"

There was a nervous chuckle from the rest, and he turned back to the door. His heart went to his mouth when he grasped the knob. It occurred to him that it might be locked, thus nullifying his plan. It wasn't. Trying to appear nonchalant, he stepped into the hall and closed the door behind him. His watch told him that less than a minute had passed, even if subjectively it felt like a year. The door to the other room remained closed. Gathering his courage, he headed down the hall at a quick walk. It took all of his self-control not to break into a mad dash. He emerged from the hall and paused to scan the terminal. It occurred to him that, although he hadn't seen anyone else, there might be other agents waiting.

There was no time to waste. The main lobby of the terminal was an open space not too much different from the one in Covington. To his left, 10 glass doors led to the departure area. To his right, 10 identical doors led outside to the front of the building. For just a moment, he was tempted to go back to his bus for the Bibles. It tore him up inside to leave them there. Sooner or later they would be found and probably confiscated. He remembered the joy of his friends in Cynthiana and Somerset when he had given them their copies. He stood there in indecision, wanting to go back and knowing he couldn't. Then he forced himself to turn right.

Once outside he paused again to get his bearings. Straight ahead was the main parking lot. At this time of night, it was practically deserted. He could see only three cars sitting there under the harsh amber lights. They were parked side by side, sitting parallel to the terminal. Beyond that was a deserted four lane street. The city of Atlanta rose up all around him. The tall skyscrapers glowed in the darkness, seeming somehow unearthly. There was a heavy silence in the cool spring air, as if the entire city was waiting for something to happen.

Scott had absolutely no idea which way to turn, and time was running out. His stop watch continued to run, now passing the three minute mark. If the agents followed their pattern, they would discover him missing in less than a minute. He forced himself not to take off in just any direction. He knew that if he panicked now, he was lost. His only hope was to do the unexpected. The problem was, he had no idea what they would *not* expect.

"Oh heck," he growled under his breath. It was the closest he had come to cursing since before that meeting in Covington. Any direction was as good as the other, he realized. He started across the parking lot, nervously looking back toward the terminal. Nothing yet. He picked up his pace a little, glancing at his watch. The tiny numbers displayed four minutes on the dot. His time had run out. He reached the edge of the lot and again looked back. Everything appeared normal, and he was just about to cross the street when the corner of his eye caught a rapid movement inside. Someone was running toward the exit.

Scott didn't have time to think. Later, he would swear that someone had ordered him to do what he did. He had simply obeyed. Just as the agent burst out of the terminal, he dove between two of the cars. Hunkering down, he cautiously peeked up through the window of the one facing the terminal. He could see the agent through the dirty glass looking wildly in every direction. He was obviously upset and angry. He began to turn to go back inside, then changed his mind. Instead he started running through the parking lot, heading straight toward Scott.

Scott ducked down out of sight. He could hear the footsteps of the approaching agent drawing closer. He would be discovered in seconds. Heart pounding, he dropped to the blacktop. Flat on his back, he slid under the center car. From his vantage point, he could see the agent's feet, still heading toward him. He held his breath as they drew even with, then passed his position and continued on out of sight. He waited, knowing they would be coming back.

Sure enough, in a few moments they returned. The agent was still running, now headed back to the terminal. Scott strained to listen as the footsteps faded away. As soon as they ceased, he dragged himself out from under the car. Tiny pieces of gravel bit into his exposed neck and arms. Slowly he lifted his eyes over the car door. He could see the agent through the window, hurrying back to the terminal. As Scott watched, he opened the door and went inside.

Scott's head slumped onto the cool metal of the car. His heart beat like a snare drum, tapping out a quick, uneven rhythm. He had to get out of here now. Soon this place would be crawling with un-friendly faces. There was nothing to do but to leg it as far away from the bus station as he could. Setting his face in a look of grim determination, he left the refuge of the cars and hit the street. There was a sidewalk running along both sides. Crossing the street, he began a fast-paced walk, continuously glancing back at the terminal. There was still no action there, but Scott knew he had a matter of minutes to clear the area. As soon as he could, he changed directions. Coming to an intersection, he turned left. The terminal was now out of sight, which helped his state of mind a little. He was following another four lane street, although there was now much more traffic despite the lateness of the hour. Atlanta did not sleep.

Again Scott changed directions at the next intersection. He was now a block away from the terminal. Just as he turned, he saw a city police car coming toward him. Quickly he ducked into a narrow alley that had just presented itself. He scurried in about 20 feet and then flattened himself against the wall. The police car passed the opening, neither stopping nor slowing. Panting, he leaned against the hard wall. This was getting him nowhere, he realized. He had never been to Atlanta, and had no idea of the layout of the city. Slowly he let his knees buckle, sliding down the wall to a crouch. *There must be some way to get safely out of this city,* he thought.

He closed his eyes and tried to think, but no ideas would come. He sat there for what seemed like an eternity. His thoughts ran in circles, chasing themselves. He was starting to get frustrated and angry. Here he was, trapped in a strange town, with no friends, and no transportation. Jeff had not given him any numbers for this area, so he had no idea where any safe houses might be. Jeff had given him the necessary passwords to access the computer network, but he did not know where to find a public terminal. In short, he was stuck — as marooned as if he had been on a deserted island. How in God's name . . . and it hit him.

Perhaps he wasn't going to get out of this. Maybe it was God's will now for him to be captured, but when was the last time he had asked God about it? When was the last time he had prayed? Not in a meeting, with other believers, but just himself, one on one with God. With something akin to shame, he realized that he had not truly asked his Saviour for guidance since Covington. Here he was, playing missionary, trying to encourage underground churches to keep believing, and he himself wasn't even praying. Too much James Bond, he realized. He had been caught up in the worry, and yes, excitement of the chase, and had forgotten the reason behind it all. *Some missionary,* he thought, disgusted with himself. Well, it might be too late to get out of this, but it wasn't too late for prayer. In fact, it was never too late. With that, Scott closed his eyes and began to talk to his Lord.

"Oh, God," he said aloud, and stopped. He could not go on. The words froze in his throat. Everything he had been through, starting with that fateful meeting in Covington, crashed through his mind. He sat there in that alley, unable to put into words what he wanted to say. His mind seemed frozen, unwilling to let his thoughts flow. Unbidden, tears formed at the corners of his eyes.

"Oh, God," he cried again, his voice breaking. "I don't know what to say! I don't know what to ask. *Please,* show me!" He shook his head violently, as if shaking off an insect that had landed in his hair. "Oh, God," he repeated, "I am Your child. You adopted me into Your family when I accepted Your Son as my Saviour. You promised that You would never leave nor forsake me. In Jesus' name, I ask that You guide me." At the mention of his Lord's name, his mind and heart were released, and the words began to flow. "Forgive me for relying on my own strength," he prayed. "In trying to do Your work, I've neglected to ask You for guidance. Forgive my arrogance and pride. Whatever You have for me to do, I will do it. Should it mean capture, or even death, I will follow You. Show me the way to go. It is in Jesus' name I ask this." Scott finished his prayer, but kept his head bowed, as if waiting for an answer.

"There somebody back here?" The voice came from just a few feet away.

Startled, Scott looked up at the entrance of the alley. A figure stood there, silhouetted by the city lights. "Hello?" repeated the voice. From the sound of it, it belonged to an old man.

Scott scrambled to his feet and brushed himself off. "Just resting," he said, walking slowly toward the figure. The thought of running did not even enter his mind. He came to the mouth of the alley and stood just a few feet away from the old man, who was leaning forward, peering into the blackness.

When he saw Scott, he rocked back on his heels. "Didn't mean to intrude, young fella," he said, looking up at Scott. "I'm the night watchman for the office building there." He pointed at the building on Scott's right. "I was just making my rounds when I saw you through that window up there. Thought I'd better check it out."

"I didn't mean any trouble," said Scott. "My bus got delayed, and I didn't want to hang around the terminal."

The old man nodded. "Can't say as I'd like to spend too much time there myself," he replied. "Filthy place. Where are you headed?"

"Florida," said Scott. The words slipped out before he realized what he was saying. He must be tired if he was being this careless. "I have friends there," he finished lamely.

The old man just stared at him for a moment, then turned and walked back out onto the street. He motioned for Scott to follow. "You might as well be comfortable then," he said over his shoulder. "Come on up to my office. I've got some hot coffee and soup. Hungry?"

Actually, Scott was famished. He had been running on adrenaline and potato chips for the last several hours. Taking a couple of quick steps, he caught up with the watchman. "You do this often?" he asked. "Take in strangers, I mean."

"Never, as a matter of fact," replied the old man.

"Then why . . . ," Scott began, but was interrupted.

"Let's just say it's something I need to do," was the vague reply. With that the old man shut up and led Scott into a darkened office building that formed one wall of the alley. There was something disquieting about the man, Scott felt. He was almost familiar, in a queer sort of way.

"Watch your step," cautioned the watchman as he led the way up two flights of stairs and into a small but cozy office. "Have a seat," he said, motioning to a comfortable looking overstuffed lounger. Scott sank gratefully into the softness, listening to the air rush out of the cushions.

His nose picked up the scent of hot bean soup simmering on a small burner that sat atop a battered desk. His mouth began to water. The watchman moved over to a small refrigerator and pulled out a can of soda. Tossing it to Scott, he then took a large plastic bowl off the top of the refrigerator and filled it to the brim with the soup. Reaching into a drawer he pulled out a big rounded spoon, and handed both to Scott.

"It's a bit hot," he warned as he turned his back and fixed himself another bowl of soup. Scott waited politely as he sat down at the desk. His stomach was beginning to growl so loudly that he knew the watchman must hear it.

"Don't wait for me, now," said his host. "This is my second bowl. You go ahead."

Scott dipped his spoon into the thick liquid and stirred slowly. He had never been so thankful for anything in his life. Carefully he brought the steaming spoon to his mouth — and stopped. It was true, he realized. He had never been so grateful for anything in his life, and no matter what the old man might say, he knew he must thank the One really responsible. He replaced the spoon and bowed his head. "Lord," he prayed silently, "Thank You so much for this food, and for the one You sent to bring it. In Jesus' name, Amen."

He looked up to see the old man regarding him thoughtfully. "Don't see much of that anymore," he said softly.

Scott merely shrugged. The old man didn't seem ready to rush out and call the police, so he let the matter rest. He took a firm grip on the spoon and this time stuffed a lion's share of soup into his mouth. It was the most wonderful thing he had ever tasted. Now that it had cooled a little, it was just warm enough to give that delightful burning sensation all the way down the throat to the stomach. Eagerly, he took another bite. Before he knew it, he had finished the bowl.

The watchman pointed to the burner. "Plenty left," he said around a full mouth. Scott obliged, and soon was working on his second bowl. They ate in silence, not talking as if by common agreement. By the time he finished his second bowl, Scott was beyond full and well on his way to being stuffed. He swallowed the last spoonful and leaned back into the chair contentedly. His tired eyes closed, and before he knew it, he was asleep.

The night watchman studied him for a moment, then reached under the desk. He pulled out an old woolen blanket and, moving on tiptoe, gently laid it over his guest. "Rest well, my friend, rest well," he said softly. "For you, the most dangerous time is yet to come."

❖ ❖ ❖

"Scott? Scott! Wake up. Come on, son. It's time to go."

Slowly Scott regained consciousness, becoming vaguely aware that the watchman was shaking his shoulder. He opened his eyes and found himself still in the office. His back was cramped from being in one position for so long, and there was a thick taste in his mouth. Blinking several times, his eyes finally focused on the old man.

"What?" he asked, not quite awake yet. Despite his recent adventures, he still wasn't used to coming to in strange places.

"I said, it's time to get up. My shift is almost over, and the people that work here will be showing up soon," replied the watchman.

Scott looked down at his watch and saw that it was past five o'clock in the morning and still dark outside. He rubbed the sleep out of his eyes and shook the blanket off. Standing, he arched his back in a huge stretch, and felt some of the kinks work themselves out. His host was gathering the soup bowls and utensils into a battered duffel bag. Casually he strolled over to the window and looked down into the alley. He could just barely see where he had hidden from the police car. The office was a bit stuffy now, and he tried to open the window to get some fresh air. It would not move, and further inspection revealed that it was permanently bolted down. He turned back and saw that the watchman had finished putting his things away.

"I never got your name," he said, the tone of his voice making it a question.

"Never gave it," was the simple reply.

Scott waited, but no further answer was forthcoming. "Well, I just wanted to say thanks. The food and the rest really helped."

The watchman merely grunted, setting the duffel bag onto the floor. Scott waited patiently as he busied himself straightening up the desk. Finally he glanced up at Scott. "By the way, just how long was that layover at the bus station? You don't seem in any particular hurry to get back there."

Scott bit his lip, wondering what to say. Before he could formulate an answer, the watchman continued. "You slept through some interesting times, last night. A lot of police action hereabouts. Some sort of agent came right to this building. He knocked loud enough to raise the dead! Know what he wanted?"

Scott could only shrug.

"He was looking for a fugitive. Seems like someone slipped right through their fingers. Isn't that interesting?"

Scott was already on his way to the door. There was no doubt that the watchman knew he was the one the police were looking for. He didn't know what he was up to, but he wasn't about to hang around long enough to find out. With surprising speed, the old man was suddenly standing in front of the door. Although Scott thought he could move him by force, he stopped.

The old man was frowning, but there was a twinkle in his eye. "I know you're tired, son," he said, a slight reprimand in his voice, "but you need to start thinking a little straighter. Do you really think I'm a threat to you? If I had wanted to turn you in, I would have done so last night."

Scott hesitated, not knowing what to do. "What do you want?" he finally thought of asking.

Now it was the old man's turn to shrug. "From you, nothing at all. You're going to have to make up your mind, son. You can walk out of here now and probably be picked up before you make two blocks, or you can believe me when I tell you that I don't mean you any harm. Believe it or not, I can help you. What's it going to be?"

Scott did not consider himself to be a good judge of people. More than once he had been hurt by so-called friends who betrayed his trust. Being on the run for the past few weeks had taught him one thing, though. He had learned to make hard, fast decisions. Before, he would always dither, not wanting to commit to any course of action until the last possible second. Those days were gone. In his current situation, if he hesitated, he was lost. He made one of those decisions now.

"All right," he said. "How can you help me, and more importantly, why would you risk trouble with the law in order to do it?"

The old man smiled and moved away from the door. "I'll answer your second question first," he said. "I want to help you because I overheard you praying last night. That's what brought me down to get you. It's been a while since I heard anyone pray like that, and I rather fancied being an answer — at least, part of your answer. As to how — well, I can't get you all the way to Florida, but I can help you find someone who *can* get you there. So how about it?"

"Okay," nodded Scott. Somehow he knew that this old man was telling the truth. "So what do you want me to do?"

"Just follow me," replied the watchman. With that, he picked up his duffel bag and walked out of the office. He led Scott through a different hall than the one he had come up in last night, and down a different flight of stairs. This led to a rear exit, which in turn led to a small, private parking lot. The only vehicle there was a powder blue compact pickup truck. The old man motioned for him to get in.

The sky was just showing a hint of daylight as they drove off. Scott was grateful for the nap he had, but he couldn't help wishing that just once he could sleep till noon. It was one luxury fugitives were not allowed, he decided. The watchman navigated the truck through the streets of Atlanta, encountering only light traffic. After a 15-minute ride, they turned onto an expressway. Scott saw that it was Interstate 75, the same one that he had used to take Beth to the airport. Once again, the feelings of loss, grief, and regret threatened to engulf him, but he ruthlessly pushed them aside.

They drove south on I-75, gradually leaving the city behind them. The watchman had not spoken during the brief trip, and Scott wondered where they were going. His question was answered soon enough. They pulled off the expressway after traveling about 10 miles. Scott had noted two state police cars passing them on the way, but neither had taken any notice of the small blue truck.

The watchman turned onto the exit ramp and gradually decreased his speed. Scott looked around, but the only places he could see were a couple of gas stations and a truck stop. They came to a stop at the end of the ramp. Checking in all directions, the watchman turned onto the two lane highway. It turned out that he was headed for the truck stop. They pulled onto the wide expanse of blacktop, carefully making their way along a row of mammoth 18-wheel monsters. Finally they reached the truck stop itself, a one story structure that housed a restaurant, showers, and gift shop. Bright neon lights ran along the top, and stood out in stark relief against the gradually lightening sky. There was a row of large windows in front, and Scott could see that the restaurant was fairly crowded. The watchman came to a complete stop.

"Inside there is a man who will take you where you're going," he said, nodding at the edifice.

"Who is he?" asked Scott, peering inside.

The watchman smiled mischievously. "You'll have to find him," he answered. "Just ask around for anyone heading to Florida."

"Excuse me?" Scott did not like the turn things were taking. The watchman knew he was a fugitive. Why take chances like this? The watchman turned to face him squarely, and he found himself looking into two dark blue pools. There was no trace of falsehood there. He knew beyond a doubt that this man was not lying to him. Strangely, the sense of familiarity increased. Scott had a very strong feeling that he had seen him before.

"Listen, Scott," said the watchman, "someone is in there who can take you safely to your destination. That someone desperately needs something that you have. Find him." He motioned for Scott to get out.

Bewildered, he complied. When he shut the door, the watchman leaned over and rolled down the window. "Trust in God, Scott," he said. "No matter what. You still have many trials ahead, but if you give Him control, you'll make it. I promise. Here." With that the watchman threw out his duffel bag. "There's enough food in there to last for a few days, as well as a change of clothes. Now get going." As Scott stood dumbfounded, the watchman put his truck in gear and with a final wave, drove off.

Scott stood there and watched him pull out of the parking lot and disappear down the road. Just who was that man? How could he possibly know about any of Scott's trials? He turned to enter the truck stop, and it hit him. Pieces fell into place with such force that it knocked the breath out of him. He had to sit down.

Sinking to the short curb that ran the length of the building, he put his head into his hands. His mouth was dry, and his heart was beating frantically. He started to shake. Something extraordinary had just happened. *The watchman had called him by name.* Not the bogus one on his current identification, but his *real* name. Twice. First was this morning, when he had awakened him, and the second was just now as he drove off. Scott knew that he had never given him *any* name, much less his real one.

Another thought hit him. The watchman had said that he had *heard* Scott praying, and had come down to invite him up. Scott remembered the window in the watchman's office. It was sealed shut. There was no way he could have heard him from that office, and he sure wasn't in the alley when Scott got there. What was going on?

He was already reeling from the one-two punch of the first two realizations when the third hit him. The watchman had looked familiar, and now he knew why. *He had seen him before.* Scott's forehead broke out into a cold sweat as he remembered the night that Beth had died. He could see her disappearing down the boarding ramp. He felt the tug at his sleeve, and an old man assuring him that he would see her again. The same man. A sudden chill ran through Scott's body. There was no denying the fact: Scott Sampson had just had an encounter with the supernatural. There was no other way to explain it. He thought of the watchman's words at the airport. "You'll see her again," he had said. Scott knew it would happen. He would meet his wife again in heaven. Still . . . there was something in the way he said it.

Suddenly, Scott's mood lightened. God had not forgotten him! He was still there, caring, watching, and protecting. All he had to do was follow His guidance. The rest would fall in place. With a newly found resolve, he stood. There was much to do.

"The Watchman," he said under his breath, looking in the direction his new friend had disappeared. "You wouldn't tell me your name, my friend, but I think "Watchman" may suit you better than anything." As the sky brightened, he shouldered the duffel bag and made his way into the truck stop. He was determined to find the mysterious man who could get him to his destination.

❖   ❖   ❖

A multitude of odors assailed him as he pushed through the glass doors and into the dining area. First and foremost was the scent of hot food. Although he had stuffed himself on soup just a few hours ago, he was ready for breakfast. The restaurant took up half the space of the building, the other half holding the gift shop and showers. A serving counter ran the length of the dining area, lined with customers sitting on cushioned metal stools. Behind the counter were three harried waitresses scurrying to fill orders. Across a narrow aisle, behind the stools, was a row of 10 red vinyl booths, all occupied. Just to his right was an old style computer cash register, and lined up in front of it were several folks waiting to pay their bill.

Scott stood there for a moment, not quite sure what to do. He could not just make an announcement to everyone in general, asking who might be going to Florida. The noise level in the restaurant certainly prevented that. The air was full of sounds, most of them loud. Utensils clinking off plates, a radio blaring out oldies of the eighties — and the conversation! It seemed everyone was talking at the same time, and no one was listening. Just how was he supposed to find someone in this mess?

With a mental shrug, he moved into the chaos. Spotting an empty stool, he slid up to the counter. The two men on either side ignored him completely, the one on the left reading a newspaper and the one on the right concentrating on his breakfast. A food-stained menu was leaning up against the sugar dispenser at his right, and he picked it up. Just as he opened it, one of the waitresses, an attractive young woman of about 25, moved to stand in front of him. Her bright blond hair was drawn up under a hair net, and her horn-rimmed glasses gave her a scholarly look.

"Coffee?" she asked in a lilting voice, holding a pot of the brew in an almost pouring position.

"Please," replied Scott, his voice carefully neutral. From somewhere under the counter she produced a cup and saucer and splashed a generous portion of the thick black fluid into it. She then pulled out a pad and pencil from her apron.

"What can I get for you today?" she asked, smiling a practiced smile. Although he had not had time to look at the menu, he pretty much knew what he wanted.

"Blueberry pancakes," he ordered, replacing the menu. The waitress wrote down the order and started to move off. Scott held up a hand to stop her. He had to begin somewhere.

"Something else?" asked the waitress. The name tag on her beige uniform read Sandy.

"I'm trying to get to Florida," he said. "Do you know anyone here that might be headed in that direction?" The man on his right glanced over in his direction. He was wearing a green John Deere cap, a plaid flannel shirt, and green work pants. His face was unshaven and dirty, and a bulging belly threatened to burst the buttons on his shirt. Scott heard him muttering something under his breath. Although he couldn't hear everything he said, one word he did pick up sounded like 'bum.' The rest was unrepeatable. Scott felt suddenly uncomfortable and out of place.

"Quiet, Nate," said the waitress, her tone reproving, just on the verge of being angry. "He's not causing any trouble. Now you just sit there and eat." With a last angry look at Scott, Nate turned back to his plate.

"Don't pay any attention to him," said Sandy. "He picked up some girl here last month. Said she was going to Macon, and needed a ride. Really came on to him. Promised that she'd be *real* grateful if you know what I mean." Sandy winked. Embarrassed, Scott only nodded. "Turned out she had a gun, though your guess is as good as mine as to where she hid it, with that outfit. Did you ever find out, Nate?"

Nate glared at her, then went back to his food.

"Anyway," continued Sandy, "she forced him to pull off the road. A bunch of her friends were waiting. They took his rig, his money, and his pants." She chuckled a little, then immediately sobered. "Most of these guys," she said, looking around the crowded restaurant, "have been held up at one time or another. These days, it's getting worse. None of them pick up hitchhikers much anymore."

"I don't want any trouble," reassured Scott. "I'm just trying to get to Florida. I've got family there." Well, it was true, he thought to himself. All Christians were family, in theory, anyway.

Sandy nodded. "Let me get your order in," she said. "Then we'll see what we can do." With that she turned and disappeared into the kitchen.

Scott sipped at the hot coffee. The bitter liquid warmed and revived him, and he felt the few remaining kinks from his short sleep ease themselves out of his neck. Next to him, Nate finished his breakfast and picked up his check. He slid off the stool, then put a meaty hand on Scott's shoulder. Scott felt the stool swivel underneath and found himself staring into two angry eyes.

"Listen you," growled Nate, his voice a menacing baritone, "stay away from here. We don't want your kind here. You bums are nothing but trouble. I see you here again, you've had it. Understand?"

Scott could only stare at him, wondering what to do or say. He tried not to flinch at his foul breath. Nate wasn't finished. "You think I'm fooling? Let's just you and me step outside, and I'll show you how much I'm fooling." With that, Nate released his arm and stood back. "Come on, bum. Let's see what you're made of."

This is all I need, thought Scott. He held up his hands in a "back off, I surrender," gesture, and swiveled back to the counter.

Nate stood there with a look of vindictive triumph on his grimy face. "Thought so," he crowed loud enough to draw attention from nearby customers. "You're all alike. No guts. You remember, bum, I see you around here again, and I'll kill you. Got it?" Without waiting for a reply, the angry man turned and shambled off. When he got to the cash register, he turned and glared back at Scott.

Scott held his glare for a moment, then looked away, hoping his face showed just the right expression of fear. Nate paid his bill and left. Scott saw him cross the blacktop and climb into one of the trucks he had passed on the way in.

"Wheeeeew," he whistled quietly. All he needed was a confrontation like that in a public place. After miraculously eluding pursuit earlier, he would be arrested because of some stupid brawl. Slowly he let the anger he felt at Nate's words run off. He hated backing down, especially to someone so obnoxious. Scott had had his share of fights growing up, thanks to a fiery temper. He had lost a lot more than he had won, but he had never backed down. It galled him, but he had no choice.

His muscles untensed, and he leaned forward on the counter. Now that the anger was out of his system, he began to feel ashamed of himself. He had walked in here after an incredible experience. God had shown him that He was still in control — He was still taking care of him. It had been a great victory over despair for Scott. Now here he was getting angry at a local who called him names and wanted to pick a fight. Some spiritual warrior he was!

Suddenly he remembered one of the many Bible stories that he learned in Sunday school. Elijah, after a great victory over the prophets of Baal, had allowed himself to become terrorized by a single woman, Queen Jezebel. He was so afraid he had run and hid under a bush. Scott found himself far more sympathetic to Elijah's plight than he had been before. *I guess it's true,* he thought ruefully. *You're the most vulnerable after a great victory.*

"Don't let him get to you." Startled out of his thoughts, he looked up to see Sandy holding a steaming plate of thick pancakes. She set them down in front of him and then refilled his coffee cup. "Nate treats everyone like that," she said, "even his friends."

"Must not have many, then," remarked Scott.

"You'd be surprised," said Sandy seriously. "Nate don't take to strangers, but once he knows you, and trusts you, then you got a friend for life."

"Oh," replied Scott, not quite sure what to say.

"I've been thinking about your problem," continued Sandy.

"Excuse me?" said Scott. He had momentarily forgotten about his reason for being there.

"Getting you to Florida," she clarified. "I think I may know someone who can help you."

Before he could reply, she looked over his shoulder at one of the booths. "Hey, Jim."

From behind him, Scott heard a tired voice respond. "Yeah, Sandy?"

"You're headed toward the 'cigar city,' aren't you?"

"Yeah. Got to be there by early this afternoon. Why?"

"You interested in some company?"

"I knew it! You're finally ready to ditch this job and hook up with a real man!"

Scott had to smile at the hint of a blush that appeared on Sandy's cheeks. She rallied gamely. "Of course," she replied lightly. "As soon as a real man comes along, I'm outta here!"

There was a groan from Jim, accompanied by hoots of laughter from the rest of the room. Slowly Scott turned to find the source of the voice. There were three men seated in the booth behind him, but he had no trouble picking out Jim. He was the one with his head in his hands.

"She doesn't love me," he cried in mock despair. "I eat her food, tip her big, and she still doesn't love me. My life is over!"

Sandy waited patiently until Jim concluded his groaning, then spoke again. "Well? How about it?" she said, nodding toward Scott.

"You want some company or not?"

Jim shrugged, then got up from the booth and moved to sit on the empty stool next to Scott. He stood about six feet in height, although his lean frame made him look taller. He gave him an appraising look. "You headed to Tampa?" he asked.

"Sort of," replied Scott slowly. "Tarpon Springs. It's in the area."

"It's a good 30 miles away," corrected Jim. He looked at Sandy. "I heard Nate giving him a rough time," he remarked. "Any good reason?"

"You know how Nate is with strangers," said Sandy. "He just overheard this fella asking about a ride."

"That would do it," agreed Jim. He stuck out his hand to Scott. "Jim Nelson," he said, introducing himself. The handshake was firm and steady. Jim appeared to be about 10 years older than Scott, although his close-cropped, prematurely gray hair gave him an aura of greater maturity.

"Gregory Andropolos," he replied, returning the grip.

Jim smiled. "Thought you were Greek," he said. "Got family in that area, do you?" Scott nodded. "You mind keeping that in the trailer?" he asked, motioning to Scott's duffel bag.

"Huh?" asked Scott.

"You seem nice enough," said Jim, "but I don't want you pulling some sort of unpleasant surprise out of there. Get my drift?"

"Oh," said Scott. "Yeah, I see what you mean. No problem."

Jim folded his arms across his chest, regarding him closely. "What do you think, Hon?" he said, looking at Sandy.

"Give the poor man a lift," she said. "Just last trip you were complaining that the company wouldn't let you have a partner."

"Yeah, I was, wasn't I? Okay, Greg, you got yourself a lift. Are you ready to pull out?"

"Now?" asked Scott, hardly daring to breathe. This was going better than he hoped.

"Yep, let's go." Jim started to turn, then wrinkled his nose. "On second thought," he said, "Why don't you take a quick shower. Got a change of clothes in that bag?"

Suddenly, Scott was aware of the fact that he had not showered since leaving Somerset. He was getting pretty ripe. "Sure," he said. "Can you give me a few minutes to eat and get cleaned up?"

"Yeah, go ahead. I got a few things to take care of myself." Clapping Scott on the shoulder, Jim turned and went back to his booth. Scott turned back to his food and dug in.

"Thanks," he said to Sandy, who remained standing in front of him.

"Glad to help," she said, smiling. This time it was genuine. "You think you'll be back this way anytime soon?" The tone of her voice was unmistakable. Now it was Scott who started to blush.

"I don't think so," he said, looking down at his food. He took a big bite of pancake.

"Too bad," sighed Sandy. "You're cute, and you seem nice. We don't get too many guys like that through here, and the ones we do are usually married."

Scott only shrugged. The idea of a romantic encounter with anyone right now, even with someone as pretty as Sandy, was repugnant to him.

"Well, I tried," said Sandy, starting to move away. "You take care now." With that, she was gone, but not before Scott heard the deep loneliness in her voice. He wished he could introduce her to the One who could take that loneliness away permanently, but it was not the right time. He could feel the Spirit tugging at him, telling him to get going.

❖   ❖   ❖

Thirty minutes later, Scott was clean, fed, and traveling south on Interstate 75 in an 18-wheel tractor trailer. As the city of Atlanta fell further and further behind, he began to relax. The mile markers sped by as he drew closer and closer to his destination. Jim turned out to be good company. He did not pry into Scott's personal life, but instead talked about everything from politics to sports. Scott found him an interesting conversationalist. He was also fascinated by Jim's rig. It was a brand new model, and the cabin of the tractor more closely resembled something out of a science fiction movie than a truck. Jim, flattered by Scott's interest, was only too happy to explain much of the equipment.

"These new babies practically drive themselves. The onboard computer there," and he pointed to a compact but complete keyboard inset into the dashboard, "keeps all sorts of helpful things at my fingertips. It's hooked in by satellite to the state police systems of every state I travel in."

"The police?" asked Scott. He did not like the sound of that.

"Yeah. It keeps me informed about road conditions, traffic problems, that sort of thing. It also monitors the vital systems of this rig. Anything goes wrong, it can tell me."

"Pretty neat," observed Scott. He was somewhat familiar with the system, of course. His former job demanded that he have a working knowledge of *all* new systems. Still, he wasn't up on the particulars, and found Jim's explanation interesting. "Bet it takes a while to learn how to handle a rig like this," he commented.

"You got that right," agreed Jim. "A lot of companies have gone back to the apprentice system in training new drivers. These monsters are just too technical to trust to a novice."

"I thought there were schools for that sort of thing," replied Scott. "I've seen ads for them on television."

Jim snorted. "Ads," he scoffed. "Let me tell you, Greg, the only way to learn how to drive a semi is to drive a semi. Those schools are great at teaching you how to drive around obstacles, or park one of these babies, but there's no substitute for experience. They can't teach you how to be out on the road for 16 or 20 hours a day. They don't tell you what to do when your electrical system starts shorting out, or you're stuck along a deserted highway at four in the morning. That's why we take on apprentices now. They get on-the-job training that way. Believe me, it's a lot better system."

"I see," said Scott. "How did you get started in this?" It was the first personal question he had asked.

Jim frowned, as if hesitating to answer.

"Hey, I'm sorry. If it's something you don't want to talk about. . . ."

"No, it's not that," interrupted Jim. "It just brings back a lot of memories. You see, I was a used car salesman. Did pretty good at it, too — made a lot of money. Had a wife, three kids, and a beautiful four bedroom house."

"Then how. . . ."

"How did I end up here, alone and on the road?" Jim pondered the question for a moment, then decided to answer. "Well, you see, I thought I had it made. Everything was going perfect. Then I find out that my oldest son has Hodgkin's disease. We found out about it too late to do anything. He died just two years ago. He — he was only five."

"I'm sorry," said Scott softly. The loss of a loved one struck home to him. He could feel Jim's deep-rooted pain.

"Thanks. I haven't talked about it since I left Maggie. I really shouldn't be talking about it now, but what the heck? Sometimes it's easier to unload to a total stranger than someone you know. Right?"

"I guess so," replied Scott uncertainly. The sudden turn of the conversation made him feel uncomfortable.

"Anyway, after it happened, I sort of went crazy. I wouldn't talk to Maggie or my other two sons. Ended up having a fling with one of the girls in my office. When Maggie found out, she left and took Eddie and Jim Jr. with her. She filed for divorce a few weeks later." He shook his head in regret. "I guess I never thought about her pain — what she must be going through. I haven't talked to her for over two years."

There was nothing Scott could say in answer, so he remained quiet.

"Since then," Jim continued, "I've been on the road. Got myself some training and got a job hauling between Detroit and Miami. In a way, I guess you could say I've been running."

"Running from what?" asked Scott.

"I honestly don't know," said Jim, his voice dropping to almost a whisper. "From the world, from my pain, maybe even from myself. Who knows? I'd give anything if I could start all over again."

"You could call your wife," suggested Scott. "If you two could talk. . . ."

He was stopped by Jim shaking his head. "It's too late," he said. "Too many things were said during the divorce — ugly things. They can't be taken back. Thanks for the advice, Greg, but I've been all over it in my mind before. You can't go back, only forward."

Scott said nothing, and silence fell in the cabin. Scott thought about his encounter with the Watchman, and what he said just before they parted.

"Someone is in there who can take you safely to your destination," he had said. "That someone desperately needs something you have." Scott did not understand then, but he was beginning to understand now. More than anything, Jim needed to be introduced to Jesus Christ. It was incredible, thought Scott. To be chased from the bus station, meet up with the Watchman, and be directed to seek out a man who needed what he had. Just 12 hours ago, he was convinced that his life was out of control. Now he knew that there was a purpose for everything. He might have lost his cargo of Bibles, but he could still witness. He had memorized more Scripture in the past two weeks than he had in his entire life. Now it was time to put it to the use for which it was intended.

"Can I ask you a personal question?" he asked.

This caused Jim to laugh. "Why not? You've earned the right after listening to me spill my guts. What is it?"

"Well," began Scott slowly, "I was just wondering where God

was during all of this. I mean, a lot of people who go through this kind of thing sometimes turn to God. You know what I mean?"

Jim looked over at him in surprise. "You got a death wish or something?" he asked, his eyebrows going up. "You could get into real trouble talking like that, you know."

"I'm just asking a question," replied Scott, holding his hands up to reassure him. "No harm in that, is there?"

"I don't know," said Jim, shaking his head. "Seems to me that it's not healthy to talk too loudly about God in the 'Land of the Free,' these days."

"What about it, though?" pressed Scott. He could sense that Jim wanted to talk about it. He just needed to be drawn out.

"Well," began Jim, "Maggie took the kids to church every Sunday — that is until they started closing. Once that happened, well, she didn't talk about it anymore. When we found out about Michael. . . ." He stopped, his voice suddenly catching in his throat. It was several seconds before he could continue.

"You see," he finally continued, "Maggie did a lot of praying during that time. She was always asking God to heal our son. She really believed it would happen. More than once I would come home and find her on her knees next to the bed. It always made me feel guilty that I didn't join her."

"You don't believe in God?" asked Scott.

"It's not that," he replied. "I just didn't think He'd be interested in my problems. When Michael died, she was devastated. She thought she had done something wrong and she was being punished. Shoot, I kinda thought the same thing myself, so I couldn't blame her, could I? Anyway, we got into a lot of big fights about it. Finally, I ended up walking out on her, and I guess I sorta walked out on God at the same time." He looked at Scott, as if inviting comment, but Scott remained silent.

"Tell me something, Greg," he asked finally. "Why didn't God heal my son? Is it my fault for not praying?"

Scott shuddered a little at Jim's question. It was uncomfortably close to the way he had been feeling since he lost Beth. If he had been a better Christian, would she still be alive? If he had been more involved in the underground church movement, they might have known about the Shepherd's Path. They could have escaped together. Maybe. . . . No! That line of reasoning led to guilt and despair. It accomplished nothing.

He realized suddenly that Jim didn't need Scott Sampson's

answers or theories. He needed his honesty, and courage — and his Saviour.

"I don't know the answer to that," he said softly. "If I did, I would be God." Jim nodded, and started to say something, but Scott rushed on. "But I can introduce you to the One who *does* have the answers. In fact, He *is* the answer. You interested?" It was the first time in his life he had ever asked anyone that question. Even though he had been a Christian for years, he had never outright witnessed to someone. He could feel his heart beating faster in both fear and expectation.

Jim stared straight ahead. His hands gripped the wheel so hard his knuckles turned white. "I guess I just never believed that God was interested in me," he repeated, his voice barely above a whisper.

Scott heard the desperation there, and made a snap decision. "You're wrong," he said, his voice firm and confident. Jim looked sideways at him, his entire face a question. "God *is* interested in you," continued Scott. "He's so interested that He pulled me off a bus in the middle of the night in order to tell you."

"I don't understand," said Jim, the confusion evident in his voice.

Scott didn't even hesitate. "My name isn't Greg, and I'm not Greek," he began. "It's Scott." With that. Scott began the story of his long odyssey. The only thing he left out were the names of his friends. He told Jim everything else — from the meeting in the furniture store to losing Beth to his escape from the bus station. He ended with the Watchman. It took the better part of an hour, and when he finished, Jim was openly weeping.

"I can't believe it," he kept saying over and over. "Things like this don't happen. They just don't."

"Believe it," said Scott gently. "God wants you, Jim. He wants you to turn to Him. He wants to be in control of your life." He paused for emphasis. "He loves you so much that He let His Son die for you so that you could live. All you have to do is believe."

"I want to," said Jim, his voice breaking. "I just don't know how."

Silently Scott said a prayer of thanks for all of the verses he had memorized over the past few weeks. Carefully he began to share them with his lost friend. The miles whisked by as they talked back and forth. Jim would listen, then ask a question. Scott would answer as best he could, but he was always totally honest. If he did not know the answer, he would admit it.

Finally, it happened. Scott could feel the Holy Spirit moving. He was a palpable presence in the cab, just as powerful as He had been that night in the furniture store, but somehow different. Then, He had moved among that tiny group, encouraging and comforting. Now, He was convicting. A life was ready to be changed.

"Well, Jim? How about it?" asked Scott. "You know what you need, or rather who you need. The only question is, are you going to accept Jesus Christ into your life? He's waiting, and it's your move."

"You know Scott," said Jim, a smile peeking out around the corners of his mouth, "I used to think that God was only for the good people, not for wrecks like me. I guess I was wrong, eh?"

Scott nodded, holding his breath. Jim did not keep him waiting. "I've been looking for this for a long time. No, that's not right. I guess I've known for a long time that I needed Jesus. I just never wanted to admit it. Now, it's time. Will you help me? I'm not sure what words to say."

Right then and there, Jim pulled the big rig over onto the emergency lane of the expressway and shut her down. Unashamedly, Scott took his strong hand and led him in the sinner's prayer.

It didn't take long, and the words weren't fancy, but the miracle of salvation happened. The change was instantaneous, and permanent. Jim looked up from praying with shining eyes. "It's real," he whispered. "It's really real! I can feel it!"

Scott said nothing. Abruptly, two huge tears rolled down his cheeks. "Yeah," he agreed, "it's real."

An air of pure joy began to fill the cab. Jim started to laugh — quietly at first, then so hard he could barely catch his breath. It was the laugh of the forgiven — the laugh of the newly cleansed. Scott joined in. If anyone had been able to peer into that small space at that particular moment, they would have wondered why two grown men were laughing like fools. Eventually they settled down. Jim checked his side mirror, then pulled back out onto the expressway.

Things were silent for a moment, then Jim spoke. "You know, Scott," he said, his voice revealing the wonder he felt, "I feel like I've got my whole life before me now. I can start over. I owe you, my friend."

"Wrong," answered Scott. "You don't owe me anything. I just followed instructions. Put the credit where it belongs, okay?"

Jim nodded, his smile threatening to stretch from ear to ear. The rest of the trip seemed to fly by. Jim began to question Scott about every aspect of living a Christian life. Scott found himself hard pressed to answer all of his questions. How he wished for just one of those Bibles he had left on the bus! He could have shared so much more! Why didn't he memorize more of that blessed Book when he had the chance? Fortunately, his memory served him well, and he shared verse after verse with Jim.

It wasn't until much later in the trip that he realized that Jim was the first soul he had ever led to Christ. It shamed him that he had been so lax before, when he had so many opportunities. Yet, it gave him an undeniable sense of happiness. Despite all of his failures, God was not finished with him. It felt good to know that.

Drawing ever closer to their destination, two believers — one brand new, the other older and somewhat battle scarred, but still very much alive — shared their Saviour with each other.

9

"Mr. Hill?"

"Yes, Doris."

"The Bradley woman has arrived. She is being held in Dr. Steiger's office."

"Excellent. Please inform Dr. Steiger he is to meet me there in exactly 10 minutes. I want to have a word with this woman."

"Yes, sir." The inter-office vid-phone went blank, and Jacob Hill allowed himself a small, predatory smile. He was seated at his desk in his suite at Mentasys, going over the latest updates to Brennon's master plan. Since he had learned of Bradley's capture 24 hours ago, he had been waiting impatiently for her arrival. All evidence pointed to her as the ringleader of this underground network called the Shepherd's Path. The information she would yield under interrogation should allow him to finish her group once and for all.

Although he would not admit it, even to himself, he was immensely relieved. Brennon and the rest of the Sextuaget were growing impatient for results. It was not good for one's health to keep them waiting too long. Turning to his monitor wall he brought up Steiger's office on the center screen. There she was, seated rigidly in one of the uncomfortable plastic chairs in the corner. Hill was surprised at how small and ordinary she looked. This was the woman who ran a national underground network right under the collective noses of his own elite organization, the Bureau of Religious Affairs? Incredible! He reached up and touched a control. The woman on the screen grew suddenly larger as the camera zoomed in. Hill examined her closely. Her face betrayed her fear and uncertainty, causing him to chuckle just a little. Abruptly, her eyes closed, and her mouth began to move slightly.

He snorted softly. "Pray to your God, woman," he growled.

"Pray all you like. It will do you no good. As far as you are concerned, *I* am your god now. *I* will decide your fate." Almost angrily he switched off the screen and swung back to his desk. Accessing his conventional private line, he entered a special 10-digit number. He waited for the answer he knew would come.

"Yes, sir," said the menacing voice on the other end.

"I'm afraid that I must ask you to cut back on your activities, Wolf," said Hill, wasting no time. "We are very close to breaking the Shepherd's Path. There must be no doubt in the minds of the public that it and the Christian Liberation Front are connected."

"Very well, sir." Hill could hear the disappointment in his voice. Wolf enjoyed killing. "Further instructions?"

"Yes," answered Hill. "You must change your method of operation and enlist new personnel. Be ready to strike within 30 days. I want everyone to believe that this is a new terrorist group. Understand?"

"Of course, sir. Suggestions on a new name?"

"Hmmmm. It should be something with either 'Christian,' or 'Believer,' or 'born again' in it. Let's see. How about the Believer's Victorious Army? That has a nice ring to it, and it fits with the militant image that a lot of those groups held in the nineties."

"Consider it done, sir," said Wolf. He now sounded pleased. "We will begin reorganizing immediately."

"Excellent," Hill approved. "And Wolf," he paused, making sure he had the man's attention, "the operatives you are using now — you understand that there can be no leaks. Keep your most trusted people. The rest. . . ." He let his voice trail off.

"I'll take care of it personally, sir."

"Good. I'll be in touch with you in two weeks. You will receive your next target then." With that Hill broke the connection, satisfied that Wolf would take care of things on his end. He stood up behind the desk and pulled on his gray suit coat. Naturally, he wanted to look his best for this interview. Just as he was leaving, the inter-office vidphone beeped for his attention. He activated the screen to find the somewhat harried features of Dr. Steiger staring back at him.

"What is it Doctor?" he asked impatiently. "Didn't you receive my message to meet me in your office?"

"Yes, sir," nodded Steiger. "I just thought you should know. We have indications that Senator Kline's implant is failing."

Hill's eyes narrowed at the disturbing news. "I thought they were failsafe," he remarked, his voice taking on a dangerous tone.

"The one we used in Kline was new," explained Steiger nervously. He had been in Hill's circle long enough to recognize that tone. "It was an experimental model, although we had it perfected in the laboratory. Its increased effectiveness allowed us a greater degree of control, while fostering in Kline a false sense of wellbeing. It appeared to be functioning perfectly at first, but lately. . . ."

"Enough, Doctor," interrupted Hill. "What is the bottom line? What can we expect from Kline?"

Steiger looked down at his notes. "Confusion, disorientation, an inability to relate properly to others. Those are the main effects we are encountering now. Others may manifest themselves." He stopped talking and looked expectantly at Hill.

"All right," replied Hill. "We need to get him here. I'll arrange it. Will a new implant solve these problems?"

"I can guarantee it," said Steiger confidently. "We can have him functioning properly again within 24 hours of his arrival."

"Set it up then," said Hill. "I'll get him here." He switched off the screen and again accessed his private line. This time the call went directly to Jack Kline's office in Washington. It turned out that the senator was unavailable at that time, Congress being in session. Hill spoke to his executive assistant, who was on Hill's payroll.

"I need Kline here within 24 hours," he said flatly. "You will take care of it."

"Yes, sir," replied the assistant reluctantly. "You must understand, sir, that Congress is in session. Besides that, the senator has been acting rather — erratic lately. He is being watched closely by several important people here. If he leaves suddenly, it will generate a lot of notice."

"I want him here *now*," repeated Hill, his voice sinking to almost a whisper. "Remind him of who he is and who made him *what* he is. That should jolt him out of his stupor."

"Yes, sir," replied the assistant again, sounding increasingly uncomfortable. "Hypothetically, though, what should I do if he refuses to come? As I said, he hasn't been entirely rational."

"Use force, then," said Hill. "You have your contacts in the bureau. I am authorizing any necessary action regarding Kline. They will know what to do. Questions?"

"No, sir. I'll handle it."

"See that you do," replied Hill, the menace in his tone unmistakable. He switched off. Pondering the blank screen, he decided to make one more call before meeting the remarkable Helen Bradley. This time he used the vid-phone, accessing an outside line. The call went through almost immediately.

"Bureau of Religious Affairs," said the pretty receptionist who answered. She obviously did not recognize Hill.

"Agent Lynch, please," he said shortly.

"Agent Lynch is in a meeting at the moment," replied the receptionist, "and specifically asked that he not be disturbed. If you will leave your name and a number where you can be reached, he will return your call as soon as possible."

"I will speak to him *NOW,*" said Hill, his voice dangerously flat. "Priority code Alpha Omicron Seven." The receptionist blanched as she heard and recognized the code. Although she did not know him, she knew by his use of that phrase he was not to be trifled with.

"I'll get him immediately, sir," she said hastily, her voice now generating much more respect. The screen went blank as he was put on hold. Less than five minutes later, Lynch himself appeared on the screen, looking somewhat haggard.

"Agent Lynch," he began, "I understand you have apprehended the head of the local FBI division on charges of conspiracy. From the report I've read he was arrested just hours after Helen Bradley. Why did you not send him here with her?" This caused Lynch to squirm a little. He shifted his position repeatedly as he spoke.

"By the time we caught up with him, Bradley was already en route to you. There were no specific instructions regarding him, so I decided to question him here first. Once his cohorts learn of his arrest, they will disappear fast. I wanted to strike quickly."

"And has he told you anything?"

"No, sir. However, we did catch him accessing the computer network that the Shepherd's Path was supposedly using."

"Indeed," replied Hill, his eyebrows raising slightly. "This is good. We should be able to get the access codes out of him and uncover the whole lot of them."

"Not really, sir," said Lynch. "It seems he became alerted to our monitoring process. Before we could stop him, he crashed the whole system. We were able to get a few names and addresses, including Helen Bradley's, but nothing else."

"Then why is he still there?" Hill was growing impatient. Lynch was a good agent, but he wasn't one of Hill's own people. Perhaps he should be replaced with someone Hill knew he could trust.

"As I said, sir, we hoped to catch his accomplices before they got wind of his arrest. Unfortunately, he refuses to cooperate — even with the threat of severe interrogation."

"I would expect no less," said Hill. "Listen, Lynch, this is not your decision. I want that man here immediately. In fact, I'm sending Ayres One out to get him. It can make the round trip faster than a conventional aircraft can travel one way. You have him ready to go when it gets there. Do you understand?"

"Yes, sir," agreed Lynch. Now the man looked downright nervous.

"That is all then. Get to it," snapped Hill. "Oh, and one more thing. I want you to come with him. See to the security arrangements yourself. That man is dangerous, and I'm holding you personally responsible." With that, he broke the connection.

He's got to go, he thought. *I'll arrange for his replacement as soon as he gets here.* Once again, Hill turned and brought up the image of Helen Bradley on the center screen.

"Now let's meet you face to face," he said softly. "I don't expect you to tell me anything yet, but after Phase Two, you will be more than ready to talk." With that, he turned off the screen and left the suite. This would be fun, he decided. He always did enjoy crowing over a defeated foe.

❖ ❖ ❖

Helen's mouth moved silently as she prayed. The past 24 hours had been a nightmare. She had been herded about like an animal, fingerprinted, photographed, and searched thoroughly. She had been degraded and humiliated. Then had come the flight to this place. She had been escorted to this office and left for almost an hour. Lack of sleep and food had left her weak and disoriented.

Lord God, what is going to happen to me? she prayed silently. *Is this the end? If it is, then please take me home quickly. Let me wake up in Your presence and see Your face. I miss Roy so much. I know he is with You. Please let me. . . .*

Abruptly the door to the office opened, startling Helen out of her prayer. *Finally,* she thought, *an end to this wretched waiting.* A woman in a white pant suit, obviously a medical technician of some sort, entered, carrying a metal tray covered by a white cloth. She smelled of disinfectant and perfume, a nauseating combination. Quickly and competently she set the tray down on the desk and pulled off the cover. Several medical instruments lay there in a neat row, although Helen did not recognize any of them. Selecting a stubby object with a top shaped like a cone, the technician placed one firm hand on top of Helen's head and forced it to turn slightly. She then inserted the pointed end of the cone into her right ear. It was a moment before Helen realized that her temperature was being taken. She repressed a sigh of relief, for she had imagined a far more sinister purpose for the high tech thermometer. In rapid order, her blood pressure, reflexes, and eye responses were all tested. Through it all, the technician said nothing. The silence finally became unbearable, and she tried to start a conversation.

"Do you think you could tell me where I am?" she asked quietly, a slight tremor threading its way into her voice. The technician ignored her completely. She tried again. "At least what part of the country. That wouldn't hurt, would it?" Again, no answer. "Please," said Helen, a hint of desperation creeping into her voice, "just *talk* to me. At least tell me. . . ." With that, the technician laid her instruments back onto the tray, covered them with the cloth, and left.

Helen felt tears of frustration beginning to form. She hadn't been ignored, she realized. Being ignored took a conscious effort on behalf of the person doing the ignoring. It required that he or she acknowledge the fact that the person they were ignoring existed — that they were human. Instead, Helen was treated as an object. To her captors, she was a non-person. At that moment, she felt very small and alone.

Once again, the door opened. Helen looked up, expecting to see the technician again. This time, however, two men entered the room. One was wearing a white coat and had the air of a doctor about him. The other . . . quickly Helen wiped her tears and sat a little straighter in the chair. The second man who entered the room and sat behind the desk was obviously in charge here. Tall and rapier thin, he wore the mantle of power like it was a second skin. His close-cropped gray hair gave him a congenial look, like everyone's favorite uncle, but his eyes — Helen looked into those steely azure eyes and saw nothing but death there — her death. She knew, with utter certainty, that this man was responsible for her being here. She knew he was her enemy.

The tall man regarded her closely from behind the desk. The doctor remained standing at the door, but Helen's attention was completely on the leader. She knew the doctor might do her harm, but it was the man behind the desk who would give the orders.

At length, he spoke. The menace in his voice was enough to freeze her heart. "Mrs. Bradley," he said, "welcome to Mentasys. I wish I could say that you will enjoy your stay here, but I'm afraid that would be a lie. In fact, I'm sure that it will be the most terrifying experience of your long life."

A chill ran up Helen's spine, and she lowered her eyes. She could not hold the stare of the man behind the desk.

"You're probably wondering where you are," he continued. "I think we can provide that little bit of information." Helen looked back up expectantly at this. The man smiled. He had the smile of a cobra ready to strike. "Yes, I thought you would be interested. You are in Los Angeles, California. This place," he said, motioning with his hand to include the entire complex, "is a research facility dedicated to uncovering truth. You are interested in truth, are you not?"

When Helen remained silent, the man continued. "You have information that I must have. You accomplished quite a feat, Helen. May I call you Helen? Maybe one person in a million could do what you have done. Do you realize that you organized and supervised a nationwide underground network right under the noses of the most efficient security force on the planet? You should be proud. I am quite impressed. So impressed that I want to hear all about it. I want you to tell me everything about your organization." The man paused for effect. "You may choose not to, of course," he said, shrugging. "It will make no difference. I *will* have the information whether you cooperate or not."

Helen remained silent. She knew that nothing she could say would bring about her freedom. She also knew something else. The attitude and actions of the man behind the desk told her plainly that she was going to die here. Strangely enough, the knowledge somehow freed her. All of her cares and worries melted away. The fear that had nipped at her heels since she had been captured disappeared. She would soon be with her Lord! True, she would have to go through the fire, but that was okay. She knew beyond a shadow of a doubt that whatever came her way, it would not be worse than what Jesus himself had endured on the cross.

A subtle battle was being waged in that room. A battle of minds, of wills. Up to this point, everything had been in favor of the man behind the desk. His every attack had thrust home, scoring a hit. Now, though, the tide of battle shifted. Helen sat a little straighter, and the slight tremble in her hands was gone. She looked up to meet the stare of her enemy, and found that she could endure it. More than endure it, as a matter of fact. She returned it with one of her own. In one of their infrequent arguments, Roy had snapped that she could stare down a praying mantis. Although outwardly the remark had infuriated her, inside she had been perversely pleased. Now it was her enemy who flinched.

"Since you know so much about me," she asked, pleased that her voice was calm and even, "perhaps you could tell me a little about yourself. I'd like to know the name of my host."

This surprised him, she saw. He was undoubtedly wondering where the frightened, cringing woman who had been brought in here was. Helen thought about explaining, but this man probably would not understand her answer. That woman was still here in this room, she knew, sitting in this chair. She was just getting a little outside help.

"All right," he agreed, after a moment's thought. "Since you ask, this is Dr. Steiger." He gestured toward the medical man. "You may call *me* Jacob."

"Well, Jacob, I think I should tell you something you need to know," said Helen calmly.

"Please," replied Jacob, holding up both hands to forestall her, "don't tell me that you have friends that know where you are, and don't lecture me about your constitutional rights. No one knows where you are, and you have no rights. You are a traitor to the state, and have thus forfeited those rights."

"I could argue about that," replied Helen, "but I won't. In any case, you misunderstand me. You don't have to pretend about your purpose. I have no doubt that I will not leave here alive."

"Then what is it that you think I should know?" asked Jacob. He was beginning to feel vaguely uncomfortable in the presence of this woman. In spite of the fact that he had her in his grasp, he had the disquieting feeling that he had somehow lost control of this interview.

"You should know that you cannot hope to win," responded Helen. Her voice was permeated with a calm certainty that, for a moment, had Jacob believing her. The tide of the battle had now shifted, and the advantage belonged to Helen. Jacob could sense this, and tried to renew his attack. He reached for the deadliest smile in his arsenal, and dialed up his most menacing tone. Even his own inner circle blanched when he used them in tandem. It usually meant that someone was going to die.

"You are obviously grossly misinformed," he said. "I have already won. Your kind can no longer practice your absurd beliefs in this country. The government is no longer your friend. The American people have realized that your religion is a pack of lies, just as is your 'Holy Book.' In another few years, people like you will simply cease to exist." *This should get a rise out of her,* he thought to himself. If he could just make her angry, he would win this little battle of wills. Anger was a close cousin to fear, and fear would defeat her. He looked at her calmly, waiting for her to respond, confident in his superior position. Even he was surprised though, when Helen started to giggle. He watched in amazement as her giggle rapidly became a full-fledged laugh.

"Oh dear," she cried, gasping for breath. "I'm sorry, I really am. I know you want me to be terrified, but. . . ." and she was off again. Now she was laughing so hard that tears began to run down her cheeks, and her face started to turn bright red. Jacob watched, convinced she had gone mad. Gradually, she brought herself back under control. "Tell me, Jacob," she asked, the merriment bright in her eyes, "what 'B' movie did you just step out of? Didn't I see you on the late show the other night? Holy Book indeed!"

Now it was Jacob who found himself getting angry. "Laugh all you want," he snapped, his voice several decibels higher. "When I am done with you, you will not possess the ability to even smile." It was the first time he had raised his voice in years. Steiger's eyebrows went up in surprise. Jacob Hill had always been icy calm — in complete control. He had handled world leaders and business giants with equal ease. Now, though, he was losing control to this absurd old woman. He watched the confrontation continue. At Jacob's threats, Helen sat straighter, her amusement gone. In its place, she now exuded a serene forcefulness that dominated the room. Steiger knew he was looking at a battle-hardened veteran who had survived a great deal.

"You poor man," she said, shaking her head. "You serve a defeated foe, and yet you think you have won." The pity in her voice was unmistakable. "Tell me, Jacob," she asked, "who is pulling *your* strings? It's obvious that you aren't behind this whole thing."

"Enough!" bellowed Jacob.

"It's not too late, you know," Helen went on with obvious sincerity. "You can still turn away from this terrible course you have set for yourself. Did you know that 'the wages of sin is death, but the gift of God is eternal life, through Jesus Christ'?" She leaned forward, intent on her message. "You can have that gift right now, Jacob. It's there for the asking." Her eyes looked up to include Steiger. "You too, Doctor. God is no respecter of persons. Why not take the gift He is offering? You might not get another chance."

That did it. Jacob stood, his eyes blazing with fury. For her to pity him was bad enough. For her to guess about the Sextuaget was even worse. But for her to sit there — preaching — it was more than he could bear. His breathing came in heavy gasps, and his hands clenched and unclenched. He could never remember being so out of control, even as a child. He had been raised to control and dominate, but now he was being dominated. He turned to Steiger, who flinched at the fury in his eyes.

"Get her out of here," he shouted. "I want her in Phase One now, and ready for Phase Two by the end of the week."

"But, sir," began Steiger, "you know what happens when an unprepared human goes into Phase Two. They go catatonic, and we can never bring them back. We put her in there without adequate time in Phase One, and she won't come out." The wild look on Jacob's face told him that this was not the time to object.

"Do it," he said, his voice now plunging to a whisper. "I don't care what happens to her as long as we get the information we need. I want you to drain it out of her — rip it out if you have to. Just do it. NOW, Doctor, unless you want to be replaced."

That was enough for Steiger. He edged his way quickly around Jacob and firmly took Helen's arm. Eager to be out of range of Jacob's wrath, he practically dragged her to the hidden elevator. Once inside, he felt the urge to sag against the wall in relief. Helen said nothing, but instead kept her eyes forward. They rode down in silence, Helen wrapped up in her own thoughts. Steiger kept his eyes averted, not wanting to have the attention of this firebrand of a woman turned on him. The doors parted, and he rushed his charge past the startled guards, down a long hall, and into the Phase One ward.

Helen scanned the ward, noting the 12 beds, only five of them now full. Four men and one woman lay totally motionless, the regular rising and falling of their chests the only indication that they were alive. Wires were attached to their heads, and several monitors sat beside each bed, keeping close watch on their conditions. Each bed had a clipboard hanging from the foot, containing the name and history of the current occupant. Without preamble, Steiger rushed her to the side of the nearest available bed.

"Stand there," he grunted, turning away.

He motioned for the nurse on duty to join them.

"Prep her," he said to the big-boned black woman. Standing back, Steiger watched as the nurse went professionally about her work. Helen was quickly and expertly undressed, her clothes going into a bin that the nurse pulled out from under the bed. Helen endured it all, trying to think of seeing Roy again in heaven. The nurse then returned to her desk for a moment, her sneakers making quiet squeaks as she left. Helen stood there, naked and alone. Even Steiger had seemingly lost interest in her. He was leaning over another patient, his back to her.

More out of a desire to take her mind off her condition than anything else, she moved closer to the bed to her right. It contained the unconscious form of a very attractive young lady. Glancing around to see if anyone was watching, she moved to the foot of the bed to read the name on the chart. She could hear the squeaking of the nurse's shoes coming toward her.

She read the name, and took a deep breath. Beth Sampson! That was Scott's wife — the one who was supposed to have been killed in that awful plane crash. How in the world. . . .

"Over here," said the nurse in a commanding voice that allowed no disobedience. Helen felt a vise of a hand grip her arm, and was led back unresisting to what was to be her own bed. The nurse had returned with a typical blue hospital gown which she now slipped over Helen's shoulders. Helen was then made to climb in and lay flat on her back.

"Doctor," said the nurse, indicating that Steiger should join them. Steiger replaced the chart he was holding and moved to stand at Helen's side. Quickly he took her pulse and blood pressure, marking on Helen's own chart.

"Okay," he said to the nurse. "She's ready. Let's hook her up." As Helen watched, Steiger attached two wires to an instrument identical to the ones next to the other beds. The nurse applied a sticky substance about the consistency of jello to her forehead. Then, Steiger carefully added round pads the size of quarters to the wires. Frowning in concentration, he pressed the other side of the pads to each side of Helen's brow. His work done, he stepped back to check the positioning. Helen remained silent through the whole process, knowing that any of her questions would go unanswered. She had no idea what this apparatus was supposed to do.

Steiger moved off for a moment, and Helen glanced over at the unconscious Beth. *Why are you here,* she asked silently. *What are they doing to you — and me?* Her first question would go unanswered, but her second would not. Steiger returned, checking her over one final time. Then he activated the instrument that was connected to Helen's forehead. Instantly, Helen felt herself losing consciousness. She found herself gazing down a long tunnel at a rapidly fading light. Knowing that she had only seconds, she made her last thoughts a prayer.

Oh God, she thought urgently, *don't let me reveal things that will get others hurt. Take me home now. Please! Don't let me . . . .* Her sentence went unfinished, and the light went out.

❖ ❖ ❖

"Jack! Jack, hold up a second." Jack Kline started as he heard his name shouted. He was making his way out of the Senate chambers, the day's session finally being finished. Normally, he lingered there long after the sessions were over. He never tired of the place. So much history had been made there, and was still being made. It made him feel alive and vital just to be in that beautiful ornate hall. Lately, though, he just couldn't seem to care. Turning, he saw Senator Ben Davidson waving at him, motioning for him to wait. Although Davidson was many years his senior, the two had formed a close friendship over the years. It was Davidson who had guided Jack through his freshman year in Congress, helping him to avoid the many pitfalls that often befell rookies. He was puffing as he caught up with Jack. His advancing years and heavy frame did not lend themselves to much exertion.

"Headed back to the office?" he asked as he drew even in the aisle with his younger friend and colleague. Jack merely nodded.

"Have you got a few minutes for an old friend?" asked Davidson. "There are some things I'd like your opinion on."

Instantly the question flashed in Jack's mind, *What does he want from me?* It was the same question he had asked for several days, anytime someone wanted to bend his ear. He answered evasively. "Sorry, Ben, but I've got a full afternoon. In fact, I'm booked the rest of the week. Why don't you call my assistant? He can probably make time for you early next week."

As he spoke, he squinted his eyes, trying to read Davidson's aura. He wanted to get a fix on where he was coming from. Unfortunately, he could see nothing. His ability to read auras was highly undependable these days.

He was startled when Davidson took his arm and began to steer him out of the chambers. "Humor me, Jack," he said as he all but led him away. "There are some things we need to talk about — important things — things that directly involve you."

"Things?" asked Jack as they left the building. He couldn't imagine what Davidson was talking about, although somewhere deep inside, he felt as if he should be able to figure it out. He shook his head to try to clear it, but the cobwebs that had clung to his mind for what seemed like forever would not go away.

It took only 15 minutes for the pair to make their way out of the Capital Building and over to Jack's office. Jack's new assistant objected to the intrusion, but Davidson had not survived in politics all these years to be put off by a glorified clerk. He swept Jack into his office and shut the door behind him. Motioning for him to sit behind his desk, Davidson took one of the blue velour chairs in front of it.

He wasted no time in getting to the reason for his visit. "Jack," he said bluntly, "what the heck is going on? Why are you self-destructing like this?"

"I don't understand, Ben," was the confused reply.

"You don't understand!?" repeated Davidson incredulously. "Have you looked in the mirror the past few days? You look terrible! When was the last time you got a real night's sleep, anyway?"

"Well," began Jack, "It was. . . ."

"Don't bother to answer that," interrupted Davidson. "And don't bother to deny that something's wrong. I've known you too long."

Suddenly, Jack felt unbearably tired. It was as if a great weight had come to rest squarely on his shoulders. Absently he rubbed the back of his neck. "What do you want, Ben?" he asked wearily. "I've got work to do."

Davidson studied him closely, the concern evident in his face. "All right," he said at last, "I'll spell it out for you. A lot of questions are being raised about your behavior over the last few months. Take your disappearance a few weeks ago. You just up and left town, and no one had any idea where you went. You've been missing appointments, not bothering to cancel them. Good grief, Jack! Today you sat next to the vice president and hardly acknowledged him! I know you don't like him, but in the past, at least you've been civil."

Davidson leaned forward in his intensity. "No one questions the fact that you've been through the wringer," he said gently. "We *all* grieved for Marcie. She was an extraordinary woman, but you've got to keep going." He paused to wipe his suddenly sweating brow. "Someone has declared war on the U.S. Congress," he continued softly. "There was Marcie, then the attempt on you. After that we lost Jackson and Kirshner, both by shooting. Jack, the whole Congress is on edge. They need someone to hold them together — to keep things moving. You've got to get your head in gear and be the leader you are capable of being."

Jack spread his hands palms up on his desk. "What can I do?" he asked plaintively. "You already said that people are starting to doubt me."

"Politicians can forgive a large bit of irregularities, Jack. Right now, Congress needs you. If you start acting like yourself again, I can almost guarantee that nothing else will be said."

"And if I don't?"

There was a look of great distaste on Davidson's face, as if he would rather contemplate suicide than what he was about to say. "If you don't," he said slowly, "then there will be a full congressional investigation into your affairs. They'll break you, Jack. Even if you have nothing to hide, they'll break you on general principles. Then they'll get someone in office who will do the job." Davidson looked Jack straight in the eye. "They *will* find something, won't they? It's obvious that you're hiding something."

Jack did not reply. Although outwardly he kept his face impassive, inside he was afraid. A full investigation could possibly uncover his association with Jacob and the Inner Circle. It could bring to light how he had used his position to benefit the circle. That would finish him. Not only would it end his career, it could bring him up on criminal charges. He realized that he was at a loss. There was only one person he could turn to. He had to get to Jacob. He would know what to do.

"All right, Ben," he said, trying to end the impromptu meeting. "I'll get it in gear, as you say. Let's call a meeting with the president and his cabinet. We need to come up with some sort of plan for dealing with these attacks. Once we get that taken care of, we'll see about getting things back to normal. How's that sound?"

"More like the Jack Kline I used to know," replied Davidson, a look of relief spreading across his ample face. He heaved himself out of the chair and made ready to leave. "You handle getting the meeting on the president's agenda, and I'll pass the word that you're back in action."

"It's a deal," said Jack with a lot more enthusiasm than he felt. He rose and stuck out his hand. "Thanks for kicking me in the tail and getting me back on track."

"Don't mention it," said Davidson, shaking the offered hand. "Better me than a congressional committee, eh? Look, I've got to get going. There's a lot to pull together. I'll be in touch." With that, he turned and left.

Jack sank into his chair and threw his head back. The ceiling stared back at him, a blank surface to match his blank mind.

He closed his eyes, trying to ward off the monster headache that always came when he tried to think straight. The last few minutes of concentration had cost him dearly. He would be paying for them for hours. There was no time to waste, he knew. Ben

THE SHEPHERD'S PATH • 255

Davidson might have bought his act, but the ruse wouldn't last for long. He had to get to Jacob now, and not just by phone.

He keyed the intercom. "Brian!"

"Yes, Senator," came the voice of Marcie's replacement.

"Arrange a flight to Los Angeles for me. Better make it a commercial flight. I need to be there by tonight."

"Uh, yes, sir." He could hear the astonishment in Brian's voice. "I'll get on it right away. Should I arrange for transportation at the airport?"

"No, I'll take care of that myself. Just get me on the next available flight."

He switched off the intercom and activated the vid-phone. In seconds, the pretty face of Doris, the receptionist at Mentasys, came on line. "Jacob Hill, please," he said with as much assurance as he could muster.

"One moment, sir," was the reply. "I'll see if he is available." The screen went blank and Jack ticked off the seconds impatiently. It was well over five minutes before the stern visage of Jacob appeared.

"Jack? You know this number is only to be used in extreme emergencies."

"Believe me, this constitutes one," said Jack quickly. "I'm flying out there tonight. Don't try to stop me. I need a car waiting at the airport."

"I wouldn't dream of trying to stop you," said Jacob.

"Good. I'll call back as soon as I know when my flight arrives. Goodbye, Jacob." Without waiting for a reply, Jack broke the connection. He slumped back into his chair, drained and in pain. The expected headache hit him so hard and suddenly that he almost cried out. It had never been so bad before. What was wrong with him? As he gritted his teeth and massaged his temples, the intercom beeped for his attention.

"What is it?" His voice came out in a harsh whisper. Even that sounded unbearably loud in his ears.

"Sir? Are you all right?" It was Brian.

"Of course I'm all right," he snapped. "What is it?"

"Your flight information, sir. State Airlines Flight 457, departing at 8:00 p.m. It's after five now, sir. You'd better get home and pack."

"Fine," Jack replied shortly. "Now leave me alone."

Once again he leaned back in the chair and closed his eyes. The headache was subsiding ever so slowly, and he could feel the familiar cobwebs settling in. He had no intention of going home, nor of packing. Jenny would understand, he hoped. He would tell no one where he was going.

Sitting up abruptly, he rose and went to the large window that dominated the wall opposite his desk. There was a ledge wide enough to sit on, which he did. Opening the heavy blue curtain, he peered out. From his vantage point, he could see the Capitol, and beyond that the Washington Monument. It was a beautiful sight, one that always inspired and comforted him. Now, though, it left him cold. Below, thousands of people scurried about. Most of them, he knew, were tourists. It was that time of year. He watched as they went to and fro, seeing the sights and generally having a good time. His eyes caught a couple walking arm in arm down the Capitol steps. The woman was carrying a toddler who had seen enough sights for one day. His head lay against his mother's shoulder.

Suddenly an intense longing seized him, wrenching his insides so hard that it was almost a physical pain. At that moment in time, all he wanted was to be one of those everyday, ordinary folk. What wouldn't he give to be able to be a part of that crowd — to be able to disappear into that mass of humanity that thronged below? Sadly he pushed the curtain back. It was not for him, he knew. He had made his choices years ago, and now he must live with them. Straightening his shoulders, he walked out of his office for the last time, and set his course for Mentasys, and his destiny.

❖ ❖ ❖

Stephen Lynch sat staring at an empty viewscreen. For the past half hour, he had the distinct impression that the walls of the small office were closing in on him. He quite literally could not believe what he had been watching. It wasn't possible. Being a part of the Bureau of Religious Affairs was a major part of his life. No — it WAS his life. Ever since he had watched his grandmother give her life savings to some smooth-talking televangelist, he had burned with a desire to see religious organizations put in their place. That particular evangelist had been indicted for fraud and embezzlement. Oh, he had gone to jail, but his grandmother had never seen her money again. She had ended her days in a cheap nursing home because his parents could not afford to keep her. She had died a broken woman, because the one person she had put her trust in was a cheap, lying, con man.

When the bureau had been formed, Lynch had joined immediately. His background in law enforcement had been a plus, and he was accepted on the spot. His zeal had allowed him to rise in the ranks, until he now dealt with the most important cases that came across the national director's desk. The bureau was everything he had believed in. Oh, maybe things had swung a little too far in one direction, but as far as he was concerned, they were evening out from a decade ago. He believed completely and wholeheartedly in what he was doing.

Until now.

Until he had apprehended the elusive Jeff Anderson and taken the video tape from him. Until he had inserted that tape into a player and had watched it. There on the screen was proof — undeniable proof — that the most important thing he believed in was not what it seemed. A half hour ago, he was convinced that the terrorist known as Scott Sampson was guilty of the bombing of Flight 407. Now he knew differently.

He had watched the tape as Scott said goodbye to his wife, as she boarded the plane, and as he walked away. He saw that Scott had not even come close to getting on that flight. Okay, he reasoned, his wife could have carried the bomb on. It would not be the first time a zealot had been willing to die for her beliefs. There could even be another accomplice the bureau didn't know about.

All of his suppositions had been shattered. They lay at his feet like broken glass, unable to be put back together. He watched as the agents came into the frame and boarded the plane. He did not need to enlarge the I.D.'s, because he knew one of them. Agent Peter Crawford was right there in front of him, carrying a small black suitcase. He carried it on, and didn't carry it off. Stephen Lynch knew that there was only one explanation possible. The bureau had bombed the flight — not the Christian Liberation Front.

Questions crowded into his dazed mind, overlapping each other. What about the bombing at Marcie Cumming's home? Crawford had been there, too, and had disappeared afterwards. Coincidence? Lynch thought not. Too many things were adding up. The shootings of two congressmen, the airport tape, the Cummings woman — all started to paint a very ugly picture. To top it all off, Jacob Hill, the national director himself, wanted him in Los Angeles, at a place called Mentasys. He thought about the phone call he had just received. Hill had ordered him to escort Anderson there personally. Lynch had barely been able to maintain his composure over the video link.

Angrily he switched off the view screen, thankful that no one else was in the office with him. In the space of half an hour, he no longer knew who to trust. There was corruption in the bureau, and who knew how high up it reached — perhaps all the way to the top. He wasn't taking any chances. There was one man close by who might have the answers he needed.

"Have Anderson brought here immediately," he said into the intercom. Slipping the incriminating tape into his pocket, Lynch waited impatiently for FBI agent Jeff Anderson to arrive.

❖ ❖ ❖

Jeff paced back and forth in the small holding room like a caged tiger. He had been brought here hours ago, and still nothing had happened. The waiting was getting to him far worse than any questioning might. He stopped in front of a large mirror that was inset into one of the walls. It was obviously two way, and he knew that there were people behind it observing him.

"Lets get on with it," he said, spreading his arms in a get-on-the-stick gesture. There was no response. He had expected none. Resuming his pacing, he tried to get his mind working on something — anything — that might aid him. They had brought him to the local Bureau of Religious Affairs office, and he did not know the layout of the building. Even if he did, escape would probably be hopeless. His face was undoubtedly burned into the circuits of every computer net in the nation. Add to that the fact that he had crashed his only source of information and it all came out to one answer — he had no where to go.

His mind turned to Helen, and he felt his heart do a double thump. He was sick with worry about her, and angry at himself because of his helplessness. If he could have stayed free, he might have. . . .

"Mr. Anderson." The voice of the matronly woman wearing the dark blue uniform of the bureau police interrupted his pacing. She was standing beside the half-open entrance looking at him expectantly. He had been so wrapped up in his thoughts that he had not heard the door open. "Come this way, please," she said, not waiting for him to respond. She disappeared through the door and he hastened to follow. Jogging a couple of steps, he drew even with her in the hall. *They must be awfully sure of themselves,* he thought. There wasn't even a guard to escort him. It stung his pride just a little. After all, he had incapacitated two agents single-handedly, and left four others eating his dust. One would think that he rated more than just this bored-looking woman.

"Where are we going?" he asked, not really expecting an answer.

"Agent Lynch wants to speak with you privately," she answered, surprising him.

He said nothing else, and followed the woman. She led him to an empty office that was only slightly larger than the holding room. He was instructed to sit in one of the two straightbacked chairs and wait. Agent Lynch would be with him in a moment. Jeff did as he was told, and was left alone. Automatically his eyes scanned the office, seeking a possible escape route. Nothing suggested itself, and it didn't matter anyway, for at that moment the door opened again and Lynch himself stepped in.

Jeff studied his adversary carefully. He saw a man a few years younger than himself, with that look of perpetual youth that would let him pass for 25 when he turned 45. Although an average person would detect nothing wrong, he sensed an air about the agent that spoke of nervousness and doubt. Jeff had made a career of reading people. He could get a picture of what they were thinking and feeling just by watching them closely. A hand movement here, a twitch of an eyebrow there, all spoke volumes to his trained mind. What he saw now confused him. This man had managed to nab both Helen and him after countless others had failed. He had proven himself to be resourceful and cunning. Jeff was sure that the tattletale in the FBI computers was authorized by him. He was equally sure that he had been the one tapping into the system when Jeff had crashed it. Yet, this same man was looking like he was the prisoner here. What was going on? Jeff leaned back in the hard chair, determined to find out.

"I'll be blunt with you, Anderson," began Lynch without preliminary. "We've got you. We have enough evidence to get you the chair for sedition and treason." There was no answer to this, so Jeff gave none. Instead he continued to observe Lynch. He was certain now that he was hiding something, and he was determined to find out what it was.

"I want answers," continued Lynch. His voice sounded firm and confident, but the rest of his body language was calling his voice a liar. "I know you're involved with the Shepherd's Path. You will give me the names of your accomplices."

Jeff continued to be silent. Partly because he had no intention of talking, but mostly because he knew very few names. That was the beauty of the system that he and Helen had designed.

"How are you organized? Who is your leader? Is it the Bradley woman?" Jeff maintained his silence, and Lynch continued the barrage of questions, not giving him a chance to speak. It was almost as if he didn't want Jeff to answer. "Is this area your home base? How do you arrange for transportation? What are the locations of your so-called safe houses?" The agent paused for a breath, staring hard at his FBI counterpart.

Jeff remained silent, waiting for him to tip his hand and discover what he really wanted.

Suddenly Lynch slammed his fist on the desk, hard. "Answer me!" Now he was shouting. "Answer me or so help me, you won't get out of this alive!"

Tell me something I don't know, thought Jeff wryly.

Lynch waited in vain for Jeff to respond. When he didn't, Lynch turned away. Jeff's eyes grew wide with amazement. The man's shoulders were shaking! He was ready to blow, and what direction that release would take, Jeff could not even guess. He half expected him to break out in tears. Whatever was sticking in this man's craw, it was eating him alive. This wasn't a professional matter, Jeff realized. This was personal. Abruptly, Lynch turned back to him. He had regained his composure, but Jeff could see the strain in his face. He reached into his pocket and pulled out the video tape.

"Where did you get this?" he asked in a dangerously low voice.

Bingo, thought Jeff. *This is the crux of the matter.*

"Get what?" answered Jeff for the first time, baiting him.

"This is serious, Anderson," said Lynch, the anger showing through his voice. "I want to know where you got this tape." Like a runaway locomotive, it hit him. Lynch truly didn't know. He didn't know that his own people were behind the bombing of Flight 407. He must have just seen that tape. He had the same resources that Jeff had. He would be able to identify the agents as easily as Jeff, probably easier.

Now Jeff leaned forward, his entire being concentrated on the man in front of him. "I don't remember where I got that," he said. "I guess I just picked it up somewhere."

His words were designed to get a reaction, not to give information. He was successful. Lynch started to turn red, and his hands resumed their trembling. Jeff knew that he was seeing pure rage, and it was only partly directed at him. Suddenly, he found himself looking down the barrel of Lynch's very large pistol. He had not even seen the bureau agent draw his weapon. The man was fast! Although he thought he was prepared to die, he could feel his eyes widening and his breath coming faster. Judging from the way the pistol jittered in Lynch's hand, anything could happen in the next few minutes.

"TELL . . . ME . . . WHERE . . . YOU . . . GOT . . . THE . . . TAPE."
His words were barely loud enough for Jeff to hear. They were an almost primal growl.

Jeff knew that the agent was ready to pull the trigger. "Airport security," he said, pleased at how calm his voice sounded. Inside, his heart was pounding like a trip hammer.

Lynch clenched his jaw and moved the gun to where it was only millimeters away from the bridge of Jeff's nose. Obviously he wasn't accepting the answer. "I saw those tapes," he said in the same low tone. "We acquired them at the beginning of the investigation. They didn't have *any* of what I just saw on them."

Jeff shrugged. The tape Lynch had taken from him was obviously genuine. He knew it, and Lynch knew it. He could see that the knowledge had sent Lynch's loyalties and values into a tailspin. Lynch's desperation was almost tangible. He could not believe that the organization he served would be involved in such an atrocity — and yet he had no choice.

"I guess you saw the edited version," he responded, never taking his eyes off Lynch's.

They spent an eternity like that, locked in each others gaze. Finally it was Lynch who turned away. Jeff took a deep, silent breath as the gun disappeared, willing his heart to slow. He was not out of the woods yet, he knew. Lynch was in a state of flux. Everything he believed in was a lie, and he was just finding that out. It made him both unstable and dangerous.

"You're one of them, aren't you?" The question was asked so softly that at first Jeff didn't understand it.

"What?" he asked.

Lynch turned back to him. "I said, you're one of them, aren't you? A part of that Shepherd's Path — a *Christian.*" Lynch spat out that last word, his contempt evident.

"You know that already," replied Jeff. "Why else would I be here?"

"Why? Why do you believe that stuff?" Jeff could hear the confusion and disbelief in his voice. "You're good, Anderson. The best I've ever seen. You took on my top men, and beat them. The only reason we got you is thanks to big brother." He jerked his finger to the sky, indicating the satellite. "Why waste your time on something that should have died out a thousand years ago?"

How do you answer a man who is about to kill you? Jeff asked himself. *Truthfully,* he decided. "It didn't die out" he replied evenly.

"It came from God. How *could* it die out?" That scored home, Jeff saw.

For an instant, Lynch let his guard down, and his face became a mirror to his soul. Jeff saw a man in pure anguish. A drowning man grasping at anything that would keep him afloat. Without another word, he jerked open the door. "Stay there!" he snarled, and left.

Jeff stared after him. "Where would I go?" he asked the empty air.

❖ ❖ ❖

Stephen Lynch forced himself to stride normally down the hall. He wanted to get as far away from Jeff Anderson as he could. Inside, he was a mess. Emotions that he had thought long erased were surfacing inside of him. Although he fought it every step of the way, he could not help remembering his grandmother. He was only 17 when she died. He had been the last person to see her alive, and that memory still haunted him. He remembered the horror of that filthy, detestable nursing home. He remembered the stench of unemptied bedpans and the loud moaning out in the hall. It was the sound of utter hopelessness — the sound of people waiting to die.

In his mind's eye, he saw his grandmother. She was not the feisty, vibrant, silver-haired woman of his pre-teen years. Now she was an eaten-out hulk, just barely alive. Her breathing came in loud rasps through her open mouth. A clear plastic tube ran into her nose, and a sickly greenish ooze trickled out around it. It had made him want to vomit. This was not his grandmother, he thought. This was a mockery of what she had been.

Her dull, lifeless brown eyes had cracked open. For a moment, they were confused. Then they settled on him, and a spark of recognition lit them. Her hand had moved feebly, tethered to the bed by intravenous needles.

Although revolted by the clammy touch of her cold skin, he had taken hold of her hand and held it tightly. "Mamaw," he had whispered, his voice choking on the words.

"Stevie," she croaked. She was the only one who called him that. "I was wrong."

"Just try to rest, Mamaw," he said, trying to soothe her.

A bit of her fiery nature surfaced, and she returned his grip. "Listen to me," she said, her voice a little firmer. "I was wrong to put my trust in a man. People will always let you down, Stevie, but God never will. He never will."

"Mamaw, please."

"Shhh. I've got to tell you. I've watched you grow cold to the things of the Lord." A fit of coughing wracked her emaciated frame. It was a moment before she could continue. "It's my fault," she said finally. "I put my trust in that television con-man. I should've trusted God. If I had listened to Him, I wouldn't be here now." Her grip grew stronger for a moment. "Do you understand, Stevie? Don't turn your back on God because His people aren't perfect. Don't give up on God. . . ." The energy she had expended exhausted her, and she fell back limp and gasping.

She slipped into unconsciousness, and less than an hour later, she was gone. Stephen had been with her the whole time. When she died, he had simply folded her hands together and walked out of the room. He decided at that moment to hate the God she wanted him to love. He would not serve any Lord who would allow this to happen. He would fight those who did with everything he had.

Lynch blew into his own office and slammed the door behind him. The interview with Anderson had unnerved him, and he was already shaky to start with. He needed answers, and he needed them now. He strode purposefully over behind his desk and sat down heavily. Thinking for a moment, he activated his computer and began to type.

Like any good agent, Lynch always made it a habit to know just a little more than he was supposed to. That little extra had saved his life more than once. Just a few short months ago, he had acquired the assistant bureau chief's access code. It had been relatively easy. He had simply looked over his shoulder as he entered it into his own terminal. Although he never planned on using it, he had filed the knowledge away for future reference. The time had come, he knew, to use it.

He entered the code into his terminal and just like that was granted access to the entire bureau system. Shoving aside the feeling that he was a traitor, he called up the personal file of Agent Peter Crawford. That was his starting point. Agent Crawford had been at both the bombing here in Cincinnati and in Washington. He was still missing and presumed dead. If he was anything else, it would show here.

Crawford's file flashed up on the screen, and Lynch knew the worst. The screen filled with personal data regarding Crawford, but it was two categories that commanded Lynch's attention. At the top of the screen was his current status. He was still listed as active. At the bottom was his current location — Geneva, Switzerland. Only two men had access to this information. The first was the assistant bureau chief. The second was Jacob Hill himself, the head of the entire Bureau of Religious Affairs.

Lynch sat back and closed his eyes. A long hiss of air escaped his lips. The corruption ran all the way to the top. He had been tracking suspected terrorists from one end of the country to the other, but members of the elusive Christian Liberation Front always remained one step ahead of him. Now he knew why. The terrorists he had been after were taking their orders from his own superiors. *One big happy family,* he thought bitterly. A sudden knock at the door startled him. Quickly he switched off the computer.

"Come in," he called. The door opened and one of his assistants, a young woman named Suzanne, entered. She was holding a small piece of paper in her hand.

"Mr. Lynch, a priority message just came in from the airport for you."

"What is it?"

"It's from the captain of an Ayres One. He's on the ground and waiting for you. He says that you were supposed to be there to meet him."

"I see," replied Lynch. "Get in touch with him and tell him that I will be delayed. Tell him something has come up. I'll be there within the hour."

"Yes, sir," said Suzanne. She went out, closing the door behind her.

Lynch drummed his fingers on the desk for a moment. He had a decision to make, one that would greatly affect the rest of his life. He could ignore what he had uncovered and continue to do his job. No one would know, and he could remain safe. The problem was, he would be living a lie. He would know that the organization he was a part of was rotten to the core, and the simple fact was, he could not abide that. He demanded total dedication and honesty from himself and those who were under him. He could not be loyal to superiors who did not subscribe to the same code of ethics. The more he thought about it, the more he realized that his decision had already been made. It had been made when he had viewed that tape. The only thing left to do was to act on that decision.

With total resolution and just a bit of apprehension, he left the office and made his way back to where Anderson was being held.

❖   ❖   ❖

Jeff started as the door to the office flew open and a very determined looking Agent Lynch walked in. He could see that something was different. Lynch had evidently come to grips with what he had learned. He had the air of a man who had just made a life changing decision.

"Let's get one thing straight, Anderson," said Lynch with characteristic directness. "I think you're wrong. I think God doesn't care about what goes on down here, and those who say He does are liars." He paused to see the effect his words were having. When Jeff made no response, he continued. "I also believe that religious groups need government supervision. Without it, they get out of control, and a lot of people get hurt. I think people who meet in secret are putting their beliefs ahead of the good of this country, and should be considered traitors. Do we understand each other?"

"Perfectly," replied Jeff, looking him in the eye. What was he getting at?

"Okay, as long as that's clear. Now, what are we going to do about this?" With that, he took the tape out of his jacket pocket and set it carefully on the desk.

Jeff looked at it, then back at Lynch. "What do you mean, 'we'?" he asked carefully.

"You know what's on there," answered Lynch. "And you know what it means. Don't you?"

Might as well be straight with him, thought Jeff. "If you mean, do I know that your people are responsible for Flight 407, and who knows what else, then yes, I know what it means," he said, a touch of anger coloring his voice.

Lynch detected it immediately and held up his hands in a defensive gesture. "I swear to you Anderson, I didn't know." His fist clenched and he looked as if he would hit something. "I'm talking to you as a fellow agent now," he said. "I've just found out that the Bureau of Religious Affairs is not what it is supposed to be."

"Oh?" Jeff's tone was mocking.

"Listen to me!" Lynch smacked the desk with his palm. "Something stinks all the way to the top of the organization. I know, beyond a shadow of a doubt, that Director Hill himself is involved."

Jeff said nothing. He knew of Jacob Hill, of course. The man had come to prominence a few years ago when he was named as chief of the Bureau of Religious Affairs. The FBI had wanted to do a routine check on him, but was flatly denied the opportunity. Even then, the bureau was a law unto itself.

"I don't know who I can trust," continued Lynch, now showing a touch of frustration. "With the top of the organization compromised, who knows how far down the corruption goes?"

Jeff had had enough. Lynch wanted something from him, and he wanted to know what it was. "Lynch," he said finally, "what do you want from me? I'm a prisoner here, in case you haven't noticed."

Lynch leaned forward eagerly. "I want you to help me expose them," he said in a low voice. "I want to prove that they are responsible for the bombings, and maybe even the murders of those two congressmen. Since I can't trust anyone within the organization, I need your help. Like I said, you're the best I've ever seen. With your help, I can pull the plug on the terrorists and nail the big guys all at once. Then we'll put the bureau back together, and have it doing the job it was originally designed to do."

"Let me get this straight," said Jeff incredulously. "You want me to help you put the bureau back on track. In other words, back to harassing innocent people — people whose only crime is to want to worship God freely. Is that right?"

"That's about it," agreed Lynch.

"Give me one good reason," demanded Jeff.

"Helen Bradley."

That stopped Jeff short. "What about her?" he asked cautiously.

"I know where she's being held," answered Lynch. "A place in Los Angeles called Mentasys. It's some kind of research facility. That's where our proof is. If you can help me get in there, then I'll get my proof, and you'll get her. How about it?"

Jeff didn't even have to think about it. He was going to get Helen back. If he could bring down the bureau chiefs in the process, so much the better. There was only one thing. "One condition," he said.

Lynch looked at him guardedly. "And that is . . . ?"

"There might be another woman in there — the one your people took off Flight 407. Her name is Beth Sampson. If she's there, we take her out, too."

"Done," said Lynch.

"Something else," added Jeff. "I want to try to get hold of her husband. He has a right to know that his wife is still alive."

"That's Scott Sampson, right?" Jeff nodded.

"You know," said Lynch conversationally, "we've been looking hard for him. Where did you send him, to the dark side of the moon?"

"Someplace like that," said Jeff. He wasn't about to give him Scott's location. He didn't trust him that far.

Lynch understood this and nodded. "Let me get some things together, and we'll go. There's a sub-orbital shuttle waiting for us at the airport. You can get a message to Sampson from there. Okay?"

"Fine," said Jeff, standing. "I don't trust you, you know."

"I'm not sure that I trust you," retorted Lynch. "I guess we're stuck with each other. Make no mistake, Anderson," and his eyes grew narrow and hard, "if I even sense that you're going to double-cross me, I'll kill you. Got it?"

"Yes."

"Fine. Wait here. I'll be back in a minute, and we'll go."

Lynch left, and Jeff was alone with his thoughts. *Lord,* he thought, *what is going on? Am I doing the right thing?* It wasn't quite a prayer, but it was the best thing he had at the moment. He certainly didn't trust Lynch, but he knew one thing. He was going to take whatever risk he had to take to get Helen — and Beth, if she was there — to safety.

Five minutes later, Lynch returned. Jeff could tell from the look on his face that something was wrong. The situation had changed. "What is it?" he asked, the tension rippling in his voice. Lynch looked at him long and hard before replying.

"I just got a report in," he said finally. "Scott Sampson was arrested in the Tampa Bay area a few hours ago. At this moment, he's in the air, on his way to Mentasys."

10

Scott sat in the middle seat of aisle 34, staring straight ahead. On either side of him sat two extremely competent representatives of the Bureau of Religious Affairs. Neither of them had spoken since the flight had taken off, which suited Scott fine. He was mad. No, he was furious. He felt like shouting at the top of his lungs "It's not fair! I was there! I made it!"

Even now he was not quite sure what had happened. Jim had taken him all the way to Tarpon Springs, even though he himself was only going to Tampa. It was a good 40 miles out of his way, but, as he told Scott, it was the least he could do for his new "big brother." A quick prayer, a firm handshake, and Jim had been on his way. Scott had examined his surroundings, already sweating from the Florida heat. By his reckoning, he had about a two mile hike ahead of him down to the docks. He had set out along U.S. 19 towards his destination.

Seeing the sponge docks of Tarpon Springs was like looking 50 years into the past. The decades-old fishing vessels lined up along one of the waterways gave the area a touch of antiquity. Scott strolled along the docks, taking in the cry of sea gulls and the smell of the ocean. Things seemed relaxed here. Life was lived day by day. The men and women who worked the docks and boats were firmly rooted in this place. Many had been here for generations. There was a sense of being, of belonging. All in all, to a man on the run, it seemed like the kind of place where he could lose himself. It was peaceful, quiet, and it put him more at ease than he had been for weeks. It also caused him to get careless.

Coming to a small hole-in-the-wall cafe, he had stopped in for lunch. Sitting at the counter, he made his first mistake. When he ordered aloud, the waiter had looked at him strangely. He realized that, although he might look Greek, he didn't *sound* Greek. The moment he opened his mouth pegged him for a Westerner. This had so flustered him that he made his second mistake almost immediately after. Thinking only of getting out and finding his contacts, he asked where the Andropolos family might be found. This had brought a look of downright anger from the waiter. He was told promptly that there were dozens of Andropolos' scattered throughout the area. The closest ones had just been arrested for holding illegal meetings. If he wanted them, then he wasn't wanted here. Quickly Scott paid his bill and left. He headed away from the cafe at a fast walk. It wasn't fast enough. The waiter must have called the police, and the police must have called the bureau. Not more than 10 minutes later, as he headed out of the area, a black sedan had squealed alongside of him. Two men, the same two that now sat on either side of him, had forced him into the car and drove off. The next thing Scott knew, he was on this flight heading to who-knew-where. It made him mad. It made him furious — so furious that he forgot to be afraid.

What was the sense of all he had been through, he kept asking himself over and over. His flight from Covington, his narrow escape in Atlanta — what difference did it make if it all ended here? *WHY, GOD?* he wanted to scream. *Why get me this far if You didn't want me safe? Why abandon me now?*

Even now he did not believe that he was caught. He half expected the Watchman to show up and get him away, or the sky to split open and a giant hand pluck him out of the bureau's clutches, or — anything. Why would God abandon him now? These and other thoughts chased themselves around and around in his mind, but always ended where they began. Why? He did not have the answer to that, so all he could do was sit quietly while the plane flew on.

It was a long flight. Almost six hours melted off his watch by the time they landed. Upon disembarking, he learned that he was at the Los Angeles International Airport. Clear across the country, he realized. He was escorted out by the goon squad, as he came to call them, and led to a waiting limousine. There his escort handed him over to two new goons. Both were tall and broad-shouldered, one was fair-skinned, the other a little darker than Jeff. *Wherever they're taking me, at least they're taking me first class,* he thought as he got in. Indeed, the limo was one of the luxury class models. Included in the rider's section was a bar, television, and small refrigerator. Scott decided that he was thirsty, but when he reached for the refrigerator,

Goon Number One, the dark-skinned one, reached out a beefy hand and grabbed his wrist. Although he said nothing, his look was clear. "Touch it and die." Scott sighed and sat back, watching the city roll past. They were cruising along one of the many expressways that honeycombed the city. He had never been to Los Angeles, but, due to his circumstances, was not especially interested in sightseeing just now.

The sun was almost down when they finally left the sprawling metropolis behind. Scott saw that they were moving into an industrial sector. He could feel that they were nearing their destination, and, for the first time, began to feel apprehensive. Whatever was in store for him would hardly be pleasant.

The limousine turned onto a busy four lane highway and began to navigate its way through the heavy traffic. Suddenly, there was a soft "pop," followed by a "thump thump thump." The whole vehicle began to wobble and shudder. Goon Number One cursed, speaking for the first time in hours.

"Flat," said Goon Number Two, his voice devoid of any emotion. Scott wondered if they ever spoke in words of more than one syllable. Slowly the massive car pulled off to the side of the road. The driver got out and went to the back to inspect the damage. Returning, he tapped on the back window.

"Yeah?" said Goon Number Two as he rolled down the window.

"Flatter than my mother's voice," said the driver, his anger coloring his speech.

"Spare me the comparisons," grumbled Goon Number One. "Just get on it."

"We're not far away," said the driver. "You could call for a ride."

"And get everyone there on my case? No thanks. We're responsible for getting Sampson there, and that's what we're gonna do. Just change it, and get us moving."

"You're the boss," shrugged the driver. "I'd appreciate it if you'd get out. I don't have a hydraulic jack, and it'd help to lighten the load."

Grumbling at the turn of circumstances, Goon One opened the door and climbed out, motioning for Scott to follow. "Don't get any ideas," he said coolly. "You wouldn't get 10 feet." The way he said it left no doubt in Scott's mind that he was correct. He nodded quietly, and moved out of the way. The driver pulled the tool kit out of the trunk and got to work. He had just unscrewed the bolts when he stiffened.

"Hey, look at this," he called to Goon One. The agent caught the urgency in his voice and glided over. "This wasn't an accident," said the driver, an edge of fear in his voice.

"What do you mean?" asked Goon One, leaning forward.

"Here," said the driver, pointing. "Look at that hole. It's on the side, not the tread. Perfectly round. That's a bullet hole." Goon One reacted instantly. He whirled around, scanning the area. His pistol appeared, almost as if by magic, in his hand.

"Danny, get him," he said, jerking a thumb at Scott. "You," he said to the driver, "get on the phone to Mentasys. Tell them to get a car and a team out here now. Tell them we're under attack."

"Right," said the driver, jumping up and heading for the door. He almost made it when, in mid-stride, he suddenly slumped over against the limousine. For a moment, he held on to the door handle. Then, without making a sound, he slumped over and fell to the ground. Scott blinked in surprise. The hair on the back of his neck was standing on end. It felt as if he had just run his shoes over heavy carpet and then had touched something metal. The air was alive with static electricity.

"Danny," shouted Goon One, "get him into the car! They're hitting us with tasers. Get on the phone and. . . ." With that, Goon One fell to the ground. His body twitched as if he were a marionette operated by someone with a bad case of hiccups.

Scott stared at the two men lying there. What was going on? Abruptly, the vise-like grip of Danny attached itself to his arm.

"Move it!" he shouted, half-leading, half-dragging him to the waiting vehicle. Scott didn't consider resisting. Whatever happened to his two captors was likely to happen to him next. In all the excitement, he didn't even think about escape or rescue. They got to the car door. Danny opened it, and dove inside.

"In! Now!" Scott started to follow. Suddenly, he could not move. Control of his body left him, and he found himself going rigid. Danny cursed and started to reach for him. Just before he blacked out, Scott saw Danny's eyes bulge in shock and surprise. He fell onto the floor of the limousine and lay still.

Now what? was Scott's last clear thought. Then a second jolt took him. He felt himself falling, and found that he couldn't even put his arms out to catch himself. He was out before he even hit the ground.

❖ ❖ ❖

"Unghhh!"

"Rest easy, Scott. You're safe now. For the moment, anyway." The voice came from the blackness that surrounded Scott's mind.

Slowly, consciousness returned. It took him a minute to realize that he hurt. Somewhere inside his head, a very little man was banging a very big drum. It throbbed painfully. Scott had never had a hangover, but thought it must surely be like this. Not only that, but his nose ached abominably. Its throbbing kept time with the little man. Moving was out of the question, but since his eyelids didn't feel any heavier than Mack trucks, he tried to open them. Immediately he was sorry. Piercing white light thrust itself all the way through his pupils and directly in to his brain.

"Owww!" he cried, squeezing them shut. His voice, although thin and weak, resounded inside his skull.

"Take it easy," said someone close by. He felt a cool damp cloth press against his forehead. "You're feeling the aftereffects of static discharge. I know it hurts worse than anything, but it'll pass. Besides that, your only injury is a bloody nose." The voice sounded vaguely familiar, and Scott struggled to place it.

"Who?" he croaked, unable to complete a sentence.

"Easy, I said. It's me, Jeff Anderson. Like I said, you're safe for the moment."

"Jeff?"

"Shhh. Rest now. You'll feel better in a few hours."

"But. . . ."

"I said rest." There was a soft hissing sound, and once more Scott felt himself losing consciousness.

When he came to again, he found he was feeling much better. The cloth was still over his eyes, but the throbbing had abated, leaving him feeling clearheaded. Memory was starting to return. The flight to Los Angeles, the long car ride, the flat tire, all came back to him. "Jeff!!" he cried out, sitting up. The cloth fell away, and he opened his eyes. Once again the light flooded in, but this time it was bearable. He was also surprised to find that he could remain in an upright position without throwing up.

"Whoah! Take it easy. You took a double charge, so don't rush things." Scott sat there blinking, getting his bearings. He was in a small motel room, lying on one of two double beds. A clock sitting on the night stand between the two beds read 10:00 p.m. A single lamp burned softly on the nightstand between the beds. Now that his eyes adjusted, it was much less bright than before. Behind him, an air conditioner hummed loudly, blowing cold air onto the back of his neck.

He took in his surroundings briefly, then centered his attention on the room's single occupant. There, sitting on the other bed, as big as life, was Jeff Anderson. He was wearing a blue cotton work shirt and denim jeans. His face showed about a day's growth of beard, and his eyes had a bleary look to them. Scott did not care in the least. Although Jeff Anderson looked a little worse for wear, he was the best thing Scott had seen in a long time.

"Jeff!" he cried aloud again, springing up. He had intended to grab the bigger man and give him the hug of his life, but his body had other ideas. Immediately the room started to spin, and the nausea returned. "Ohhh" he said, grabbing his stomach with one hand and his head with the other.

"I told you to take it easy," admonished Jeff. Instantly he was on his feet, supporting Scott by the shoulders. Gently he eased him back down on the bed.

Scott sat there for a moment, regaining his equilibrium. "What happened?" he finally managed to get out. He wasn't sure if he was asking what was wrong with him, or how he had been rescued. Since talking was still a chore, he let Jeff decide how to answer.

"We had to stun you," said Jeff. "It was the only way to get you safely away from those thugs.

"Stun me?"

"With this," said Jeff, pulling a small metal cylinder from his jeans pocket. "A taser. It emits a charge of static electricity that will put you out cold. Its range is limited, but within 30 feet, it's quite effective. Unfortunately you got in the way of a blast meant for one of your guards. You took that as well as one for you. That's why you're feeling so out of it, now." He shrugged. "Like I said, it will pass."

Scott took a deep, cleansing breath. He was starting to feel almost human again. "Thank you," he said after a moment. It sounded lame in his own ears. This man had literally snatched him from the grasp of the enemy. *How does one say thank you for a life?* he wondered.

"Don't thank me yet," said Jeff, a grin suddenly splitting his brown face. "The worst is yet to come." He sobered a little, becoming serious. "There's something you need to know, Scott, and there's a decision you're going to have to make." He shook his head back and forth. "To be honest, I don't quite know how to tell you."

"Tell me what?" asked Scott curiously. Memory was fully returning, and the events of his flight from Covington sprang into his mind. "Listen," he said, interrupting Jeff before he could answer, "have I got some things to tell you. You're not going to believe some of the stuff that's happened to me. There was. . . ."

"Later, Scott," said Jeff, cutting in.

"But. . . ."

"I said later. What I've got to tell you won't wait."

At that moment, the door behind Scott opened. Scott spun around to see a tall, blond man enter carrying a large green knapsack. He stared as the stranger closed the door behind him and nodded to Jeff. Then he turned his full attention on Scott. "So you're Sampson," he said, lowering the knapsack to the floor. Taken aback, Scott only nodded. His eyes followed the newcomer as he walked across the room to the dresser. There, he opened the ice bucket that was sitting next to a television set and popped a piece of ice into his mouth.

"The limo's out of sight," he said, obviously talking to Jeff. "And our two guests are in the next room."

"How long will they be out?" asked Jeff, keeping his eyes on Scott.

"With the dose I gave them, at least 24 hours."

"Good. Scott Sampson, meet Agent Stephen Lynch."

Scott nodded in Lynch's direction, then turned a questioning gaze at Jeff.

"Stephen is going to help us with a little project," said Jeff. His face grew very solemn, and he spoke quietly. Scott felt a chill go up his spine at his tone.

"Show him," he said, looking back at Lynch. As Scott watched in confusion, Lynch went back to the knapsack. Dipping inside, he pulled out a small black case. When he opened it, Scott saw that it was a mini video player, not much bigger than a wallet. He flipped open the top to reveal a small screen. Pulling a tiny cassette out of his pocket, he slid it into the player. Then he handed it to Scott.

"So what am I supposed to be looking at?" he asked, eyeing Jeff.

"Just watch," replied his friend gently. There was a look of utmost compassion on his face as he waited for Scott to push the play button.

Still not sure where this was leading, Scott pushed the tiny control. Instantly a picture came on to the screen. It took a moment for him to realize what he was seeing. There was some sort of waiting room, like a terminal, with people standing and . . . recognition blindsided him.

He drew in a sharp breath and looked up at Jeff. "Is this the gate. . . ." He could not finish the sentence. Jeff only nodded.

Scott's eyes returned to the screen just in time to see the likeness of himself and Beth walk into view. A soft groan permeated his entire being. "Jeff," he whispered desperately, "don't do this to me. Don't make me go through this again."

"Scott, trust me," said Jeff, reaching across the empty space and gripping his arm. His firm touch was like an anchor that Scott could cling to. "Just watch the tape." He released his arm and sat back.

Scott licked his lips as he watched the drama play itself out. He almost could not bear to look at his wife. She seemed so full of life. Even with the poor quality of the tape her vitality nearly jumped off the screen. In the past days, other things had forced him to put his grief in the back of his mind. Now, once again, it hit him with gale force, leaving him weak and dazed.

"I'd almost forgotten how beautiful you were, darling," he half-thought, half-said. With tears in his eyes, he watched as the couple said their heartbreaking goodbyes. Once again he felt as if his very soul would be ripped out of him as Beth disappeared down the boarding ramp. He wanted to drag her back, to shout at her not to get on that plane, but he was helpless. The past could not be changed. He looked up at Jeff, as if to say "Is this over now? Can the pain stop?" Jeff motioned for him to keep watching.

Even in his grief, Scott had to smile a little at his likeness talking to seemingly thin air. *Where are you now, my friend?* he thought as he saw himself turn and walk out of the shot. *Wherever you are, you have my gratitude, and my thanks.* He was not the least surprised that the Watchman could not be seen on the security camera. The past few weeks had taught him to accept such things on faith alone. He leaned back and looked questioningly at both Jeff and Stephen. For some reason, Stephen looked ashamed. Jeff was staring at him intently.

"All right, Jeff," he said, his voice a little steadier. "What's this all about? Why are you putting me through this?" In answer, Jeff reached over and touched another control on the player. As Scott watched, the tape fast forwarded. After a few seconds, Jeff released the control and the tape resumed its normal speed.

"I swear to you, Scott," Jeff said, his voice tense with emotion, "I didn't know. If I did, I would have never sent you away." He lowered his eyes. "I could have done *something* — at least tried."

"What are you. . . ."

"Just watch," said Stephen roughly, and turned away. Scott could feel his chest tightening as he fixed his eyes back on the screen. He could hear his heart pounding in his ears as he watched. He saw the three agents pass the camera and go onto the plane. He looked questioningly at the two other men in the room.

"Bureau of Religious Affairs," explained Jeff tightly. He said no more. Scott returned his attention to the screen. Finally he saw what Jeff wanted him to see.

"Oh no," he cried, his voice barely above a whisper. "Oh God, no." There was no doubt. That woman between the agents was his wife, *and she was being taken off the plane!* "Jeff." He looked helplessly at his friend, not knowing what to think or do.

"I know Scott. Believe me, I know."

"She wasn't on the plane." Even as he spoke the words, he couldn't believe them. He had been having dreams like this for weeks. Every time he slept, it was always the same. Beth would be alive, and they would be back in their house, safe and sound. No one was hunting them, or trying to hurt them. Her death was all a mistake. She was really alive, and they were together. Then he would wake up to bitter reality, and have to realize all over again that it was all just a dream, that Beth was dead, and he was on the run. He would have to pull himself together and get on with the business of surviving.

"Where is she? Where is she, Jeff?" The emotions that had been repressed came flooding back, threatening to overwhelm him. His hand shot out and gripped Jeff's arm. All at once a tremendous weight seemed to lift from his shoulders, while at the same time the bite of renewed care and worry clamped itself around his heart. His voice took on a twinge of panic.

"Scott," said Jeff gently.

"My God, she's alive! Beth's alive. Where *IS* she, Jeff? Where have they taken her?"

"SCOTT!" Jeff's voice suddenly became stern and commanding. It jolted Scott back into reality. "I know that this is rough," continued Jeff in the same tone, "But if you will let me talk, I'll let you in on everything." Scott took a deep breath and nodded. He sat back, releasing Jeff's arm. His thoughts whirled around and around inside of his head, and it took a Herculean effort to concentrate on what Jeff was saying.

"Better," nodded Jeff. "Now, we think we know where Beth has been taken, and if we're right, it's going to take a major miracle to get her out."

"I don't understand."

"The chances are that she is being held at a place called Mentasys. It's a research facility not far from here."

"Research," said Scott, wrinkling his brow. The thought kept pounding at his mind. Beth was alive! He struggled to ask an intelligent question. "What kind of research?"

It was Lynch who answered. "Officially, mental disorders, like paranoia, schizophrenia, things like that. Unofficially, it's used for interrogating prisoners of the bureau."

"I don't understand," said Scott. He was rapidly coming back to earth. Beth might be alive, but she was a prisoner, and still in very great danger. "Why would anyone want to interrogate her?"

"Because you were both associated with the Shepherd's Path," said Jeff.

Scott shook his head vehemently. "No way!" he said firmly. "We didn't even know about you guys when we went to that meeting, and I wasn't involved until after the plane crash. Beth doesn't know anything."

"The bureau didn't know that," said Lynch. "They only knew that you two were the only ones that escaped their net. They also knew that someone from the Shepherd's Path was supposed to be there at that meeting. At the time, it probably looked like a good bet to question your wife."

The certainty with which Lynch explained bureau thinking caused Scott to study the other man closely. "Just who are you?" he asked. When Lynch didn't answer, he turned to Jeff. The look on his face demanded a response.

"He's a special operative for the Bureau of Religious Affairs," replied Jeff bluntly.

Scott stared at his friend in disbelief. "And you trust him? Are you crazy?" He pointed an accusing finger at Lynch. "He's one of the reasons my wife is de — missing! People like him put us in prison, Jeff. People like him are *killing us.*"

Lynch, who had been standing with his eyes downcast, jerked his head up. Scott's last remark had struck home. "And you're one of the people who used to preach to everyone that they were going straight to hell," snapped Lynch. In three quick strides he crossed the small room and stood in front of Scott, who remained seated on the bed. His body was taut, like a piano wire strung too tight. Scott suddenly realized that he had just angered a very dangerous man.

"Let me tell you something," said Lynch, looking down in disgust at him. "I watched you and your kind rake it in when I was growing up. I watched you care more for your building projects and television programs than for the people who lived next door to you. I watched you almost wreck this country by trying to impose your morals on it. Now, I'm sorry about your wife. What's been going on here is wrong — dead wrong, but as for the rest . . ." here Lynch turned away and walked back to the dresser, "you brought it on yourselves. And as far as I'm concerned, when it's fulfilling its original purpose, the bureau serves a useful function."

He turned back to face Scott. "Okay, so you don't trust me. I don't care. You need my help. You either accept that, or I'm gone."

His harsh words stung Scott's pride, and his long dormant temper aroused itself. "You arrogant, selfish. . . ."

"Knock it off, Scott," said Jeff sternly. "It's not for you to judge. Besides, he's right about a few things. Isn't he?" Jeff caught Scott's eye and held it. "Isn't he?" he asked more softly.

Slowly the anger that Lynch had aroused began to ebb. He began to feel ashamed of his outburst and looked away. He had to admit that some of the things Lynch said hit too close to home. For a large part of his life, *he* had been one of those who had cared too much about things and not enough about people.

Jeff saw Scott's face relax and nodded. "Good," he nodded. Looking over his shoulder to Lynch, he raised an eyebrow. Lynch was obviously still upset, but he was too good an agent to allow personal feelings to get in the way of a job he had to do. He nodded once, sharply. "All right," said Jeff, clapping Scott on the shoulder. "Maybe when this is over," he said in a conspiratorial tone to Scott, "we can show him what it *really* means to be a Christian. How about it?"

"Okay," said Scott.

"Don't count on it," retorted Lynch. "If we're successful, I'll give you both a head start, but once things are back to normal, I'll be after you again."

"Whatever," said Jeff, dismissing Lynch's threat with a wave of his hand. "Right now we've got things to do, and you have a very important decision to make, Scott."

"Decision?"

"Uh huh. Are you with us in this?"

"You're going to go get Beth?" Scott asked. He had guessed as much from the way they were talking.

"Partially," said Jeff cautiously. "To be honest, we don't know for sure that she's in there. We *think* so, but we're not 100 percent sure."

"And you want to know if I'm in?" Scott laughed once sharply. It was not a humorous laugh. "That's my wife in there, Jeff. Of course I'm in."

"There's more," said Jeff, holding up a hand to quiet Scott. His face grew hard. "They've got Helen, too."

That brought Scott up short. Helen Bradley had literally saved his life. The thought of her in unfriendly hands burned him as much as the thought of Beth being held.

"The fact is," continued Jeff, "we probably won't get away with it. Stephen here tells me that security at Mentasys is pretty tight." Now he looked Scott directly in the eye. "That's why we rescued you, Scott. We need you to help us get in there."

"ME?" asked Scott, surprised. "You guys are the professionals. What do I know about this sort of thing?"

"The bureau wants you," answered Jeff. "We want to use you as a decoy to get us through the outer perimeters. Once inside, we'll do the rest. I'll tell you right now, Scott, if we're caught, we won't have a chance of coming out alive. It's your decision."

"Let me get this straight," said Scott. "It's just the three of us against this place?"

"Well, I think there might be one more person involved," corrected Jeff, his eyes motioning upward.

Lynch caught the gesture and snorted.

"Fine," replied Scott. "Let's go get them." Just like that, he said it. Even he was surprised at the lack of hesitation in his voice. There was a time when Scott Sampson would not have committed to *anything,* much less something as dangerous as this, but there had been some changes in the past three weeks. *Perhaps,* Scott reflected, *it is called growing up.*

Jeff continued to study him closely, only now his eyes were twinkling. "Yes, I see," he said after a moment. "All right, let's get going. Stephen, if you would."

Lynch nodded and once again dug into his knapsack.

"What do you want me to do?" Scott asked anxiously. Now that he had agreed to help, he was impatient to get started.

"Lift up your chin," answered Lynch. Puzzled, Scott complied. Lynch came over to stand next to him, holding a high pressure syringe.

"Wait a minute," objected Scott, "you didn't say anything about drugging me. I want to be awake for this."

"This isn't a drug," reassured Jeff. "We're implanting you with a micro-transmitter and beacon."

"Say what?"

Even as he asked, Lynch placed the syringe against his bared neck and pressed the control. There was a hiss as the high pressure spray forced its way through his pores. It felt like he had been stung by a hornet. "Ouch!" he cried, jerking back.

"There are undoubtedly sensors at Mentasys that will pick up any bugs we try to plant on you, but chances are they won't pick up anything *in* you," said Lynch.

Scott rubbed his neck, waiting for Jeff to explain the rest.

"Stephen will get you inside" said Jeff. "You will be his prisoner. We think that you will be taken to wherever they are holding Beth and Helen. The transmitter you're carrying will give us the exact location."

"Where will you be?" asked Scott.

"We're going to use the limo you were being moved in. I'll be assuming the identity of one of your guards. Hopefully they won't look too closely at my identification since they're expecting me." Jeff smiled a predator's smile. "Stephen and I have been comparing notes on bureau procedures. Although security on the outer perimeter will be tight, once we're inside, things will probably loosen up."

"Probably?" asked Scott, raising an eyebrow.

"We can only hope and pray," replied Jeff. "Certain areas will be heavily guarded I'm sure, but once we're through the front gate, I may be able to move around in relative freedom — at least in the more public spots."

"Okay," said Scott. "So what happens when I find them?"

In answer, Jeff held up a tiny earpiece. "I'll be able to hear everything you say through this," he said. *"Only* you, by the way. Because the transmitter is internal, I can't hear anyone who may talk to you. Hopefully you can give me instructions on how to get to you."

"There's an awful lot of 'hopefullys' in this plan," grumbled Scott.

"If you have any better ideas," snapped Lynch, "now's the time." His dislike for Scott was obvious. Scott remained silent, his attention on Jeff.

"I know," agreed Jeff. "that there are a lot of things we don't know. We'll have to play it by ear." He looked back at Lynch, then continued, "Sooner or later the bureau will catch up to us, Scott. With the computer network gone, the Shepherd's Path is limping badly. That's my fault. I should never have convinced Helen to rely on technology. The first Christians did quite well without it, and so should we. I used to think we could operate the system right under the bureau's nose." He shook his head in regret. "I was wrong, and because of my mistake, none of us can hide for very long."

"It sounds like you're giving up," said Scott. "If we're going to be caught, then why bother trying to rescue Helen and Beth?"

"Giving up?" Jeff shook his head in dismissal. "No, I'm not giving up. We can start over. The Shepherd's Path can reorganize, bypassing the network. I want to get Helen back for two reasons. One," he said, holding up an index finger, "she knows better than anyone how to pull this off and get us back in business. We *need* her. Two," and his voice sank to a whisper, "she's my friend — probably the best friend I've ever had. I'm not going to let her go without a fight. If we can get Beth out in the bargain, so much the better."

"And after we get them," asked Scott pointedly, "how do we get away? Tell me one place on this planet where we can hide?"

"Like I said," smiled Jeff, "most of the Shepherd's Path is still intact. We only need to reorganize a bit and we're back in business. I promise you, if we can pull this off, we'll find a way to disappear. Just trust me, okay?" Scott nodded, and Jeff clamped him on the shoulder. "All right," he grinned, "let's go bring them out."

Scott jumped off the bed, and helped his two allies clear the room of anything that could be used to identify them. After that, Lynch led them to where he had hidden the limousine. While he drove, Jeff reviewed their plan with Scott, making sure he understood what he had to do. Together, the two believers and their uneasy ally headed into the stronghold of the enemy.

❖ ❖ ❖

Jack Kline stepped out of the boarding ramp and into Los Angeles International Airport. He was immediately met by two plainclothes security guards from Mentasys. His mental state could only be described as unstable. He was led, unresisting, to a waiting car and hustled into the back seat. One of the guards sat next to him while the other got in the driver's seat. Just as they drove off, a young woman stepped out of the terminal. She watched as they disappeared, then opened her purse and pulled out a small communicator.

"He's on his way," she reported quietly. "Have you got him?"

"Affirmative," came the male voice through the tiny earpiece she wore. "The transmitter is functioning properly. Good work."

"Thanks," she replied. "It wasn't all that hard planting it on him since I sat next to him all the way. With any luck, we should have an answer for Senator Davidson soon."

"I have a feeling he's not going to like what we find," said her fellow detective.

"Count on it," she snorted, "but it's not our job to worry about it.

We just find out things, and let the big guys make the decisions."

"Roger that. Looks like he's heading for the freeway. I'll get back to you."

"Affirmative. I'm going to see about renting a car now. You tell that chopper pilot to take it easy up there." There was a chuckle, then the communicator went dead. The young woman set her course for the car rental agency, wondering what dirt they were about to dig up on one of the most powerful men in the nation.

❖ ❖ ❖

The black limousine pulled to a stop at the outer gate of Mentasys. Jeff casually rolled down his window and handed the guard the plastic identification he had taken off one of the now sleeping agents. He was careful to keep his face averted. The professional make-up kit provided by Lynch had given him an approximate appearance to the picture on the card, but the flimsy disguise would not hold up under close examination. The fact that one of Scott's guards was black was indeed fortunate. Their main hope was that the very audacity of their little raid would catch security off guard. Jeff knew from experience that sometimes the more elaborate the system, the greater the overconfidence. Sometimes.

He waited impatiently as the guard inserted his stolen card into an impressive looking terminal. It only took a second for the light to glow green. The guard returned the card and motioned for him to open the rear window. Jeff complied, and Lynch handed over his own identification. There was no need to worry here, Jeff knew. Lynch's card was valid, and he was expected.

"Thank you, sir," said the guard, handing the card back. Jeff was just about to move forward when the guard leaned over and aimed his flashlight into the back seat. The beam came to rest on Scott's face. "You're a little late, Mr. Lynch," he said, examining Scott closely. "We were told to expect you almost two hours ago. Also, aren't you supposed to be bringing in a black man? My supervisor said to expect someone by the name of Jeff Anderson." Jeff tensed, waiting for Lynch to answer. If he decided to turn on them, they would be finished. Lynch was armed, as were the guards at the gate.

"Anderson made the mistake of trying to take me out," replied Lynch evenly. "He's back in Cincinnati in the morgue. This," he said, jerking a thumb at Scott, "is Scott Sampson. I'm sure you've heard the name."

The guard's eyes grew a fraction of an inch wider in recognition.

He frowned suspiciously. "I know the name, sir," he said. "We are expecting him also, but he's supposed to be accompanied by Dieter and Washington — in this very car, as a matter of fact. I see Washington," he said, nodding to the front, "but where's Dieter?" As he asked the question, the guard carefully put his hand on his holstered pistol. He did not draw it, but the meaning was clear.

"I re-assigned Dieter," answered Lynch calmly. Jeff, listening, had to admire the man's boldness. What an asset he could be if he would come to know the Lord! Jeff didn't think he could convince him, but he said a quick prayer to the One who could.

"We arranged a meeting at the airport," Lynch continued without missing a beat. "I've sent him on a courier mission. The driver is with him. Check your command authorization codes. Mine is Victor Zulu November Tango, three three seven. That gives me the authority to reassign agents in class three and below."

The guard hesitated, clearly undecided.

"Look, Martin," said Lynch sternly, reading the guard's name tag, "this is official bureau business. Now, if you don't want my code, then you'd better check with the bureau director himself. My direct line to him is 555-4427. Do it now, please. I don't appreciate being kept waiting here at the gate."

The guard blanched at the thought of calling Jacob Hill direct. He weighed his options a moment, trying to decide whether to trust Lynch or risk the wrath of a man who had total control of his life. He made a decision. "If you will wait here just a moment longer, Mr. Lynch, I'll check your code."

He moved off to the small guardhouse and busied himself with his terminal. It took just a few moments for him to verify his information. "All clear, sir," he said, trying to smile and not quite succeeding. "Your code checks out. Should I be expecting Dieter soon, then?"

"He should be back within three hours. He has orders to report to me directly, so I'd appreciate it if you would notify me the minute he gets here."

"Consider it done, sir," said the guard, now eager to please. His check of Lynch's code had told him that Lynch was not a man to be trifled with. Stepping back, he nodded to the guard standing at the control of the gate. He touched a button and the heavy structure began to move aside. Within seconds they were through and heading into one of the many parking lots.

Scott fell back into the cushioned seat and let out a long sigh.

"Wheeew!" he exclaimed. "I thought we had had it!" He turned to Lynch and admitted grudgingly, "It's a good thing you're in so good with your boss. That phone number saved us!"

"You mean it's a good thing that idiot of a guard didn't call the number" replied Lynch wryly. "He'd have gotten 'Date Rapp.' If I were his supervisor, he'd be cleaning out toilets tomorrow." He glanced over at Scott to see his mouth hanging open in amazement. "Close your mouth, Sampson. You're ugly enough as it is!"

"You mean," Scott stammered, and found he couldn't go on. He took a deep breath. He seemed to be doing a lot of that lately. "You mean," he tried again, "that number you gave isn't the bureau director's?"

"Will you live in the real world?" retorted Lynch. "You think that every agent on the bureau's payroll can just call him up any time? Sure, I've been in contact with him, but he's always called me."

Scott could hardly believe what he was hearing. "Of all the stupid, harebrained stunts. . . ." he started, but Lynch chimed in on top of him.

"Look, Sampson, we're in, aren't we. Now if you don't shut up. . . ."

"Children!" Jeff's voice cut in from the front seat. "What say we get our friends out of here? Then you two can tear into each other all you want, although if you get physical, Scott, I'm putting money on Stephen. In other words, gentlemen, SHUT UP!" His rebuke had the desired effect. Both Scott and Lynch fell silent, glaring at each other. The limo pulled into an empty parking place about 50 yards from the main entrance.

"Would you look at the size of this place?" murmured Scott. His heart was beating rapidly as he scanned the immense structure. Beth was in there! Even if Jeff was not absolutely sure, he could feel it. She was here, and she was alive. He started to get out of the limo, but felt Jeff's strong hand on his shoulder.

"Hold up, Scott," he said, inserting a tiny plug into his ear. Lynch was doing the same. "We need to make sure your transmitter is working. Count softly to 10" Scott complied, turning his back on his two allies. He got to five when Lynch stopped him.

"I've got him," he said, looking at Jeff. "How about you?"

"Sounds a little muffled, but I can hear him," answered Jeff.

"One more thing," said Lynch, producing a pair of sinister looking handcuffs. He clicked them open.

"Now wait a minute," began Scott, but saw Jeff's reassuring nod.

"It's necessary, Scott," he said. "Standard bureau procedure. Anything else will be noticed." Scott hesitated briefly, then allowed his hands to be fastened securely behind him.

"These are security cuffs," explained Lynch. "Don't try to get them off by yourself. There's a micro chip embedded in the lock that will activate a small battery. It's not lethal, but it delivers a substantial shock. They're quite effective."

"Charming," said Scott sarcastically. There was nothing else to be said.

They began to cross the distance to the main entrance, trying to keep watch in all directions at once. Scott was awed by the sheer size of the building. If not for the transmitter he now carried under his skin, the chances of locating anyone in that huge, cube-shaped structure would have been non-existent. To him, it felt as if they were entering a dark, evil fortress of ancient times, except that no fortress could possibly compare to this.

No one seemed to notice them as they opened the large glass doors and entered the empty lobby. At this time of night, the receptionist was not on duty. Only a single security guard sat behind the long counter.

He saw them enter and waved them over. They approached cautiously, Jeff hanging several feet back.

"Mr. Lynch?" he said, looking from one to another.

"I'm Detective Lynch," answered Stephen.

"Yes, sir. Just a moment, sir." He activated the vid-phone at the desk. "Detective Lynch is here, sir," he said. He listened for a moment, then nodded. Switching off the phone, he looked back up at Stephen. "Mr. Taylor will be right out, sir."

They waited a nerve-wracking five minutes, then one of the elevators opened and a short, bull-faced man appeared. Jeff pegged him as the security chief. "Lynch," said the man without preamble, "the guard at the gate just filled me in. What the devil do you mean, reassigning my people? I don't care what codes you may have, you don't have the right to. . . ."

"Mr. Taylor," interrupted Lynch, "I'll be glad to justify my actions to both you and Mr. Hill. Things have developed rapidly. I had no choice."

Taylor stopped short, considering what Lynch had said. Although he resented him usurping his authority, Lynch had the reputation of being the best in the bureau. He usually had a good reason for what he did. *Best,* he thought, *to let Mr. Hill handle this.* He nodded in response, curbing his temper.

"Mr. Hill wants to see you first thing in the morning. We'll put you up in one of the guest quarters. I'll get someone down here to show you to them."

"Fine," said Lynch. Unnoticed by both Taylor and the guard, he reached into his back pocket and pulled out a tiny, pistol-shaped device. He looked around casually, noting the position of the security cameras. There was one in the corner to his left, and another directly in front of him. He would have to get this right the first time. Taylor turned his attention on Scott. His lips tightened with distaste as he nodded to the guard behind the desk. The guard activated the vidphone again.

"I need an escort in the main lobby," he said quickly. "Also, inform Dr. Steiger that Sampson has arrived." There was a muted response, then the guard clicked off the monitor. Almost instantly, two tall, muscular uniformed men appeared. They stopped on either side of Scott.

"This him?" one of them asked Lynch, who nodded. "We'll take it from here."

Without a word, Lynch handed over the key to the handcuffs. Scott was taken by either arm and led off. A look of panic crossed his face as he was led away.

Keep it together, urged Jeff silently in his departing friend's direction. *Stay calm. We'll get you back, I promise.* He watched closely as Scott was led to a single door across the lobby. Although he could not read the name plate on the door, Jeff guessed the office behind it belonged to Dr. Steiger, the name the guard had just mentioned. He turned back to Lynch and Taylor. The security chief's attention had so far been centered on Stephen and Scott. Now he really noticed Jeff for the first time. His brow wrinkled in confusion for a moment, then he took a step backward.

"You're not Washington," he stammered. Instantly, Lynch pointed the device, covered by the top of his hand, and pressed the trigger. There was a hiss of escaping air and Taylor froze. Almost casually, he turned back to the guard and fired. The effect was the same — the guard froze, his muscles rigid by the drugged dart. Jeff swung into action, moving easily but quickly to stand between the camera and Taylor. He continued to nod at the paralyzed security chief as if he were carrying on a conversation.

"How long?" he asked Lynch, keeping his eyes on Taylor.

"Paralysis wears off in 30 seconds," replied Lynch under his breath. "After that, they'll be susceptible to suggestion for about an hour."

"Get going, then," ordered Jeff. "They'll be on to us long before that."

"You don't have to tell me my job," growled Lynch. He moved to stand next to Taylor. "Can you hear me?" he asked him.

"Yes," came the dull reply.

"Take me to Central Control," he ordered. Taylor did not reply, but instead walked off at a steady, even pace. Lynch fell into step beside him, and the two moved off across the lobby and disappeared down one of the two halls that led into the bowels of the building.

Jeff turned his attention to the guard behind the desk. He was sitting very still, his face totally devoid of expression. He resisted the temptation to check his pulse. Lynch had promised that the Hyper-Pentothal tipped darts were harmless. The darts themselves dissolved on impact, injecting the drug directly into the blood system. The only side effect, Lynch insisted, was a headache when the drug wore off. Jeff studied the guard closely, but could see no evidence that he might be in distress.

"Can you hear me?" he asked softly.

"Yes," was the emotionless reply.

"Uh, right," stammered Jeff. It was like talking to a department store mannequin. "Continue to do your job. Situation normal. Do you understand?"

"Yes," replied the guard. He continued to sit quietly.

Jeff took a deep breath and expelled it slowly. It was all up to Lynch now. If he could neutralize security, they might just have a chance. If not. . . . He decided not to contemplate the alternative. Instead, he concentrated on listening for Scott, who had remained silent since being led away. He felt alone and exposed as he leaned over the desk, pretending to talk with the guard. All he could do was wait.

❖　❖　❖

Scott was led into a rather plain looking office. The only furniture was a desk, several plastic chairs, and a plastic bookshelf that looked like wood. It certainly did not look like the office of a doctor. Behind the desk sat a dark-haired, broad-shouldered man in his fifties. His harsh face and stern, humorless look made Scott shudder.

"Bring him in," he said, glancing up from some sort of file folder. Scott was pushed forward and made to sit in one of the plastic chairs.

His handcuffs were removed, and he rubbed his wrist to restore the circulation. One of the guards left, while the other took up a position next to the door. The man, who Scott assumed from the name on the door was Dr. Steiger, turned his attention back to the folder. Long seconds ticked by, and the silence in the room grew intense.

"Well, Scott," said Steiger finally, closing the folder, "You've led us on a merry chase." He smiled congenially, folding his hands on the top of the desk and leaning forward. He looked for all practical purposes like a concerned friend. Scott was not fooled. The minute he entered the office, he recognized his enemy. The spirit emanating from the doctor was that of pure evil. It assaulted his own spirit, making him feel slightly nauseous. He said nothing. His silence seemed to disappoint Steiger.

"Actually," he continued, "we really don't need you now. We have Helen Bradley, so that makes you rather superfluous." Scott remained silent. "Still," said Steiger, cocking his head to one side, "we may find a use for you. We have another guest that you might find interesting." The thought seemed to amuse him. "In fact, I'd venture a guess that it's the last person you would expect to see alive."

It was only with a supreme effort that Scott remained calm. Inside he soared. Steiger's attempt to confuse and taunt him had just confirmed that Beth was here! Scott had been close to panic when he entered this room, but now the fear fell away like a discarded piece of clothing. It was not quite the same as when he had been to that fateful church meeting in Covington. Then, his fear had been replaced with a great peace. Now, he felt a tremendous sense of purpose fill him. Beth was here, and by all that was holy, he was going to get her out!

Steiger saw that he was not going to speak. "Very well, Scott, we'll do this the hard way." He got up from the desk and turned to the bookcase. As Scott watched, he pressed his hand against a section of wall. Instantly a small square became visible, outlining his hand in a bright white light. There was a slight whine, and a small panel opened to reveal some sort of lens.

"Good evening, Dr. Steiger," came an emotionless, feminine voice that Scott recognized as computer generated. "Please step forward for retina scan." Steiger obeyed, bringing his eye to within a few inches of the lens. There was a red glow. "Identity confirmed," said the computer. "I scan two other occupants in the room. Please identify."

"Haines, security," said Steiger. "Identity on file. Third occupant — Scott Sampson. Accept command override zero zero alpha zero."

"Command override accepted," said the computer. With that, the entire bookcase slid back to reveal a single door. In turn, it opened to a spacious elevator. Steiger motioned to the guard, who moved to stand next to Scott. Roughly he took him by the arm and stood him up.

Scott felt his heart do a flip. The panic that had subsided began to rear its head again. They had expected Beth and Helen to be held in some kind of ward. At worst, there would be guards to be taken out. This was an entirely different matter. Scott was no security expert, but he knew about retina scans and palm readers. There was no way that Jeff and Stephen could follow him to wherever he was being taken.

The elevator became a gaping maw as he was practically dragged toward it. He felt like a drowning man, and he grasped at the only idea he could think of. He had to warn Jeff.

"Retina scan," he said aloud, hoping it would pick up on the transmitter he was carrying. "Palm reader." Steiger heard this and froze.

"What did you say?" he demanded. Scott only looked at him blankly. Steiger reached out a hand and grabbed Scott's shirt by the collar. His grip was surprisingly strong. "WHAT DID YOU SAY?"

"I heard him," said the guard. "He said 'retina scan' and 'palm reader.' " Steiger released Scott's shirt and whirled on the guard.

"He said it like he was sending a message," he snapped. "Was he checked for bugs?"

"Of course he was," said the guard defensively. "We checked him just before we came in. He was clean."

"Idiot!" exclaimed Steiger. "Did you check for internals?"

"Internals?" The guard was incredulous. "Where would he get them? Only federal agencies have access. . . ."

"One of his contacts is with the FBI!" Steiger was practically shrieking. He whirled to his desk. "Hold him while I get a scanner in here!" Scott felt two vise-like hands grip his arms as Steiger activated the vid-phone. He watched helplessly as the doctor called security.

❖   ❖   ❖

Stephen Lynch followed the drugged Taylor down the long hall toward Central Control. He felt cut off and alone — cast out. For the first time ever, he was operating on his own. He had passed the point of no return. Even if he blew the whistle now, and turned Sampson and Anderson in to Mentasys, he could not hide his own participation. He had deliberately entered Mentasys in a covert fashion, in league with two known conspirators. He had also drugged a guard and the chief of security himself.

These thoughts chased themselves around inside his head as he followed Taylor. Somehow, deep inside his soul, he knew he was doing the right thing, but it didn't make his course of action any easier. He had been loyal to the bureau ever since he had signed on. Now, he was discovering that it was not what it seemed. The people he worked for had blown up a passenger plane, and blamed it on innocent people. His one hope was that he could find enough evidence on this raid to expose the corruption in the bureau. Admittedly, freeing Bradley and Sampson's wife was an added bonus, but he was here to nail his superiors.

A cold, seething anger settled in his stomach as he followed Taylor. He had been used! Used and then summoned here by Hill himself — no doubt to be terminated. His loyalty and dedication counted for nothing! He was simply a pawn in Hill's war on Christianity. *Well, Mr. Hill,* he thought grimly, *pawns can sometimes bring down kings.*

Taylor turned a corner and stopped at what Lynch initially took to be an elevator. Without pausing, he pressed his hand against a section of the wall, which glowed bright white. Lynch sucked in a sudden breath. A palm reader! If these were used in other parts of the building, they were in trouble. Almost silently the doors slid back. Taylor stepped through, with Lynch right behind. The doors closed as soon as they were through.

Central Control was a large, octagon shaped room lit dimly with track lighting. Rows of monitors lined two of the walls, which glowed brightly. Directly under the monitors was a control board much like the one in Jacob Hill's suite. Two bored guards sat in comfortable looking swivel chairs in front of the board. The large center screen showed the lobby. Lynch could see Jeff leaning over, pretending to talk to the drugged guard. One of the guards swiveled around to face them as they entered. Lynch didn't hesitate. Pushing Taylor out of the way, he aimed and fired the dart pistol. It caught the guard squarely in the chest, penetrating his clothes and the skin underneath. He froze, his muscles rigid.

"What the. . . ." The second guard did not even finish his sentence. As he turned, Lynch fired, and the guard was paralyzed. Just as he stepped up to the control board, Lynch heard Scott's transmission, confirming not only the presence of another palm reader, but a retinal scan as well. He wasted a second on a curse, then began to examine the monitors. There was the lobby on the center screen. He could see that Jeff had heard Scott's transmission as well, but he could do nothing until Lynch had taken security. It took him a few moments to find Scott, and once he did, he realized that they were all in trouble. Scott was being held by one of his guards, while the other man, probably Steiger, was running a small object in front of his neck. They had discovered the transmitter! Even as he watched, Steiger grabbed Scott by the throat, his face a mask of rage. They were out of time. He pulled his communicator out of his back pocket and thumbed the "on" button.

"Security neutralized," he said quickly. "Go!" There was nothing else he could do now except watch. They had only one dart gun, and it was now out of ammunition. Either Anderson was good enough to take out both Steiger and the guard, or he wasn't. His eyes glanced back to the lobby monitor, but Jeff was nowhere to be seen.

❖ ❖ ❖

Scott was thrown roughly back into the chair by the guard. Steiger glared hatefully at him as he activated the vid-phone. "I don't know who you are working with," he spat, "but your little game is over." He looked meaningfully at the guard hovering next to Scott. "If he tries to speak, kill him." The guard didn't answer. Instead he drew his pistol and pressed the muzzle hard against Scott's neck. Scott had no doubt that he would pull the trigger if he uttered one single word. He watched as the doctor punched in a code and waited. Seconds dragged past, but there was no answer.

"Now what?" growled Steiger, re-entering the number. Again there was no response. Realization dawned on him. "Haines! They've taken Central." He looked wildly at the camera perched in the far corner of the room. "Come on! We've got to. . . ."

Instantly several things happened at once. The door flew open, slamming against the wall with a loud bang. Scott felt the weight of the gun leave his neck, and he turned his head toward the disturbance. Jeff barrelled into the room, taking in the situation. As if in slow motion, the guard brought his weapon around to center on Jeff's chest. Scott could tell that Jeff would not be fast enough to reach the guard before he fired. He didn't stop to think. Bolting from the chair, he threw himself against the guard. Physically he was no match for this trained killer, but he gave Jeff the split second he needed. The pistol, miraculously, did not fire. Jeff sprang across the room and landed a sharp upper cut against the guard's jaw. He followed it with a right jab, and the guard went down. In one smooth motion, he grabbed the guard's pistol and pointed it straight at Steiger.

"Stay there, Doctor," he snapped, his breath coming in short gasps. Steiger froze.

Jeff looked over at Scott. "Thanks."

"So what now?" asked Scott. He glanced over at the still open elevator. "We didn't count on this."

"I know," agreed Jeff grimly. "Doctor, please sit down."

His face distorted with pure hatred, Steiger complied. "There is no way you can succeed," he growled, his voice raspy.

"You're probably right," said Jeff, relaxing his grip on the pistol just a little.

He pulled out his communicator. "You there?" he asked.

"Yeah," came the reply through his earpiece. "Nice piece of work there."

"Right," said Jeff. He did not like being congratulated for knocking people out. "We've got a problem."

"I know — and we can't use the dart gun, so we can't force Steiger to lead you to them."

"It wouldn't matter," answered Jeff. "The first person who talks to him would know something is wrong. Besides, we have no idea what's on the other end of that elevator." There was silence at the other end.

Finally, "You want to pull out? Cut our losses and run?" Although Scott could not hear Lynch, the look on Jeff's face was plain. He looked at Jeff desperately. The pain on his face was almost more than Jeff could bear.

"No. Not when we're this close. Listen, can you find out where this thing leads?"

"There's a layout on the back wall here. Give me a minute," replied Lynch.

"We may not have that long," said Jeff grimly.

"Yeah, right. Okay, I've found you. Hmmm, according to this, it doesn't lead anywhere. The elevator is marked, but that's all. The only way out of that office is the way you came in." Jeff shook his head in frustration. His mind raced for possible solutions, but none presented themselves. Their time was running out.

Suddenly Helen's smiling face popped into his mind. He remembered a conversation they had had years ago, when they had been setting up the computer network.

"You have a tendency to be too subtle, Jeff," she had said after listening to some of his suggestions. "Sometimes the simplest way is the best." He had blushed when she said that, because it was the same concept he had taught others over the years. It struck home now. The only way to get Helen and Beth out was going to be the simple, direct way.

Laying the pistol aside and pocketing the communicator, he approached Steiger. "Where are they?" he asked menacingly. He put every ounce of threat he could into his voice, hoping his bluff would work. As he came close to the doctor, he pulled another piece of equipment out of his back pocket. Without looking at it, he turned it on. Steiger glared at him defiantly.

"Do you really think you can just waltz in here and take them out?" he asked, his voice breaking in anger. "This isn't the local jail, *Boy.*" The last word was spat out so vehemently that Jeff wasn't sure if it was a racial slur or just Steiger's way of talking. Not that it mattered. He had what he needed. Grinning, he held up the small box he had activated and pressed a button.

"Do you really think you can just waltz in here and take them out? This isn't the local jail, *Boy.*" Steiger's eyes widened in shock as his voice, perfect in every detail, resounded from the box. It was the digital voice recorder, the same one Jeff had used to fool Scott in the warehouse.

"Thank you, Doctor," he said in satisfaction.

Once more he used his communicator. "Can you mess that place up fairly well?" he asked.

"Sure," was the quick reply.

"Do it, and get down here."

"On my way." The communicator went dead. Jeff went behind the desk and firmly moved Steiger out of the way. Next to the vid-phone was a single page directory of inter-office numbers.

"What are you looking for?" asked Scott, moving to stand in front of the desk.

"There has to be some kind of communication with whatever is on the other end of that elevator," answered Jeff. "I was hoping it might be listed here with the other numbers, but it isn't. It's just the normal, run-of-the-mill directory." The frustration in his voice was evident.

"Let me see," said Scott. He slid in front of a surprised Jeff and examined the vid-phone closely. "I used to help design systems like this," he explained. "Nothing this elaborate, but the same principles." He ran his index finger down the list of numbers while Jeff watched with growing impatience. "Yeah!" Scott's exclamation coincided exactly with the door opening. Both men jerked their heads up, but relaxed when they saw it was Lynch.

"YOU!" Steiger's tone was both accusing and amazed. "I should have known. I told Jacob not to trust you."

Lynch ignored the outburst and moved to join Jeff and Scott.

"Have you got it?" Jeff was asking.

"I think so," replied Scott. "The numbers might not be listed, but they usually follow a pattern. Find the pattern in the existing directory and you can fill in the missing codes. Since these are only four digit numbers, it's fairly obvious."

"What about the video link?" asked Jeff. "I can fake his voice, but I can't fake him."

Scott pointed to a control. "That's a privacy button," he said. "Push it, and it cuts out the video. They're common on executive lines." Jeff stood there for a moment, then nodded. He busied himself with the tiny keyboard on the recorder. He paused only long enough to ask Scott about the code Steiger used to open the elevator doors. It took him a moment of panicky memory searching, but he remembered.

"All right, Scott," Jeff said finally, "if you think you've got it, punch it in." Scott took a deep breath, then entered the code. There was a soft beeping, then a feminine voice answered.

"Phase One." The three allies looked at each other. *This had to be it,* their looks said. Jeff pushed in front of Scott and held the recorder up to the phone.

"This is Dr. Steiger." The voice was perfect, down to Steiger's inflection. Quickly Jeff hit the pause button.

"Yes, Doctor," replied the voice on the other end.

"Prepare Bradley and Sampson for immediate departure."

"Doctor?" They could hear the surprise in the voice. Pressing his lips together, Jeff played his last card.

"Accept command override zero zero alpha zero." He held his breath, hoping that Steiger's code for the computer applied to humans as well.

"Very well, Doctor," said the voice, although it sounded suspicious. "They'll be ready for transport in five minutes."

"I'm sending in Agent Lynch to get them," said Steiger's voice. "He will have proper identification."

"Yes, Doctor. Anything else?"

"That is all." The line went dead.

Jeff looked from Scott to Lynch. "It's up to you Stephen," he said gently. He glanced down at his watch to see that almost half an hour had passed since they had arrived. "We're running out of time."

Lynch nodded, and without another word, entered the elevator.

"I'm going with him," said Scott, moving forward.

"No, Scott," said Jeff firmly, taking him by the elbow. "They might recognize you. Let Stephen handle this." Scott looked at the bureau agent. Their eyes met. Despite their mutual dislike, there was a moment of understanding.

Lynch nodded. "I'll bring her back," he said softly. He looked at Jeff. "Both of them." With that, the door slid shut and he was gone.

"Now we wait," said Jeff to Scott. They did not have to wait long. Somewhere in the distance, an alarm began to blare. They heard the sound of running feet. Then someone began to pound on the door. Jeff bowed his head, and Scott's shoulders slumped. Their time had run out.

11

Jacob Hill jolted out of his light sleep, instantly awake. The second the alarm sounded in the dimness of his suite he rolled out of bed. He did not sleep as most men. He had long ago trained himself only to doze, no matter how tired he might be. His rationalization for this was that a man in his position must be alert at all times, but deep inside, so deep even he did not realize it, was the fear that if he slept too deep, he would never wake up.

His movements catlike and subtle, he glided over to his desk. He was wearing pastel silk pajamas that rustled softly as he walked. A touch of a single button, and the monitors behind the desk came to life, filling the suite with an eerie glow. He would call security momentarily, but first wanted to see the situation for himself. He had access to areas of Mentasys that security did not.

Quickly his eyes darted from screen to screen as each one came on line. Everything appeared normal in both Phase One and Two. The duty nurse was on station in Phase One and the four-man staff was in place in Two. Satisfied, he punched up Steiger's office. Although he never permitted himself to show surprise, what he saw caused an almost silent gasp to escape his lips. Steiger was there, but he had company. For a moment, Hill did not recognize the two other men that flanked him. He turned the camera control and focused on the tall black man.

"Jeff Anderson, I presume," he muttered under his breath. Even though he was wearing an obvious disguise, Hill had no trouble recognizing the former FBI agent. He had been sent his complete file the moment of his capture. The man next to him . . . Jacob studied the smaller man's features carefully, then allowed himself a small smile.

"Welcome to Mentasys, Mr. Sampson," he said softly. Despite

the darkened hair and skin, he easily identified the man who had eluded his best people time and time again. A third man, probably a bureau agent or a security guard, sat slumped in one of the office chairs, obviously unconscious. Hill only gave him a cursory glance.

"Excellent," he muttered to himself. Looking up at the rest of the monitors, he noted several security guards running toward Steiger's office. The reason for the commotion was clear when he checked Security Central. One of the staff doctors was examining two unconscious guards and his security chief. They looked as if they had been drugged. Hill sat back and regarded the panoramic scene before him. Somehow, he realized, Anderson and Sampson had escaped capture and made it all the way to Mentasys. Even more amazingly, they had penetrated outer security, immobilized Central Control, and evidently discovered where Phase One was located — quite an achievement. From the looks of things, they had only been discovered due to the regular security shift rotation.

The question is, Hill thought, *just how did those two get so far?* They were obviously here for Helen Bradley and Beth Sampson — except that they should not know where the two women were being held. How did they learn so much? He touched a control, and the only area he had not yet checked appeared on the center screen. For a moment, he simply stared, then his shoulders slumped slightly.

"I should have known," he said to himself. There, in the elevator that led to the entire underground interrogation complex, was Stephen Lynch. Somehow, one of his best agents had been turned. The mistake was his, Hill knew. Lynch should have been brought into his confidence years ago, or else terminated. There was no room in his organization for someone who was not totally committed to him. Now, there he was, headed straight into the deepest secrets Mentasys had to offer.

Angrily, Hill activated the all-page on the intercom. "Security, this is Hill," he snapped. He noted with satisfaction how fast every guard stopped in his or her tracks, waiting for his instructions. "Immobilize the two men in Steiger's office, and hold them there. I'll be down in 10 minutes."

He shut off the intercom and watched as the guards reached the door to Steiger's office. It took them only seconds to force an entry and capture Anderson and Sampson. They were held at gunpoint and made to sit in two of the plastic chairs. Nodding tightly, he turned his attention to Lynch. The renegade bureau agent obviously could not hear the alarm. That was fine with Hill. He used the vid-phone to call

Phase One. The security guard who answered looked nervous, under-standable since the alarm had sounded there as well. His eyes widened a little when he saw who it was who was calling.

"In a moment," said Hill, not waiting for him to talk, "a bureau agent will be there."

"Yes, sir," nodded the guard. "An Agent Lynch, Dr. Steiger said."

"Indeed," said Jacob, his own eyes widening in turn. This was an interesting development. What was Steiger up to?

"Yes, sir," said the guard. "He told us to have Bradley and Sampson ready for transport. He was very adamant about it, sir."

"I see," mused Jacob, rubbing his chin absently. "Follow those instructions, then," he continued. "Are they awake?" The guard looked over to one of his security monitors that showed the Phase One ward. Jacob could see on his own monitor that two nurses were going through the delicate process of reviving the two women.

"Just becoming conscious now, sir," replied the guard. "Bradley is showing signs of disorientation, probably due to her advanced age. Sampson is still groggy, but otherwise seems fine."

"Very well," said Jacob. "Allow Lynch to take both women out. Oh, and tell the staff there to make three extra beds ready. You will be receiving new patients soon."

With that, he broke the connection. He was just starting to change his clothes when his vid-phone beeped. Not wanting anyone to see him in a state of undress, he only activated the audio link. "Hill here."

"Security here, sir," said the voice of Taylor's assistant. "We know your orders were to admit Kline tonight and inform you tomorrow, but — well, with everything else going on, I thought you should know that he's here now. We just let him past the front gate."

Hill considered this bit of information for a moment. "Very good. Bring him to Steiger's office immediately. Oh, and send me the names of the guards on duty when Anderson and Sampson got in."

"Y-Yes, sir," said the assistant, and broke the connection. Hill stood staring at the blank screen for a moment, then went to the bedroom to finish changing. The next few hours would be quite interesting.

❖　❖　❖

"Come on, come on!" Lynch bounced up and down on the balls of his feet impatiently, waiting for the elevator to stop. Every muscle in his body was wired for action, and he was ready to lash out at the first person who got in his way. This little operation was getting more complicated by the moment. First the unexpected security measures, then a secret elevator that went down instead of up. He hated surprises. He knew that in an operation like this, they could be fatal. It was all he could do to keep from pacing anxiously. The ride seemed to go on forever, taking him deep into the earth. He could only hope that Bradley and Sampson would be able to travel. Who knew what they had been through down here?

His questions were answered almost immediately. The elevator finally bumped to a stop, and the door opened. A guard was waiting for him as he stepped out into a small square room. Quickly and confidently he handed his identification to the guard, who nodded.

"They'll be ready in just a moment, sir," said the guard offhandedly, returning the I.D.

Lynch said nothing, and moved back to stand next to the elevator doors, facing the guard. Trying to appear relaxed and bored, he did a quick but thorough survey of the room. It was totally empty of any furnishings, and lit only with fluorescent lights. Covertly he looked at his watch and gritted his teeth. Too much time! They had been here for over 40 minutes. It could not be too much longer before someone discovered that Central Control had been taken out. Once that happened, they were dead in the water. Their only hope was a fast strike — to get in and out so quickly that the staff would not have a chance to react.

His wait was suddenly ended as two very pale and weak looking women were brought out in wheelchairs. He had no trouble recognizing Helen and Beth, but it was obvious that they were still suffering from whatever had been done to them. Without a word, the two nurses wheeled them into the elevator and returned the way they came.

"They're all yours, sir," said the guard, motioning with his hand. "Do you need any help?"

"Thanks, but no," he replied, getting into the elevator. He had to get out now. He could not put his finger on it, but something was wrong. Every sense he had developed as an agent over the past few years was screaming at him. "The boss is waiting upstairs," he added.

With that, he punched the button, the door closing behind him. Immediately they began the long ride back to Steiger's office. Helen and Beth looked around at their new surroundings, but neither spoke to him. He wondered idly if they might be permanently damaged. No telling what they had been through. He hoped that would not be the case. It would destroy Sampson, he knew, if he got this far only to discover that his wife was now a vegetable. While he disliked Scott, and perceived him to be a self-righteous jerk, he did not want to see that happen. He was just thankful that everything had gone well so far. The people below did not seem to suspect anything yet. In fact . . . and it hit him.

"Oh no," he groaned under his breath. Things had gone *too* easily, he realized. He remembered the conversation Anderson had faked with his little toy. The nurse on the other end had fairly reeked of suspicion, and yet, when he got down there, no one questioned him. The guard merely glanced at his identification and then brought out Helen and Beth — *as if he were following instructions!* Lynch realized too late what it was that had been nagging him since he started back up. If he were a guard who had received suspicious instructions, he would call to confirm them. That would blow everything. In fact, it probably already had. He closed his eyes and slumped back against the cold elevator door. It had to be that, he knew. Someone else had gotten in touch with them down below. That meant he was probably heading straight into a trap. Something like a primal growl escaped his lips.

In frustration he lashed out, striking the hard metal wall. So close! They were so close. They had Sampson and Bradley, and all they had to do was get out.

"Think, Stephen, think," he urged himself. There had to be a way out of this, he knew, but try as he might, no idea or inspiration presented itself. He could only watch helplessly as the elevator continued its inevitable climb.

❖ ❖ ❖

When Jack Kline arrived in Los Angeles, his head was beginning to hurt. When he reached the outer perimeter of Mentasys, it had started to throb. By the time he was brought unceremoniously inside, he was in agony. He paid no attention to anything as he was led to the office of Dr. Samuel Steiger. It did not matter to him that one of the guards ran some kind of sensor in front of him. When it started to beep, he was roughly searched. He did not care. Only months ago he would have been outraged at this treatment, but now, all he cared about was getting rid of the pain. His implant was failing, and it was destroying what little was left of his mind. He could hardly walk by the time he was ushered into the office.

There were others there who watched curiously as he entered, but he did not notice. He was pushed roughly into an uncomfortable chair and told to wait. Leaning forward, he put his head in his hands and groaned in misery.

Jack's past was gone. He no longer remembered Jenny, or his children. Marcie was lost to him, as was his career. His future no longer existed. All he was, all he ever hoped to be, lay in ashes at his feet. Jacob Hill had systematically destroyed him. Even this did not matter now. All that mattered was the pain.

"Well, I must say, this is certainly an interesting gathering. Mr. Anderson and Mr. Sampson — good to see you at last. And of course I know our famous senator here." The soft, steel-in-velvet voice thrust its way through Jack's agony. He knew that voice. Slowly, every movement a major undertaking, he raised his head to the door. Jacob himself stood framed there, flanked by two of the ever-present guards. He was smiling that same smile that he had smiled all those years ago, when Jack had first met him. The man had not changed one iota since then.

Uncontrollably, Jack raised his arms to the man who ruined him, pleading. *Jacob!* he wanted to shout, *Help me! I've done everything you asked. I've sold my very soul to be your friend. Please help me!* The words would not form. His body betrayed him. When he found he could not even speak, he gave a strangled, desperate cry and fell to the floor. There, writhing in pain and helplessness, one of the most powerful men in the nation began to sob like a lost child.

❖ ❖ ❖

Scott watched the scene play itself out before him. Although not a great follower of politics, he certainly recognized Jack Kline. The senator was a media favorite, and had been on television frequently. The sight of him wallowing on the floor out of control was unnerving. Scott glanced over at Jeff, and saw his own fear mirrored in his friend's face. He felt a sinking sensation in the pit of his stomach. His eyes darted to the tall, gray-haired man who still stood in the door. Just who *was* he? Certainly he carried himself with an air of great power, and the senator had treated him like some sort of god. Not only that, but he knew both Scott and Jeff by name. Scott had not always been the most perceptive person, but he did not need instinct to tell him that the man responsible for much of his grief stood before him.

As he watched, the newcomer stepped all the way into the room, surveying it like a conquering general would survey a won battle. Scott tensed, waiting. The tall man stopped beside the quivering mass of flesh that was Jack Kline. A look of distaste flashed across those stern features.

Delicately, he toed Jack in the ribs. "Oh, get up, Jack," said the steely, cultured voice. The sheer lack of emotion sent a chill down Scott's back. When Jack did not respond, the tall man looked over to where Steiger stood. His eyebrows arched in an unspoken question.

"Complete implant failure," said the doctor evenly. "We knew it was happening, but did not expect it to happen so fast."

"Is he totally gone, then?"

Steiger shook his head. "It's more like Alzheimer's disease," Steiger replied. "The pain will come and go. There will be brief periods of lucidity followed by complete disorientation."

"Can he be salvaged?" asked the tall man.

"No," answered the doctor. "At the rate he's losing it, he'll be a complete vegetable within 12 hours. If we could have gotten to him a few days ago, maybe. Now — well, it looks like a complete neurological breakdown."

"Hmmm," said the tall man. "Pity. We could still have used him." He motioned to one of the two guards in the room, who promptly picked the senator off of the floor and deposited him into one of the chairs. Jack stopped begging for help and put his head in his hands. A soft groaning escaped his lips. Ignoring him, the tall man turned his attention on Scott.

When he had met Steiger, Scott had been repelled by the malicious spirit within the man. It had nauseated and revolted him. This was different. Scott found that he could not look this man in the eye. The power, the pure force that permeated his spirit made Scott want to crawl under the desk and hide. He had thought that his recent experiences had made him strong in the Lord — a spiritual warrior to be reckoned with. Now he saw that he was out of his league. One didn't oppose power of this magnitude — one submitted to it. Feeling ashamed and weak, he bowed his head, and lowered his eyes to the floor. The tall man smiled at Scott's capitulation, gloating silently over an easy victory. Scott felt his cheeks beginning to burn with shame.

The stranger then strode over to where the open bookcase still revealed the closed elevator doors. "I see Agent Lynch is returning with his two charges," he remarked in the same calm voice. He glanced back at Scott. "This should make a touching reunion."

At that last comment, Scott jerked his head back up. The stranger could only mean one thing. Lynch had Beth and Helen — and he was walking straight into a trap! Eyes widening in panic, he looked at Jeff. Surely there must be *something* they could do! Maybe Jeff could . . . his wild hope died when he caught the former FBI man's eye. Jeff only shook his head negatively. The look on his face was plain. *Don't do anything stupid. Wait.* Scott's shoulders slumped, and he felt the bitter taste of defeat in his mouth.

The stranger, watching carefully, caught the exchange. "Very good, Mr. Anderson," he said, his voice filled with sarcasm. Slowly he began to clap his hands together in mocking applause. "I like a man who knows when to fight, and when to accept defeat."

Even Jeff's dark complexion was not enough to hide the flush that started to rise in his face. At first, Scott thought it was from the shame of giving up, but one look at his eyes told him otherwise. There was a fire there, and it was burning bright. Jeff Anderson hated being helpless, but he was far from giving up!

"Stephen should be here in just a few minutes. I'm afraid that elevator is dreadfully slow," said the tall man as he sat behind the desk. "In the meantime, allow me to introduce myself."

"Spare us the theatricals, Mister Jacob Hill," said Jeff, speaking for the first time. Scott looked at him in surprise. Somehow, Jeff had mastered his anger and rage. His voice mirrored the same cool, mocking tone that Hill had been using since he had entered the room. "You're not so invisible that I wouldn't know you."

"Indeed," said Jacob, his eyes narrowing as he studied Jeff with renewed interest. "And just what do you know of me?" he asked.

"Other than the fact that you're at the top of an organization that makes Hitler's S.S. look like a Sunday school class, not much," replied Jeff, now looking straight at Hill. "You're probably one of the most powerful people in the nation, if not the world. You have enough politicians in your hip pocket to make the government do what you want it to do. As far as the private sector is concerned, you control the people who control the economy. You have worked behind the scenes for years, only now emerging into the public eye as head of the Bureau of Religious Affairs. How's that?" He looked defiantly at Hill.

Scott could see that Jeff's mini-biography had scored a direct hit. Now it was Jacob Hill's cheeks that were slightly flushed, and his breathing was coming just a little faster.

"Interesting," he said softly. Scott shuddered from the sheer venom that now permeated that cold voice. "It seems that I am going to have to redesign my security measures. Tell me, Anderson, just how do you know so much about me?"

Jeff shrugged his shoulders. He knew he had nothing to lose by talking. "Not too hard," he answered with a grim smile. "I make it a point to know *all* of the heads of *all* of the government agencies that directly affect mine. I've been building a file on you ever since you assumed control of the Bureau of Religious Affairs. All evidence points to the fact that you, and probably a selected group, have had a lot to do with what's been going on in this country for the past several years."

He leaned forward in his chair, his features intense. "The thing I don't understand," he said with honest curiosity, "is why you allowed yourself to become visible by heading up the bureau. That's why I was able to find out about you. The only thing I can figure is that the people who pull your strings must have told you to." His grim smile became a full-fledged grin. "How about it, Hill? Did your masters order you to step up your attacks on Christianity? That's what this is all about, after all. Isn't it?"

Scott watched in amazement as Hill grew livid with rage. All of a sudden, he saw not a man, but a coiled cobra ready to strike. For a moment, he was sure that Hill would order the guard to shoot Jeff right then and there. Even as he thought this, though, something else was revealed to his senses.

At first, Scott had been cowed by the power and authority Jacob Hill carried. It had washed over him and left him weak and submissive in its wake. Now he saw the truth. Jeff's tirade had shaken him out of his stupor. Certainly Hill was a powerful man in this world. Perhaps Jeff was right, perhaps he had caused much of the persecution that was even now happening, but now Scott saw with spiritual eyes . . . *and he saw a defeated foe!* The man before him wasn't all powerful. He had masters, and ultimately, he had one master. *We wrestle not against flesh and blood,* Scott thought, and knew that it was never truer than now. His real enemy was not Jacob Hill, but rather Jacob Hill's master, and that master had been defeated over 2,000 years ago on the cross of Calvary.

His new insight filled and overflowed inside of him. Scott threw off the shackles of defeat and sat tall and straight in the chair. Submit? When the victory was already his? What was he thinking? His eyes sought Hill's. Jacob still stood there, seething, and Scott realized that his whole train of thought had taken a matter of seconds. Jacob turned to him, and their gazes locked.

Theirs was a contest that was no contest.

Scott looked Hill directly in the eye and said evenly, "Do what you want. You can't stop the spread of the gospel of Jesus Christ. People like you haven't been able to stop it for 2,000 years, and you're no different."

Jeff looked over at him, his face showing amazement and delight. *Me, too,* Scott thought in wonderment. *Where in the world did that come from?* When he looked back at Hill, he was even more surprised. The man was standing with his mouth open. It moved, but no sound emerged. His face was becoming an even deeper shade of red. Jacob Hill seemed about ready to explode with rage! From the way the security guard was fidgeting noisily behind him, Scott guessed that this did not happen often. Time froze for an instant, everyone in the office motionless. Then Hill took a deep breath and started to talk.

What he would have said was never known, for at that moment, the elevator opened. Even though they knew it was coming, it still took everyone in the room by surprise. Jack Kline remained slumped in his chair, but everyone else turned and looked. Two women in wheelchairs sat there, facing out into the office side by side. Both were pale and wan. Scott's heart stopped. Even though he knew that Beth was still alive, up until this moment he had not quite believed it. Deep inside, he had feared that this was all a cruel joke, or a case of mistaken identity. Now he saw the truth. He had never moved so fast in his life. Before anyone could stop him, he sprang out of his chair and bounded across the room.

"BETH!" He practically fell into her lap. Grabbing her around the neck fiercely, he pulled her close and held her tight. She smelled of hospital disinfectant, and Scott could tell that she had lost a lot of weight. Her slender frame pressed against his chest, and he eased his grip a little in fear of hurting her.

"Scott?" It was the first time he had heard her voice in an eternity. Even though it was soft and weak, it sounded like a heavenly chorus to him.

"It's okay, Hon," he whispered. He slid his hand behind her head and gently gathered in a handful of her beautiful auburn hair. Tears stung the corners of his eyes as he stroked her gently. "Everything's okay now."

"Scott, they told me you were dead. Or was that a dream?" She pulled away from him just a little, and looked at him as if she had never seen him before. Hesitantly she touched his cheek with a trembling hand, affirming that he was indeed here with her. Smiling with joy, he reached up and grasped her hand tightly. He was just about to lean forward and kiss her when two strong, rough hands grabbed his shoulders and he was pulled roughly away.

"Scott!" cried Beth, straining forward. In her weakened condition, she did not have the strength even to stand up. She watched helplessly as Scott was torn from her and thrown back into his seat. The guard then returned, stepping in front of the elevator, his face a mixture of anger and confusion. He surveyed the two women — Beth looking up at him in apprehension and Helen simply staring straight ahead — and then the rest of the elevator. Then he turned reluctantly around to face Hill.

"Well?" demanded Jacob.

"He's not in here, sir," replied the guard, his voice a frightened squeak.

"What do you mean, he's not in there? Did you check — oh, never mind, I'll do it myself. Watch them," he said, jerking his thumb at the prisoners. He started to punch in the code to call below, and the guard took a step forward.

Without warning, the ceiling of the elevator caved in. At least, that is what it seemed like to Scott. He watched in amazement as a 200-pound blond projectile hurtled down from above. The guard was thrown forward, slamming into the desk. Jacob stumbled back in surprise and confusion. Jeff was on his feet instantly. He swung his leg in a roundhouse kick that knocked the dazed guard back toward the elevator and right into the waiting arms of Stephen Lynch. Lynch, who had climbed up through the service hatch during the ride up, caught the now unconscious guard and dropped him roughly to the floor. Swiftly he pulled the guard's holstered pistol out and aimed it squarely at Jacob. He looked up at where he knew the hidden security camera would be. "Try anything and he dies," he said to the guards in Central Control.

"No!" shouted Jeff, swinging to face Lynch. "We don't work that way." He started to say more, but shut up as Lynch turned the gun on him.

From the look on his face, Jeff had no doubt that Lynch would pull the trigger if provoked. The bureau agent had been used and deceived. He was here for one thing — to expose the bureau and get his revenge. He would allow *nothing* to stand in his way, even his erstwhile allies.

"Quiet!" he shouted at Jeff, then looked around at the rest of the group. His face registered shock and surprise when he saw Jack Kline.

"Senator, what the devil are you doing here?" There was no response from the human wreck slumped in the chair. Lynch's eyes narrowed and he pressed his lips firmly together. "I should have known you'd be on his payroll," he growled, indicating Hill.

As he spoke, Scott moved back to kneel next to Beth, while Jeff checked Helen over worriedly. "Helen? Helen! It's me, Jeff. We've come to take you home." No response. Helen stared vacantly ahead at nothing.

Jeff looked up at Scott, his face revealing his fear. Scott could only shake his head helplessly. It was obvious that Helen needed medical attention, but they were still trapped in this hellish place. Beth gripped Scott's arm, still unsure of what was going on. Scott turned to see what Lynch was up to. The bureau agent was busy fiddling with the vid-phone on Steiger's desk. In frustration, he looked up from the blank screen to the camera.

"It won't work," he said grimly. With a single movement, he grabbed Jacob Hill by the collar and dragged him behind the desk. Carefully and deliberately, he pushed the gun barrel against the back of his head. "I've got nothing to lose," he said in Jacob's ear. "Tell your people to open up an outside line, or you're a dead man." He paused a beat, but Jacob remained silent. "Okay, Boss," shrugged Lynch, "It's your choice." His fingers began to tighten on the trigger.

Jacob realized suddenly that he was going to die. "Wait!" he cried in panic. "Open an outside line to this office. Now!"

The pressure eased against his neck as the screen came to life. "Better," nodded Lynch, and shoved him aside. Jacob stumbled, and fell to his knees. He remained there, watching Lynch. Lynch sat down at the desk and began to punch in a number. He shot a quick look at Jeff. "Watch them," he snapped, then turned his attention back to the screen.

"Who are you calling?" Jeff asked as he moved over.

"Not all of the people I work with are monsters like that," he replied, indicating Jacob. "Most of them are just trying to do their jobs the best they know how. I know a few I can trust. If I can get a message to them, and let them know what's going on here, they can blow the lid off this place."

"NO!" The cry came from across the room, and both Lynch and Jeff looked up in surprise.

Jack Kline stood up on unsteady legs and stumbled over to lean across the desk. "No," he said again, this time in a lower voice. Although his eyes were laced with pain, somehow he had regained control of his mind. It was obvious to both men that every word he spoke required a great effort. "Let me do it. I know who to call. Please." He looked desperately at the two men.

"What do you think?" Lynch asked Jeff, who shook his head.

"Are you sure about these people of yours?" he asked Lynch. "Completely sure? We only get one shot at this."

Lynch thought about it for a moment, then shook his head. "No, I'm not sure," he admitted. "But can we trust him?" Both men looked back at Jack, who was obviously in pain.

"Please," he repeated, his voice trembling. "My mind is going. I can feel it! I don't have much time. I *know* who to talk to. You don't. Let me make that call."

Jeff shrugged. "Why not?" he said. "What have we got to lose? The whole place is alerted, and we'll probably never get out of here. Let's see if we can bring them down with us."

"Fine." Lynch moved away from the desk. "Okay, Senator, it's all yours."

Jack did not reply. It took all of his effort just to concentrate on what he was doing. He sat down and very carefully typed in a private number that only he and a handful of others knew. He could only hope that the person he was calling would answer.

"Hello?" The craggy features of Ben Davidson appeared on the screen.

"Ben? It's me, Jack."

"Jack?" Davidson looked closely at the screen. What he saw alarmed him. "Jack! What's wrong? You look terrible!"

"Ben, I don't have much time left," said Jack, his voice barely above a whisper. "Listen to me, please. I've made a horrible mistake, and it's going to cost me."

"Okay, Jack, I'm listening," said Davidson, making a visible effort to control his emotions. "You might as well know, I've had you followed. What are you doing at this place called . . ." and here he looked offscreen, "Mentasys?"

"Thank God," said Jack quietly. "And thank you, Ben, for being such a good friend. Listen, you've got to launch a full scale investigation here. What's going on — I've seen it myself. People are being tortured, Ben. Arghhhh!" Jack's head shot back, screaming in pain. Jeff moved closer to help, but was waved violently off.

"Jack!" shouted Davidson, "Get out of there! We'll get you to a hospital. Whatever's wrong, we'll take care of it!"

"It . . . it's too late for me, Ben," replied Jack, his voice now barely a whisper. Beads of sweat began to roll off his forehead. His words came in short bursts, like a broken machine gun. "Just close this place down. Listen to me. Things have gotten out of hand. The bureau is too powerful. I was wrong to push for government control of churches. It's turned us into a police state. Oh, Jenny, I'm sorry!" His last words came out in a sob.

"Jack, listen to me!" shouted Ben. "I've got some of my people just outside. If you can get out of there, they'll get you home. Do you understand me? They have a helicopter waiting. Get out of that building, and they'll get you home."

"Sorry, Ben," said Jack, infinite sadness in his voice. "I can't make it." He looked at the others in the room, his gaze resting at last on Helen and Beth. He turned back to his friend on the screen. "Tell your people to land on the grounds here. Help the ones here with me. Get them out, and then let them go. Do you understand? Get them out, and then let them go."

"We'll get you all out," said Davidson. "Just hang on, Jack."

"Goodbye, Ben. Please tell Jen that I love her, and the kids. It's my own fault, you know." With that, he broke the connection and the screen went blank.

Jeff, who had been listening closely, moved forward. "Come on, Senator," he said gently. "Let's get out of here." He looked up at the hidden camera. "I'm sure you monitored that call," he said to the invisible security force. "You know that this place is going to be a hotbed of activity soon. I'd advise you to get out now, while you can. In any case, Lynch here has a gun trained on your boss, and frankly, I'm not good enough to take it away from him. I have a feeling that you'd better not try to stop us from leaving."

"You got that right," growled Lynch. "Let's go, 'Boss.' "

With that, he grabbed Jacob roughly by the collar and yanked him up on his feet and toward the door. Jeff helped the senator up, then turned to push Helen's wheelchair. Scott, of course, saw to Beth. Once at the door, Lynch put both Hill and Steiger in front of him.

Together, the odd procession moved out of the office and into the lobby. As expected, there were over a dozen security guards there, guns drawn and aimed. The two groups faced each other, neither one backing off. Both Jeff and Stephen knew that one wrong move would start a massacre. Lynch took the lead, his stolen pistol pointed at Jacob Hill's head. The guards gave ground, opening an aisle that led to the main entrance. Huddled together, the escapees moved as one toward the outer doors. In just a few moments they were outside. Scott found himself breathing the fresh night air deeply. After the sterile atmosphere of Mentasys, it tasted sweet beyond words! He looked up at the twinkling stars, feeling somehow comforted by their presence.

Followed closely by the knot of guards, everyone edged slowly into one of the deserted parking lots. Scott could see the limo parked far across the grounds. It seemed distant and inaccessible.

"Senator, I hope your friend is true to his word," said Jeff, pushing Helen's chair. Jack did not answer. Indeed, he now seemed oblivious to everything. They stopped in the center of the lot and waited. As they watched helplessly, the guards, now reinforced by men from the outer perimeter, began to encircle them. No one as yet made a threatening move, but the message was clear. Release Hill and Steiger now!

"Jeff?" Scott was trying to look in all directions at once. Everywhere he looked, escape was cut off. They were completely ringed in. They stood there helplessly, watching the guards close in the circle.

Then, just as if it looked like they would charge, the entire group was bathed in a blinding light. It formed a sharp circle around them. For one instant, Scott thought of all those science fiction movies he had loved as a teenager. Just when everything seemed hopeless, benevolent aliens would appear from above to save the day. He looked up, trying to see past the blinding light.

"Attention!" The male voice sounded from overhead, amplified and bigger than life. "The people in the center, stay where you are. The rest of you, back off. Now!" Scott could now hear the dull roar of a helicopter. It was getting louder, preparing to land. He looked away from the light, trying to see past the spots that danced before his eyes. The guards were still there, and they were not backing up. Lynch moved to stand in full view of them, still holding Hill by the throat. He reached behind him and pulled up Steiger as well.

"BACK OFF!" he shouted at the top of his lungs. He nudged Hill with the pistol.

"Do as he says!" shouted Jacob Hill. It was the first time in years he had shouted. His orders got results. The guards backed up several yards, although they still kept their weapons trained on the group. The helicopter pilot, seeing the circle enlarge, brought his craft down to a soft landing, less than 10 yards away. The wind from the rotors almost threw them to the ground. It wasn't a large craft, and Scott wondered if it could carry all of them.

"This is it, folks!" shouted Jeff. "Let's get out of here." He began to trot toward the helicopter, pushing Helen ahead of him. Scott took

Beth, and Jack followed on wobbly legs. Lynch saw the rest of the group begin to board, and he started to back up, still holding the gun on both Hill and Steiger, forcing them to follow. When he reached the chopper, only Jack Kline and two empty wheelchairs remained on the ground.

"Get moving, Senator!" shouted Lynch over the roar of the rotors.

"Let me help you with them," returned Jack. He put his hands on Steiger's shoulders and began to move him to the helicopter's opening. Lynch continued to back up with Hill. He never saw the blow coming. A desperate fist slammed into the side of his head. Darkness rushed in from the edges of his vision for just a moment, but it was all Jack needed. He reached in front of the staggered Lynch and grabbed the gun.

When Lynch recovered, he found himself looking at the business end of his stolen pistol. "Senator, what are you doing? Give me that toy and let's get out of here."

Jack only shook his head. His hands were trembling, causing the pistol to waver uncertainly. Normally, he would never have considered taking on a man like Lynch, but now he had no choice. He had flown in enough helicopters to know that there was not enough room for all of them to escape. He motioned with the pistol.

"Get on board!" he yelled. He could feel his strength rapidly fading. His single burst of energy had cost him. Not only that, but he could feel his mind sinking back into a painful fog. His time was gone. "GO!" he shouted, waving the pistol for effect.

Lynch hesitated. He thought he could safely disarm the senator and physically drag him into the chopper, but what would that accomplish? He had heard Steiger's assessment of Jack's condition, and knew that there was no hope for him. *Maybe it's best,* he thought, *to let him face death on his own terms.* He made his decision and nodded at Jack.

"All right, Senator. It's your choice." With that, he turned and jumped on board. Jack could hear arguing going on in the cabin, but within a few seconds it stopped. The door slid shut, and the engines revved. He turned to see Hill and Steiger watching him.

"S — stay there, Jacob," he shouted, each word becoming more and more painful. He remembered what Steiger had said about his condition. Brief periods of lucidity followed by disorientation. Within 12 hours, he would be a vegetable. *Best to end it here,* he thought. Behind him, the chopper's engines reached full power. He glanced over his shoulder to see it take off quickly. Its running lights winked out and it disappeared into the night. Soon, silence descended over the parking lot. He looked back to see the guards now running toward them.

"Okay, Jack," said Jacob, his calm demeanor starting to reassert itself. "It's over. Give me the gun."

Jack nodded, allowing himself a small smile. "You're right, Jacob. It *is* over — for all of us." He looked down at the pistol, now hanging limp in his hand. He could hear the shouts of the guards as they ran forward. They would be there in seconds. Carefully, deliberately, he brought the weapon up and centered it on Steiger's chest.

"No, Jack!" Jacob shouted, springing forward. Almost casually, Jack swung the pistol in a arc, bringing it across to smash into Jacob's face. He crumpled to the ground, dazed. Again Jack brought the pistol to bear on Steiger.

"Monsters like you have to die," he said quietly.

Steiger, his face white with horror, stumbled back. "No! Wait, Jack!" he cried. "We can help you. We can get that implant out, and you'll be as good as new. I promise. . . ."

The report of the pistol shattered the silence. Steiger was thrown back onto the pavement, a red stain growing right over his heart. He looked shocked and angered for a moment, as if death was beneath his dignity. Then his eyes glazed over and his heart stopped.

Jack swung the pistol over to where Jacob lay. Slowly he aimed for his head, but he was too late. As soon as they heard the shot and saw Steiger fall, three of the guards stopped and aimed. Jack looked straight at them, wanting to shout some kind of defiance, something to show that he was not afraid. Then he decided that he didn't have the right to speak any last heroic words. He thought of his wife and children.

"Jenny," he whispered. Three shots rang out in unison. Three bullets, perfectly aimed, smashed into his chest. Senator Jack Kline was thrown to the ground by the force of the impact. He lay there, looking up at the stars, his life rapidly fading into nothingness. Not surprisingly, his last thoughts were of the people he had helped to escape. There was something about them. They had something special, unique. It set them apart. *I wonder what it was?* was his last clear thought. *I wonder if I could have had it?* Then it was too late for anything else. Jack Kline stepped out of his life, and into a Christless eternity.

❖   ❖   ❖

Scott lurched violently to his left as the chopper banked hard. He was grateful that *this* helicopter, at least, had seats. The one he had ridden in before was nothing more than a flying boxcar. This one was also much quieter, being soundproofed. He checked the rest of the passengers as they leveled out. Beth was next to him on his right. She gripped his arm with a desperate strength, as if afraid he might disappear. Behind him sat Jeff and Helen. Scott could see that Helen was still in some sort of stupor. She was not responding at all to Jeff, who was speaking quietly to her. The worry on his face was evident. Behind them was the enigmatic Lynch, alone and aloof. Scott knew that their success so far was due to the courage and resourcefulness of the volatile agent, but still he found that he did not trust him fully. Lynch was there to accomplish his own agenda. Helping them was secondary.

In front sat the pilot and one other man who had introduced himself only as Ted. Scott could only guess that they were working for the man Jack Kline had spoken to on the vid-phone. Whether that meant they were friend or foe was still uncertain. All they could do was hang on and wait. He slid his arm around his wife and held her close. She leaned into his shoulder, and he felt her breath on his cheek as she gently kissed him. *Thank You, Lord,* he prayed silently as he nuzzled her. *Thank You for these few moments together. Whatever happens now, we can face it together. Thank You.* He held her tightly as the chopper lurched again, this time to the right.

"Hold on tight, folks," shouted the pilot over his shoulder. "We've got to put a lot of distance between us and that place you were in. They may try to track us by satellite, so the next few minutes could be rough!" With that, he turned back and concentrated on his flying. Scott felt the bite of renewed fear. Once away from Mentasys, he had thought the hard part of their escape was over. He looked back at Jeff and raised his eyebrows in question.

"That's how they got me," explained Jeff grimly. "If they can lock on to us, we can pretty much forget it."

Ted, the man next to the pilot heard Jeff and turned to respond. "It's not over yet," he said. "This bird can do a lot. If we can steer an erratic enough course, we might be able to slip past their scan." He looked at the small band of passengers for a moment. "Whoever you people are, I hope you're worth it," he said. "All we were supposed to do was to follow Senator Kline. Then word came down from the top to pull him out of that building if we could. Now, all of a sudden, we're minus the one man we were supposed to keep an eye on, and we've got a load of refugees. Senator Davidson's not going to be too happy about this. I just hope we can get to Kline before anything happens to him."

Scott did not reply. He had heard Steiger's assessment of Jack. According to him, there was no hope. He might be wrong, but he didn't think that anyone would be seeing Jack Kline again.

He was jolted out of his thoughts as the helicopter lurched yet again. When they finally leveled out, he could hear a loud Beep! Beep! Beep! coming from the cockpit. There was a blinking yellow light in the upper left corner of the control panel.

The pilot began to mutter under his breath, and even in the dark, Scott could see that Ted was beginning to look afraid. "What is it?" he demanded, already knowing the answer.

"They nailed us," said Ted. "Satellite surveillance has locked on to us." He looked back at the anxious passengers. "If anyone has any ideas, now's the time. Otherwise," he looked back at the blinking light, "we might as well set down at the nearest police station." He looked back at the control panel and pushed a series of buttons. Suddenly the beeping changed. It became quicker, more urgent. Scott did not think that it was possible, but Ted began to look even more frightened. "Oh no!," he said softly, almost under his breath.

"Now what?" demanded Scott.

"It's not surveillance," said Ted, his face taking on a sickly yellow hue from the light on the control panel. "Somehow, your friends have tapped into a defense satellite. Those monsters are equipped with enough firepower to take out a small army, and accurate enough to vaporize a single soldier." He looked directly at Scott. "They're not just tracking us, they're going to shoot us down."

❖ ❖ ❖

The situation room was located deep in the heart of Mentasys. In function, it was identical to its counterpart in Ayres One. It had the capability to enter *any* defense network in the world. It could call for a nuclear strike, or disable a nation's defenses, all without outside help. In form, it was quite large, being over 100 feet wide and just as long. Banks of equipment were manned by a group of hand-picked technicians around the clock. In the front of the room were two huge screens. The one on the left displayed a computer generated map of the United States, while the one of the right showed the entire planet. The technicians worked on the main floor, while a second level allowed those in charge a complete view of the entire area. A Master Control center, manned by a single technician, stood alone on the upper level. There were five other rooms like this in the world, each one commanded by a member of the Sextuaget. Only they, and the technicians who operated them, knew of their existence. Even Hill's own Inner Circle did not know about them.

When Hill blew into the Situation Room like an angry hurricane, everyone sat a little straighter. The technicians were totally loyal to the Bureau of Religious Affairs, and thus to Jacob Hill. Nevertheless, they paid greater attention to their assigned task when he was present. They all knew the consequences of failure.

Hill stormed up to the second level and surveyed the map of the United States briefly. "Get the defense net on line for this location, plus a diameter of 50 miles," he said through gritted teeth. The tech at the Central Control board hurried to comply, and within seconds a glowing map of the area appeared on the left screen.

"A chopper left here 10 minutes ago," Hill told him. "Heading unknown. Find it." The tech blanched a little at these instructions. He wanted to tell him that, even with state-of-the-art tracking equipment, that was still almost impossible. Instead he kept his silence. His only hope was that, at this time of night, there would be very little air traffic. A tiny bead of sweat appeared on his forehead as he bent to his task.

He could feel Hill behind him, a dark and foreboding presence. He tried to concentrate, knowing that the man behind him held total control of his life. Quickly, systematically, he divided the area into ten sections. Then he instructed the computer what to look for and where to search. He waited anxiously as the seconds ticked by.

When the blip appeared on the main screen, he suppressed a sigh of relief, knowing that his job, and life, were secure for at least a little while longer. "Got them, sir," he said, eager to please his boss.

"Are you sure?" asked Hill, his eyes fixed on the screen.

"Yes, sir," said the tech confidently. "It's the only chopper *not* in an assigned flight path for over 50 miles."

"Good," said Hill. He watched as the blip representing the fleeing craft moved slowly across the screen. He allowed himself a small smile. The people in that helicopter had humbled and humiliated him, but the final blow would be his. "Bring it down," he said softly.

"Sir?" The tech was not sure he heard right.

"I said, bring that chopper down. Use the satellite defense

systems. They *are* capable of that, are they not?" Jacob fixed his cold stare on the tech.

"Yes, sir," agreed the tech nervously. "The lasers have enough accuracy to destroy a target that size — even one much smaller. You must understand though, that I can't disable something that small. The laser blast will totally destroy it."

Jacob looked back up at the screen. "Do it," he commanded.

The tech didn't dare discuss it further. He entered the proper commands and accessed the proper programs. It took only seconds. "Target acquired, sir," he said in a level voice. "Locked on and ready to fire."

Jacob folded his hands across his chest and smiled. "Time to pay the price for your audacity," he said softly to the group of people who had caused him so much grief. He looked down at the tech. "Fire!"

❖   ❖   ❖

Scott watched helplessly as the pilot tried maneuver after maneuver. The chopper shuddered with the effort, but still the yellow light continued to blink. Finally he looked at Ted and shook his head. Scott knew that their death warrants had just been signed.

Ted looked back at the frightened group. "They've got us," he said bitterly.

"Can't we land?" asked Scott. "Take our chances on the ground." Ted shook his head and he felt a gentle hand on his shoulder. He looked behind to see that it was Jeff.

"They tracked me on foot, Scott," he said, his voice flat with finality. "There's nothing we can do. It's in God's hands."

Their gazes locked for a moment, then Scott reached up and gripped Jeff's hand hard. "For what it's worth, thanks," he said. "I owe you more than I can put into words."

Jeff nodded, then broke into a big smile. His teeth gleamed in the dimness of the cabin. "Hey, thank me on the other side," he said, a glint of joy peeking through his grim demeanor. It was contagious. Scott started to smile, then chuckle. Beth had overheard, and the tiniest of giggles wormed its way through her lips. Helen did not react, but Scott was sure that he could see a sparkle in her eyes that wasn't there before. Soon, they were laughing for the sheer joy of it — Scott, Beth, and Jeff. They knew that this was not the end, but the beginning. Soon they would see their Saviour, and all of their troubles would be behind them.

Lynch followed everything from the back of the cabin. He stared uncomprehendingly at the scene in front of him. He had known before the pilot started his evasive maneuvering that they were finished, but kept his silence. He had faced death before, but not quite like this. He could not even scream some final gesture of defiance at his killers. Death would fall from the sky, taking them all efficiently and impersonally. He chose to spend his final moments studying the people he was giving his life to save. He did not know Beth Sampson at all, so he could make no judgment. Scott, on the other hand, he still thought of as a total jerk. Maybe it was the fact that their personalities clashed so violently. Still, he admitted grudgingly, there was something about him. He had certainly shown guts in their ill-fated raid on Mentasys. When it counted, he had come through. Helen he knew and respected by reputation. Now that he knew the truth about the Shepherd's Path, his admiration for the seemingly-frail woman grew immensely. Anyone who could run an operation like hers, in this day and age, not only had brains, but a great deal of courage as well.

Mostly he identified with Jeff Anderson.

Both of them were agents — well, former agents. Anderson was one of the best Lynch had ever worked with. Thorough, professional, and totally dedicated, he was the man Lynch had always aspired to be. He admired Jeff, and would have been proud to call him "friend." The realization surprised him.

He looked at them all, holding each other, laughing in the face of certain disaster. *What is it?* he wondered to himself. *They're about to die, and yet they act as if they've been given the one thing they want most.* He swallowed hard as the one question that had been laying under the surface of his mind since this little venture started finally surfaced. *Could it be true?* he finally asked himself. *Could it actually be true? God, heaven, all of it?* The more he watched them, the more he thought it just might be — and if it was, then maybe he had better do something about it right now, before it was too late. He leaned toward Jeff, but just as he tried to speak, the chopper lurched hard for one final time.

❖ ❖ ❖

"Fire," said Jacob Hill, his voice ice and steel. The tech hesitated barely a fraction of a second, then entered the command. He looked up at the screen just in time to see it go blank. There was no warning. The map simply winked out. The tech's eyes grew wide as the second screen went dead. Frantically he checked his readouts.

At the same time, the technicians on the main floor began to notice that something was amiss.

"I have a partial power failure on the defense net. . . ."

"Get someone down to main power now. . . ."

"We're deaf and blind here! All lines are down. Repeat, all lines are. . . ."

The overlapping warnings were punctuated with a loud WHOOP! WHOOP! WHOOP! As everyone watched, system after system failed. The Situation Room, once linked to the world, became cut off and isolated.

Jacob Hill watched it all, then stepped forward to grip the shoulder of the tech in front of him with vise-like hands. "Explanation," he demanded tightly.

"Total power loss on the main grid, sir," replied the tech in a shaky voice. "Cause unknown."

"Did the laser fire?"

The tech checked his board, then reluctantly shook his head. "I don't think so. We've lost access to the defense net, and if contact is lost, the firing sequence is automatically aborted."

Jacob stared at the now impotent room, his rage barely contained. With a quick, angry motion, he activated the vid-screen next to the main control panel.

"Security!" he snapped. Taylor's face appeared, drawn and haggard. He had evidently not recovered from the effects of Lynch's dart gun. "What's happening?" demanded Jacob.

"We've got red lines across the board," said Taylor, his voice betraying his fear. "It looks like a general power failure."

"How?" snapped Jacob. "This building has multiple backup systems that automatically come on line in such an event."

"Sir, we're trying to find out now," said Taylor. "I've got a team. . . ."

"Sir! Full power restored!" The tech's excited report interrupted Taylor. Jacob looked up to see the maps reappear. On the main level, techs scurried to and fro as each system returned to full operational status.

Forgetting about Taylor, Jacob returned to the main control panel. "Get them back!" he practically shouted. The tech was already re-accessing the network. It took less than a minute to recall the area map, and only seconds for everyone to realize that their quarry had eluded them. The blip had disappeared entirely. The tech went through the entire procedure twice, but with no better results.

"Well?" Hill's voice was quiet as death.

The tech swallowed hard and replied. "They're gone, sir. They must have landed. I can maybe find the chopper, but without anything else to go on, I won't be able to track the passengers." He waited nervously for a reply. Jacob Hill stood there for a moment, staring at the now empty screen. Then, hands clenched, he turned and left the room.

❖ ❖ ❖

The aged maintenance worker stepped out of the main power room of Mentasys. It was located far across the complex, in the second sub-basement. He began to walk slowly up the concrete stairs, his work finished. He was a nondescript man, gray-haired, and clad in dark blue coveralls. Just as he reached the halfway point, the doors overhead burst open. Several technicians and a handful of guards came barreling down towards him, and he had to press up against the wall to keep from being run over. No one noticed him, so intent were they on their destination. He watched them go, shaking his head in amazement. He didn't think he would ever comprehend the human race. Always rushing around, trying to solve problems, never realizing that the causes, and solutions, were usually right under their noses.

The little bit of sabotage he had accomplished was just enough to carry out his mission. It was nothing fancy. In fact, the people who had just passed him would have things running again in no time. The vehicle they were tracking in the situation room, though, would be long gone. He allowed himself a small smile. The more intricately people designed things, the simpler it was to jam the works. A cut wire here and a thrown switch there, and the most expensive and sophisticated equipment built became useless. If they had relied simply on their own inventiveness and intelligence, they might have caught the escapees — but then again, he would probably have been there to stop them in any case. It was his job, after all. Speaking of jobs, he had many others to see to. Things were coming to a head soon, and there was much to do. After all, everything was in place. The Return was eminent. With energy belying his appearance, the Watchman bounded up the stairs, and made his exit. No one saw him leave.

❖ ❖ ❖

"Now what?" thought Scott as the chopper continued to bounce around the atmosphere like a baby's mobile. He was waiting patiently to die, but for some unknown reason, the dying had not started yet. It did not seem quite fair, he thought, to get all geared up for the Big

Event, then to continue instead to hang on tightly while the pilot tried one insane maneuver after another. He wasn't frightened anymore. He wasn't even apprehensive. In fact, he was getting a little air sick.

He was just about to complain when the man known as Ted let out a sharp yell. "They lost us!" he cried, disbelief mixing with relief.

"Impossible," said the pilot. "Once they're locked on, it would take a miracle. . . ."

"Who cares?" shouted Ted. "Just get us down. With enough head start, they'll never be able to find us again."

"Are you crazy?" retorted the pilot. "Look out the window, for cryin' out loud! That's a suburb of greater Los Angeles out there! I set down in the middle of someone's backyard and I guarantee they'll find you again!"

"Oh for the love of . . . there, off to the left. See it? That dark splotch of ground."

"What? I don't . . . oh yeah, now I do." The pilot checked his controls, then quickly changed course. "Okay, people," he said over his shoulder, "we're landing. We've spotted what looks like a small park. Hang on tight. There's no points for neatness on this one!"

As the pilot began his descent, Ted grabbed the microphone that hung nearby. He checked the frequency, then spoke. "Madalyne! Madalyne, do you read?"

"I'm here, Ted. What's going on? Did you get Kline out of there?"

Ted pressed his lips together, not wanting to answer. "Madalyne, just listen. We're landing in a small park at. . . ." He looked at the pilot expectantly.

"Just north of Glendale," was the answer. "That's a suburb east of Los Angeles proper."

"Did you get that?" asked Ted.

"Yeah, I got it."

"What's your location?"

"Heading away from Mentasys as fast as I can push this car," was the sarcastic reply. "Just a second. Let me check the map they gave me with this rental." There was a moment's silence, then Madalyne spoke again. "Okay, I've got you. See if you can get to the west entrance. That's the one that runs along Elm Street. I should be there in about an hour."

"We'll be there," said Ted, and replaced the microphone on its hook. He nodded to the pilot. "Okay, go for it!"

To Scott, it seemed like forever, but the actual landing took only minutes. The pilot flicked on the landing lights and circled the park once. There was a crude baseball diamond in one corner, and he headed for it. Scott braced himself for impact, but the pilot was good at his job. The passengers barely felt the bump as the craft came gently to rest. Ted jumped out of the co-pilot's side and opened the rear door for the rest of them. Lynch was the next one out. Without a word, he disappeared into the darkness.

"Where's he going?" Scott asked Jeff as both men climbed out.

"Checking out the area," was the answer. "Here, Scott, give me a hand." Scott assisted Jeff in getting Helen out onto the ground where she slumped to her knees. He turned back to help Beth, but his wife had regained enough strength to jump down herself.

"Come on," urged Ted. "Let's get away from here." He grabbed Helen on one side, and Jeff grabbed the other. Scott took Beth's hand, and the tiny group stumbled away from the helicopter. They were barely clear when the engine revved and the small craft practically leaped into the sky.

"Shouldn't he have stayed on the ground?" Jeff asked Ted, who shook his head.

"He'll be back to the small airfield we rented it from in less than 10 minutes," he said. "I don't think anyone will lock on to him before then."

Just then, Lynch came trotting back up. "All clear," he told Jeff, panting slightly. "I found the west entrance. It's not far. Come on!"

Not far to Lynch turned out to be a good distance to Scott and Jeff, who were now helping Helen. Finally, though, they were there. They waited in a growth of bushes for over an hour before Ted's friend finally showed. She pulled up in an old four-door sedan that rattled ominously.

"Sorry," she said as everyone squeezed in. "Best I could do on short notice." She was a large-boned, blond woman of about 25. She eyed the refugees warily. Scott got in first. He slid into the back seat and put Beth on his lap. Next was Helen, then Jeff. Ted and Lynch got up front. "Where's Kline?" she asked as Lynch shut the door.

"Never mind," said Ted shortly. "Just get us out of here."

Madalyne obviously wanted to discuss it further, but something in Ted's voice told her to drop it. She put the car in gear and started forward.

They drove in silence for a few minutes, then Ted spoke. He kept his eyes forward. "My orders were to get you people out of Mentasys and let you go. I'm going to do just that, even though I recognize one of you." Because he would not look at anyone, it was uncertain whether he was speaking about Jeff or Scott. "Anyway, we'll take you anywhere in this area you want to go, as long as it's within reason. How about it?"

Everyone was silent for a moment. Jeff and Stephen just looked at each other. Their original plans were shattered. Neither of them had any idea where to go in this area.

"How about the Network?" asked Scott finally. "Didn't you tell me you could access it anywhere? We can get a name and address from it and. . . ."

He stopped as Jeff shook his head. "Sorry, Scott, but I had to crash it. The system had been breached, and it was the only way to keep it from falling into the wrong hands." He looked over at Ted. "I don't suppose you could get us out of the state?" he asked hopefully.

Ted shook his head emphatically. "Sorry, but not a chance. I'm to get you out, and let you go, and that's it."

Jeff slumped back into the seat. It looked as if they were going to be let out on the next street corner.

"Access code seven, seven, nine, two. Password, Grandmother."

Madalyne kept her eyes on the road, but everyone else turned in shock to stare at the owner of the soft voice that had just spoken.

"Helen?" Jeff grabbed her arm with one hand and turned her head to face him with the other. "Helen?" he repeated, hope and worry coloring his voice.

"Ouch," said Helen. "That's my arm, Jeff, not a side of beef." Her voice was weak, and it had a slight tremor to it, but it was there.

"Helen!" cried Jeff. Despite their cramped quarters, he and Scott, somehow both managed to hug her.

"You're back!" exclaimed Scott joyously.

"I guess so," replied Helen, a hint of her old humor showing through. "Sometime maybe one of you can tell me why I woke up in a helicopter that landed in a park in the middle of the night."

"Later," said Lynch, who was watching the whole scene from the front. "For now, what was that about an access code?"

"It's my own personal code for the network," she replied. "Any terminal will access it. There should be several safe houses in this area that will take us in."

Jeff shook his head gently. "Sorry, Helen. Right after you were captured, I crashed the whole system. It doesn't exist anymore."

"I heard you say that," replied Helen. "The thing is, I copied the whole system into another file."

It took a moment for this to register with Jeff. "You — what?" Jeff asked slowly, not quite believing what he had just heard.

"I said I copied the system into another file," replied Helen. "I did it right after we set the thing up." She saw that Jeff was staring at her, his mouth open. "What's the big deal, Jeff? You told me that we should do that. It was dangerous to have just one file to rely on."

"Do you mean that the network. . . ." began Jeff.

"Should be alive and well," finished Helen. "The file name is Grandmother. Now, be a dear and take care of getting us someplace safe. I'm awfully tired." She leaned her head back and closed her eyes.

Jeff continued to stare at her, while Lynch simply shook his head. "You realize, Anderson," he said, "that if she was on *my* side, you wouldn't stand a chance."

Jeff let out a small chuckle. "Don't I know it," he said, his voice filled with an infinite tenderness. He took a deep breath, then spoke to Madalyne and Ted. "If you can get us to a public access terminal, I think we can take it from there."

Unnoticed by everyone, Helen allowed herself a small, contented smile.

❖ ❖ ❖

Scott leaned back in the soft reclining easy chair and sipped cautiously at the steaming mug of hot chocolate. He was in the family room of the Henderson family. The older couple had taken them in instantly, after giving and receiving the proper recognition verses. Next to him, on an overstuffed couch, Beth lay quietly sleeping. Jeff was softly snoring on the floor, and Helen was one room over in the guest bedroom. Ted and Madalyne had dropped them off a few miles away and they had taken a bus the rest of the distance.

No sense, they agreed, in letting too many people know that this location was part of the Shepherd's Path. Lynch had stayed with the other two. They would drive him back to the airport where he would catch the next flight to Washington. There he would meet with this Senator Davidson. He was determined to be in the thick of things when the investigation of Mentasys began.

Scott sighed contentedly. He reflected back on everything that had happened since that meeting in Covington. One thing was obvious, he knew. God had been in control all the way. His entire journey was a testimony to that fact. He had been protected and guided with each step. They were safe now, at least for the time being. He wanted to believe that their adventures were over, but Jeff cautioned him not to be overly optimistic. They were all still wanted on charges of conspiracy and treason. The laws had not changed. It was still illegal to worship freely, and, according to both Jeff and Helen, things had gone too far to turn around now. At the most, the persecution would ease off for a short time, while the mess at Mentasys sorted itself out. They might be able to find a place to start over.

Scott felt a yawn coming, and welcomed it. He stretched, feeling clean and comfortable in the borrowed night clothes. He felt his eyelids drooping, and set the mug aside. Let tomorrow's worries take care of themselves tomorrow, he decided. Right now, he and Beth were free and together. That was all that mattered. This part of his life might be over, but a new phase was starting. What direction it might take, he had no idea, but as long as God was in control, he wasn't afraid. He knew now that he would serve his Saviour no matter what the cost. It was a good feeling to know that. Pulling a comfortable afghan over him, he snuggled down into the chair, and quietly went to sleep.

EPILOGUE

ONE DAY LATER

Jacob Hill sat at his desk, watching intently as a series of file names crept up the screen before him. Behind him, as always, the security monitors kept watch on the entire complex of Mentasys. One difference they showed today was the lack of patients in either Phase One or Phase Two. Phase One patients had been evacuated during the night and flown to a more secure location. Those in Phase Two had died after being removed from the life support cylinders.

Jacob was dressed impeccably, as always, in a gray business suit, although the left side of his face was purple and swollen, thanks to Jack Kline's blow the day before. As the files went by, he stopped the scrolling for a closer look at one of them. It was entitled simply "Wolf." He debated accessing it, then decided not to. Instead he touched the control that would erase it. There was a second's delay, then the file disappeared forever.

These were his most personal files, protected by the most intricate and complicated security systems in existence. There probably was no need to take such drastic measures, but he was taking no chances. He had thought Mentasys a secure base for his activities, but it had been penetrated. Three men, using little more than their wits, had successfully gotten in, and out. In the process, they had freed two "patients," disrupted an entire security force, and drawn national attention to his operation. While Hill was certain that he owned enough senators and congressmen to ward off total disaster, things were going to get sticky for a while. Best to destroy any incriminating evidence before it could be brought to light.

Another file drew his attention, this one dealing with the Christian Liberation Front. Again he deleted it, then continued the search. He was so intent on his task that he did not notice when the central monitor blinked behind him. It flickered a moment, then came back on. Now, though, the cold, emotionless face of Brennon stared out at him. The head of the Sextuaget regarded his minion impassively.

"Things should never have been allowed to go this far, Jacob," he said finally. Jacob started, then swiveled around to come face to face with the only man he feared. His eyes flicked to the control panel. This system was secure, he knew. How could Brennon access it?

Brennon caught his look and answered the unasked question. "Of course I have access to your little secrets," he said scornfully. "I have access to *all* of the Sextuaget. Did you think me a total incompetent?" Jacob only stared at the sinister apparition before him. A cold shiver of fear ran through him. If Brennon was able to tap in to his private quarters, then he could have . . . .

Again Brennon nodded. "And of course I know about the fiasco that happened here last night." He shook his head sadly. "You have become a liability, Jacob. While your bungling has not set the plan back significantly, it *has* caused us some inconvenience."

"Dr. Steiger can be replaced," said Jacob quickly. "There are several people on our payroll who have the qualifications."

"Enough, Jacob! Steiger's loss is inconsequential. Even the coming investigation is not a serious impediment to us. The real problem is that your little bureau has been discredited." Again he shook his head. "Your plan was too subtle. You tried to turn the public against Christianity by blaming them for certain terrorist actions. This has now blown up in your face, and it is you who is under suspicion."

"I can still make it work," said Jacob desperately. "Once this investigation is over, I can start again."

"Sorry, Jacob," said Brennon, "but as I said, you have become a liability." With that, the door opened to Jacob's suite and two guards stepped in. Between them was Christine Smythe. She looked at Jacob with a mixture of disgust and pity.

"Ms. Smythe will be a worthy successor to you, Jacob," continued Brennon. In disbelief, Jacob watched as the two guards moved to stand on either side of him. He was lifted to his feet, his arms held tightly, and moved toward the door. Christine walked over to sit behind his desk.

"What are you doing?" cried Jacob, his voice rising in unaccustomed panic.

"Replacing you," answered Christine shortly. Brennon watched the scene play itself out before him, a small smile playing about his thin lips.

"You can't do this!" shouted Jacob as he was led away. "Brennon, I've served you well! You can't just cast me out!" Still shouting, he was led out of the suite. The door slid shut behind him and silence descended.

"What about the investigation?" asked Brennon to his new lieutenant.

Christine swiveled to face him. "We'll give them a sacrifice," she said confidently.

"Jacob," replied Brennon.

"Yes, sir," said Christine. "We have new interrogation facilities set up in New York. He'll be taken there and reprogrammed. When we turn him over to the government, he will make a full confession, accepting complete responsibility."

"And what of Mentasys?"

"We'll let the investigating team get into Phase One and Two, just to confirm Jacob's story. The Situation Room will remain hidden and functional."

"And the mysterious power failure?"

"Unknown," said Christine. "We are still looking into it."

"Hmmmmm," mused Brennon. "It could be that the Enemy had a direct hand in it."

"Yes, sir," agreed Christine carefully. Privately she did not believe in a supernatural foe. With the power Brennon wielded, however, that was something she would keep to herself.

"No matter," said Brennon. "His followers are few and scattered. I expect *you* to see to it that they are eliminated once and for all."

"I have already begun," said Christine. "And what of Wolf?"

"Give him a free hand," Brennon said, smiling. Christine suppressed a shudder. Brennon's smile was not a pleasant sight. "As I told Jacob, his plan was too subtle. Turn Wolf loose. No more arresting hidden churches. Let him simply destroy them — wipe them out. Understood?"

"Yes, sir."

"And Christine."

"Sir?"

"Do not fail me." With that, the screen went blank. Christine Smythe sat there for a moment, resisting a sudden urge to run. Then she turned back to the desk and got to work.

❖ ❖ ❖

ONE MONTH LATER

Jeff Anderson leaned forward in intense concentration, his face lit only by the dim glow of the small computer screen. He sat before a makeshift desk placed in the center of an otherwise empty room. To his left, a single window admitted a thousand odors and noises, all of them man-made. It was well past midnight, but New York City was as busy as ever. He could hear the distinctive sounds of the docks just a few miles away. A single, solitary streetlight shone just outside the window, casting a harsh, sterile glare over the street three stories below.

"Come on, sweetheart, come on," he murmured to the screen. His "new" terminal was a far cry from what he was used to working with, but it was all he had. If the contact he had made was telling the truth, it should be enough. Around him, the deserted office building he had chosen for his new headquarters was silent, as if waiting with him. There was little or no traffic in this part of the city, and most of the surrounding buildings were deserted as well. It was a perfect base for the operation . . . provided he could get a secured channel.

"That's it, baby. I know you can do it!" Suddenly, as if it were responding to his cajoling, the screen came to life. The dim glow was replaced by a series of codes that marched across the screen too fast to see. Then the symbol for SKYCOM-12, the nation's newest and most efficient communications satellite, appeared. The screen portrayed a computer rendition of the satellite itself, with a lazily spinning globe beneath it. Below the graphic, the word MENU flashed.

"Yeah," whispered Jeff in satisfaction. It had taken hundreds of hours to get this setup working. Every step, from running power from the street light, to hiding an uplink transmitter on the roof, to getting a secured channel from one of his old FBI contacts, had been dangerous and potentially disastrous. Now, though, he had it. Here, in the most run-down and deserted part of the city, he was in touch with the world.

A small smile wormed its way to his lips as he called up the menu and continued to type. The public networks were there, just as his contact had promised. Everything he needed was at his fingertips. "Helen, old friend, you would be proud," he said to his absent companion as he explored the menu. He was careful, cautiously skirting the edges of the main system. He did not dare activate the satellite's security system. He only needed to access the public nets, and they were the easiest to get to.

In just 15 minutes he had found what he was looking for. There before him, whole and complete, was the computer network of the Shepherd's Path — thousands of safe houses, linked together to form a network of escape for hunted believers. He continued to work. Two hours later he was in business. A few carefully exchanged passwords and the rest of the network knew he was there. Double checking everything, he exited the system and shut down his terminal. From now on he would only spend a few minutes a day uplinked. More than that could possibly be traceable.

Slowly the glow of the monitor faded, leaving only the illumination from the street light. Jeff continued to sit there, his thoughts traveling to friends he knew he would possibly never see again in this lifetime. Helen, Scott, Beth . . . and others he had worked with, seemed far away in both time and space. A wave of loneliness washed over him, and he felt the stirrings of self-pity.

"Enough!" he exclaimed aloud. Abruptly he stood, pushing his chair away with determination. There was work to do. Contacts had to be established, escape routes drawn out and rehearsed, a thousand details waiting for his attention. As suddenly as it had come, the loneliness left and he felt his spirit lift. God had given him a job to do and it did not matter if hell itself stood in his way. He was going to do it. A sense of excitement filled him. Certainly, the months ahead were going to be interesting! Besides, no matter what happened, he knew with an utter and complete certainty that God was in control.

He gave his new headquarters a quick once-over, making sure that everything was secure. Then he stepped out of the room and made his way to the street below. It was going to be a busy night.

❖   ❖   ❖

ONE YEAR LATER

Scott strolled slowly down the neighborhood street, hand in hand with Beth. It was early evening, the sun just beginning to set. The cool, summer evening air wafted about gently, and the large oak trees that lined the quiet street cast long shadows across somewhat dilapidated houses. Both of them kept watchful eyes in every direction, alert for possible threats.

The past year had seen the word "persecution" take on a whole new meaning. Each week seemed to bring news about another underground meeting that ended in tragedy. Government officials would be tipped off as to the time and location of the meetings, only to arrive to find the members murdered. It was a wholesale massacre of the Church. Law enforcement agencies swore that they were trying to find the ones responsible, but they never seemed to make any progress. Still, Christians continued to meet, and the gospel continued to spread. Scott had personally led over 30 people to Christ in the past months, and Beth even more.

Despite everything, Scott was content — at peace with himself and God. War still raged in the Middle East, food shortages were becoming more and more harsh, but he was where God wanted him. That was enough. He knew that his Heavenly Father was in control, and that was all that mattered. Both he and Beth were working now. They had adequate food and shelter. Also, thanks to the network, their new identities were holding up well under routine scrutiny.

In his hip pocket he carried a much read letter that had arrived by courier that morning. It was from Helen, who was back in Cincinnati living with friends. Stephen Lynch had helped establish a whole new identity for her. Privately, Scott thought it was dangerous for her to be back in that area, but Helen insisted.

Everything was fine, she assured them, although she was getting progressively weaker. Her ordeal in Mentasys had not been without its effects. She no longer had the strength to oversee the Shepherd's Path. Fortunately, it did not matter. The last 12 months had seen the network take deep root in the nation. It had survived its infancy and was growing quite well on its own. Thousands of cells were scattered from California to New York, each one a link in a lifesaving chain. The Church, and the Shepherd's Path, were alive and well.

Unfortunately, all of Helen's news was not good. Jeff Anderson's whereabouts were, at the moment, unknown. He had set up shop somewhere in New York and, by all accounts, had been doing well. Then something had happened. All Scott could find out was that a former bureau agent had been involved. Jeff had been forced to abandon his headquarters and disappear. Hopefully he would resurface soon. Until then, all they could do was pray . . . and hope.

Helen's next news item was far better. Stephen Lynch had finally put aside his pride and accepted Christ as his Saviour. Scott had to chuckle a little at the change in the fiery agent. After aiding the Senate in their investigation of Mentasys, he had resigned from the Bureau of Religious Affairs and gone into private practice. The sign on his front door read Stephen Lynch Investigations. As far as the world was concerned he was just another private investigator, but to many hunted Christians he was a vital link in the Shepherd's Path. No one, not even Stephen himself, knew how many people he had hidden over the past year. It made Scott smile to think that even when he had not yet made a commitment to Christ, he was still helping believers. It was good to know that he had settled matters at last.

As they walked, Scott released Beth's hand and slid his arm around her waist. Last night was the first night in months that she had not screamed herself awake. Her stay in Mentasys had left its mark as well.

Together they turned a corner and arrived at their destination — a small, wood frame house that looked exactly like its neighbors lining the street. Scott felt his leg muscles cramp as they climbed the four steps to the front door. He had just started his new job with the city road department last week, and the hard physical labor made him sore. Still, it paid the rent on the small, one bedroom apartment he shared with his wife. It also allowed them to carry on their true work.

They stopped at the front door and rang the bell. There was no answer, as usual. They waited a moment, then heard a soft tap from the other side. It was their signal.

"He that overcometh, the same shall be clothed in white raiment; and I will not blot his name out of the book of life," said Scott, lowering his voice and leaning into the door. This month, the recognition verses were being taken from the first four chapters of Revelation.

From inside, the answer came muffled through the wood. "But I will confess his name before my Father, and before his angels."

The door opened, and they were admitted. Inside, in a small living room, the rest of the little church he led waited patiently. There were eight of them in all, and they met once a week in secret to pray and encourage each other. Scott smiled as he stepped into their midst. It never failed to thrill him. These people were sold out to God, and would follow Him no matter what the cost. To be a part of them was an honor. To be chosen to lead them was both thrilling and humbling. Beth stepped up beside him, smiling a greeting. There were murmured hellos. Then Scott straightened his shoulders and spoke in a strong, confident voice, very much different from the Scott Sampson of a year ago. It was the voice of a man who was committed to follow the Saviour to death and beyond. It was the voice of a man who had grown up.

"The Lord is risen!" he said, grinning at the sheer wonder of serving a living God.

And, as it had in centuries past, the reply came back in perfect unison. "The Lord is risen indeed!"

AMEN!